The End Begins
Book 1

The Dragon Roars
Book 2

The Morning Star Rises
Book 3

About *The End Begins*

"The first book in Davison's Seven trilogy grips the reader from page one and holds on until the very end. Meryn O'Reilly is a believable character, and—though dreadful—the story is plausible. Thought-provoking, relevant and suspenseful, *The End Begins* is a must-read."
—*RT Book Reviews*, 4 ½ Stars, *Top Pick*

"It's a compelling and scary read you won't soon forget."
—SANDRA ORCHARD, Author of the Award-Winning Port Aster Secrets series

"Sara Davison takes 'what if' to a chilling level that is all too real. Yet wrapped in love, both human and divine, this novel gives us hope. Book Two can't come out soon enough."
—NANCY RUE, Author of *One Last Thing* and *The Merciful Scar*

About *The Dragon Roars*

"The second book in the Seven trilogy is more exciting than the first. The suspense is well-placed and the timing is spot on, giving readers enough breaks to not be overwhelmed while never losing the tension."
—*RT Book Reviews*, 4 Stars

"*The Dragon Roars* is a riveting, well-written novel with an engaging storyline that draws the reader into futuristic world where it's dangerous to be a follower of Christ. Davison is a master at weaving the faith elements of the story into a beautiful tapestry that highlights rather than detracts from the underlying message of survival in a dangerous new world of unbelief. Readers will not be disappointed in Davison's second book in the trilogy; it delivers!"
—LUANA EHRLICH, Author of *Titus Ray Thrillers*

"*The Dragon Roars* is an edge-of-your-seat romantic thriller that will give your emotions a roller coaster workout."
—BARBARA ELLEN BRINK, Author of *Roadkill*, Double Barrel Mysteries, Book 1

"Sara Davison's vision of a dystopian Canadian future has refreshingly smart and courageous characters with a lot of heart."
—MAGGIE K. BLACK, Author of over 8 novels including *Tactical Rescue* and *Kidnapped at Christmas*

About *The Morning Star Rises*

"The final installment of Davison's Seven trilogy does not disappoint. The sense of foreboding is palpable …. Davison answers many mysteries presented throughout the series, all culminating in a shocking and satisfying end."
—*RT Book Reviews*, 4 Stars

"*The Morning Star Rises* is a deeply satisfying conclusion to Sara Davison's Seven trilogy. Full of twists and turns, equal parts suspense and romance, it keeps you guessing till the end. Davison has created a believable world that turns the tables on today's most pressing issues, and peopled that world with vivid, heartbreakingly real characters. A thoroughly enjoyable read."
—ERIN E.M. HATTON, Award-Winning Author of *Across the Deep*

"Another thrilling read from Sara Davison. Thrust into the midst of intrigue, terror, and a heartrending love story, you will sit on the edge of your seat. Sara propels the reader into the battle between good and evil, where Christians must choose—Christ or their life. Don't miss this final episode in the Seven trilogy."
—BONNIE LEON Best-Selling Author of the Northern Lights series

THE MORNING STAR RISES

The Seven Trilogy
Book 3

SARA DAVISON

Ashberry Lane

© 2016 by Sara Davison
Published by Ashberry Lane
P.O. Box 665, Gaston, OR 97119
www.ashberrylane.com
Printed in the USA

All rights reserved. No part of this publication may be reproduced, stored in a retrieval system, or transmitted in any form or by any means without the prior written permission of the publisher. The only exception is brief quotations in printed reviews.

All characters and some locations appearing in this work are fictitious. Any resemblance to real persons, living or dead, or places is purely coincidental.

Canadian spelling is frequently used.

Published in association with the literary agency of WordServe Literary Group, www.wordserveliterary.com.

ISBN 9781941720233

Library of Congress Control Number: 2016948057

Cover design by Miller Media Solutions
Edited by Rachel Lulich, Christina Tarabochia, Kristen Johnson, Sherrie Ashcraft, Andrea Cox, and Amy Smith

THE HOLY BIBLE, NEW INTERNATIONAL VERSION®, NIV®
© 1973, 1978, 1984, 2011 by Biblica, Inc.™ Used by permission. All rights reserved worldwide.

FICTION / Christian / Romantic Suspense

To Seth, my youngest and my fellow sports fan in the family. It is an indescribable joy to watch you grow into a godly man with a heart for others. I love the way you embrace life and are always ready for another adventure. Go, Blue Jays!

To all my brothers and sisters in the body of Christ. Stand strong in the Word, regardless of opposition or cost. Heaven and earth will pass away, but the Word of God will endure forever.

And always and above all, to the One who gives the stories, and who alone can provide the strength and courage to endure to the end. It is all from you and for you.

The light shines in the darkness,
and the darkness has not overcome it.
John 1:5

1

Jesse Christensen stopped in the hallway between the farmhouse living room and kitchen and drew in a deep breath. He pressed a palm to the doorframe and stuck his head into the kitchen. The lingering aroma of roasted chicken, mashed potatoes, and gravy permeated the room. Comfort food that had failed to bring him any comfort that evening.

Meryn O'Reilly stood at the sink, hands immersed in soapy water, apparently trying to scrub the lining off a pot.

"Can I talk to you for a minute?"

She jerked and dropped the pot, sending a spray of water shooting across the front of her red shirt.

Jesse grimaced. *Not a great way to start this conversation.* "Sorry. Didn't mean to startle you."

Meryn shook the water from her hands and stalked to the stove to grab the dishtowel hanging on the handle. "I didn't hear you coming."

She wouldn't have seen him either, given the way she'd studiously avoided glancing in his direction since he'd responded to her brothers' invitation to come for dinner and shown up at her door earlier that evening. Not that he blamed her. How *did* a woman look at the man she'd just found out had gunned down her husband? There was no handbook for that kind of thing. Jesse pushed away from the doorframe and stepped into the room.

Meryn scrubbed at her shirt with the towel, still not looking at him. The fact that they both stood in almost the exact spots they'd been a couple of weeks earlier when she had ordered him out of her life for good had to be registering in her consciousness right about now.

Please look at me. Jesse repressed a sigh. He wasn't any more comfortable than she was. He likely shouldn't have come out here, but if he was going to work with her brothers, he, Shane, and Brendan had to get together. They all agreed the farm was the best place. At least here they were out of sight of the authorities, if still in range of the GPS embedded in the bracelets that identified them as believers.

Besides, Meryn wanted to be involved in any plan they devised to fight against Gallagher, who had recently been promoted to major, making him the commander of the Kingston base. Or, in his mind, king. After Gallagher had executed Jesse's best friend and commanding officer, Caleb Donevan, and kicked Jesse out of the army at the same time, Jesse and Meryn's family had agreed to band together to stand up to him. How did she think she could work with him if she couldn't even look at him?

He took a tentative step closer. "So this is okay?"

"Sure." She stopped the frenetic scrubbing and shoved the towel back over the handle. "It's fine."

Her trapped-animal look suggested it was anything but. "If you want me to bring Kate or Shane in here, I can."

Meryn looked over at him. Finally.

Jesse was drawn immediately into the ocean-blue depths of her eyes. *Be careful what you wish for.*

"That's not necessary. We're both adults. I'm sure we're capable of having a civilized conversation." She crossed the room and sank down on a chair, pulled one knee up to her chest, and clasped her arms tightly around her leg.

Great. A civilized conversation. Just what he wanted from her. Jesse shook off the thought. He had to let go of wanting anything more than that. A pang shot through him, but he worked to keep his features even as he leaned back against the counter. "I know you told me not to come back here, but it's the safest place for us to meet."

"Really?" Her lips twitched slightly. "Way out in the middle of nowhere? Aren't you just asking for trouble, coming out here?"

The muscles across his back relaxed. Was she actually joking around with him? That would make things easier. And a lot harder. "I think I'll risk it. After all, you survived four years out here all by yourself."

Her smile didn't reach anywhere but her mouth, and barely there. Like a restless butterfly, landing lightly and flitting away almost immediately. "In spite of your dire predictions to the contrary."

"Exactly." His own lips twitched, but he couldn't manufacture a real smile either. "Anyway, I just wanted to make sure you were okay with me coming here so we can make plans."

She studied him for a moment, then flipped her long, dark hair back over one shoulder. "I don't really have a choice, do I? There are things that need to be done, and we have to work together to accomplish them. You don't always get to choose the people you're going to work with; you just put your head down and focus on completing the task."

Did she know how far she was pushing the blade in with every word? She'd always been able to read him, to see on his face everything he was thinking and feeling. Could she see it now, or had even that connection been severed? "So we're co-workers."

"Yes." She shifted. "Is there anything else?"

"Actually, there is. I'm sure Kate told you she and Ethan offered me the use of the in-law suite in their backyard. I'm working on some other arrangements, but until those come together, I hope you don't mind that I took them up on it."

Meryn shrugged, as though nothing he did could possibly concern her. "You have to have a place to live. I'm glad you aren't on the streets. Whatever you might think, I don't want you to suffer any more than you already have."

Then you might want to lose the nonchalance. Jesse pushed the thought away. She was hurting as much as he was. He shoved his hands into the front pockets of his jeans, trying to match her attitude with a detached one of his own. And failing miserably. His fingers closed around a hard, cold object. The silver heart she'd given him before everything between them had been smashed into pieces. He glanced at her throat. It was bare. The gold necklace he'd fastened around her neck—twice—along with the promise that she would always have his heart, was gone. Jesse pushed back his shoulders. "All right. As long as you're okay with everything."

The shadow that crossed her face before her guard shot back up suggested that she wasn't as nonchalant as she was pretending to be. Hope ignited, a fragile spark dropping from flint struck against flint onto sparse tinder below.

"You didn't change your name."

She blinked. "What?"

"When you got married. You didn't change your last name."

"Oh. No, I didn't. Like I told you, everything happened so fast. Logan and I decided we could do that when he came back and we had our big wedding."

"Too bad. It would have saved us a lot of … confusion if you had."

She exhaled. "I know."

Jesse pulled his hands from his pockets and gripped the edges of the counter on either side of him as he studied her. She looked thinner and there were shadows under her eyes. Was she all right? He bit his tongue to keep from asking. Of course she wasn't all right. She was a widow, thanks to him, and in mourning. Did she grieve the loss of him a little, or were her thoughts only for her husband? He cleared his throat. "If we're going to work together, it would be great if it wasn't awkward for everyone. Do you think we could be *friends*, at least?" He almost choked over the word.

"We could try." Her voice softened slightly.

That would have to do. For now. Her feigned disinterest seemed to be gone anyway.

God, let it be feigned.

Otherwise the hope he clung to would extinguish quickly, leaving nothing but a curling tendril of smoke in its wake. His gaze settled on her mouth. A rush of longing poured through him. If things had gone according to his plan, they'd be married by now. Jesse clenched his jaw. *Don't go there.* None of this was his plan; it was God's plan. Which meant it had to be better. Something Jesse was sure he'd come to see. Eventually.

Meryn lowered her foot to the floor. "It's almost curfew. You should go."

He lifted his eyes quickly. "Yeah, you're probably right."

She stood and headed for the hallway as if she had been released from a cage.

When she reached him, Jesse touched her elbow. He'd told her once that she didn't feel like glass, all hard and cold. Now, with every muscle in her body tense, that's exactly how she felt.

She stopped but didn't turn in his direction.

"I really am sorry, Meryn. More sorry than I can say."

"I know you are." Her gaze dropped to his fingers, still resting on her arm. "Are we through here?"

Jesse pulled back his hand. "I guess so." For several seconds, all he could do was stare at the doorway where she had disappeared.

2

Bells jangled above the door of Meryn's secondhand bookstore. She looked up from dusting the shelves.

"Aunt Meryn!" Three-and-a-half-year-old Gracie ran down the aisle toward her.

Meryn set the feather duster on top of a row of books and crouched down. Gracie flew into her arms, nearly knocking her backward. Meryn pulled her close and looked over the strawberry curls at Kate, the friend who was more of a sister to Meryn and her brothers than their half-sister, Annaliese, had ever been. Still holding Gracie, Meryn straightened up. "This is a nice surprise."

Kate tucked her short red hair behind one ear. "Gracie's been begging me to bring her to see you for a couple of days, so I finally gave in."

"I'm fine, Kate. You don't have to keep checking up on me."

Kate cupped Meryn's chin, studying her. "*Fine* is clearly a bit of an overstatement." She let go of her. "I am glad to see you back at work, though."

Meryn set Gracie down and reached for her hand. "Want to go to the kids' section, Gracie?" She led the little girl down a long aisle between rows of books, toward the area in the back corner she'd recently set up for children who came into the store with their parents. Two-foot-high bookshelves formed a rectangular area, a small break between a couple of the shelves allowing kids to come and go. Inside the rectangle, a large, brightly-coloured rug covered the wooden floor. Bins of toys lined the back wall of the area, and soft cushions were strewn every few feet.

Gracie tugged her hand free and ran through the opening.

Meryn waited until Kate came up alongside her. "I had to get back to work. There's a lot to do here. Besides, I was climbing the walls at home. Way too much time to think."

"Who were you thinking about?"

"Not who, what. My life, mostly. Where I'm at and what I should do now that so much has changed." *How I'm going to keep going after losing everything.* She shook off the negativity. She still had so much to be thankful for. God, family, friends, and—she glanced around the store—resources. What more did she need? She mentally blocked that answer before it could even cross her mind.

Kate stopped at the entrance to the kids' area and turned to her. "And?"

"I have one or two ideas. I have time, now that I'm not involved with anyone, and I want to do something meaningful."

"Are you going to share those ideas with me?"

"Soon. When I have all the details worked out."

"All right. I'm assuming you're talking about the list of things Jesse wants us to do."

His name still stung but Meryn worked to keep the jolt that shot through her like a current of electricity from showing on her face.

Unfortunately, Kate knew her too well. "Would you rather I not talk about him?"

Meryn waved a hand through the air. "Of course not. It's fine. He asked me last night if the two of us could be friends. He's obviously still part of our lives. I'm going to be hearing his name all the time."

"And you're ..."

"Perfectly fine with that."

Kate smiled. "Just seeing how many times you're going to work the word *fine* into this conversation. You do understand what it means, right?"

Meryn shot her a dark look. "Yes, I understand what it means. And yes, I guess Jesse is the one who's got me thinking about what I can do. But I'm not doing this for him; I'm doing it for God, and all of us, and for the Christians in Kingston. At least in some small way, I'd like to try and make things better."

"You sound pretty passionate about this, Mer. So go for it. It will help take your mind off ... everything."

"That's the plan."

"And it's a fine one."

Meryn scrunched up her face, and Kate laughed.

A buzzer sounded from the rear of the store.

Meryn glanced in that direction and bit her lip. "I'm expecting a delivery this morning. I'll be right back, okay?"

"Sure." Kate slipped through the opening in the shelves and sank down, cross-legged, on the area rug.

Clutching a picture book to her chest, Gracie ran over to Kate and turned around to drop into her lap. "Read, Mama."

Meryn grinned. Nothing made her happier than kids enjoying her huge collection of children's books. The thrill that gave her was one reason she was so thankful the army had allowed her to re-open her store, even after she'd been arrested for using the place to smuggle Bibles.

Her smile faded as she headed for the back room and marched through the swinging doors. The table where she did her unpacking and sorting dominated the small space. Meryn walked around it and made her way to the door. A medium-sized cardboard box sat on the stoop outside. After glancing up and down the alley and not seeing anyone, she bent down and lifted the box to carry it inside. She shifted it onto one hip, so she could pull the door shut and lock it.

Her hands shook a little when she set the box down on the table. She ran her fingers over the top of it. *Father, I know this is what you want me to do. Give me courage.* She'd open it later, when Kate and Gracie were gone. Meryn turned the handle to close the blinds over the one small window in the room, stuck the box in a cupboard she'd cleared out in preparation for the delivery, and closed the doors firmly.

When she got back to the children's area, Gracie was snuggled in Kate's lap, but the little girl must have gotten up a few times since Meryn had left as the pile of books on the floor beside Kate had grown to at least ten.

The ache in Meryn's chest drove in deep. Would she ever have a child of her own? The prospect appeared less and less likely. Maybe that wasn't God's will for her. *Which is fine.* She winced as the word crossed her mind. Kate was right, as usual. The truth was nothing was fine. She certainly wasn't. She scooped a stuffed animal up off the floor and tossed it into a red bin. "Want me to take a turn?"

"Sure." Gracie went for more books, and Kate took the opportunity to stand up and dust off the back of her pants. "I want to browse around for a bit anyway. I need something to read."

"Okay." Meryn settled on the carpet and patted her knees. "Come on, Gracie. Aunt Meryn will read you a story."

The little girl trotted over with a book in each hand.

For the next twenty minutes, Meryn read book after book to Gracie, delighting in the little girl's laughter and the chubby fingers pointing out animals and objects on the pages. What would her family have done if Jesse hadn't been able to get Gracie and her brother, Matthew, back after the army removed them from Kate and Ethan's home a few weeks earlier?

Her arms tightened around the little girl. They would have gone on, somehow. Still, two bright rays of light in their family would have been extinguished. The dark shadows that remained might never have lifted. Meryn pressed a kiss to the top of Gracie's head.

"Had enough?"

She looked up. Kate was watching the two of them, an amused smile on her face.

"Are you talking to me or Gracie?"

"You. Gracie could never have enough stories. She'd listen to you read for hours if you were willing."

The bells above the front door jangled again. Meryn lifted Gracie from her lap and rose with a groan. "I am willing, but I better take care of my customers. Did you find a book?"

Kate held up a paperback. "This should last me a couple of days. Then we'll be back, so I can find another one."

"And check up on me."

"We'd never do that, would we, Gracie?" Kate hoisted her daughter up into her arms. "And why would we need to? Aunt Meryn's just *fine*, isn't she?"

Gracie nodded and rested her head on Kate's shoulder.

Meryn picked up the pile of books and set them on a shelf. "I better go see if anyone needs help."

Kate caught her arm as she walked by them, leaned in close, and whispered, "Did that delivery you just got have something to do with one of those ideas you mentioned earlier?"

Meryn glanced toward the front of the store. "Maybe."

"You're not going to get yourself in trouble again, are you?"

"It seems like just about anything we do these days can get us into trouble."

"That's pretty evasive." Kate let go of her. "Okay, Mer, I'll wait until you're ready to tell me about it. Just promise me you'll be careful, okay?"

"I will." Meryn followed her to the front door.

Two customers, a man and a woman, were perusing books in the historical fiction section.

"Thanks for coming by. I really do appreciate it."

Kate opened the door and turned back, her hazel eyes serious. "I mean it. Be careful."

"You worry too much. I'm …"

Kate held up a hand. "Don't say it."

Meryn laughed and went out onto the front stoop as Kate set Gracie down and helped her climb down the steps. When they reached the bottom, the two of them headed for the van parked at the curb. Although it wasn't quite ten in the morning, the early August heat was already oppressive, rising in shimmering waves from the sidewalk.

Meryn turned to go back inside. Sunlight glinted off the silver fish symbol screwed above the door of the store, and her chest tightened. Would having her store marked as a Christian business make it easier or harder for her to carry out her plans? She drew in a breath of humidity-laden air. Only time would tell. That part was out of her hands.

The bells jangled softly as she went in and closed the door behind her.

3

Light flooded through the stained-glass window, casting a soft glow over the parishioners gathered in the old limestone church. Shane's eyes were drawn to a mass of curls, which, other than a few, wayward ringlets, was gathered up in a clip at the neck of a woman. Rays of sun turned the strands a shimmering gold. *Who is that?* In spite of the government crackdown on Christian activities, it wasn't unusual for new people to show up at the church. It *was* unusual for one to capture his attention so completely.

Brendan kicked him in the foot.

Shane tore his gaze from the woman and focused on the red-headed preacher in the pulpit. When his brother kicked him again, he gritted his teeth. Twenty-five years ago he would have responded to the harassment without a thought, except to consider whether a punch to his brother's thigh or a sharp elbow to the ribs would hurt more. Of course, they both would have paid for it—in church with a glare from their mother, and at home with some one-on-one time with their dad.

When a movement at floor-level caught his eye, he shot out his hand and gripped his brother's knee. Hard. "Back off," he hissed from the corner of his mouth.

Brendan grinned.

After the service, Shane followed Meryn and Brendan to the fellowship hall for refreshments.

The woman with the curls was already in the room when they arrived. She sat at a table, talking to the Sunday school superintendent—no doubt being conscripted into service—and Shane studied her surreptitiously while filling his mug at the coffee machine.

Brendan elbowed him in the side, and Shane jumped back as coffee splashed over the top of the mug, narrowly missing his jeans. He set down the mug and whirled on his brother. Brendan's smug look suggested that maybe Shane hadn't been as surreptitious as he'd thought. "Do you want to take this outside?"

"She's pretty cute."

"Who?" Shane reached for a napkin and crouched down to swipe at the puddle of coffee on the floor.

His brother didn't answer.

Shane straightened up and tossed the napkin into a garbage can. "I've got eyes, Brendan."

"What about feet? Why don't you go over and talk to her?"

"Talk to whom?" Meryn grabbed the jug of milk and splashed some into her cup of tea.

Shane sighed. "No one. Hey, where's Kate? I didn't see her in the service."

His sister's eyes narrowed. "Gracie has a cold, so Kate stayed home with her. Why are you changing the subject?" She turned and scanned the room. "Who should he go talk to, Bren?"

"The new girl over there in the corner, the one with the curly hair. He couldn't take his eyes off her the whole service."

Shane let out his breath in exasperation. "What is the matter with you? I looked over once or twice maybe. Just wondering who she is, since she hasn't been here before."

"So go ask her."

"I'm not going to go over there to ask her who she is. Besides, she's busy talking to someone."

"Oh, for Pete's sake, I'll go ask her." Meryn brushed past him and started toward the woman.

"No, don't."

Meryn didn't stop.

Shane frowned and turned back to his brother. "You're never happy unless you're stirring things up, are you?"

"Nope." Brendan grabbed a couple of chocolate chip cookies and jerked his head toward an empty table. "Want to sit?"

"Actually, I was thinking I might head out. I need to check a couple of things on the truck."

Brendan gave him a lopsided smile. "Might as well stay and get it over with. You know Meryn won't rest now until she introduces the two of you."

"And whose fault is that?"

"Mine." Brendan looked more pleased with himself than sorry. "Come on. I'm sure she doesn't bite." He glanced in the direction Meryn had gone off in. "And I doubt she'd do much damage if she did. She's just a little thing."

"Everyone's a little thing compared to you, ya big lump."

Brendan laughed and headed for the empty table.

Shaking his head, Shane followed him. His brother was right. If Meryn suspected the remotest amount of interest on his part—and, thanks to his big-mouthed brother, she obviously did—she would move heaven and earth to get him and the mystery woman together.

He set his coffee down on the table and pulled out a chair. "I wonder where Jesse was this morning."

"He was here. He sat in the back, though, and left right after."

"Too bad. I didn't even see him."

"Of course not. Your eyes were firmly riveted on—"

"Shane, Brendan, I'd like you to meet Abby Wells. She's new to town."

Shane's face warmed as he stood up. Mercifully, Meryn had cut Brendan off before he finished the sentence. Shane held out his hand. "Hi, Abby. Nice to meet you."

"You too." She slid her hand, small and warm, into his. When she smiled, her eyes, grey with flecks of jade, glowed like an evening sky.

Shane swallowed and forced himself to let go.

Brendan shook her hand too, but the amused smile was directed at Shane, not her.

Meryn touched Abby's elbow. "Do you have plans for lunch? If not, we'd love to have you join us at the farm."

Shane resisted the urge—barely—to send his sister an icy look. Meryn was going through a rough time; he'd cut her some slack. Once.

A startled look crossed Abby's face, then she smiled again.

The effect on Shane's stomach was new and more than a little disconcerting. *What is the matter with you?*

"I'd like that. I just have to talk to someone for a minute. Can I meet you there?"

"Sure." Meryn gave her the directions.

Abby thanked her and headed for the exit.

Shane's gaze edged back to his sister. "Really?"

"I invited her to lunch for me, not you. She seems nice and I'd like to get to know her better."

"Uh-huh."

Meryn pulled a chair out and sat down. "It's true. Although …"

"Here it comes."

She tapped his arm with her fist. "I was just going to say that it wouldn't hurt you to keep an open mind. Abby's pretty and friendly. And it would be good for you to think about something besides work for a change. That's all you do anymore."

"I don't have much of a choice. Our boss gave Brendan and me a couple of big projects to get done, and Jesse asked me to …" He pressed his lips together.

"Don't do that."

"What?"

"Try to avoid saying his name around me. It's all right. I know you're working with him, and I'm glad." She ran a finger around the rim of the ceramic mug, her gaze fixed on the steaming tea.

He leaned back in his chair. "In case you were wondering, Jesse's not doing great. He's devastated by what happened."

Meryn shoved back her chair, the legs scraping on the cement floor. "We should get home, so we're there when Abby arrives."

Shane grasped her arm. "I'm sorry. But you said I could talk about him."

"I know." Meryn tugged free of his grasp. "It's not a problem. I just think we should go." She carried her still-full mug over to the cart that held the grey buckets for dirty dishes.

Seeing his sister in pain drove something sharp deep into Shane's gut. Especially when there was nothing he could do to make it better.

Brendan stood and reached across the table to punch him in the upper arm. "Let's go."

Shane glared at him. "You are really asking for it today."

"What are you going to do about it?"

Since his brother had a couple of inches on him, and was a solid two hundred and fifty pounds of muscle to his two twenty, likely not much. "Just watch your back."

Brendan snorted. "I'm shaking now."

"You should be."

Shane walked over to set his cup inside one of the buckets. Meryn had waited for them by the cart, and he slid an arm around her shoulders. "Ready to go?"

Her smile looked forced. "Definitely. Let's go find out what Abby is like. It would be good if at least one of the three of us wasn't lonely and pathetic."

Shane was relieved to see the usual spark of good humour in her eyes, even if it burnt out quickly. "I thought you invited her for you, not me."

"Oh, right. I did, of course."

He shook his head. "You're a terrible liar, kid."

She flashed him a smile as she pushed open the door.

Shane followed her out, blinking in the bright sunshine.

Abby stood beside a blue compact car in the parking lot, talking to a tall man in tan shorts and a striped golf shirt.

The man didn't look happy. Abby said something to him, and he shook his head.

Shane frowned. *Something doesn't feel right.* He took a step toward them, but the man flung open the door of the car and climbed behind the wheel.

Abby stepped back as he slammed the door and reversed out of the parking space. Her eyes met Shane's across the lawn, and she managed a smile that looked as forced as Meryn's.

Another woman going through a rough time? Not sure he could handle two of those right now. And who was the guy? The unfamiliar surge of jealousy startled Shane. *Maybe this is a bad idea.* He might be lonely and pathetic, but his life was reasonably uncomplicated. The idea of keeping it that way was appealing.

He followed Meryn as she walked over to Abby. His sister looked concerned as she touched Abby's elbow. "Is something wrong?"

"No." Abby threw a look in the direction the man had gone. "Just a little misunderstanding with my brother. No big deal."

Her brother. The muscles across Shane's shoulders loosened.

"Then we'll see you out at the farm?"

"Absolutely." Abby pulled an i-com from the pocket of her dress pants. "I just have to make a quick call. I'll be right behind you."

Resigned, Shane climbed up into the cab of his truck. It was just one lunch. No big deal. He blinked as Abby's words echoed through his mind. Their one lunch together might not be a big deal.

But, despite her assertion to the contrary, the disagreement between her and her brother seemed to be.

4

Jesse leaned back against the cold stone of the church building, drawing in deep breaths of humid summer air in an attempt to ease the pounding in his chest. It was torture, being this close to Meryn but feeling the distance between them. Maybe he shouldn't have come. He wanted to go to this church, though. He'd only been in Kingston for ten months, nine and a half of which had been spent enforcing the restrictions imposed on the Christians, and dealing with drug dealers and gang members when the army came down on both. He winced and touched a hand to his ribs, still tender from the beating he'd taken after Gallagher had tossed him into a cell a couple of weeks earlier with several of the men Jesse had arrested since being sent to the area.

He needed to be here, with his friends. Besides, this was one of the few churches left in Kingston that still taught boldly from the Bible. Every time he attended he left challenged, convicted, and empowered. He had found life through coming to this place.

The only problem was being here just might kill him.

"Mr. Christensen!" A flash of red shirt and blue jeans hurtled toward him.

Jesse braced himself for impact as Kate and Ethan's son barrelled into his legs. For someone who wouldn't be six for another couple of months, the kid threw a pretty mean tackle. Jesse chuckled as he took a step backward. "Hey, Matthew." Jesse grasped the boy's shoulders to steady them both, and crouched in front of him. "How was Sunday school?"

"Great. We learned about Gideon hiding down in a hole and an angel finding him and hauling him out to lead an army."

"That's a good one." And a powerful reminder that no one could accomplish anything while in hiding. Coming out of the dark, even to face a vastly superior army, was the only way to be of any use to anyone. And, like Gideon, Jesse and his "ragtag band of rebels"—as

Caleb had dubbed them just before he died—had God fighting on their side.

Jesse straightened up and rested a hand on Matthew's head as Ethan strode toward them.

"Sorry about that."

"It's not a problem. He's excited about what he learned in church today. Can't fault him for that." Jesse dropped his hand as Matthew took off, headed for his dad's car. "And, Ethan, I'll respect whatever you want your kids to call me, but I'd be good with Jesse. I'm kind of done with titles these days."

"I get it. Jesse it is. Should we head home for lunch?"

Jesse trailed along after Ethan. He noticed Meryn in the front seat of Shane's truck as they drove out of the parking lot, but she didn't look in his direction.

He'd sat at the back of the church that morning, so she wouldn't see him and he could make a quick getaway afterward. The problem was the back pew afforded him the perfect view of her. He'd worked to keep his eyes on the pastor, but his gaze strayed occasionally to the hair that gleamed almost black as it flowed over her shoulders. At one point she turned toward her brothers, and he caught a glimpse of the curve of her neck, the soft skin he'd once been free to press his lips to.

His eyes followed the truck as it turned out of the parking lot and headed down the street. A hand clamped down on his shoulder, and he swallowed and tore his gaze away.

"You good?" Ethan's eyes held a hint of sympathy.

Jesse managed a tight smile. "Sure. Just hungry."

"Right." Ethan's mouth quirked as he held out a hand toward the car. "Let's head out, then."

Jesse nodded and slid onto the passenger seat. He was hungry, all right, but he was going to have to stop wanting what he couldn't have and direct that desire toward something productive, like defeating Major Thomas Gallagher.

5

Shane shoved his chair back from the table. "That was delicious, Brendan, thanks. I'll help with the dishes, then I need to go out and do the chores."

Abby's eyebrows rose. "This is a working farm?"

"It hasn't been for a while, but we've just started getting a few animals."

Brendan reached for their plates. "Meryn and I will clean up. Why don't you take Abby out and show her around?"

"I'm sure Abby isn't interested in seeing a couple of cows."

"Actually, I wouldn't mind. I spent a lot of time at my grandparents' farm as a kid, but I haven't been on one in a few years. Seems like almost no one farms anymore." Abby sounded almost wistful.

Shane grabbed the empty glasses from the table and carried them to the dishwasher. "All right, then, if you're sure. I'll give you the big tour. Should take all of about thirty seconds." In spite of the objection he'd made, on principle, to his brother's attempt to get him and Abby alone, Shane was glad she was coming with him. The conversation at lunch had mainly centred around the sermon that morning, which had inspired them all. Meryn had asked Abby a little about herself, but not nearly enough to suit Shane. He'd been hoping to hear more about her past, who she was, and what had brought her to town. *And maybe what that scene in the parking lot was all about.*

"Wear my boots, Abby." Meryn waved a hand at a pair of black rubber boots in the corner by the door.

"Thanks." Abby helped clear the table, then pulled on the boots and followed Shane out the door. It had rained the night before, and neither of them spoke as they concentrated on avoiding the large puddles in the driveway. When they got to the opening in the cedar rail fence, Shane held out his hand for her to go on ahead. She reached the top of the hill that led down to the pond and stopped to gaze at the view. "It's beautiful here. Peaceful. That's what I miss the most about living in the country. It's so busy and chaotic in town, but I guess you get used to it after a while. I forget until I come back to the country that there are actually places like this that still exist in the world."

"It is pretty nice." Shane moved to her side. A faint floral scent drifted from her. "You couldn't pay me enough to live in a city. Way too much noise and dirt for me."

Abby looked down.

Shane followed her gaze. Streaks of mud were splattered across the top of Meryn's boots. When Abby looked back at him, he grinned. "That's good clean dirt, though. Not town dirt."

"Oh well, as long as it's clean dirt." She smiled. "Has this farm been in your family long?"

"Actually, no." Shane started for the barn, and Abby fell into step beside him. "Meryn married a guy named Logan Phillips four years ago. This was his place. Brendan and I moved here in April, when we came back from working out west." They reached the big barn doors, and Shane lifted the wooden bar that held them closed and leaned it up against the wall.

"Where is Logan now?"

He heaved on the doors to swing them open. "He served overseas as a peacekeeper, and he was killed in action shortly after they were married."

Abby looked stricken. "Poor Meryn."

"Yeah. It's been rough." Shane stopped in the middle of the barn floor.

Dust motes hung thick in the beams of sunlight that streamed through the windows set high on all four walls. The smell of warm animals and straw drifted on the air. He waved an arm around. "Well, this is it. Some stalls, four beef cows, and a workout area. That's the extent of our operation so far."

"Are you planning to get more animals?"

"A few. We'd like to eventually be self-sufficient out here. Probably get a few pigs, a couple of goats for milk, maybe some ducks for eggs and meat."

"Not chickens?"

"No. Meryn won't have live chickens on her place."

"Why not?"

Shane grabbed a hay bale from the stack in the corner, hauled it over, and dropped it in front of the stalls. "She had a bad experience with them as a kid. Still can't be around them." He pulled a knife from his pocket and flipped it open. "We have an older sister who's always been mean to her. She locked Meryn in our chicken coop one time just as a big storm hit. The chickens went wild and attacked Meryn. She still has nightmares about it."

He caught the shiver that moved through her as he crouched in front of the bale and slid the blade under the twine.

Memories of a childhood trauma of her own, or just a high degree of empathy for others?

"Where does your other sister live?"

Shane shrugged. "Here in town. We don't see her much."

"What's her name?"

"Annaliese."

"Annaliese O'Reilly. Interesting combination."

He looked up from trying to saw his way through the binder twine. Definitely had to invest in a new knife one of these days. "It's Pettersson, actually. She's a half sister. Her father was Swedish." Boy, Abby did a lot of digging around for information. What was she, some kind of reporter? The last thing he felt like talking about was his older sister. His gaze dropped back down to the bale, and he finally managed to snap the last strand of the twine holding it together. "What about you? What brought you and your brother to this area?"

"Work. We bought a little coffee shop downtown, and we're going to run it together."

Shane grabbed a handful of hay and tossed it into the trough in front of the cows. "Which coffee shop, Brewski's?"

"That's the one. Although we're calling it Maeve's, after my grandmother. Something we've always wanted to do. We saw it advertised one day and decided it was finally time to jump in." She leaned down and grabbed some of the hay. "May I?"

"Sure."

She pulled the hay apart and dropped it into the trough. She was only about five foot two or three, too short to reach over the top of the rail, but she stuck a hand between the bars and rubbed the forehead of one of the cows. The cow mooed softly and Abby's face lit up. More of her curls had come loose from the clip and bounced around her face. She shoved them back with her free hand.

Shane fought the ridiculous urge to reach out and unfurl one with his finger. What colour was that anyway? Bronze? Copper?

"So do you have another job or is this your full-time …?" She turned and caught him looking at her.

His neck warmed but he stepped closer. "You have some hay here." He pulled a couple of strands from her hair and tossed them onto the floor. The curls were as soft as he'd imagined.

She swallowed, her eyes still fastened on his. "Thanks."

"You're welcome." His voice had gone a little husky. He cleared his throat as he forced himself to turn away and grab another handful of hay. "Brendan and I work for a construction company during the week. This is definitely a part-time occupation for now." He dropped the hay in front of the last stall.

Abby sat down on another bale. "Tell me about Kingston."

He leaned back against the haymow, facing her, and crossed his arms. "What do you want to know?"

"Mostly what it's like here for Christians."

Shane rubbed his hands together to brush off the dust. "It was about the same here as everywhere else in Canada, I guess, until a few weeks ago."

"What happened then?"

"Our friend, Jesse Christensen, was a captain here. His best friend was the major and commanding officer. Things were okay under them, especially after Jesse became a believer. Unfortunately, there was a mutiny of sorts, and the lieutenant on the base, Gallagher, executed the major and got Jesse kicked out of the army at the same time. Gallagher's been promoted to major now and has taken over. Since he hates Christians, and Jesse in particular, we're expecting things to get a lot worse fast."

She pointed at the stalls. "Hence the cows."

"Exactly."

"So your friend hadn't done anything wrong?"

"Other than getting in Gallagher's way? No. Except for becoming a Christian, of course, which didn't go over well."

"No, I guess it wouldn't. And the major? What was he charged with?"

"The official charge was treason, although that was manufactured too." Shane frowned. Maybe he was wrong to tell her all this. Was it confidential information or public knowledge? His gaze dropped to her wrist. She wore an identity bracelet, but he probably shouldn't count on that. After all, he really didn't know anything about her. "Tell me about the conversation you had with your brother in the church parking lot. What was that about?"

A shadow crossed her face. "Nothing serious. Cameron isn't a believer and doesn't get why I feel the need to go to church. And he wasn't thrilled when I told him I was coming here."

"Because we're Christians."

"Yes. It's his philosophy that the less time spent with *Bible fanatics*—his term—the better." She offered him a wry grin. "I think he still holds out hope that I will overcome my own fanaticism one of these days, like an addiction I need to recover from."

"Hmm. Is there a twelve-step program for that kind of thing?"

"If there isn't, I'm sure he thinks there should be."

Shane pushed away from the bales. "Does it make him feel better that we're Bible fanatics without Bibles?"

Her smile faded. "It helps a bit. He thought that was a step in the right direction anyway."

Shane held out his hands. Abby reached up and he closed his fingers around hers, engulfing them, and pulled her to her feet. Her skin was warm and soft, and Shane struggled to draw in a breath. *Slow down, Shane.* What if she turned out to be a horrible person? He bit back a laugh. Nothing about her suggested she was capable of being horrible. He might not know her well, but he'd looked into her eyes, and they were guileless and trusting. And she'd shown obvious compassion for Meryn when he'd told her about Logan and the chicken coop story. Abby had a good heart. The rest was just details. Shane forced himself to let go of her.

Abby's cheeks had gone pink. "Thanks for the tour. I should probably head out now, though. The coffee shop needs work before we can open it up, so I have to go in for a while this afternoon to help out or Cameron will be even more upset with me."

He nodded and followed her out of the barn. Shane dropped the wooden bar back into the slots on the door. The two of them crossed the driveway again and stopped beside her car.

Meryn got up from the porch swing and came down the stairs.

When she reached them, Abby hugged her. "Meryn, thank you so much for inviting me for lunch."

His sister smiled. "You're welcome. It was great to have you. Do you have to go already?"

"Yes. I have a busy week ahead."

"Hey, it's Shane's birthday on Saturday, and I'm having a dinner for him, just a few friends. Can you come?"

Abby glanced over at him, as though she wasn't sure he'd want her there.

All of this was so new and unexpected. Part of him wanted a little time to figure out if this was something he was ready to pursue.

His eyes met hers. Maybe he didn't need any time. "If Meryn's cooking, you might want to come full, but if you're free, it would be great if you could join us."

Meryn punched him in the arm. "Actually, Kate's cooking and it's at her and Ethan's house."

"And how, exactly, is that you having a dinner for me?"

"It was my idea."

"Ah." Shane turned to Abby. "You're safe. Kate's a great cook."

Abby laughed. "All right, thanks. I'd love to."

"Good." Meryn clapped her hands. "We'll see you Saturday, six o'clock. Shane can tell you where it is." She retreated up the walkway and slipped into the house. The screen door banged shut behind her.

Shane turned back to Abby. "Sorry about that. I love my brother and sister, but they're about as subtle as a hurricane. Please don't feel you have to come."

"No, I'd really like to. Unless it would make you uncomfortable."

"Not at all. To be honest, I'd ..." *Might as well jump in with both feet.* "I'd like to get to know you better."

Her smile lit up her eyes. "I'd like that too."

For a moment, neither of them moved. Then she pulled open her car door and slid behind the wheel. "You were going to tell me where the party is?"

"Oh, yeah." When he gave her the address, she entered it into her dashboard GPS.

"Who are Kate and Ethan anyway?"

"Kate was a stray Meryn brought home from university one day. We all basically adopted her, and now she's more of a sister to us than Annaliese is. Ethan's her husband, and they have two kids, Matthew and Gracie."

"Any other family I should know about?"

"Our parents are in Ottawa, but that's it."

Abby pushed the button to start the car. "I'm looking forward to meeting everyone. See you at the party."

"Yeah." Shane lifted a hand. "See you." He closed the door.

He stood at the end of the walkway to the house for several minutes after her car had disappeared down the road. *What just happened?* He'd woken up that morning thinking it was going to be another ordinary day, and suddenly life had gotten very interesting.

6

Meryn carried the cake, ten flames flickering above thick white icing, out to the table on Kate and Ethan's back deck and set it in front of Shane. She rested a hand on his shoulder while everyone sang to him, then went back to her chair as he blew out the candles.

He cut the cake and Kate added a scoop of ice cream to each plate before handing them out to everyone.

Meryn forced herself to eat. *Don't look.* It was painful, knowing that Jesse was in the in-law suite forty feet away and not being able to see him, not even wanting to glance in his direction. Yet wanting it more than anything. Kate had invited him to join them, but he'd declined. Did he think it would bother her if he came?

Would it?

Meryn shook her head. Tonight was about Shane, not her. She pulled her wandering attention back to her brother.

He'd already finished his cake and opened several presents, as a growing pile of ripped paper on the ground by his chair attested.

Abby held out a small box.

Shane took it, smiling at her in a way Meryn hadn't seen before. "Thanks, Abby. You didn't need to bring me a gift."

"It's not much. I just saw it and thought of you."

Shane looked at her a moment longer, then down at the box in his hand. Carefully removing the blue paper, he lifted the lid and grinned. "Wow. Exactly what I needed." He lifted a Swiss army knife out of the box. "How did you know?"

"I saw you working away at that binder twine last week. Looked like you were in need of an upgrade."

"I am. Or was." Shane touched the back of his hand to hers. "Seriously, this is great. Thank you."

"You're welcome." Her eyes held his for a moment before she looked away.

Still holding the knife, Shane cleared his throat. "I appreciate everyone coming out to help me celebrate. And dinner was fabulous, Kate."

Kate held up her water bottle in salute as Ethan reached over and squeezed her hand. She smiled at him.

Meryn's chest tightened. Kate and Ethan were so happy together, so in love. And now Shane might have found someone ... She was happy for all of them, but seeing them together made her feel more alone than ever. At least Brendan was still single, so she wasn't the only one.

Kate waved a hand over the table. "There's plenty more food, so help—"

"Excuse me?"

Meryn looked up.

A woman stood at the corner of the house, suitcase in hand.

When she started toward them, Kate set down her bottle of water and walked to the top of the stairs.

The woman stopped at the bottom, one slender hand resting on the railing. Her honey-coloured hair hung straight and sleek past her shoulders. Long lashes framed bright-blue eyes. She looked stunning in a short denim skirt and pale-green blouse.

And somehow familiar ...

"I'm sorry to bother you. I'm looking for Jesse Christensen. I was told he lived at this address?"

Meryn jerked slightly.

The woman's gaze shifted to her.

Meryn forced a smile.

The woman smiled back before looking at Kate again.

"Yes, that's right." Kate pointed to the small building. "He lives out there, in the in-law suite."

The woman let go of the railing and gripped the suitcase in both hands as she looked over her shoulder. When she turned back, relief crossed her delicate features. "Thank you."

"You're welcome." Kate sat down beside Meryn. Her fingers gripped Meryn's arm as the woman started up the stairs to Jesse's place.

The woman rapped lightly on the door.

Meryn struggled to draw in a breath. Who was that? And what did she want with Jesse? She straightened in her chair. It wasn't her business who the woman was or what her connection to Jesse could be. Still, Meryn couldn't tear her eyes away as the door opened.

"Hope!" Jesse's exclamation echoed across the yard. He pulled the woman to him briefly before glancing over at the deck and letting her go.

Meryn looked away quickly. *I need to get out of here.* She patted Kate's hand then pulled her arm away. "Since you did the cooking, Kate, I'll clean up." She reached for everyone's plates and piled them up with a clatter, then shoved back her chair and stood. Without a glance in the direction of the yard, she strode toward the house.

Brendan slid open the glass doors. "I'll help you with the dishes."

"Thanks, Brendan." Meryn stepped through the doors and crossed the kitchen with the pile of plates and forks. Her fingers shook as she set them down on the counter and yanked open the door of the dishwasher. After shoving the plates her brother handed her into the slots, she straightened up and turned around, nearly banging into Brendan.

"You okay, kid?"

"Of course. Why wouldn't I be?" Meryn started to walk around him, but he held out an arm to stop her.

"Brendan, seriously."

"I'm sure she's just a friend."

"It doesn't matter. I'm the one who told him to go. I have no right to care about what he does or who he does it with."

"So you don't."

"That's right."

He waited a few more seconds before dropping his arm.

Kate came into the kitchen with a platter of food in each hand. "Mer, are you—?"

Meryn glared at her. "Can everyone stop asking me if I'm okay? I'm fine, all right?"

"Um, I was just going to ask if you are planning to take the leftover cake home."

Heat rushed into her cheeks. "Cake?"

"Yes. Cake." Kate lifted up the plate with the remaining pieces on it.

"Oh. Yes, sure. I'll take it home for Shane." She pressed trembling lips together. "Sorry."

Kate set down the dishes and hugged her. "It's okay. Totally get it. And I don't blame you. Did you see those legs?"

Brendan snorted a laugh.

Meryn shoved her away. "Kate!"

"What?" Kate lifted both hands in the air. "I thought you said you were fine."

"I am. But not fine enough to want to hear about her *legs*."

Kate reached for the dishtowel hanging on the oven door. "I'm sorry. I didn't realize there were degrees of fineness."

"Well, there are. Apparently." Meryn turned on the hot water tap and rinsed off a bowl. She handed it to Brendan to dry.

Kate grimaced and clutched the edge of the countertop as she pressed the hand holding the towel to her stomach.

Brendan set down the bowl and moved to her side. "What is it?"

"Nothing. Just ate a little too much for supper, I think."

Brendan frowned. "Why don't you go lie down? Meryn and I can finish up here."

"Yes, go Kate." Meryn turned off the tap. "You're not supposed to be cleaning up anyway, since you did all the cooking."

Kate waved a hand through the air. "I'm okay." She picked up a dripping pot. "Don't look so concerned, Brendan. It's nothing."

He didn't look convinced, but he didn't press her any further, just picked up the bowl and continued swiping the towel over it. He didn't move too far away from her, though.

Meryn turned the tap back on and ran a soapy pot under it, turning the water off again as quickly as possible. Water usage was at the orange stage, meaning restrictions like no watering lawns or washing cars, and limited usage inside the house was in effect as well. She didn't want to be the one to push Ethan and Kate over their quota for the week and get their water shut off. Although Canada still had a plentiful supply of clean water—relative to much of the rest of the world anyway—its increased value made it a precious commodity, and government regulations regarding its use were strictly enforced.

Brendan continued to hover around Kate, and Meryn repressed a smile. There were worse things in the world than having an overprotective brother. Or brothers. Shane and Brendan had always looked out for her, trying to shield her from Annaliese or anyone else who might try to hurt her. And they'd done the same for Kate after Meryn had brought her home.

Meryn glanced out the window at the building in the backyard.

Unfortunately, sometimes, despite their best efforts, there was nothing her brothers could do to keep either of the women from getting hurt.

7

Jesse followed Caleb's sister into his apartment and shut the door. "I can't believe you're here."

She set down the suitcase and turned to face him. "I got your message about Caleb." Her eyes misted. "Of course I had to come. He was …" Her voice broke.

Jesse wrapped his arms around her and held her tight, grief welling in his chest.

After a few moments, she stepped back and brushed her hair from her face. Her eyes were red, but she mustered a weak smile. "Sorry."

"Don't be. I still can't believe he's gone."

"Neither can I. I'll never forgive myself for not coming home to see him more often. I wasted so much time …"

"Don't do that." Jesse grasped her elbow and led her toward the couch. "You'll drive yourself crazy. Caleb knew you loved him, and he loved you too."

She sat down and crossed one leg over the other, then leaned forward and clasped her hands together on top of her knee. "What happened, Jess?"

He dropped onto the other end of the couch and turned to face her. "It was my fault."

"Your fault? How?"

"The lieutenant on the base, Gallagher, always hated me. When Caleb went to Germany to provide security for the G7 Summit, Gallagher saw his chance and arrested me. He managed to get a commission to find me guilty of treason and sentence me to death."

"But …"

He held up a hand. He had to get this out now, or he wouldn't be able to finish the story. "An hour before I was to be executed, Gallagher brought in another prisoner."

"Caleb."

Jesse nodded. "Instead of killing me, he executed Caleb in my place, right in front of me."

Hope's eyelids fluttered closed.

Jesse gave her a minute.

She opened her eyes. "How?"

The sight, the deafening sound, ripped through him as if it had happened seconds earlier. "He shot him in the back of the head."

She choked out a sob.

Jesse reached for her hand. "I'm so sorry, Hope. It should have been me."

"No. It wasn't your fault. Gallagher is to blame. And Caleb wouldn't have wanted it any other way. He promised Rory he'd take care of you. If you had been killed, he never would have been able to forgive himself."

"I'm not sure I can forgive myself either." He let go of her and ran his fingers through his hair.

"You have to find a way, Jess. You know he would never have wanted you to carry this around."

"No, he didn't. He told me this was the way it was supposed to happen, that his job was the easier one, and my work here was just beginning."

"And I know he meant it." Hope wiped away the moisture under her eyes with her fingers. "Where is he buried?"

"The army has designated an area for executed prisoners, a field just outside of town. I'll take you there next week."

"Thank you. I need to say goodbye." Hope stood and wandered around the room. "This is a nice place."

Jesse propped a shoulder against the back of the couch. "It's temporary. It belongs to friends of mine, Kate and Ethan. You probably saw them on your way out here. She was the one with the short red hair."

"Yeah, she told me where to find you." Hope ran a hand across the spine of the few books of his that Treyvon Adams, his one remaining potential ally in the army, had packed up and brought to him. Jesse had stacked them on one of the wooden shelves that lined the walls on either side of the television set. "And what about the other one?"

"What other one?"

"The one with the long, dark hair." She turned and leaned back against the shelf. "What's going on between the two of you?"

"Nothing."

She tilted her head.

Jesse sighed and pushed to his feet. "All right. There was something, but it's over now."

"It was serious."

He hesitated. "Yes. I wanted to marry her."

"What happened?"

"When I proposed to her a few weeks ago, she informed me she was already married. Or had been. Turns out her husband was a soldier too, a peacekeeper, and he went missing shortly after being deployed to the Middle East four years ago. Last year the army sent her his death certificate, but she still had doubts, because they were so vague on details. When I said I might be able to find out something about him, she gave me his name."

"Which was?"

"Logan Phillips."

"Not the guy you …"

"That's the one."

Her eyes widened. "Jess, no. That nightmare is never going to end for you, is it?"

He let out a humourless laugh. "Apparently not. Anyway, when she found out I was the one who killed her husband, she told me, understandably, to leave and never come back, so here I am." He waved a hand around the room.

"So you lost …"

"Everyone? Everything? In one fell swoop? Yep, that's about it."

She squeezed his arm. "That's awful."

He shrugged, an attempt at Meryn's default defence mechanism. "How did you know?"

"What?"

"That there had been something between us?"

"When I mentioned I was looking for you, something flashed

across her face. It was there and gone almost at once, but it was pretty telling. I felt her eyes on me the whole time I was walking out here. Then, just before we came inside, you glanced over at her, as though you didn't want her to see me with you."

"Awfully smart, aren't you?"

"That's what I've been telling you for years." A small smile played around her mouth. "Anyway, next time I see her, I'll tell her there is not now, and never has been, anything between us. Because, eww." She shuddered.

Jesse snickered. He knew exactly what she meant. He loved Hope, always had, but he would never be able to get past feeling like she was his sister. Somehow Rory had done it, but ... The thought of his older brother sent more grief flooding through him.

Hope touched his arm. "I still miss him too."

He narrowed his eyes. "What is it with you and Caleb? I have never been able to hide anything from you. It's maddening, to be honest."

She laughed. "Too bad. You're going to have to get used to it, my friend."

"Why? Are you staying for a while?"

She scuffed the floor with the toe of one of her white sandals. "Actually, I thought I might stay for good."

Joy flooded through him, tempering the grief. "Hope. That would be fantastic."

"Do you really think so?"

"Yes. Absolutely. But what made you decide to leave L.A.?"

Hope lifted slender shoulders. "After I heard about Caleb, I took a long overdue look at my life. It struck me that it was pretty empty, that I'd spent the last few years pursuing something that wasn't even real, and that definitely hadn't brought me any fulfillment or joy. I was running away, Jess." She tucked a strand of hair behind one ear. "The worst of it is that I traded all of that for time with Caleb, time I can never get back now. I realized then that I needed to come home, even if it was a little late." She squeezed his arm. "I know Rory and I never actually made it to the altar, but you're still my brother. You're still family to me. The only family I have left."

"You're family to me too." He covered her hand with his. "And I can't tell you how happy I am that you're staying." He glanced around the room. "The only problem is …"

"I can't stay here." She dropped her hand. "It would look bad, and it might cause even more trouble between you and your lady love."

"First of all, it's not possible for there to be more trouble between us than there already is. She's made it clear that whatever we had is over. Which means she is also not my lady love. Not anymore. And finally, and most importantly, you will not, under any circumstances, tell her that there is nothing between you and me. I don't want her thinking we were talking about her, or that you are suggesting that the absence of any romantic feelings between us means that she and I are free to get together again. Do you understand?"

Hope's eyes held a mischievous glint, and his heart sank. She was too much like her brother. Nothing delighted either of them more than giving him a hard time.

"Hope, I'm not kidding."

She held three fingers to her temple. "Scout's honour."

Jesse shook his head. "I've known you all your life, and you were never a Scout. Besides"—he reached for her other arm and pulled it out from behind her back—"I'm not falling for the old fingers-crossed-behind-your-back trick again."

"Too bad. I used to get you with that one all the time."

"I remember. There's a reason I used to call you Hope the Dope, you know. Unfortunately for you, I'm not eleven anymore."

"I can see that. And I'm sure …" She gestured back toward the house.

"Meryn."

"Oh, pretty name. I like it. Anyway, I'm sure Meryn can see it as well. If you two were that close, there's no way she can keep pushing you out of her life forever. You're one of the last of the great ones, not to mention ridiculously good-looking—at least some women have told me they think so. Maybe she just needs a little nudge to help her remember how things were with you. How they could be again."

"No." Jesse pointed a finger at her. "No nudging. I mean it."

Hope tossed her hair back over one shoulder and laughed. "All right. No nudging. Whatever you say."

He bit his lip and studied her. Something was up. Hope never capitulated to him that easily. "I mean it."

"So you said." Her face grew serious. "I'm just teasing you, Jess. I'd never do anything to hurt you. You know that, right? I want you to be happy."

"I know. I want you to be happy too."

"What would make me happy at the moment would be finding a nice hotel and climbing into bed and sleeping for a couple of days."

"You don't need to go to a hotel. Not for tonight anyway. Kate and Ethan have a spare room, and I'm sure they'd be happy to let you use it."

"Really? That sounds amazing. I actually hate hotels. Living with a family, even just for a day or two, sounds like the greatest thing in the world right now."

"See if you feel the same way when you have a five-year-old and a three-year-old bouncing on your bed at seven o'clock in the morning."

Sadness welled in her eyes. "Sounds perfect."

His chest clenched. She and Rory had gotten engaged just before Rory headed out for his last tour. They'd talked about having a whole bunch of kids. Then Rory left and never came back, and, as far as he knew, she'd never let herself get involved with anyone else.

"I'd love to be in a house that's filled with the sound of children giggling and playing. Even at seven in the morning."

"All right, then." Jesse picked up her suitcase. "Let's go get you settled." He pointed to her identity bracelet as they walked toward the door. "How did you get that so quickly?"

"Apparently my name was on some kind of list. When I checked in at the airport, I must have been red-flagged, because they were waiting for me when I got off the plane in Toronto. They took me into a room and gave me my options—to renounce my faith or put on a bracelet." She held up her wrist. "I went with this one." Hope lowered her arm when they reached the door and tapped his bracelet. "There's a story here, isn't there?"

"There is."

"Does it involve the dark-haired beauty on the deck?"

"It does."

"I'd like to hear it someday."

"I'd like to tell it to you."

She wrapped her fingers around his bracelet. "You and Caleb both. Rory would have been so happy."

"I like to think he is."

Hope smiled and let go of him.

Jesse grasped the doorknob. "I'm really glad you're here, Hope. I have to admit I've been feeling pretty alone in the world lately."

She touched his cheek with one finger. "Well, you're not alone anymore."

He nodded and opened the door. "Neither are you."

She gave him a sad smile, and his heart warmed. Even if she did give him a hard time at every possible opportunity, Hope was family.

And at the moment, family was just what he needed.

8

Meryn wiped the last of the crumbs off the counter and shook the cloth into the sink. "There. Dishes are done, finally."

Brendan hung the towel over the stove. "Good. I think the guys and Abby are out in the garage, so I'm going to join them."

"I need to talk to Kate for a few minutes. I'll be out soon."

Brendan kissed Kate on the cheek. "Thanks for dinner. Get some rest."

"I will." Kate slid an arm around Meryn's shoulders as Brendan disappeared out the patio doors. "At the risk of my health and well-being, are you really okay?"

"I don't have a choice, Kate. Jesse and I are done. I have to find a way to move on and to not resent him for doing the same."

"I just wish—"

A tapping sounded on the glass doors.

They both turned and Meryn froze.

Jesse and his friend, whoever she was, stood on the other side.

Kate shot Meryn a quick look before heading over and sliding the door open. "Jesse, hi. Come on in."

"Thanks, Kate." He held out his hand and the woman stepped inside.

Meryn contemplated her. Why did she look so familiar? Had they met somewhere before?

Jesse followed her into the kitchen. "Kate, Meryn, I'd like you to meet Hope Donevan, Caleb's sister."

Shock tingled across her skin. *Caleb's sister.* Not someone he had just met, then. Meryn drew in a shaky breath, crossed the room, and laid a hand on the woman's arm. "Hope. I'm so sorry for your loss. We were all devastated by what happened to Caleb. He was such a great guy."

"Yes, he was. Thank you, Meryn."

Meryn nodded and pulled her hand back.

Jesse cleared his throat. "Hope just arrived here from California. She was going to go to a hotel, but I wondered if she might be able to use your guest room, Kate, just for a night or two."

"Of course. You're more than welcome, Hope. And you can stay as long as you want. Did Jesse warn you that we have two little ones, though? It might not be the best place to recover from jet lag."

"That's not a problem. I love kids."

"They're in bed now, but I'm sure you'll meet them bright and early in the morning. Come with me and I'll show you where everything is."

Meryn shoved back a surge of panic as the two of them left the room. As she'd told Jesse before, they weren't children. And they were going to have to see each other sometimes. If they were planning to move on with their lives, they'd have to find a way to be together without it being awkward and uncomfortable.

And she had to figure out how to not let it bother her when women from California with perfect hair and great legs showed up at his door and ... Her head jerked. *Wait. Hope Donevan? From California? It couldn't be.* Her eyes met Jesse's emerald ones.

He was watching her intently. "What?"

"Is that *the* Hope Donevan? As in the *The Last Treasure Hunter* show?"

"Yeah, she was on that for a couple of years."

"Why didn't you ever mention that Caleb's sister was a big television star?"

He shrugged. "I guess because I don't think of her that way. To me, she'll always be pesky little Hope the Dope in pigtails."

"Well, she's all grown up now," Meryn said dryly.

"I've known her all my life, Meryn. We grew up together. She's like a sister to me. In fact, she nearly was. She and Rory were engaged. They were supposed to get married when he came back from his last tour."

Her shoulders slumped. "That must have been terrible for her." She pressed a palm to the counter to steady herself. "Still, what the two of you are to each other isn't really my business."

"Right. Always best not to get too involved in the personal lives of your *co-workers*."

"Exactly." Meryn turned away and opened a cupboard door, searching for a container for the leftover cake. She found one but had to crouch down and reach into the back of the cupboard to retrieve the lid. The back of her head burned. As aware of his presence in the room as she had always been, she had never felt it as keenly as she did at that moment, when he stood silently behind her, watching. Was he waiting for her to throw herself at him and beg him to give them another chance? Or was he counting the seconds, like she was, until Kate and Hope came back?

Meryn scraped the cake from the platter into the container and shoved the lid down hard to snap it into place.

A rosy glow fell across the counter. Sunset.

Gripping the container in both hands, she spun around. "It's getting dark. Please tell Kate I had to leave."

Jesse nodded but didn't move out of her way as she approached the door.

Meryn stopped and looked up at him.

"I thought we were going to be friends."

She clutched the container tighter. "I said I'd try, and I am."

"By running away?"

"I'm not running away. I just don't want to get caught out after curfew. I have no desire to get arrested again and go through what I went through the last time."

He flinched. A direct hit.

Meryn closed her eyes for a few seconds. That wasn't fair. She opened her eyes. "I apologize, I shouldn't have—"

"No, you're right; you'd never want to go through all that again." His voice was tight. "You should go." He stepped to the side and held his arm toward the door.

As badly as she wanted to escape, she hadn't wanted to leave that way. Hadn't meant to hurt him any more than she already had. But maybe it was for the best. Meryn nodded and slipped past him and out the door. Heart pounding, she made her way around the house to the garage.

The hood of Ethan's car was up, and both he and Shane were bent over the engine.

Brendan stood by the workbench at the back of the garage. He looked over when she approached. "What's up?"

"Nothing. Can we go?" Her voice shook.

Brendan set the screwdriver he'd been holding down on the bench. "You're right, we should."

Shane twisted to look back at her, flashlight in hand. "Could you give me a couple of minutes? Ethan's car wouldn't start this morning, so we're trying to figure out why."

Abby had been leaning against the wall, but she stepped forward. "I can drive Shane home if you want to get going, Meryn."

Shane looked over at her. "Would you mind?"

"Not at all."

Brendan glanced at Meryn and shrugged.

Meryn didn't really care who took whom at that point. She just wanted to leave. "Thanks, Abby."

"No problem."

Meryn spun around and headed for the truck.

Her brother's footsteps echoed behind her, but she didn't look back. *I'm fine. I'm fine. I'm fine.*

The word had lost all meaning.

9

Shane held his breath as Ethan pressed the ignition button to start the car.

Nothing happened.

He sighed. They could be here all night. Except … He turned around to look outside. It was really starting to get dark now. He had no right to keep Abby out after curfew.

"We should get going, Ethan. It's getting late."

Ethan wiped his hands with a rag. "No problem. I'll keep playing with it."

Abby moved out of the shadows where she'd been waiting. "Would you mind if I took a look?"

Ethan looked surprised, but he gestured toward the engine. "Be my guest."

"I need to check something on the computer first." Abby waited for Ethan's nod, then climbed into the passenger seat of the car and touched the screen set into the dash.

Shane shot a look at Ethan as they waited.

Ethan lifted his shoulders.

After a couple of minutes, Abby jumped out and walked around to the front of the vehicle. She leaned in and fiddled with a couple of wires. "Could someone grab that screwdriver Brendan left on the workbench?"

"I'll get it." Shane's mind whirled as he strode to the bench and grabbed the tool. Did she really know what she was doing? "Here." She held out her hand, and he set the screwdriver on it.

Abby tightened something on the alternator and straightened up. "Want to give it a go?"

Ethan slid behind the wheel and pushed the button.

The engine roared to life before settling into an even idle.

"Ha!" He smacked the steering wheel. "I can't believe it." He climbed out of the car. "No offence, but I wouldn't have taken you for someone who knows her way around an engine. How did you know what to do?"

Abby's gaze was fixed on the hood as she slammed it closed. "My dad was a mechanic. I started hanging around in the garage, watching him, when I was three or four. By the time I was a teenager, I was the one fixing the cars, and he was watching me."

"Well, I'm extremely impressed."

"Me too." Shane grabbed another rag from a nail on the wall and handed it to her.

His fingers brushed hers as she took it from him. Shane swallowed and stepped back.

Abby wiped her hands and inclined her head toward the doorway. "We should probably head out."

"Yes, we should." Shane reached for the rag and hung it back up on the wall.

Abby started for the driveway.

Ethan jabbed Shane in the ribs. "Definite keeper," he whispered.

Shane sent him a warning look before exiting the garage behind Abby. She'd brought the blue car her brother had been driving on Sunday, a Kev, like Meryn's, only a newer and slightly larger model.

Ethan followed her around the front of the vehicle. "So, Abby."

She stopped at the driver's side door and turned back to face him.

He held out his hand. "Seriously, thank you. I likely would have had the car towed to a garage tomorrow. You saved me a big bill. I owe you one."

She slid her hand into his. "You don't owe me anything, Ethan. I had a wonderful time tonight. It's been awhile since I've been with a big family. It was really nice." The wistful tone was back in her voice.

"You're welcome here any time." Ethan let go of her.

"Thanks. Please tell Kate I said goodbye."

"I will."

She opened the door and got in.

Ethan shut it behind her. Over the top of the car, he mouthed the word *keeper* to Shane, which, in the rapidly fading twilight, looked more like a command. *Keep her.*

Shut up, Shane mouthed back as he pulled his door open.

Ethan grinned and backed away from the car.

Shane climbed into the passenger seat, grunting as his knees hit the dashboard.

"Sorry." Abby giggled. "That's usually my seat. There's a button on the panel on the door to move it back. The one closest to the front of the car."

Shane studied what looked like a cockpit display mounted on the door. He found the one she'd described to him and held the button for several seconds as the seat slowly retreated toward the back. "Good grief. Are you even tall enough to be sitting in the front seat?"

She smacked him on the arm with the back of her hand. "Hey, I've been tall enough to sit up here since I was sixteen years old."

He laughed. A woman who could fix cars *and* make fun of herself. Maybe she *was* a keeper. The thought sobered him and he grabbed for his seatbelt. It didn't give when he pulled on it.

"Everything's automatic in this car. The button for the seatbelt is on the same panel. It's in the middle somewhere. There." Abby pointed.

Shane took a stab at one. The sunroof slid open. He looked helplessly at Abby.

Her lips were pressed together as if she was trying not to laugh. "A little to the right. Here." She reached across him and tapped the button.

Shane breathed in the same light floral scent he'd noticed the day she came to the farm.

She straightened and he pressed his thumb to the button. The seat belt slid across his chest and locked into place. "Okay, that's pretty cool."

"I know. It's Cameron's car, so I'm still getting used to it, but when I'm driving it, I always feel like it might take off and start flying or something."

"I can see why."

Abby pressed the ignition button, and the car purred to life.

"What do the rest of the buttons do?"

"One lowers the window, of course, and another one darkens and lightens the tint."

Shane's eyebrows rose. "Really?"

"Yep. And one of them warms the seat and one cools it off. One changes the colour of the exterior of the car. And one makes coffee ..."

He turned to her, eyes widening.

Abby laughed. "All right, I'm kidding about that one, but it would be awesome, wouldn't it?"

"Definitely. I might actually be able to break my Tim Hortons' habit if I could get in my car, hit a button, and order a double-double."

She grinned as she pulled out onto the street. "Me too. Although it wouldn't be good for my new business."

"So, your dad was a mechanic?"

"That's right." She gripped the steering wheel and stared out the front window.

Come to think of it, she hadn't looked at him or Ethan the first time she said it either. What was up with that? She *was* driving. But she hadn't been driving in the garage. "What about your mother? What did she do?"

"She was a doctor. A surgeon. Still is, actually."

"Oh, good. Then, if we get in an accident and I suffer a life-threatening injury, you can perform the operation, on the side of the road, that will save my life?"

She did look over at him then, a smile playing across her lips. "Absolutely. As long as you don't mind me getting blood all over that new knife of yours."

"It is a pretty great knife. For such a worthy cause, though, I think I'd forgive you."

"I'm glad to hear it." The headlights of her vehicle arced across the trees when she turned into the driveway of the farm.

Shane winced. It had gotten dark fast. "This wasn't the best idea. You shouldn't drive home in the dark, in case you get pulled over."

"I'll be okay."

"No, really, Abby. You're new to town, but you should know that they don't take it lightly here when Christians ignore the curfew."

She circled the vehicle around the farmyard and pulled up to the walkway.

Shane reached over and grasped her arm. "I'd feel sick if you got in trouble because of me. Could you spend the night?"

She shot him a look.

"We have extra rooms," he added quickly. "You could use one of them and go to your place first thing in the morning. And Meryn's home, so she could loan you whatever you needed."

"All right." Abby powered down the vehicle and nodded at the panel on his door. "It's the button to the right of the one you used to put it on."

"Thanks." He pressed the one she'd indicated and the seatbelt released.

Abby followed him to the house. "I need to let Cameron know what's going on. I'll call him out here, so I don't bother anyone." She pointed to the porch swing.

"Okay. Come on in when you're done. I'll put the kettle on."

She nodded and pulled an i-com from her pocket.

Once inside, Shane filled the kettle and plugged it in. The window was closed and he couldn't make out the words, but he could hear her voice rise occasionally. Cameron probably wasn't too happy about her spending the night with the *Bible fanatics*. Or maybe he didn't believe his sister when she told him she'd be sleeping in the spare room. *Stay out of it, Shane.* He didn't like the idea of someone giving Abby a hard time. He might need to have a chat with that guy at some point.

The kettle whistled and he dropped two tea bags from the canister into the teapot and poured the boiling water over it.

Abby yanked open the door. Her forehead was creased and her eyes stormy.

Shane shoved back the urge to take her in his arms and hold her until the muscles that were clearly all tensed up relaxed. "That didn't go over well with Cameron, I assume?"

"Not at all. Most of the time he's a great brother, but the whole Christian thing is definitely his hot button, and it's been coming up a lot since we arrived in town."

"Would tea help?"

"Maybe. Do you want to go for a walk first?" She shook her hands in front of her. "I need to burn off a little excess adrenaline."

"Sure." Shane set the lid on the ceramic pot and followed her back out onto the porch. "Meryn was heading up to bed, but she said she'd leave pyjamas and a toothbrush in the spare room for you." They walked across the yard in silence. He had to work to keep up with her, in spite of the fact that his stride was twice as long.

She really must be worked up.

When they reached the bench at the top of the hill overlooking the pond, he inclined his head toward it. "Want to sit?"

"All right." She dropped onto the bench. Her toes barely touched the tips of the grass, and he laughed.

Abby followed his gaze, then looked up and pointed a finger at him. "No short jokes. Believe me, I've heard them all."

Shane sat down beside her. "Oh yeah? What's your favourite?"

"You mean which one do I hate the least? How about, 'I'd short-sheet your bed, Abby, but you probably wouldn't notice.' Or, 'Your family tree must be a bonsai.'"

Shane chuckled. "Sorry, but those are pretty good."

"It's okay. I'm sure you get lots of tall jokes."

"Not as many as Brendan, but I would be quite happy if no one ever asked me what the weather's like up here again."

"I'm sure." She pulled both knees to her chest and wrapped her arms around them as she tilted back her head. The sky had gone ink-black while she'd been on the phone with her brother. "It's a gorgeous night. I always forget how many stars there actually are in the sky."

The light of the half-moon that had risen over the top of the barn bathed her face in a warm glow. The lines were gone now, and she looked completely at peace.

Shane swallowed. "You're beautiful in the moonlight."

Abby looked over at him.

He winced. "That sounded like a cheesy pick-up line or something."

"No, it didn't. It was nice. It just caught me by surprise. That's another drawback of being short. I get 'cute' most of the time, the odd 'adorable,' sometimes even accompanied by a pat on the head, but not a lot of 'beautiful.' Not that I would expect to. I mean ..." She looked down at her clasped hands. "I do have a mirror, even if I have to jump up and down to see into it." She offered him a self-deprecating smile. "Anyway, I know how I look, and I'm not exactly—"

"You're beautiful."

"Okay. Thank you." Abby slid to the front of the bench. "I should probably get some sleep. I need to be at the shop early in the morning, or Cameron will have my head. And I can't afford to lose six inches." She wrinkled her nose. "Sorry. I tell jokes when I'm nervous."

"Why are you nervous?"

"I ... I wasn't expecting this."

"Neither was I."

"My life is crazy right now, with moving to town and starting up a business. It really isn't the best time ..."

"Sounds like the perfect time to me. A time for new beginnings."

She pursed her lips. "Maybe."

"My life is a bit crazy too." Shane brushed the back of his fingers across her cheek. "But I don't think that's a good enough reason to run from something that might be truly great."

"I guess not."

"Look, why don't we start by spending some time together." He took one of her curls between his fingers and slowly unfurled it, like he'd wanted to since the day they'd met. "We can take this slow and see where it goes. No pressure. Okay?"

She studied him for a moment. "All right, O'Reilly. Slow is good."

Shane let go of the curl, and it sprang back into place. He stood up. "Let's go inside. I don't want to *short-change* you on your sleep." He reached for her hand and pulled her to her feet.

She rolled her eyes. "Really?"

"Sorry. I couldn't resist."

They climbed the stairs to the porch, and Shane pulled open the screen and turned the knob on the inside door. It was locked. He groaned. "Oh no. Brendan must have heard me come in earlier and thought I was still inside. He knows Meryn never locks the door, so he's gotten into the habit of coming down right before he goes to bed to do it for her."

"She doesn't lock her door?"

"No. When she and Jesse were together, that drove him crazy, especially when she lived here alone."

"Meryn and Jesse were together?"

"Oh yeah, I forgot you didn't know that."

"That does clear up a lot of things about tonight."

He let go of the screen door, and it swung closed. "Even though she was the one who ended it between them, I think it really threw her when another woman showed up on his doorstep. Especially since it's been less than a month since they broke up."

"What happened?"

"It's a long story. I'll tell you sometime, but for now, I'm going to see if I can get a hold of Brendan, so he can let us in." He started to pull his i-com from his pocket, but she stepped in front of him.

"Don't bother him." Abby pulled out one of the pins holding her curls in place. "I've got this." She stuck the pin into the keyhole and wriggled it around until it clicked. "Ta-da." She turned the knob and pushed open the door.

Shane stared at her. "You're full of surprises, aren't you?"

"It's not that big an accomplishment. This lock is probably as old as the house. Not exactly foolproof."

"Let me guess, your uncle was a locksmith." He held the door open for her and she went into the kitchen.

She laughed. "No, that little trick I figured out on my own."

"Have a seat. I'll get the tea." Shane grabbed two mugs out of the cupboard and filled them from the pot. He carried them over to the table and set them down. "Here you go."

"Thanks." Abby pulled her mug closer and inhaled. "Mmm. Peppermint, my favourite."

"Mine too. Should be well-steeped by now." He took the chair beside her. "So, tell me how you learned to break into houses like that."

She leaned back in her chair. "Do you remember that show that came out in the late twenties, *The Unstoppables*?"

"Oh yeah. Brendan and I loved that one."

"Me too. So did Cameron. We were in awe of those kids who could get past any locked door. We studied everything they did and practised for hours on any door we could find. We got pretty good at it, especially me, which probably wasn't for the best, because …"

"What?"

"You'll find this hard to believe, but I was a bit of a troublemaker when I was a kid."

"Actually, I don't find that hard to believe at all."

She smiled. "Anyway, when none of the locks in our house provided a challenge anymore, I started, with Cameron egging me on, to try my newfound talent out on the neighbours' doors. We'd wait until we were sure no one was home, then go to work. Eventually we broke into every single house on the block."

"Wow. A little criminal. Who knew?"

Humour danced in her eyes. "No one. We never got caught, and nobody ever reported it, because we didn't take anything. We didn't even go inside. We just wanted to see if we could do it."

"Since we're confessing, I'll tell you that Brendan and I once tried the same thing. We were more interested in cars than houses, so one time, when friends of my parents were visiting, we snuck out to their vehicle and tried breaking in. Unfortunately, my dad came out and caught us. He …" Shane looked down at his cup of tea. "Well, never mind what he did. Long story short, our criminal career came to an abrupt and painful end."

"Ah." Her eyes glinted with amusement. "Old-school parenting."

"My dad was old school all the way. Something I can appreciate now, although I definitely didn't at the time."

"I bet that show got sued for millions by all the people whose homes were broken into by ten-year-old delinquents."

"I bet it did. Probably why it was only on the air for a couple of years. Just long enough for you to garner all the skills you needed to make you a proficient little thief."

She held up a finger. "Not a thief. Just a potential thief. And is it necessary to attach the adjective *little* before every name you call me?"

"Sorry." Shane drained the last of his tea and set down his mug. "I'm going to have to keep an eye on you, aren't I?"

"I could make a joke about how that would be tricky for you to do when your head is so high up it's covered with snow even in the summertime, but I'll refrain."

"Thank you. I'll try to limit the height jokes too, then."

"I'd appreciate it." She yawned and covered her mouth with her hand.

"Right. Time for bed. I'll show you to the spare room. As soon as I perform what I now realize is no more than a symbolic gesture." He carried their mugs over to the sink, then turned the lock in the door handle. He had no doubt Abby could get past any closed door she wanted. She'd definitely crashed through all his defences with far less effort than she'd expended getting them into the house tonight.

He followed her through the kitchen and into the living room, mulling over that thought, surprised at how little—he grinned as the word entered his mind—that actually scared him.

10

The i-com on Jesse's nightstand buzzed, and he grabbed for it. Still half asleep, he blinked, trying to make out the name of the sender.

Treyvon Adams. *Can we meet? It's urgent.*

Jesse ran a hand over his face before tossing off the blankets and sitting up. He switched on the audio function, not trusting himself to find the right keys in the pitch black of his room, even though the screen was dimly lit.

"When and where?" His voice was hoarse but the device transcribed and sent out the words correctly.

The answer came back immediately. *Now. I'll come to you.*

Jesse hesitated, then inputted the address. He sighed and tossed the i-com onto the table. He still wasn't sure if he could trust Trey, but he really hoped so, since he had led him straight to the backyard of Ethan and Kate's place.

Although Trey could probably have gotten that information from a tracking centre if he'd wanted to.

He stood up and pulled on jeans and a T-shirt, then headed into the bathroom to brush his teeth and splash cold water on his face. His hair was growing longer, now that he didn't have to conform to army standards, and he ran his fingers through it before grabbing his i-com and going out into the living area. That was the best an unexpected visitor in the middle of the night was going to get.

A quiet knock on the door startled him. Where had Trey messaged him from? He couldn't have gotten there from the base that quickly.

Jesse pressed the switch on the lamp beside the couch to fill the room with soft light before striding to the door.

Trey stood on the top step, his beret clutched in both hands. "I was parked down the street, where I dropped you off. I figured you'd be somewhere in this neighbourhood. I didn't want to look up your GPS coordinates, in case I drew anyone's attention to your location, or to the fact that I was coming here."

Jesse stepped back. "Come on in."

The two star shapes on the shoulders of Trey's uniform jacket caught Jesse's eye, and his stomach clenched. Trey had been promoted to lieutenant. What did that mean? That Gallagher was rewarding him for his loyalty, or that he had Gallagher completely fooled?

Trey followed his gaze. "Oh yeah, apparently I'm still on the major's good side, so he doesn't suspect anything yet. Hopefully I can keep that going for a while."

"Why?"

"Why what?"

"Why are you so willing to help us? Take risks like coming here in the middle of the night. Gallagher will kill you if he finds out."

"I know, but I have to. I've been reading a Bible and finding out everything I can about Jesus Christ. I'm not sure what I believe yet, but everything I'm reading makes sense, and nothing that is happening to the Christians right now does. I feel like I have to do something to help make things right. And like I told you, I owe it to Major Donevan after what I did to him."

"He forgave you, you know."

Trey's dark eyes met his. "Do you really think so?"

"I know it. He asked me to talk to you, to answer any questions you might have, because he wanted you to hear the truth."

"That helps a lot, thank you." Trey nodded toward the couch. "Can we sit?"

"Sure." Jesse sat down on the chair across from him and balanced his i-com on the arm. "What's this about?"

Trey pulled his own unit from his jacket pocket. "Have you had your TV or computer on during the last couple of hours?"

"No, I've been asleep since twenty-three hundred or so."

"Well, something's going on. Looks like another terrorist attack."

"What kind?"

"Medical centres from about twenty-five cities across the country started reporting a sudden surge in people coming in with strange symptoms today. Early speculation was some kind of violent flu or E.

coli outbreak. A couple of hours ago, confirmation came in that the water in The Great Lakes Company bottles had been tampered with at their main facility in Toronto."

Jesse winced. The Great Lakes Company had been formed in the 2030s, after global water scarcity reached a critical level. The government saw an opportunity and took over the bottled water industry in Canada. The facility in Toronto was the largest bottled water producer in the world, shipping tens of thousands of cases a day across Canada and around the planet. "Tampered with? You mean poisoned?"

"Yes. They're advising everyone to avoid drinking any bottled water purchased in the last seven days. A hundred thousand cases here and around the world have been recalled."

Meryn. Jesse pushed back the fear that rose at the thought that something could happen to her. They had a well out at the farm and drank mainly tap water, since the price of bottled water had quadrupled in the last ten years. The only cases he'd ever seen at the farm were with her emergency supplies in the basement, and they'd been there a lot longer than a week. She and Brendan and Shane should be all right. Although they had been here for dinner. His gut twisted. Kate and Ethan did buy bottled water sometimes. Had they purchased any recently? Did anyone drink any tonight? Jesse's mind whirled. He had other friends in town that could be in danger. He'd have to warn Pastor John. He could let the people of his church know to be careful.

"The worst part is that we know who's responsible." Trey turned his i-com toward Jesse.

Jesse read the message quickly, then closed his eyes and exhaled. "The Horsemen." He pressed his fingertips to his temples to push back a surging headache. The Horsemen claimed to be a radical Christian group, responsible for the bombing of seven mosques across the country in an attack a little more than ten months ago, known as 10/10. No one had heard anything from them since, and Jesse's hope was that they had disbanded and would eventually be identified and proven not to have an affiliation with Christianity at all.

In spite of the fact that the link was based on an unsubstantiated claim by an unknown group, that attack had brought the military storming into cities across the country and accounted for the martial law still in effect, including the curfew and other restrictions imposed on Christians. And for the horrific sentences that continued to be meted out if any of them were found to have defied those restrictions, like the flogging Meryn had received for smuggling Bibles.

Jesse dropped his hands and opened his eyes. "How do you have clearance to receive a memo like that?"

Trey shoved the i-com back in his pocket. "I don't. A couple of weeks ago I managed to hack into the message centre on Gallagher's i-com. This came to him thirty minutes ago."

The unit on the arm of Jesse's chair vibrated. One three a.m. message signalled bad news. Two of them could only signal a very bad night, and possibly a lot of bad nights ahead. He picked it up and looked at the screen, his heart sinking.

Ethan.

Trey's warning had come too late.

Kate's really sick and I don't want to ask your friend to stay with the kids. Could you come?

On my way. Jesse stood up. "I have to go over to the main house. The woman who lives there, a good friend, is sick, and her husband is taking her to the hospital."

Trey followed him to the door. "Make sure they tell them as soon as they arrive if she had any bottled water to drink in the last couple of days. The hospital should have received the alert outlining what they are dealing with. There is an antidote and it's already being shipped out across the country, so tell your friends that if it hasn't arrived already, it should be there soon."

"Is this poison deadly?"

Trey hesitated. "Not usually, if the patient receives the antidote in time."

"Which is?"

"Three to four hours after exhibiting severe symptoms."

Three to four hours. How long had Kate been sick? He'd seen her last around nine o'clock, and she might have looked a little pale, but she hadn't been experiencing severe symptoms. When had they manifested themselves? If they had the antidote at the hospital, she should be okay. If not … "Why did you come and tell me all this? What were you hoping I would do?"

"I read the message exchange between Gallagher and the general at Headquarters after that memo came down. The general is furious and humiliated that the plant was infiltrated. He figures it must have been an inside job, that someone, or maybe more than one person, working at the plant is either affiliated with The Horsemen or was bribed or threatened by that group to carry this out. I don't know yet what the government is going to do to retaliate against Christians in order to demonstrate a zero tolerance for terrorism, but it will definitely do something. Gallagher assured the general he would do his part and come down hard on the believers in Kingston. So I came to give you a message to pass along to every Christian you know as fast as you possibly can."

"And what message is that?"

"To brace yourselves."

11

Jesse went around to the front of the house and met Ethan as he was coming out.

Kate leaned against him heavily. Her face was white and her red hair was plastered to her damp forehead.

Jesse swallowed and went ahead of them to open the car door.

"Thanks." Ethan helped Kate into the car and shut the door behind her. "Appreciate you staying with the kids. Meryn's going to come and get them in the morning and take them to the farm."

"Okay." Jesse grabbed Ethan's sleeve as Ethan started for the front of the vehicle. "They think there's been another terrorist attack."

"What's happened?"

"The government is warning everyone not to drink any bottled water purchased recently. A lot of people have gotten sick in the last twenty-four hours. The government suspects that someone poisoned the water at The Great Lakes Company facility in Toronto."

Ethan's face went as pale as his wife's. "Poisoned?"

"Yes. Did Kate drink any bottled water in the last couple of days?"

"I just brought home a case yesterday. I know she had one at dinner, but I have no idea if she's had more than that." He pressed his palm against the hood of the car. "Is it … life-threatening?"

"Not usually, as long as the patient receives the antidote in time. Tell them at the hospital she's had bottled water, and they'll know how to treat it. If they don't already have the antidote there, it's on its way." Jesse stepped up onto the curb. "Did anyone else in your family drink the water?"

Ethan shook his head. "The kids and I usually have milk or juice. Everyone else had lemonade or coffee or tea at dinner, made with tap water." He wiped his mouth with trembling fingers.

Jesse waved a hand toward the car. "Go. Get Kate some help. I'll put the case of water bottles in my apartment for now, until we can return it. And I'll keep an eye on the kids, so don't worry about anything but her, okay?"

"I'll try." Ethan strode around the front of the vehicle and jumped into the driver's seat.

Jesse watched until the car disappeared down the street. *God, let her get the help she needs in time.* With a heavy sigh, he turned and went into the house. After checking on the kids, and listening outside the guest room door for a moment and hearing nothing, he went to the kitchen, pulled the case of water bottles from the cupboard, and carried it out to his place. The government would likely set up depots where they could be safely disposed of. Hopefully people wouldn't dump them down the drain and contaminate the water supply.

When he came back into the main house, he sat down at the kitchen table to send out a couple of messages, beginning with one to the pastor of their church.

John, warn everyone you can think of that any bottled water purchased in the last week might have been poisoned. Gallagher will come down hard on Christians after this latest attack. Must prepare ourselves for what is to come. Can you meet at Meryn's house this afternoon, 3 p.m.?

He pressed the send button. *God, please let this line still be secure.* He'd feel terrible if Trey got in trouble for taking a chance and coming to warn them. He sent another message to Shane before leaning back in his chair. Until Gallagher acted, it was difficult to know how to prepare, but they could at least discuss possibilities and pray. He looked over at the sunflower clock on the kitchen wall.

3:45.

There wasn't much more he could do before the sun came up. Jesse pushed to his feet and made his way to the living room. Not sure he'd be able to sleep, he stretched out on the couch and pulled the knitted blanket hanging over the back of it on top of himself.

Something brushing across his cheek startled him awake.

Instinctively, he raised an arm to defend himself, but the sight of round, dimpled cheeks, framed by soft red curls, stopped him. Dull light penetrated the darkness he'd fallen asleep in, and Jesse turned his wrist to check the time.

Just after six.

He turned onto his side and propped his head on his hand. "Morning, Gracie."

"Where's Mama?"

His chest clenched. The last thing in the world he would ever want to have to do is tell this sweet, innocent child that her mama was gone and wouldn't be coming back. *God, help Kate. Keep her safe. And all the others. Please.* He rested a hand on Gracie's head. "Mama's sick, honey, but your dad has taken her to the hospital, so she can get better. Aunt Meryn will be here in a little while to take you to her place, and you can hang out with her and Uncle Shane and Uncle Brendan, okay?"

She nodded, eyes wide. "I sleep with you?"

"Sure." Jesse moved back on the couch and patted the cushion in front of him.

She crawled up beside him and stretched out, her little back pressed to his chest, warm through her pink cotton pyjamas.

Awed by the trust she was showing him, Jesse swallowed the lump in his throat. Would he ever have a child of his own? Like Rory and Hope, he'd always wanted a houseful. Seemed like maybe that wasn't God's plan for any of them. He tugged on the blanket to cover the little girl, and wrapped an arm around her as he closed his eyes again.

When he woke up, Gracie was still snuggled up next to him, and Hope sat in the chair across from the couch, an amused smile on her face.

Jesse grinned. "Every time I open my eyes, there's another beautiful girl in the room. I think I might sleep on this couch more often."

Hope laughed. "Why *are* you sleeping in here? Did you get lonely out there all by yourself?"

Jesse glanced down at Gracie to make sure she was still asleep before he said, wryly, "That's pretty much a given."

Hope's sympathetic look was undermined by the glint in her eyes. "Poor Jesse. If all those women out there could see you now, that problem would be rectified pretty quickly. Not that you'd be interested in any but one of them."

"Hope."

"I'm teasing, but I have to say she does seem really lovely."

"She is really lovely."

"That was incredibly sweet of her to offer me sympathy on my loss when she's still grieving a terrible loss herself. Losses, actually."

"She's incredibly sweet as well." Talking about Meryn hurt somewhere way down deep inside, although it helped too. "But she is also mind-numbingly stubborn. Once she makes her mind up about something, it takes an act of God to change it."

"Good. Now I know what to pray for."

Incorrigible. "I came inside because Kate got sick in the night and Ethan had to take her to the hospital."

The amusement disappeared from Hope's face. "Really? What's wrong?"

Gracie stirred in his arms, and Jesse lowered his voice. "There's been another terrorist attack. Someone infiltrated a bottling plant in Toronto and tampered with the water. I think that's what happened to Kate."

Fear flickered in Hope's eyes. "You're kidding."

"I wish I was."

"Will she be okay?"

"I hope so. There's an antidote, thankfully."

Gracie sat up and rubbed her eyes. She looked over at Hope, then back at Jesse. "Is Mama home?"

Jesse sat up too. "Not yet, Gracie. But Aunt Meryn will be here soon to get you. And I want you to meet a friend of mine. This is Miss Donevan."

Hope made a face. "Hope, please. Miss Donevan makes me sound old."

"Believe me, the last thing you look is old." He touched Gracie's arm. "Can you say hi to Hope?"

"Hi, Hope."

Hope came over and knelt in front of the couch, resting both hands on the girl's knees. "Hi, Gracie. It's a pleasure to meet you."

"You too."

"I'm going to be staying here for a little while. I hope that's okay."

"Sure. Want to see my dollhouse?"

Hope looked delighted. "I'd love to. I used to have a dollhouse too, when I was your age. I miss playing with it."

Gracie bounced to the front of the couch. "I show you."

"Okay. And maybe you can tell me where your clothes are, so we can get you dressed." Hope stood up and held out her hand.

Gracie hopped off the couch and slid her hand into Hope's.

Jesse stood up and tossed the blanket over the back of the couch. "Thanks, Hope. I'll make us some breakfast while the two of you are playing."

She flashed him a smile as Gracie tugged on her hand and pulled her toward the stairs.

Jesse's gaze lingered on them until they had disappeared into the hallway. Neither of them shared his blood, but they couldn't feel more related to him if they did. A fierce protectiveness rose up in him. Whatever Gallagher's plans were, Jesse would do whatever it took to keep Gracie and Hope, and the rest of the family, safe.

12

Meryn's i-com vibrated and she snatched it up off of the kitchen counter. Shane and Brendan sat at the table, watching her. "It's Ethan." She read the message out loud, voice trembling. "'Kate got antidote in time. Recovering well. Should be able to come home in a couple of days.'" Relief poured through her and she steadied herself against the counter.

Shane dropped his head into his hands. "Thank you, Lord."

"Amen." Brendan drove his fingers through his dark hair. "You girls really have to stop doing this to us."

Shane lifted his head. "Yes, please."

Meryn winced. It hadn't occurred to her that this situation with Kate would have brought back bad memories for her brothers. Now she felt even worse for putting them in the position three months ago of having to wait an agonizing forty-eight hours to hear whether or not she had survived the Red Virus. "I'm sorry."

Brendan walked over to the window. "It's not exactly your fault, either of you, but if you could try to avoid flirting with death for a couple of years at least, that would be great. Shane and I need a little recovery time." He brushed back the white lace curtains to look outside. "What time are we supposed to be meeting?"

"Three o'clock." Shane glanced at his watch. "Any minute now, actually."

"Who's coming?"

"Pastor John and Jesse, of course, and Jesse asked if it was okay to bring Hope. Apparently, she's planning to stay in Kingston, and she wants to help out any way she can."

"Hope's staying in town?" Brendan continued to peer out through the glass.

"That's what Jesse said."

The unit in her hand vibrated, and Meryn looked down.

Ethan again. *Kids okay?*

She touched the screen. *They're great. They can stay as long as you need. We love having them.*

Thank you. Kate sends her love.

Tell her we love her too.

She set the device down on the kitchen counter.

Brendan looked over his shoulder at her. "A rental car just drove up. Must be Hope and Jesse."

Her stomach tightened. *This is going to get easier, isn't it?*

"Pastor John is with them too. That's everybody, then, until Kate and Ethan get back home." Brendan let the curtain drop back into place.

"I'll put water on for tea." Meryn grabbed the kettle and turned on the tap. A cold chill shivered through her as water gushed into the sink. What if someone decided to tamper with their well? They'd have easy access to it. Even though it was unlikely, it wasn't impossible.

Brendan rested a hand on her shoulder. "Our water's clean, kid."

"I know." She stuck the kettle under the tap. "And stop calling me *kid*."

He kissed her cheek. "Sorry."

Meryn turned off the tap and looked at him.

He shrugged. "What? I'm glad you're alive. You and Kate both. I don't know what I'd do if anything happened to either of you."

"Well, it looks like you're stuck with us for a while longer."

"Okay by me."

She smiled at him, then set the kettle on the counter and plugged it in.

A knock sounded at the door.

Brendan pulled it open. "Come on in."

Meryn turned and leaned against the counter as Hope came into the kitchen, followed by John and Jesse. The pastor's hair and beard gleamed in the sunlight pouring through the window, the flaming red colour belying his calm, steady nature.

Jesse shut the door. "Any word on Kate?"

Brendan nodded. "Ethan just messaged us that she's doing well. She should be able to come home soon."

"That's great news." Jesse touched Hope's back lightly as they walked over to the table. "Shane, Brendan, I don't think you officially met Hope yesterday."

Meryn bit her lip at the familiar gesture and turned around to grab mugs out of the cupboard.

"Can I help?"

Startled by Jesse's voice, Meryn jumped. One of the mugs slipped from her grasp and crashed onto the counter.

"Sorry." He looked sheepish as he came up beside her and started picking up the pieces. "I really have to stop sneaking up on you like that."

"Yes, you do." In spite of herself, Meryn's lips twitched.

"Go sit. I'll clean this up." Jesse took the other mug from her and nodded at the table.

"I was just going to make tea."

"I've got it." Brendan reached for the canister on the counter.

Her legs were a little weak. She pulled out the chair beside Hope and sank onto it.

Hope touched her hand. "How are the kids doing?"

"Great. Shane and Brendan wore them out playing with the train set, so Gracie's sleeping and Matthew's watching a movie."

"They are adorable. Gracie and I played with her dollhouse for an hour this morning."

Meryn shook off the petty thought that Hope seemed to be moving into every area of her life and taking over.

"Coming up on your left, Meryn." Jesse set a steaming mug of tea down on the table in front of her.

Shane laughed.

Meryn shot Jesse a mock dark look. "Are you going to warn me every time you walk up to me now?"

"I think I have to." His green eyes gleamed in a way she hadn't seen for a while. "I've ruined a shirt and a mug of yours in the last few weeks. If you're going to have any possessions left, I'll have to start letting you know when I'm in the vicinity."

Meryn pulled the mug closer. She'd missed this, the easy rapport they used to have with each other. Maybe they could be friends after all.

He walked around to the far side of the table and sat down opposite Hope.

Brendan handed Hope a mug, and she smiled at him as he took the seat at the end of the table.

John settled his tall, lanky frame onto the chair beside Jesse.

"So what's going on, Jesse?" Brendan clasped his hands together on the table and leaned forward.

"The government has informed the army that they believe the water tampering is a terrorist attack. So far, over a hundred people have died across the country, eight of them here in Kingston. Hundreds, possibly thousands, more have been affected in other countries. The Horsemen have officially claimed responsibility."

Meryn pressed her knuckles to her lips. A group claiming to be Christians carrying out another attack could only make things worse for them. "What's going to happen?"

"I'm not sure. Since Toronto isn't that far from here, Gallagher has promised the general that he is going to do something to show everyone that he won't tolerate any acts of terrorism. All kinds of Christian activities will be subject to scrutiny and possibly severe retribution."

Brendan shifted in his chair. "More than what we've already faced?"

"I believe so. If I know Gallagher, and unfortunately I know him far better than I'd like to, he'll act fast and he'll come down hard. My guess is he'll be desperate to make some kind of massive statement, set a precedent that the military in other cities will decide to follow. This is his chance to rise to prominence, and I doubt he'll let it pass by."

Shane rubbed the side of his hand hard across his forehead. "Can he act unilaterally, without authority from the government or the army?"

"He's already shown he's more than willing to do that."

Or Caleb would still be alive. Meryn glanced at Hope. The pain that flashed across her face suggested she'd just had the same thought.

Jesse looked at Hope too, and cleared his throat. "These days, the military is stretched so thin, the commanding officers in each city are given an incredible amount of leeway. As long as they stay within the confines of the law or, in Gallagher's case, manage to keep any instances where they bend or break the law from becoming public knowledge, it seems like no one has the time or desire to interfere with what they're doing."

Meryn wrapped her hands around the yellow-and-white-striped mug, hoping the warmth would drain some of the chill that had settled in her core. "How do you know about Gallagher's interaction with the general?"

"There's a guy on the base, Treyvon Adams, who professes to be working with us."

"Professes?"

"Yes. I think he can be trusted, but I'm still being cautious. He's on Gallagher's good side—enough to get himself promoted to lieutenant—because he has him convinced that he is a yes-man, Gallagher's favourite kind of subordinate. Trey came to see me last night, to let me know what was happening and to warn us to be ready for something big."

Meryn gripped her mug tighter. *Are we ready for something else big to happen? What could Gallagher possibly be contemplating?*

Jesse shifted in his seat. "In the meantime, we need to get moving on some of the things we've been talking about, like making sure we have access to food and supplies if it starts to get hard to buy things, and setting up an underground system to bring in Bibles and other resources."

Meryn took a deep breath. "I can help with that."

Everyone looked at her.

Brendan tilted his head. "What are you talking about?"

She got up and went over to the counter where she'd set the novel she had brought home from the store the day before. She grabbed it and sat back down, propping the book up on the table, so everyone could see it. "Here." Her eyes met Jesse's briefly, before she looked away.

Shane's brow furrowed. "I don't get it. How is a copy of *A Tale of Two Cities* going to help us?"

"Well, it wouldn't. Except that this isn't exactly Charles Dickens." She flipped through the yellowed pages and handed the opened book to Shane. "Look."

His eyes scanned the page. When he looked up, his expression was incredulous. "It's the Bible." He held it out and Brendan grabbed it.

"That's right. I contacted the person who supplied the Bibles to me the last time, to see if they were still shipping them out. She told me they were, but that they had come up with a way of printing them inside the covers of other books, all classics. The first and last chapters match the cover, as well as the odd excerpt throughout, but, otherwise, each book has about a quarter of the Bible printed inside. Three other titles by the same author contain the rest."

Brendan turned another page. "There are no chapter or verse numbers, though."

"No, their thought was that if anyone picked it up and leafed through it quickly, nothing would leap off the pages at them as being anything other than what the cover suggested. The names of the books are included, but in the same font as the rest of the text, so they don't stand out."

"Wow." Brendan handed the book to Jesse. "That's ingenious."

Jesse flipped through it for a moment. "It really is." Hope held out her hand, and he reached across the table to give the book to her. "I don't think you should bring these in through the store, Meryn. Not after you've already been convicted of smuggling Bibles."

Shane shook his head. "I don't either. There has to be another way to get them out."

"How? As far as I know, I'm the only bookstore owner in town who's a believer. And no one else can take shipments of books and pass them on to people without arousing suspicion. It has to be me. Besides, it's too late to change the plan. Ten of these, with various covers, arrived at the store a few days ago. You've already seen them, Brendan."

"I have?"

"Yes. You helped me screw that case into the wall outside the break room, where I can see it from the front counter, remember? The one with the glass lid that lifts up? And we unloaded the first shipment into it. I didn't tell you that you were handling Bibles, because I wanted to see if anything about them made you suspicious. And nothing did, did it? That's the great thing about this idea. These books look like they are rare editions. They've even managed to age them somehow, so not only do they seem to be regular books, they appear quite valuable, so they can be kept under lock and key. If anyone asks me if I can get them a Bible—and people do sometimes—I can feel them out to see if the request is legitimate, and, if so, I'll go and get them one."

Brendan's jaw was tight. "I don't like it."

"Me neither." Shane's voice sounded strained.

Meryn set her mug down with a thud. "Look. Eight of us signed up to be part of this team. That means eight people working and taking risks together, not five people out there getting things done while three of us sit at home and applaud your efforts. We all bring different skills and connections to the table, and this is what I have to offer. I'm not going to sit around doing nothing. You know Kate won't want to do that when she gets back, and I think I know Hope well enough already to guess that she didn't have playing it safe in mind when she volunteered to get involved."

"That's right." Hope nodded.

Meryn caught the *not helping* look Jesse sent Hope, but she pressed on. "I would like to have your support, all of you, but with or without it, I *am* going to do this. I already have. I prayed about this long and hard before I moved forward on it, and I believe I have God's blessing. And, frankly, that's the only permission I need."

For a moment, no one spoke. Then John clasped his hands together. "Amen."

Hope laughed, and even Shane managed a weak grin.

Brendan and Jesse still didn't look happy, but neither of them offered any further protests.

"These really are remarkable, Meryn." Hope gave the book back to her. "Ingenious, like Brendan said. I think it could work, giving Bibles out this way."

"I hope so."

An i-com buzzed. The pastor pulled a device from his shirt pocket. He perused the screen before looking up at them, a grim look on his face. "You were right, Jesse." Even the faint Scottish accent couldn't soften the harshness in his tone. "Gallagher has acted fast and he has definitely made a statement."

"What has he done?" Jesse's voice was equally grim.

John took a deep breath, as though inhaling strength. "He's closed all the churches."

13

Shocked silence greeted his words. Before anyone could speak, the crunching of gravel announced the arrival of another vehicle.

Soldiers. The panicked thought ripped through Meryn before she dismissed it. Other than the camouflaged Bible lying on the table, they weren't doing anything wrong. The churches might be closed, but as far as she knew, they weren't forbidden to gather together. Not yet. "I'll see who it is."

She carried the book back to the kitchen counter, where it wouldn't be so obvious, and set it down as she looked out the window by the door.

Drew Hammond slammed the door of his car and started up the walkway.

Meryn turned back to the group gathered around the table. "It's Drew." Something flickered across Jesse's face, but disappeared so quickly she wasn't sure she'd seen it. "I'll go talk to him, see what he wants." No one answered as she strode toward the door and slipped outside, closing both the wooden and screen doors behind her.

She and Drew had been friends for years, since they were in university together. The last year or two he had made it clear he would like to be more than friends, but Meryn wasn't sure she felt the same way. And then she'd met Jesse ... She pushed back her shoulders as she went down the porch stairs.

Drew stopped when he reached her. "You're okay."

"Yes."

"I was worried about you, with everything that's been going on. I had to check on you and your family for myself."

"Kate did get sick, but they were able to give her the antidote in time, and she's much better."

"I'm glad to hear it. The kids are all right?"

"Yes, thankfully." It was thoughtful of Drew to come by. He had stopped in to see her after she'd nearly died from the Red Virus too. But was he concerned about her as a friend, or did he want something more?

He gestured toward the hill on the other side of the driveway. "Do you have time for a walk?"

Meryn hesitated. She wanted to be inside with the others, but maybe taking Drew into the house when Jesse was there wasn't the best idea. Although he had brought Hope …

Stop it. This wasn't the prom. They didn't all need to show up with someone on their arms, trying to outdo each other.

"If you're too busy …"

"No. A walk sounds good." They strolled side by side across the driveway and through the opening in the cedar-rail fence that lined the far side. The wrought-iron bench to the right sent a pang twisting through Meryn. She and Jesse had sat there and talked about their future after she came home from being held for a week in his quarters. He had kissed her that night, and promised her …

Meryn pushed away the memory. It didn't matter what they had talked about or what they had done. It certainly didn't matter what promises he had made to her. Those promises were all shattered now.

Drew stopped at the top of the hill leading down to the pond.

"Let's walk to the water." Meryn started down the small incline. The air was damp and thick, and she gathered her hair up in one hand and lifted it away from her neck as she walked. Her favourite tree at the edge of the pond had blown down in a severe thunderstorm months earlier. When Jesse realized she was terrified of the weather, he had spent the night holding her in his arms and consoling her until the fear went away.

Meryn dropped her hair. If she was going to move on, she'd have to stop letting memories of her time with Jesse linger in her mind.

Two bright-yellow Muskoka chairs sat near the pond, and Meryn made her way over to them. She dropped down on one and patted the arm of the other.

Drew sat down beside her. His light-brown hair was tousled from the breeze, and the sun had brought out a smattering of freckles across his nose. He grinned at her, and suddenly the years fell away and they were old friends in school again, hanging out at his parents' place while he tried to coax life back into his dad's old car. And laughing. They'd laughed a lot, hadn't they?

When was the last time she had laughed, really laughed? Not in spite of pain and fear, but in the absence of it? Just for the sheer, blissful, ignorant-of-what-lay-ahead joy of it?

Drew tapped his fingers on her chair. "What are you thinking about?"

"We had fun, didn't we?"

His smile was warm and went deep into his eyes. "Yes. We did. A lot of fun." He shifted in his seat to face her. "The last time we spoke, Meryn, you told me you were seeing someone else."

"I'm not anymore."

He touched her arm, but pulled his hand back quickly. "I'm sure that was hard for you, when it ended, and I'm sorry for that. But I admit I'm not sorry to hear you are free again."

"To be honest, Drew, I don't feel free yet. Not that things aren't completely over. They are, but it hasn't been that long. I still need time."

"I understand. I promised you before that I wouldn't push you, and I won't, but keep me in mind when you are ready to think about seeing someone else."

"I don't know when that will be."

"That's okay. I'm willing to wait as long as it takes."

"It's not fair for me to ask you to wait, when I can't promise when or if I'll be ready to move on."

He reached out and took her hand. "You're not asking, Meryn. I'm offering. There's never been anyone else for me, and I can't imagine there ever will be, so I will wait. As long as there is the slightest bit of hope, I'll keep on waiting."

When the sound of a car door slamming drifted down the hill to them, she gently pulled her hand from his grasp and looked over.

Jesse rounded the back of Hope's rental car and pulled open the passenger side door. He hesitated for a few seconds, his hand on the roof of the car.

Meryn held her breath. She had always been able to read him.

Would he look her way? Would she know what he was thinking if he did? What he was asking of her?

He didn't look over, just climbed into the car.

Her throat tightened as the vehicle pulled down the driveway and disappeared from view behind the barn.

When she looked at Drew, he was studying her closely, the look on his face that of a defendant watching the jury file back into the box.

Meryn rested a hand on his arm. "I can't give you much right now, Drew. But I can do this. If the time comes that I am ready to move on, I promise you will be the first to know."

14

Jesse reached over and covered one of Hope's hands, white-knuckled where she gripped the steering wheel. "Ready?"

She drew in a quivering breath. "Not really. But let's do this."

He nodded and pushed open the car door. Ever since the day before, when he'd seen Meryn and Drew together down by the pond, he'd worked to block the image from his mind, with little success. Thinking a distraction might help, he'd suggested to Hope over breakfast that they come visit Caleb's grave today, and she'd readily agreed.

Jesse had only been out to this field once, a few days after Caleb's death. It had helped to come and see his best friend's final resting place, to clear the weeds a little around the generic metal nameplate in the ground, and to say goodbye.

"It isn't much, I'm afraid." He waited at the front of the car for Hope.

When she reached him, she slipped a hand into the crook of his elbow and offered him a sad smile. "I didn't expect it would be." The sun beat down from a cloudless sky, but still she shivered as she leaned against him.

Jesse led her up a small hill, their shoes crunching over blades of grass turning brown in the mid-August heat. Neither of them spoke until they reached the crest.

Hope lifted a hand to her forehead to shield her eyes.

A flat area spread out before them. One lone tree at the top of the hill they stood on offered several feet of shade around its trunk, but no other foliage broke the long stretch of desolate ground. Rocks were scattered around the surface of the graveyard, and puffs of dust swirled over it with every breath of wind. The area looked more like something out of an early-century movie set on Mars than ground consecrated to honour the dead.

Of course, these dead were not to be honoured, not as far as the army was concerned. Certainly not as far as Major Gallagher was concerned. If government and military regulations hadn't dictated it, it was unlikely he would have afforded them even this minimal amount of decency. As it was, he had clearly searched diligently to find the most worthless piece of property in the area.

Hope's grip on his arm tightened. "It looks like an empty field."

"It practically is, although I'm sure it will fill up alarmingly quickly. Here …" Jesse pointed a little ways out into the field and then led her to the spot.

Caleb's was the only nameplate in the makeshift cemetery. So far.

Jesse felt rather than heard the sigh that shuddered through her.

"I don't supposed they'd let us put up a headstone. Or plant anything."

"No, I'm sorry." Jesse reached across his body to squeeze her trembling fingers. "He's not here, Hope."

"I know. Still …" Her hand slid out from under his, and she knelt down at the plate. Bending forward, she brushed away the dust that covered the inscription.

1
Caleb Edward Donevan
2016 - 2054

"What does the one mean?"

His stomach roiled. "It means he was convicted of being a terrorist."

"Ah." She glanced down at her own bracelet. "And the five on mine?"

"That you've never been in trouble with the law."

"What number is on yours?"

"Three. Arrested and convicted of a hate crime other than terrorism. In my case, assault and attempted murder of Gallagher. Somehow, he managed to have that left on my record, even though he dropped the charges."

Hope frowned. "From what I've heard, that should have garnered you a medal, not a sentence." She traced Caleb's name with one finger. A drop of moisture splashed onto the metal.

Jesse's throat tightened. "I'll give you a minute."

Hope nodded and he retreated the way they had come, stopping in the shade of the big red maple. He propped a shoulder against the gnarled trunk as he watched her.

She lifted her hands to her face. Was she praying? Weeping? Talking to the brother she had been robbed of the chance to say goodbye to? All of those, probably.

After several minutes, she rose.

Jesse pushed away from the tree and went to her. When he wrapped an arm around her, she rested her head on his shoulder.

"Is it wrong to question what God does?" Her words hung in the thick, humid air.

Jesse sighed. "I think God can handle it when we ask him *why*. Or get angry."

"I am angry. Rory and Caleb and Natalie all trusted in a God who claims to love justice, and they all suffered the worst kind of injustice in return." She swiped at a tear sliding down her cheek. "Rory and I were going to have children to play with the kids Caleb and Natalie would have, and we all should have died in old age, leaving a legacy of grandchildren and great-grandchildren. Now they're all gone, and there are no children or …" She pressed her knuckles to her lips. After a few seconds, she dropped her hand. "It's all wrong, Jess. Nothing happened like it was supposed to."

"I know." He pressed his lips to the top of her head before looking out over the barren landscape. "I used to be sure of so many things in life."

She lifted her head and looked at him. "And now?"

"Now I only know two things to be absolutely true: God is still on his throne. And he has not abandoned us."

For a moment, her bright-blue eyes searched his. Then she nodded. "I'm clinging to that."

Jesse pulled his arm from her shoulders and held it out for her. She clutched it tightly. He cast one look back at the place where Caleb's body lay, and then they turned and walked away.

15

A car door slammed. *Finally.* Shane and Brendan had dropped Meryn and the kids off at Kate and Ethan's house on their way to work, so they would be there when Kate arrived home.

Meryn scooped up Gracie and headed down the hallway to Kate and Ethan's front door. Just before she reached it, the door opened, and Kate came into the house.

"Mama!" Gracie leaned toward her, both arms outstretched.

Kate took her from Meryn and pulled her close. Her eyes met Meryn's over the little girl's shoulder, and Kate held out one hand.

Meryn grabbed it. "I'm so glad you're home."

Kate's smile was a shadow of her usual one. "Me too." She squeezed Meryn's fingers before letting go. "Don't worry. I just need to spend some time with the kids and sleep in my own bed. In a couple of days, I'll be as good as new."

Ethan came into the house.

Meryn led the way back up the hallway to the kitchen. "Do you want tea?"

"That would be wonderful."

Ethan pulled out a chair for Kate, and she sank onto it, still clutching Gracie to her. "Where's Matthew?"

"I sent him upstairs to put on his pyjamas. I said I'd come up and read him a story in a few minutes, but if you feel up to it, I'm sure he'd prefer for you to tuck him in."

"I'd like that." Weariness lined Kate's face as she rested her cheek on Gracie's head.

Meryn exchanged a look with Ethan. He appeared as concerned as she felt. Being poisoned had, not surprisingly, taken a lot out of Kate. Meryn clenched her jaw as the kettle whistled, and she went to make the tea. What kind of human beings did this to innocent people? The most vulnerable—the elderly, children, babies—had been hit the hardest by this latest attack. How could anyone be so cowardly? She set the pot and two mugs on the table.

Ethan had sat down on the chair beside Kate, his hand resting on her knee. He didn't look much better than she did. He probably hadn't slept at all until he knew that she was going to be all right.

"Do you need anything else?"

"No, Mer. You've done so much already. Thank you for taking care of the kids." Kate handed Gracie to Ethan. "I'm sorry. I'm too tired to even drink that tea." She stood up and swayed on her feet.

Meryn grabbed her elbow to steady her.

Ethan stood too and shifted his daughter to one hip, so he could put an arm around Kate. "I'll take you upstairs. Then I can drive you home, Meryn."

"No, that's okay. One of my brothers is coming for me any minute now. You two get some rest."

"All right. Thanks again for watching the kids."

"No problem. We had a great time, didn't we, Gracie?" Meryn cupped the little girl's chubby cheeks in her hands and pressed a kiss to her forehead. "I'll come by tomorrow to check on you, Kate."

Kate nodded and leaned against Ethan as he guided her toward the stairs.

Meryn dumped the tea into the sink and set the mugs in the dishwasher. A slight headache niggled behind her eyes. *I need some air.* She'd wait for whoever was going to pick her up out on the back deck. *Or you could wait on the front porch, where you are far less likely to run into Jesse.* She slid open the patio doors to the deck.

The orange-red sun grazed the top of the building in the backyard, but Meryn only gave the in-law suite a cursory glance before walking to the railing and drawing in a deep breath of cool air. For a few moments, the only sounds were the distant hum of traffic from the highway a half-mile away and the occasional bark of a neighbourhood dog. Then the sound of a vehicle pulling into the driveway disturbed the tranquility of the evening. A door slammed, followed by another.

Meryn started for the stairs but the sound of a woman's voice stopped her.

Hope stood at the edge of the driveway, where they had first seen her during Shane's birthday party. Her back was to Meryn as she spoke to someone Meryn couldn't see around the corner of the house. Whoever it was murmured a reply to what Hope had said, and she laughed.

Meryn froze. She couldn't make out the words, but the voice was male. Was Hope with Jesse?

Hope reached out as though resting a hand on the chest of whomever she was talking to. Then she shifted toward him.

Meryn bit her lip. Were they about to kiss? Whatever was going on, it was obviously an intimate moment she should not be privy to. Heart pounding, she stepped backward. Her foot caught the leg of a patio chair, sending it crashing onto its side. She steadied herself with a hand on the table. Heat flooded her cheeks as Hope turned and their eyes met. "I'm sorry. I didn't know anyone was out here." Meryn circled a finger through the air. "Just carry on with … whatever you were doing. I'm leaving." She stumbled backward another step. *Where is the door?*

"It's okay. I need to go in anyway. It's getting late." Hope walked toward the deck stairs.

Panic seized Meryn. *I can't see Jesse.* Not after he was about to kiss another woman.

The man came around the corner of the house.

Meryn's eyes widened. *Brendan?* She stepped forward and gripped the porch railing, knees weak.

Her brother followed Hope up the stairs.

At the top, Hope turned to face him and held out her hand. "I'll see you tomorrow?"

Brendan took her hand in his. "Absolutely."

She smiled at him before nodding at Meryn. "Good night, Meryn."

"Good night."

Brendan came over to stand beside her. Neither of them spoke for a moment, then he nudged her shoulder. "Nice timing."

She grimaced. "I'm sorry. I had no idea you and Hope were coming here together. In fact, I had no idea you and Hope were anything. What is going on?"

He shrugged. "When you left the meeting to walk with Drew the other day, Hope and I got talking. We hit it off and I came over tonight to take her for a drive. We just got back when you made your dramatic entrance onto the scene."

Meryn wrinkled her nose at him. "I was *not* trying to make an entrance. I just came out here to …"

"To what?"

"Get some fresh air."

Brendan glanced over at the building in the backyard. "Yeah, I'm sure that was it."

A shadow moved past the curtains, and Meryn averted her eyes. "It was. And we better get home. It's almost dark." She started for the sliding doors.

Brendan grasped her arm. "Meryn. Go talk to him."

"I can't."

"Why not?"

"I just can't, Bren. It's too complicated."

He studied her face for a moment before letting go. "Okay, it's your decision. It's just that you're both so miserable. It's hard to watch."

"I'm not—"

Brendan held up a hand. "Don't say it. You can lie to yourself all you want, but don't lie to me. You haven't been the same since the day you found out what happened to Logan and kicked Jesse out of your life."

Heat rushed into her chest. "Of course I haven't been the same. Now I know for sure my husband is dead, and I also know who killed him."

"I know that. And I'm sorrier than I can say. And so is Jesse. How long are you going to make him pay?"

She gaped at him. "I didn't send him away because I wanted to make him pay. I sent him away because he killed Logan. How can I betray my husband by being with the man who ended his life?" Her voice broke.

Brendan's expression softened, and he wrapped his arms around her. "I'm sorry, kid. I know you're going through a lot, and I'm not helping. It just kills me to see you unhappy."

"I'll get through this. I just need …"

"What?"

Meryn stepped back and lifted one shoulder. "I don't know. Time, I guess." She shot another look at the in-law suite. "Distance, maybe. But maybe not." She offered him a wry grin. "No wonder you're frustrated. I don't have any idea what would help me at this point."

"Well, getting caught out after curfew definitely won't. Let's go home. A good night's sleep might help a bit."

A good night's sleep? What would that be like? Meryn hadn't slept soundly in weeks. Every time she crawled into bed, she tossed and turned, afraid to close her eyes, because, when she did, images flashed through her mind. Of Logan, young and full of laughter like he had been the few brief days they'd spent together after they got married. Or Jesse, strong but gentle as he doctored her wounds or comforted her the night she was attacked by masked strangers in his quarters. How was it possible that they had both been torn from her life? What had she done that was so terribly bad that God would …? Meryn shook her head. God hadn't taken either man from her because she had done anything wrong. He didn't work like that.

Brendan directed her through the kitchen and into the hallway.

The sound of children giggling rolled down the stairs.

Kate and Ethan must be putting the kids to bed. Meryn pressed her fingers to her mouth. Jesse had wanted to marry her. By now, they could have been husband and wife and starting to talk about having kids of their own. If she had never married Logan, or if she'd been honest with Jesse from the beginning and told him she'd been married before, or if Jesse hadn't been the one to pull the trigger that killed … Meryn grabbed her purse and went out the front door.

What had happened had happened. She couldn't do anything to change the past. She just had to live with the present and let go of any dreams she might have had about the future.

16

Shane opened the door of Maeve's Coffee Shop and stepped inside. The aroma of brewing coffee permeated the air.

Other than his mother's apple pies baking, that had to be the greatest smell in the world.

The walls of the shop glistened with fresh white paint. Booths lined three walls, and tables covered with red-checked cloths filled the room. A vase of fresh daisies sat in the centre of each table.

Abby came through the swinging doors, clutching a pan of freshly baked cinnamon buns in both hands. "Hey." She set the pan down and came around the counter, rubbing her hands on the front of her full-length, royal-blue apron and leaving flour marks on the front of it. Her smile still floored him every time. "What brings you into town?"

"You." He handed her the bouquet of carnations he'd brought. "To celebrate your grand opening." On impulse, he leaned in and kissed her on the cheek.

"Aw. That's sweet. Thank you." She waved a hand toward the red leather stools at the front of the shop. "Do you have time for coffee? You can be our first customer. Those cinnamon buns are our special feature today."

"I won't turn down one of those." Shane bent over the tray and inhaled on his way to the stool.

Abby took a spare vase off a shelf and dropped the flowers into it. She filled the vase from a sink in the counter along the back wall, then set it by the cash register. When she finished, she came back over and scooped out a bun dripping with glaze and transferred it to a plate. She set it in front of him and reached for a mug and the coffeepot on the back counter behind her. "Double-double, right?"

"You got it."

"Same as me." She doctored it up and nudged the mug toward him.

"It's amazing in here, Abby. Seriously. This has got to be what heaven smells like."

Abby laughed. "Good enough to compete with all the other coffee shops in town, do you think?"

"I'm sure you'll be overrun before you know it. It's my new favourite place already."

"Just because of the smells?" She propped her elbows on the counter and clasped her hands under her chin, her grey-green eyes teasing.

"As good as they are, not the biggest draw for me." He slid forward on the stool to move in closer to her.

"No? What would that—?"

"Abby, the dishwasher's done. Can you come grab some plates?" Cameron came through the swinging doors and stopped. "Oh."

Abby straightened up quickly.

"Sorry, I didn't realize we had a customer." He shoved the packages of napkins and takeout containers he'd been carrying under the counter and came over to stand beside Abby.

She cleared her throat. "Cameron, this is Shane O'Reilly. I had lunch with him and his brother and sister a week ago Sunday?"

Shane held out his hand. "Good to meet you, Cameron."

Cameron shook his hand briefly before dropping it. "Things between you and my sister are moving pretty quickly."

"Um …"

"I mean, you've known each other for what, a week or two? And you've already spent the night together?"

"Cameron!" Abby's face reddened. "Not that I have to explain myself to you, but we did *not* spend the night together."

"Really?" His eyebrows rose. "Didn't you call to tell me you were staying at his place on Saturday night?"

"That was my fault." Shane managed to keep his voice even. "We were working on a friend's car, and I didn't realize how late it was. By the time Abby drove me home, it was past curfew."

"Convenient."

Shane's fists tightened behind the counter.

"All right, that's enough." Abby grabbed her brother's elbow and dragged him toward the swinging doors. "I need to see you in the back."

For several seconds after the two of them disappeared, Shane stared at the doors still gently swinging back and forth. How did a girl as great as Abby end up with a brother like that? The two of them were speaking in low tones, and light rock music played in the background, so Shane couldn't catch more than the odd hiss of words between them, but a banging noise, like someone slamming something down on a counter, made him wince. Should he go back there? Cameron was a couple of inches shorter than Shane, but he was lean and fit, and his muscles appeared to be as hard as his head. Should be a reasonably fair fight. Easier than taking on Brendan anyway.

Before he could decide what to do, Abby came out into the shop. She stopped on the other side of the counter and pressed her hands to her still-flaming cheeks. "O'Reilly, I'm so sorry. I don't know what has gotten into him."

"Don't be sorry. His people skills might need a little work, but he's probably just trying to protect you, in his way. I get that. And he doesn't know me at all, so I don't blame him for not trusting me. I'll just have to win him over with my devastating wit and charm."

"Thank you for understanding. And for not leaping over the counter and grabbing him by the throat."

"I can't say the thought didn't occur to me."

"I know it did."

He cocked his head. "How do you know?"

"You've got this little vein here"—she reached over and traced from his hairline down to his temple—"that throbs when you're mad."

Her touch sent vibrations thrumming across his skin. "I'm not going to be able to hide much from you, am I?"

"Would you want to?"

"No, actually. I'm not big on hiding things. Pretty huge fan of transparency."

A shadow flickered over her face. "That's good. And speaking of huge fans, what do you think of the cinnamon buns?"

"Honestly? They're the main reason I didn't throttle your brother. I was worried about getting banned from the place and having my supply cut off."

"Hmm. 'Maeve's cinnamon buns. Better than ploughing your fist into the face of a jerk.' Do you mind if we use that line in our advertising?"

"It's all yours."

Abby turned her wrist and checked her watch. When she looked up, she had a pained expression on her face. "I'm sorry. I have an appointment with a delivery service in a few minutes." She shoved her copper curls off her face with both hands. "I should get going."

"No problem." Shane tipped back his head to catch every drop of the rich-tasting coffee before setting the mug down. "Brendan and I came into town together. He had a couple of errands to run while I popped in here, but he's probably done by now."

"Here." Abby grabbed a take-out container from under the counter and put the rest of his bun in it, then added two more. "For Meryn and Brendan." She snapped the lid down and handed him the container.

"Thanks. They'll appreciate that." He slid off the stool and reached into his back pocket.

Abby shook her head. "No, please. It's on the house."

"But …"

"Really. It's our policy. Whenever a customer is unjustly accosted and accused by one of the owners, they get their order for free."

"That's your policy?"

"Part of it. It's in the fine print."

Shane laughed. "Well worth the damage to my reputation, then. Although I'm sorry about yours."

She waved a hand through the air. "He knows me. He's well aware that nothing happened, but he's trying to establish the ground rules with you. An alpha male kind of thing."

"Yeah, I got that."

Abby walked with him over to the door. "Thanks for coming by. It means a lot to me to have your support."

"You do." Shane looked around the little shop. "I'm really proud of you. You've done a great job with this place. It's a vast improvement over the old one."

"Thank you." Her eyes met and held his.

The door opened, and a group of people came inside. Shane moved out of the way as Abby greeted them. Before they were settled, three college-age girls walked in and took another table.

"See?" He nudged her. "You're overrun already."

"I guess I'm going to have to hire someone to help out. I have a lot of administration work to do, and Cameron's busy in the back."

"Hey, what about Hope, the woman who was looking for Jesse the other night? She's decided to stay in town, apparently, so I'm sure she'll be looking for work."

"Will Meryn mind?"

"I don't think so. Hope and Jesse are more like sister and brother, apparently. In fact, Hope and Brendan have been spending time together, so I have a feeling Meryn's going to be seeing quite a bit of her anyway."

"Okay. If you see Hope, tell her to come by and talk to me if she's interested."

"I will." He glanced at the customers in the room. As happy as he was to see them, he wouldn't have minded a couple of more minutes alone with her. "Meryn asked me to invite you to dinner Friday evening, a celebration for your new venture. Are you free?"

"We don't close until five, but I could come after that."

"Cameron's welcome too." He hadn't noticed it before, but a tiny dimple to the right of her mouth formed when she smiled.

"Thank you. I'll tell him, but I suspect it will just be me this time."

The door opened again and Brendan stepped into the coffee shop. "Ready to go?"

"Yep. I was just coming out."

"Looks great in here, Abby." He tipped back his head. "Are those cinnamon buns I smell?"

Shane lifted the container. "I have one for you here. Compliments of Abby's brother."

Abby elbowed him in the ribs.

"Great. Thanks. And good luck on your opening." Brendan turned and went out the door.

Shane touched Abby's elbow. "I better go too, but I'll see you Friday?"

"Count on it." Abby smiled at him.

Shane went out the door and strode down the sidewalk after his brother, already counting the hours until Friday.

17

"Did you get everything done that you wanted to?" Shane pulled his seatbelt across his chest and snapped it into the holder. No automatic anything for him in this truck. He grinned wryly.

"Yes. How about you?" Brendan jerked his head toward Abby's shop. "Did you get everything you wanted?"

"Cute."

"Yes, she is."

Shane sent him a sideways glance. "Be careful where you're looking, buddy."

"That bad, huh? Well, don't worry. I only have eyes for one woman these days."

"So Meryn told me. That didn't take long."

"No, it didn't, pot."

Shane laughed. "Touché."

"Was there anything else you needed to do in town?"

"I have to stop at the hardware store for a couple of items." Shane started the engine. "And I should do one other thing after that." He grimaced. "You might not want to come with me, though."

"Why? What do you have to do?"

"Go see Annaliese."

"What? Why?" Shock flashed across Brendan's face.

"Mom asked me to. She wants me to check in on her once in a while, see if she's okay."

"Our dear sister is more than capable of taking care of herself."

Shane pulled the truck out onto the street. "I know that, and you know that, but Mom worries about her."

"So you go see her often?"

"This is the second time. Mom would like me to go more than I do. Every few months is all I can stomach."

"I don't even know where she lives. Where do you meet with

her?"

"She works out of some warehouse in the industrial district. Creepy place, but she says it suits her needs, whatever those might be."

"What does she even do?"

"You don't have any idea where your own sister lives or works or what she does? Maybe you should drop in and see her yourself once in a while."

"I doubt she'd welcome me with open arms."

"No, that's definitely not her style. Still, on some level, I'm sure she'd appreciate it if you showed a little interest in her life."

Brendan snorted. "Now you sound like our mother."

"I could do worse."

"She never has given up on Annaliese, has she?"

"No. Although Annaliese has given Mom every reason to." Shane turned into the parking lot of the hardware store.

Brendan reached for the takeout container on the seat between them. "All right, if we're going to do this, I need to fortify myself while you're gone."

"If anything can do it, those cinnamon buns can. They're amazing."

Brendan lifted out one of the buns and took a bite. He swallowed it and licked the icing from his lips. "Man. You weren't kidding. This is incredible."

"Told you." Shane opened his door and jumped out of the truck. "I'll be right back." Once inside the dimly lit store, he grabbed a box of nails and two packs of batteries and paid for them. When he got back to the truck, he tossed the bag onto the passenger floor and climbed behind the wheel.

Brendan snapped the lid of the takeout container closed. "If you'd been one more minute, I'd have eaten Meryn's too."

Shane grinned and pulled out of the parking lot, headed for the far side of town. Houses grew fewer and farther between, and the scattered ones at this end of town were badly in need of paint and repairs. He pulled into a parking lot behind a row of warehouses.

Brendan leaned forward to look out the front window. "Uh, Shane?"

"Yeah?" He looked where his brother pointed.

A woman emerged from the narrow alley between two of the buildings. She paused at the entrance to Annaliese's warehouse for a moment, her back to them, then she pulled open the door.

Abby. Shane held his breath, but she didn't look around before slipping inside and letting the door slam shut behind her.

The air had been sucked out of his lungs, as though he'd been punched in the gut.

"Is that Annaliese's place?"

"Yes." Why on earth was Abby meeting with his sister? A delivery service, she'd said. Annaliese's business affairs were varied and nothing Shane wanted to know too much about, but he did know enough to be quite sure that delivering cookies was not among them. He gripped the steering wheel, rising anger tightening up his chest.

"Why would Abby—?"

"I don't know, Brendan." The words came out more sharply than he'd intended. "Sorry. But something isn't right here. There's no way she can be seeing Annaliese for anything to do with the bakery, which is what she told me her meeting this morning was about."

Flashes of their conversations whirled through his mind, the moments where she had seemed to be a little less than forthcoming or wouldn't look at him when she was talking. Had Abby been lying to him about what she was doing here in town? Had she been lying to him about everything? Was there a more ominous reason Cameron didn't want him coming around, sticking his nose in their affairs?

The coffee and pastry weren't sitting well.

"Let's get out of here. I'll see Annaliese another time."

"What about Abby? Are you going to ask her what she's doing here?"

"Seriously, Brendan, I don't know what I'm going to do. I don't have any idea what to think at the moment." He cranked hard on the steering wheel and pulled out of the parking lot, the back tires spinning in the gravel.

For once, his brother had the sense to keep his mouth shut. He didn't speak until they were nearly home, then he tapped Shane lightly on the arm with his fist. "I'm sure there's a logical explanation. No one who bakes like that could possibly be involved in anything nefarious."

"I hope you're right." Shane turned into their driveway and parked the truck near the barn. "Don't mention this to Meryn, okay? Or anyone else, for that matter. We don't have any idea what we're dealing with here, and I don't want to jump to any conclusions."

"But what if Abby is involved in something dangerous? Shouldn't we tell Meryn to be careful?"

"Abby's coming out here for dinner Friday night. I'll catch her before she goes into the house and ask her what she was doing at Annaliese's place. If she does have a good explanation, then there's no reason to involve Meryn in this at all."

"All right. I'll wait until you talk to her before I say anything." Brendan started to open the door of the truck, then stopped. "I can't believe Abby would do anything dangerous or illegal. She's way too nice, and she knows how serious the penalties are now for breaking the law. Especially for believers."

"I'm sure she wouldn't." Shane shoved open the door of the truck and hopped out. The problem was he *wasn't* sure. About anything.

18

Jesse stopped in front of the deli counter. "What should we have for dinner?"

Hope tapped the glass display case with a soft-pink painted nail. "Those steaks look good. I haven't had red meat in ages. Do you have a barbeque?"

"Kate and Ethan do, and they told me I was welcome to use it anytime." He lifted a finger to get the attention of the attendant behind the counter.

"Why don't you grab a couple of those for us, and I'll go over to the produce section and get potatoes and stuff for salad?"

"Sounds good."

The Hundred Mile Market was Jesse's favourite place in town to buy food—a small, market-style shop with fresh products all grown within a hundred miles of Kingston. The best part was he could usually be in and out in less than ten minutes, because everything was close together and easy to find.

Twenty feet away, Hope paused in front of an assortment of cucumbers, tomatoes, and carrots, delivered from local farms that day.

"What can I get ya?"

Jesse pointed at the steaks, advertised as the Thursday special. "Two of the T-bones, please."

The attendant, a middle-aged man in a full white apron, pulled on a pair of disposable plastic gloves and reached inside the display. He lifted up two of the steaks and paused for Jesse's approval. When he nodded, the attendant carried them over to the counter to wrap them in brown paper.

"Well, well, well. Who do we have here?"

Jesse's jaw tightened. He hadn't heard that voice since the night Caleb was killed, and if he'd never heard it again, he would have been quite happy. He turned around slowly.

Dressed in full camouflage gear, Gallagher stood, arms crossed, a smirk plastered on his face. As usual, his two little minions, Privates Whittaker and Smallman, lurked in his shadow.

Gallagher had been greying at the temples since Jesse had known him, but in the last few weeks, his hair had become liberally salted. *The burden of trying to rule the world must weigh heavily on his shoulders.* Jesse bit back a sardonic grin. "What do you want, Lieutenant?"

Gallagher's features hardened. "It's *Major*."

Jesse shrugged. "If you say so." He wasn't in the army anymore, thanks to the man in front of him. Jesse was under no obligation to follow protocol. He started to turn back to the display.

Gallagher grabbed him by the shoulder and spun him around, sending him crashing backward against the glass counter. "Don't ever turn your back on me."

Jesse caught a glimpse of the startled face of the attendant as he pushed himself away from the glass, fists clenched. "What is your problem, Gallagher?"

Both Whittaker and Smallman rested their hands on the weapons strapped to their waists.

The major stepped closer, until his face was inches from Jesse's. Stark hatred swirled in his eyes. "You. You are my problem, Christensen. And you should know I have all kinds of plans for ways to deal with you once and for all."

Stay calm. Do not get yourself arrested. Jesse forced himself to draw in deep, even breaths. If he gave Gallagher the slightest reason to take him in, it was highly unlikely Jesse would ever come out, except to keep Caleb company in that desolate field on the edge of town.

A movement to his right caught his attention. Hope edged toward them, her gaze riveted on Gallagher. *No. Stay away.*

Slowly and deliberately she walked toward them. Her eyes were colder and harder than Jesse had ever seen them.

Everything in him screamed at him to call out her name, to order her away or tell her to run. But if Gallagher knew the two of them were as closely connected as they were, he'd ... *I have no idea what he'd do, but it wouldn't be good.*

She stopped five feet from them.

Gallagher's gaze slid to her and back to him. "Friend of yours?" When Jesse didn't answer, the major gestured to her. "Come join the party, sweetheart."

Hope moved a couple of feet closer.

Gallagher tapped a finger against his chin as he studied her. "Interesting. What happened to the other one, Christensen? She finally come to her senses and decide she'd rather be with a real man?"

The privates snickered behind him.

Jesse's fists tightened.

"Actually, this is good news. The three of us have always been great admirers of hers, you know." Gallagher half-turned toward the men behind him. "Make a note of that. The one with the long, dark hair, what was her name?"

Whittaker leaned forward. "Meryn O'Reilly."

"That's right. Meryn O'Reilly. Maybe the three of us should pay her a little visit one of these nights, help her to get over this broken relationship. Not that it would take much, I'm sure, after that." He waved a hand dismissively in Jesse's direction.

"Stay away from her, Gallagher." Jesse ground the words out between clenched teeth.

The major's laugh was mocking. "Still haven't figured it out, have you? I run this town now, and I can do anything I want to anyone I want, and there isn't a single thing you can do about it."

"I'll find a way."

"Hmm. Still not over one, but moving on with another. That seems like too many beautiful women for one man, doesn't it, gentlemen?" He walked over to stand in front of Hope. His eyes narrowed as they travelled slowly up and down the length of her.

Jesse's heart pounded. *God, help us. Protect Hope and let us get out of this, preferably before I murder Gallagher with my bare hands. Or before Hope does.*

She looked capable of anything at the moment.

"Who are you?" Gallagher cupped her chin. "You look familiar. Have we met before?"

Hope jerked away from his touch. "I doubt it. I rarely visit reptile zoos."

Gallagher laughed. "Looks, spirit, and wit. I like that. I have to give credit where credit is due, Christensen. You do know how to pick them." He shot out a hand and grabbed her wrist. Hope tried to yank it away, but he held on tight and pulled an i-com from his shirt pocket.

When Jesse started toward them, Whittaker cut him off. The private yanked out his pistol and shoved it against Jesse's ribs.

Gallagher touched the screen with his thumb before lowering the i-com to Hope's identity bracelet.

Jesse's heart sank. Now he would know her name and everything about her.

Still clutching Hope's wrist, Gallagher scanned the screen. When he looked up, his face was smug. "Hope Donevan. You wouldn't, by any chance, be related to the late Caleb Donevan, would you?"

Hope glared at him.

Gallagher pursed his lips. "Let's see. You're too young to be his mother and too old to be his daughter, and his wife is as dead as he is, so that would make you his sister, am I right?"

She yanked her wrist from his grasp. "Who I am is someone who will see you pay, one way or another, for the cold-blooded murder of my brother." Her voice was as hard as her eyes.

"You're new to town, Ms. Donevan, so you might not realize we don't take threats like that lightly around here. Easy enough to teach you that lesson, though. While I might pay someday, you will pay right now. Or, to be more accurate, your friend will pay for you, just like your brother paid for him." He spun toward Jesse and lifted the i-com. Light flashed from the device before Jesse could look away.

He blinked away the spots in front of his eyes as Hope lunged toward Gallagher.

Smallman, who had moved around behind her while Gallagher was talking, grabbed both elbows and yanked her backward.

Whittaker jammed the pistol farther into Jesse's ribs.

Impotent fury poured through Jesse.

Gallagher inputted something into the unit, then strode toward the attendant, still standing, wide-eyed, behind the counter. "Get me the manager of this store."

The man nodded and disappeared through the strips of thick

plastic that hung in the doorway behind him.

Hope gave Jesse an apologetic look.

He shook his head slightly. It wasn't her fault. He'd known as soon as he heard Gallagher's voice behind him that he wouldn't emerge from the encounter unscathed. Just what the major had in mind, though, Jesse had no idea. As long as Gallagher focused on Jesse and not Hope, Jesse didn't particularly care.

A large man in a rumpled blue shirt, red-striped tie askew, punched through the strips of plastic, shoving them out of his way with both arms. "You wanted to see me, Major?"

"Yes." Gallagher jerked his head toward Jesse. "This man here, Jesse Christensen, is a convicted criminal and is also suspected of terrorist activities in this town."

The manager looked at Jesse, a scornful look on his face. "Is that right? He's a regular in here."

"Well, for the safety of your other customers, I am officially revoking that privilege from him."

You have got to be kidding me. Jesse rolled his eyes in disgust.

Gallagher held up the device in his hand. "Do you have an i-com?"

The manager scrambled to pull one of out of the pocket of his dress pants, nearly dropping it in the process. "Here."

"Good. Scan this photograph."

The manager complied.

"Post it where all your workers can see it, and let them know they are not to serve him. If he sets foot on the premises, you should notify the military immediately, and he will be arrested. Do you understand?"

The man nodded.

Gallagher shoved the i-com back in his shirt pocket. "And consider passing that picture along to your fellow merchants in town. I'm sure you agree that, in the interests of public safety, we cannot allow criminals and terrorists to roam freely through our streets and our places of business."

"Absolutely not." The manager's voice dripped with contempt.

Gallagher looked at Jesse, face triumphant.

Jesse gritted his teeth.

The major turned to Hope and ran a finger down her cheek. "As for you, sweetheart, I certainly hope our paths cross again soon." He nodded at the two privates. "Let them go, gentlemen. If Christensen doesn't vacate the property in thirty seconds, we will be forced to arrest him for trespassing."

Smallman let go of Hope as Whittaker, clearly reluctantly, lowered the weapon he'd been holding on Jesse.

"Come on, Hope." Jesse took her arm and they started for the door, customers all over the store frozen in place, staring at them.

"Oh, Miss Donevan, I almost forgot." Gallagher waited for Hope to stop and look back at him. "Always a pleasure to have a big star move to town. Welcome to Kingston."

19

Jesse slid an arm around Hope as they exited the store. She trembled slightly and he tightened his grip. "There's a new coffee shop down the block that a friend of Shane's just opened up. She was on the deck having dinner with everyone when you first came by the house. The one with the curly hair?"

"Oh yeah. I remember her."

"She's new to town too. Her name's Abby. Came to church for the first time a week or two ago, and she and Shane have been seeing each other a bit since then. I've been meaning to drop by her shop, since he told me how nice it was, but I haven't had a chance yet." He guided her across the street. When he opened the door of the coffee shop, a blast of warm, spice-laden air wrapped itself around him, and his muscles instinctively relaxed.

Abby stood at a table across the room, refreshing the cups of two patrons. She said something to them, and they both laughed. When she started back to the counter, she caught sight of Jesse and Hope, and her smile faded. Still holding the coffeepot, she changed direction and headed toward them. "Is everything all right?"

Was it that obvious? Jesse nodded. "We're good."

"It's Jesse, right? And Hope?"

"That's right." Jesse looked around the shop. "It's amazing what you've done with this place, Abby. It looks great."

Abby flashed a smile. "Thanks. It's going well so far. Business has been steady."

"I'm not surprised."

She waved a hand around the room. "Sit anywhere you like." She lifted the pot in her hand. "Coffee?"

"That would be great, thanks."

Hope sat down in a booth in the corner, and Jesse slid onto the chocolate-brown leather bench across from her.

Abby went to the counter and grabbed a couple of mugs. She set them on their table and filled them from the pot, then she rested a hand on one hip. "I don't mean to pry, but did something happen before you came in? You both look a little shaken up."

Jesse exhaled. "It's no big deal. We just had a run-in with Major Gallagher."

Abby winced. "That would do it." She glanced around the shop and lowered her voice. "Shane told me a little about your history with the major, so I'm sure that encounter wasn't pleasant. At least you're both here and not behind bars."

"Not yet." Jesse offered her a wry grin.

"Please let me bring you something to eat, on the house. We have homemade minestrone soup today."

"That sounds amazing, Abby, but we'd be happy to pay for it."

"No, really, I insist. I'll bring it right over."

After Abby had gone, Hope reached across the table and grasped his arm. "Jesse. I'm so sorry about what happened in the store. I should have stayed away. I knew you wanted me to, but I couldn't stop myself from coming over and looking that man directly in the face." A shudder moved through her. "Not that I expected anything else, but he is a complete monster."

"Yes, he is. So don't apologize, it's not your fault. He was going to do something to me in there regardless of whether or not you got involved. You just helped him narrow down his choices. But, Hope ..."

"What?"

"You're going to have to be really careful. You're on his radar now. Not just because beautiful women have a tendency to catch his eye, but because he knows you're part of my life. His resentment toward me has morphed into this sick, twisted hatred, and he knows the best way to get to me is to threaten the people I care about." He hesitated. "Are you sure you want to stay here, now that you know what we're up against?"

She pulled back her hand. "Of course I'm staying. I'm not letting that horrible man run me out of town. Besides, he may be particularly evil, but things really aren't much better anywhere else."

"It was this bad in California?"

"Pretty much. Christians are generally despised there too, and marginalized. The U.S. government hasn't resorted to handing out bracelets yet, but I've heard a lot of rumours about various methods they're considering to identify believers. And it's harder for Christians to buy and sell products there, although maybe not as hard as it's going to be for you now."

Jesse waved a hand through the air. "Don't worry about that. I'll figure something out. But you make a good point. It's easy to get caught up in what's happening directly to us, but I know it's happening all over the world. Europe, Africa, Asia, the Middle East. Christians are suffering and dying for their faith on almost every continent, and have been for a lot longer than they have here." A memory washed over him. "Meryn reminded me of that once. I asked her if she wanted to run away together, find a safe place and start a new life."

"What did she say?"

"That there was no safe place."

Hope sighed. "Unfortunately, she's right. If there ever was, there isn't anymore."

"She also told me that we needed to stay here because we had work to do, and she was right about that too."

"Speaking of which, I need to find a job." Hope pulled back as Abby set a tray down on the table and unloaded a basket of bread and two steaming bowls of rich-looking soup.

Jesse inhaled deeply. "Man, that smells good."

"It has gotten favourable reviews today. I hope you enjoy it."

Hope smiled at her. "I'm sure we will."

Abby picked the tray up. "Did I hear you say you were looking for a job?"

"I am, actually. I just arrived in town, so I haven't had a chance to look around and see what's available, but I need to do that soon."

"I mentioned to Shane yesterday that I needed someone to help out here, and he suggested I ask you. It might not be what you're looking for, but if you want to think about it, I'd be happy to have you."

Hope leaned against the back of the bench. "I will think about it, thanks, Abby."

"No problem. Enjoy your dinner."

Hope wrapped her hands around her mug as if, after the trauma of what had just happened, she needed the warm comfort of it. "She's nice. It's not hard to understand what Shane sees in her."

"No, it's not."

She raised her eyebrows.

Jesse made a face at her. "Not like that. I would never, in a million years, go after a woman a friend of mine …" He blinked as another memory struck him. The hominess of the café must be making him nostalgic.

"What?"

"Sorry. That just reminded me of something Caleb once did to me."

A small smile played across her lips. "What did he do?"

Jesse peeled back the cover on a creamer and dumped the liquid into his coffee. "I met Meryn the day after we arrived in town, when the army stormed her church. Caleb knew right away that I was drawn to her, and he wasn't happy about it. I don't blame him. We'd just been sent to Kingston to contain what we had been told were a bunch of potential terrorists. Then, second day in, I go and fall for one of them. He ordered me to stay away from her, and I tried, but somehow we kept getting thrown together." Intermingled pleasure and pain twisted through him. "Then one day he told me that he thought there was more of a connection between him and Meryn than between her and me."

"Ouch."

"Exactly. I was furious. I've never come so close to shoving my fist down his throat. When he saw how upset I was, he told me he would never go after a woman I was interested in."

"He was testing you."

"Yep. To see how much trouble I was in, he said."

"And you were in a lot of trouble."

"Apparently."

Hope absently swirled a spoon through her soup. "So you didn't punch him?"

"Actually, I did. Not in the face, though. On the arm. For messing with me."

"What did he do?"

"He laughed."

She grinned. "That sounds about right."

Jesse reached for a packet of sugar and shook it to settle the contents. "I really miss him."

"You miss her too."

"Yeah, I do."

"You're still in a lot of trouble."

"I know. But I am happy for Shane. I don't think he's dated anyone since he and Brendan moved here a few months ago, and Abby does seem great. What do you think of the idea of working here with her?"

Her gaze travelled around the room. "The last few years, I spent a lot of nights alone in my trailer on the set of one television show or another, thinking about what it would be like to have a regular job. You know, one where I could be with people who weren't trying to boost my ego or tell me things like how I was so much more talented and gorgeous and brilliant than the other women in the cast, when I knew very well they were telling those other women the exact same thing. Being around people who don't want anything from me, except a cup of coffee and a kind word, sounds pretty appealing right now."

Jesse picked up his spoon. "You've really been unhappy, haven't you?"

"I have. And the sad part is I didn't realize it until I heard the news about Caleb. His death put everything in perspective for me."

"I'm sorry, Hope. I had no idea. Caleb didn't either, or he would have caught the first flight out west and dragged you back here."

"I wish he had." Her voice caught and she took a sip of coffee. When she set down her mug, she offered him a shaky smile. "Anyway, I'm here now. And it feels right. It feels like I have come home."

"Good. I feel like you have too."

"Which is why I'm staying in Kingston. Everything important to me is here, including the opportunity to finally take a stand and put some action behind my faith. And you, of course."

"And Brendan." He flicked his fingers against the back of her hand.

Her cheeks coloured. "Are you okay with me seeing him? Because if it bothers you, I won't."

"Why would it bother me?"

"Do you feel like I'm betraying Rory?"

He blinked. "No, of course not. Why would you even ask that?"

"I feel that way sometimes. Even though we never did get married, I promised Rory, when we got engaged, that I would love him for the rest of my life. And I will. I do. Until I met Brendan, I never had any interest in dating anyone else. But as happy as I am, part of me feels like I am not keeping my word to Rory."

"You aren't betraying him. Don't think that for a second. Rory would never have wanted you to think you had to go through life alone, turning down every chance at happiness because of what the two of you had. He loved you far too much for that."

Tears glistened in her eyes. "It means a lot to me that you're okay with this, and that you believe Rory would be as well."

"I do. And you can't do better than an O'Reilly, trust me."

"I wasn't looking for this."

"I know you weren't. So take it for what it is, Hope. A gift from God. For what it's worth, you have my blessing."

Abby came over to their table. "How are you two doing?"

Hope looked up at her. "Everything about this place is wonderful, Abby. I'd be thrilled to take you up on your offer to work here. When do you want me to start?"

Abby's eyes lit up. "How's tomorrow, eight a.m.? That will give me time to get you oriented, then I have a meeting in the afternoon, and you can watch the shop for me. And just so you know, I brought you and Jesse your food because you're friends and we're not very busy at the moment, and I've been refilling coffees for customers this week since it's our grand opening, but we don't normally wait on tables. Customers order and pick up their food at the counter, which will make things easier for you. And Cameron will be here too, so you won't be completely on your own."

"Sounds good. I'll be here at eight."

Abby squeezed her shoulder. "I'm looking forward to working with you. We'll have fun."

"I'm looking forward to it too."

When Abby had disappeared behind the swinging doors, Hope looked around the coffee shop. "I feel like this is exactly where God wants me right now." She clasped her hands together on the table. "It's time to put the past behind me and embrace whatever he has for me this day, and in the days to come."

That resonated. Jesse leaned across the table and covered her hands with his. "I couldn't agree more."

20

Shane watched as Abby parked her brother's navy Kev at the side of the driveway and climbed out of the vehicle. A gust of wind caught her curls and whipped them around her face. She brushed them back as she rounded the front of the vehicle.

The desire to chuckle at the now-familiar gesture caught him by surprise, and he pushed it back fiercely.

Abby reached the end of the walkway and bounded up the stairs. Either she was excited about spending the evening with his family or her meeting with his sister two days earlier had gone extremely well.

Shane gritted his teeth at the thought and stepped out of the shadows before she reached the door.

Abby came to an abrupt stop and pressed a hand to her chest. "I didn't see you there." She smiled up at him. When he didn't speak, her smile faltered. "Are we going in?"

"Can we talk first?"

She must have caught something in his voice, because the last of her smile faded as she crossed her arms over her chest. "Okay. What are we talking about?"

"You. And what you were doing at my sister's warehouse this week."

Her face paled. "Were you spying on me?"

"Don't turn this back on me. I was there to check up on my sister, not to spy on you. But I want to know what business you had with a woman whose sole mission in life is to torment my family and as many Christians as possible. If you are involved with her in any way, then you are a traitor and a threat to everyone I care about in the world, especially Meryn, since she is Annaliese's favourite target."

"I'm not *involved* with her. I know exactly who she is, and I don't want any part of her."

"The first time you came out here, you asked me my sister's name like you had no idea who she was. So how do you know her so well now? And why were you at her place of work? Nothing legitimate happens in that building, so it follows that, since you were there, you must be involved in something highly questionable. What is it?"

Silence stretched out between them.

Shane waited, willing her to give him something, anything that would explain what he had seen.

She uncrossed her arms. When she spoke, her voice was low and soft. "You know me, O'Reilly. Can't you just trust that I would never do anything to hurt you or your family?"

Not good enough. "If you can't give me a reasonable explanation, then clearly I can't trust you. Which means that I don't really know you at all." He reached out and circled her wrist with his fingers, lifting it and pointing to the grey bracelet with his thumb. "Is this thing even real or part of an elaborate scheme to infiltrate the Christians and cause us some kind of grief?"

Abby regarded him coolly. "Why don't you cut it off with that fancy new knife of yours, and we'll find out?"

"Fine." Still holding her wrist, he fumbled in his back pocket for the knife. "Then when the authorities get here, I can be a good citizen and tell them what I saw the other day, see if they can get any answers out of you." He pressed the button on the handle of the knife, snapped it open, and slid the thin blade under the grey plastic.

Abby didn't make any attempt to pull away.

Shane met her gaze. He couldn't read a single emotion in her eyes. Another skill he hadn't realized she possessed. The woman was capable of exhibiting more self-control than anyone he'd ever met.

Except maybe Annaliese.

The comparison didn't help to cool the blood coursing through his veins.

A sudden awareness of the softness of her skin beneath his fingers struck him. The feel of her sent tingles of electricity through his hands and up his arm. Not great timing. And why wasn't she trying to stop him? Either she knew the bracelet wasn't real or she trusted him not to put her in that kind of danger.

His jaw tightened. If he cut through the bracelet and the thing *was* real, one or both of them would go to jail. Given the conflicting feelings churning through him at the moment, having a wall of bars between them didn't seem like such a bad idea. The knife edged into the plastic. Her eyes widened slightly, almost imperceptibly. If he hadn't been searching for it, he wouldn't have seen her react at all. It was enough, though, to tell him the truth. *Too bad.* It would have been easier if the thing hadn't been real.

Shane pulled the knife out from under the bracelet, snapped it shut, and shoved it back into his pocket. After what had happened to Meryn, he wouldn't send Abby to jail. Not unless he found out for sure that she was somehow connected to Annaliese. Then he'd drag her down to the base himself and hand her over to the military without a single qualm. Tightening his grip on her wrist, he leaned in closer. "I don't know what you're up to, but I'll tell you this—if you hurt my family, you will regret it. I promise you."

She yanked her wrist out of his grasp. "You know what? You're right. This has all been a huge mistake. From now on, O'Reilly, you stay out of my life and I'll stay out of yours."

"Done."

"Shane?" The screen door creaked open behind him.

Shane swung around to face Meryn.

Confusion flickered on her face. "Are the two of you going to come inside?"

Abby didn't look at Shane as she stepped around him and walked toward his sister. "I'm sorry, Meryn. I can't stay. I have a terrible headache all of a sudden, and I need to go home."

Meryn reached for Abby's hands. "Maybe you shouldn't drive. Shane …" She started to turn to him, but Abby shook her head.

"No, I can drive. I'm sorry I can't stay, though."

"So am I. Another time, okay?"

Abby didn't respond to that, just squeezed Meryn's hands and let her go.

Shane leaned against the post at the top of the stairs as Abby strode across the lawn toward her vehicle. His fingers, where they had touched her skin, still burned and he wiped them on his jeans, to no avail.

He felt Meryn's eyes on him and forced a grin as he turned to her.

"What did you do?"

His grin faded. "What do you mean, what did I do? She has a headache."

"That looked a lot more like emotional distress than a headache. Did the two of you have a fight?"

"Not exactly. We just came to the mutual conclusion that things aren't going to work out between us." His chest tightened at the sound of Abby's car speeding down the driveway, but he didn't look behind him.

"Oh no. She seemed so great."

"Maybe so, but we're not right for each other." Shane shoved himself away from the post. "And I really don't feel like talking about it right now, kid. Can we drop it?"

She studied his face for a moment. "All right, I'm going in to finish dinner. I'll call you when it's ready."

"Thanks." As soon as the screen door slammed, he pressed both palms to the top of the railing. *Really hoped that would go differently.* Why couldn't Abby just tell him what she was doing? Although he'd racked his brain to come up with any possible explanation that would exonerate her and hadn't been able to, he'd still held out hope that she would be able to provide one. Her refusal to speak in her own defence was maddening.

The front door swung open and Brendan came out onto the porch. "I take it that didn't go well?"

Shane slumped back against the railing. "You could say that. I told Abby I saw her at Annaliese's warehouse. She didn't deny it. She accused me of spying on her."

"Did you come right out and ask her what she was doing there?"

"Yes, and she wouldn't tell me. All she would say was that I knew her and I needed to trust that she would never hurt our family."

"I don't suppose you can do that."

"Of course not. I'm not foolish enough to trust anyone who has anything to do with our sister."

"So she's gone."

"Yes. And she won't be back."

"We need to tell Meryn and Hope."

Shane sighed. "I guess so." The look on Abby's face when she asked him to trust her flashed through his mind. It was that look that was twisting his insides into knots.

"You *guess* so?"

"We still have no idea what Abby is up to. I don't want to start any wild rumours about her."

"Meryn and Hope aren't prone to gossiping. But we have to warn them. If Meryn thinks you ended things with Abby because you weren't compatible or you didn't feel a spark or whatever, she won't feel the need to be careful around her. And Hope just started working at the coffee shop yesterday. If Abby is involved with anything questionable, I sure don't want to see her working there now. They both need to know the truth, at least as much as we know of it, so they can have their guard up around her, or preferably stay away from her altogether."

"All right. We have to make it clear we don't know anything for sure, though."

"Got it. Come inside. We'll talk about it while we eat."

Shane pushed away from the railing and trudged to the door after his brother. He'd been so looking forward to dinner, and now all he looked forward to was bringing an end to this day. A heavy weight settled in his gut.

You hardly knew Abby, and you obviously can't trust her, so why are you having such a hard time letting her go?

Shane stalked toward the table and their *celebration* dinner.

He'd always been a pretty decent judge of character, but obviously his instincts had failed him this time. Or, to be more accurate, his attraction to Abby had caused him to throw away the caution and common sense he relied on to protect his family.

That wouldn't happen again.

21

Meryn lifted a piece of lasagna from the pan and set it on a plate. The aroma of garlic and tomatoes curled around her.

Brendan took the plate from her and carried it over to Hope's place at the table.

Hope smiled up at him. "Thanks, Brendan."

He touched her shoulder. "No problem."

Meryn watched their interaction, the easy way they had with each other and the obvious enjoyment they took in each other's company. She and Jesse had been that way too, until … She swallowed hard and carried the last two plates of lasagna over to the table. After she sat down, she looked at Shane. "Are you saying grace?"

The slight hesitation was unusual, but he nodded. "Sure."

Everyone bowed their heads.

"God, we thank you for faith, family, friends, and food. May all of these blessings from you give us courage and an extra measure of strength to face what lies ahead. Amen."

"Amen." Brendan reached for the basket of bread.

Meryn contemplated her older brother. Interesting choice of words. Of course they all needed courage and strength, but why pray for an extra measure tonight, right after he ended things with Abby? Was he worried that he would change his mind and go after her? Would it be so terrible if he did?

Shane met her questioning gaze. He winked but there was nothing lighthearted in his eyes to back up the gesture.

Meryn handed him the bowl of salad. "What is it?"

"What is what?"

"You seem concerned about something. Do you want to talk about it?"

Shane set down the bowl without taking anything out of it. "Actually, I do. Brendan and I want to talk to both you and Hope."

Hope tilted her head. "About what?"

"Earlier this week, Brendan and I went to see Annaliese."

Shock jolted through Meryn. "You did? Why?"

"Mom asked me to check in on her occasionally, so I thought I'd drop by while I was in town, and Brendan came with me."

She gripped her water glass. "How is she?"

"I don't know. We didn't actually go inside her building, because, when we pulled into the parking lot, Abby was going in the back door."

"What? Why would Abby be there?"

"Excellent question."

Meryn leaned back in her chair. "That's what your fight with her was about, wasn't it?"

"Yes. I confronted her when she got here, told her that Brendan and I had seen her."

"What reason did she give you?"

"That's the problem. She didn't even try to give me a reason, just asked me to trust her."

Hope took the basket of bread Brendan held out to her and set it down. "And you can't."

"No, he can't." Brendan pushed his plate away, as though the subject of their older sister took away his appetite. "I know I haven't told you much about our half sister, but she is bad news. She's involved in all kinds of things we don't know much about, and don't want to. We do know enough to be ninety-nine percent sure that if Abby is working with her on any level, then she cannot be trusted."

Meryn was still trying to process the fact that her brother was keeping an eye on Annaliese. Her throat had tightened and she reached for her glass and took a sip of water. "But you don't know, do you?"

Shane looked at Meryn. "We don't know what?"

"If Abby is actually working with Annaliese, or if she is doing anything shady. Maybe she was meeting with her about some aspect of her new business. Brendan just admitted you don't know much about what Annaliese does; it's possible her business interests are legitimate. Some of them at least."

"First of all, while it is possible, it's highly unlikely that Annaliese is doing anything legitimate, unless it is as a front for something illegitimate. But if she is, and Abby's dealings with her are completely aboveboard, then why wouldn't she just tell me so?"

She set down her glass. "Did you give her a chance to?"

"Of course I did. What did you think we were talking about out there?"

"You said yourself that you confronted her as soon as she got here. And you looked pretty angry when I went out. Did you jump on her the second she arrived at what she thought was a celebration dinner for her new business? You're usually so calm, not at all aggressive. I'm sure she already knows that about you. It would have taken her by surprise when you came at her like that. You are a lot bigger than she is, you know, and you must have caught her off guard. Maybe she was a little flustered or intimidated or even scared."

He flinched, as though that thought caused him physical pain. "Maybe I could have handled the situation better. Abby didn't seem at all flustered or scared, though. In fact, she didn't really show any emotion at all. The bottom line is something is going on with her and our sister, something she isn't willing to talk about."

Hope picked up her fork. "Why are you telling us about this?"

"If Abby is involved in something she shouldn't be, then it could be dangerous for you to be around her. You should probably avoid that if possible."

Hope's perfectly manicured eyebrows drew together. "Dangerous? I don't know her well, but the last thing Abby strikes me as is dangerous."

"Even so, if she is in business with Annaliese, that's exactly what she is."

Hope pursed her lips. "All right, then. I'll be careful when I'm at work. And I can keep an eye on her, see if she does anything at all suspicious. I would like to state for the record, though, that my motivation will be to prove her innocence, not her guilt."

Brendan frowned as he touched Hope's hand. "Are you sure you still want to work there?"

"Of course. When Abby offered me the job yesterday, I knew that was where God wanted me to be. Maybe that's so I can warn you if I think something is going on, but I suspect it's so I can ease your mind.

Either way, like I said, I'll be careful."

Meryn nodded. "So will I, when I see her."

The salad tongs Shane had grabbed clattered into the glass bowl. "What do you mean, when you see her?"

"I told her I'd drop by Maeve's so we could have a visit, get to know each other better."

"Let me get this straight. Brendan and I tell you both about Abby, so that you will be on your guard against her and stay away from her, and your response is to decide to spend as much time as possible with her?"

Meryn snagged a piece of garlic bread from the basket. "If Abby is involved in anything shady, wouldn't it be better if one of us was keeping an eye on her, so we could find out what it was?"

Shane and Brendan exchanged a look, but neither of them answered.

Meryn almost laughed. If Hope hadn't been there, her brothers would have come down on her a lot harder, been adamant in their insistence that she stay away from Abby. Not that she necessarily would have, but it would have made them both feel better to be able to make the demand. With Hope there, Brendan's hands especially were tied. He had no right to tell Hope what to do, and from the look on her face, she wouldn't have done it, even if he had tried.

Especially if he had tried, probably.

She scrutinized Hope from a fresh perspective. As disconcerting as it had been to watch her arrive at Jesse's door and to see him welcome her with such obvious affection, Meryn was glad now that she was here.

Her eyes met Hope's and she saw the glint of humour in them.

A kindred spirit. Meryn pressed her lips together. Her brothers definitely wouldn't appreciate either of them being amused by what was going on. She squeezed Shane's arm. "If anything doesn't feel right, I'll let you know right away, okay?"

Hope nodded. "So will I."

Shane picked up the tongs again. "Maybe it would be good to have someone staying close to Abby, watching to see if she does anything we should be concerned about."

"Maybe." Brendan didn't sound convinced. He and Shane were pretty quiet as they all finished eating.

Hope reached for the plates and piled them up. "Thanks for dinner, Meryn. I don't know what Brendan is talking about ... I think you're a wonderful cook."

Shane smiled wanly as Brendan threw both hands in the air.

Meryn threw him a dark look. "Getting a little tired of the shots everyone is taking at my cooking lately. I think I'll let the two of you do all the meal preparations from now on."

Brendan elbowed Hope lightly. "Thanks a lot."

She grinned at him as she stood to carry the dishes over to the counter. "I'll clean up, Meryn."

"I'll help you." Brendan grabbed the bowl of salad and basket of bread from the centre of the table.

"I'm going out to feed the cows. Supper really was great, Meryn, thanks." Shane grabbed his ball cap from the hook by the door.

Meryn lifted her hand. "I'll come out too. I just need to change my clothes."

He nodded and headed outside.

When Meryn got to the barn, Shane was following the last of the cows in through the side door that opened into an outdoor pen. He steered the animal into the stall and closed the metal gate. A melancholy look crossed his face before he turned back to pull the barn door closed, but when he returned, he offered her a tired smile.

She touched his elbow. "You look beat."

Shane ran a hand over his face. "I've had better days."

"I'll help you with the chores." Meryn threw hay down in front of the cows.

They worked in silence for a few minute, then he looked around the barn. "I think everything's done here. Let's walk."

"All right." Meryn stepped into the yard and waited as Shane came out behind her and drop the bar into the slots of the door.

Neither of them spoke as they crossed the farmyard and walked through the opening in the cedar-rail fence. Meryn nodded at the bench. "Want to sit down?"

"Sure." He followed her and settled onto the bench.

"Look, Shane, I was hard on you earlier, about Abby. I know you're just trying to watch out for us, so I'm sorry."

"No, you made some good points. Now that I think about it, I did kind of attack her, and I don't usually react that way."

"You really like her."

"Yeah. I guess I do. Or did."

"Then you weren't only worried about her hurting us, you felt personally betrayed." *I know that feeling.* A pang darted through her.

He looked over at her. "That's a lot of psychoanalysis for one day."

"It's just that you and Abby really seemed to have something, you know? A connection. I felt it that first moment in church. That's not something that comes along every day, you know." Her voice quivered.

Shane wrapped an arm around her. "I know."

"I hate to see you throw that away because of a possible misunderstanding. Will you talk to her again?"

Shane didn't answer for a long moment, then he nodded. "Yeah. I'm sure it won't change anything, but I'll go talk to her."

"Good." Feeling completely drained, Meryn rested her head on her brother's shoulder as the sun that had shone brightly earlier in the day, succumbed to the dusk and sank below the trees.

She managed a grim smile at the sight, a fitting metaphor for the way their evening had gone.

22

Planes roared overhead. The whistling sound of a bomb hurtling through the air toward them filled Jesse's ears, and he dove behind a pile of rubble and threw an arm over his helmet. A deafening crash assaulted his ear drums. The world shrank down to five feet around him in every direction, filled with flying gravel and dirt and a thick dust that clogged his nose and throat until he could barely draw in a breath. Stinging debris pummelled every bit of exposed skin. His heart pounded.

Someone touched his shoulder.

One of Jesse's hands gripped an automatic rifle, but he shot out his other hand, his fingers closing tightly around the man's wrist.

"Jesse."

He hesitated. How would an enemy soldier know his name?

"It's okay, it's me. It's Trey."

Consciousness slowly came for him, and he opened his eyes. He still held Trey in a tight grasp, but he let go and dropped his hand. "Sorry."

"It's okay." Trey stepped back, rubbing his wrist. "I shouldn't have snuck up on you in the dark. I know better than that."

Jesse sat up. "What time is it?"

"Oh five hundred hours."

He glanced at his bedroom window. A thick grey fog pressed against the glass. "What are you doing here?"

"I'm supposed to be out patrolling, so I took the opportunity to drop by. I need to talk to you."

"You couldn't knock?"

"I did, but there was no answer, and I didn't want to pound on the door and wake up the neighbourhood. I tried the handle and it wasn't locked. I'm sorry to burst in on you like this, but it's important."

Jesse swung his legs over the side of the bed. "Give me one

minute. I'll meet you in the living room."

Trey nodded and retreated from the bedroom.

With a low groan, Jesse stood. He grabbed jeans and a T-shirt off a chair and pulled them on, then went into the little washroom. Splashing cold water on his face, he tried to bring himself back from where he'd been. The images continued to assault him, the cries echoing in his ears, but he'd learned a few techniques for blocking them out over the years, so he was mostly able to shove them back. For now.

Meryn could help, but since she wasn't here, and wasn't likely to be again, he was on his own.

Jesse wiped his face on a towel and headed out to see what Trey Adams was doing in his home so early in the morning.

Trey sat on the couch, an ankle crossed over one knee.

Jesse dropped onto the armchair across from him. "What's up?"

"I wanted to update you on what's happening at the base. You know Gallagher ordered all the churches closed after the water was poisoned."

"Yeah, I know." Jesse had driven past their church a few times in the two weeks since, and the heavy padlock on the door, the unusual darkness cloaking the building, had torn at his chest.

"What are you doing instead?"

"Instead?"

"Instead of getting together at the church. Are you meeting somewhere else?"

Jesse studied him. There had been talk of trying to meet in smaller groups, in houses maybe, but nothing had been decided yet. Why did Trey want to know?

Trey sighed. "Still have some work to do, don't I? The reason I'm asking is I couldn't have come to a big church meeting, but if there's something smaller going on offsite, I might be able to sneak in. I'm still reading the Bible and have a lot of questions. Just need a place to go for answers."

Jesse had undergone extensive training in interrogating prisoners. He scrutinized Trey now, analyzing his body language, his tone of voice, his eyes. No red flags. Still … "I haven't heard about anything yet. If I do, I'll try to let you know."

"I'd appreciate it. I check all the time, and the line to my i-com is still secure. You can send me a message that way."

"All right. What else is Gallagher up to these days?"

"Still trying to prove himself to Headquarters, according to the messages flying back and forth between the two. There's been a massive upsurge in the number of arrests he's making or ordering. There's a flogging at the base pretty much every day now."

Jesse's stomach lurched. "What about executions?"

"Surprisingly, no. None since the major. Maybe, because the circumstances surrounding that one were so questionable, Gallagher's decided to lay low for a while."

"I had a run-in with him recently."

"Oh? What happened?"

"He cornered me in a grocery store. We exchanged a few words. He ended up bringing out the manager and having me banned from that store and probably others."

Trey snorted. "Games. He's toying with you."

"Believe me, I know."

"I guess you would. He sure does not like you. Talks about you all the time. He even has a different tone of voice he reserves just for you."

"No doubt."

"Why does he hate you so much?"

"I have no idea. I asked him that once, and all he would tell me was that I had gotten in his way. He is a few years older than me, so he was pretty upset when I was promoted and he wasn't. Especially since he's apparently been passed over for a few promotions over the years. I've talked to several guys who've worked with him longer than I have, and he's gotten a reputation for causing dissension. Probably why he was a lieutenant for so long, in spite of all his efforts to move up. But, if he was angry with me because I got promoted ahead of him, why is he still so antagonistic? I'm no threat to him anymore."

"Aren't you?"

"Well, not in any professional capacity."

"That's what I wanted to hear." Trey dug into the pocket of his camouflage pants and pulled out a small box. "I brought these for you."

Jesse reached across the coffee table for the box and lifted the lid.

Four tiny round pieces of metal were slotted into the velvet lining the bottom.

"What are these?"

"They're scramblers. These are prototypes a friend of mine is working on."

"Scramblers?"

"Yeah. They're magnetic, so they stick to the underside of an identity bracelet, and they throw off the GPS coordinates."

"Really." Jesse studied the metal objects with renewed interest.

"Yes. Usually by about seven kilometres, but it varies. Use them sparingly. If someone tried to find you and you weren't where your bracelet indicated you would be, there would be huge consequences. In an emergency situation, or, say, a rescue or pick-up of some kind, it would be worth the risk, because it could save your life. Best to keep them for that kind of situation, though."

"Do I owe you?"

Trey laughed. "Sorry, but I doubt you could pay. They're worth about ten thousand apiece on the black market. I only got these because the guy who made them is a buddy, but I won't be able to get any more. Treat them like gold."

"I will. Thanks." Jesse replaced the lid on the box and set it on the coffee table.

"You know"—Trey drummed his fingers on the arm of the couch—"a lot of people have come to the base asking for an identity bracelet. It's shocked everyone, especially since fewer than half the people from the original list actually agreed to put one on, but apparently it's happening all over the country. People have just started showing up, claiming to be Christians and wanting to put on a bracelet."

"Why would anyone voluntarily …?" The truth hit Jesse immediately. *I know why.*

"What?"

Jesse took a deep breath. "Actually, I get it. When I was still on the base, and no one knew I was a believer yet, it bothered me not to wear a bracelet. A lot. It was a solidarity thing, I guess. Or maybe more like a declaration-of-allegiance thing. In any case, when Gallagher finally did put one on me, it was an enormous relief, as though I had come in out of the dark."

Trey looked thoughtful. "I wonder why he didn't arrest you."

"At the store?"

"Yeah. He's bringing people in for next to no reason these days. He just makes up the charges if there aren't any real ones. Why wouldn't he have hauled you to jail when he had the chance?"

"I don't know. Although he did say something about having plans for me."

"That's what I'm afraid of." Trey tapped a knuckle against his chin. "If I hear anything specific, I'll message you."

"I'd appreciate it."

"Anyway, I better get back out there, or someone will notice I'm not patrolling." Trey stood up and pulled on his beret.

Jesse followed him to the door. "What is the army doing to make sure nothing like the infiltration of the water bottling plant happens again?"

"I've heard rumours that the government is looking into hiring some big international security firm, but nothing definite yet. And we've been ordered to be extra-vigilant, but it's hard to even know what to watch for, to imagine what kind of heinous thing could be coming next. My mind just doesn't work that way."

"Probably a good thing."

"I guess."

Jesse contemplated him. Something in Trey's steady gaze reassured him. He held out his hand. *God, help me if this is a mistake.* "Thanks, Trey. For the scramblers and for coming by to let me know what's going on. It's good to know that someone at the base is on our side."

Trey gripped his hand. "I'm glad. I really do want to help, so just let me know if there is anything else I can do."

"I will." Jesse let go of him and opened the door.

Trey slipped out into the cool, misty morning.

Jesse shivered as dampness seeped into the room. It felt more like November than the first day of September. Strange weather. He closed the door, his mind whirling. Hopefully Trey would pick something up about what Gallagher's plans for Jesse might be. It would be useful to know what might be coming, so he could avoid it if possible. He headed for his bedroom to get dressed and ready for the day.

It was time to move ahead with a few plans of his own.

23

Meryn reached over the rails to scratch one of the cows between the ears.

"No chicken coop on your property, Meryn? Why ever not?"

She whirled toward the voice.

Annaliese stood in the doorway of the barn. Her long, blonde curls tumbled over a leather jacket, and she wore tight jeans tucked into high-heeled black boots.

Heat rushed through Meryn. "What are you doing here?"

"I didn't realize you were going all country hick again."

"Shane thought we should get a few animals. In case we need to … well, he just thought it would be good for us to produce some of our own food."

Her sister's smile was knowing. "Still expecting the apocalypse, isn't he?"

"You never know."

"I suppose not."

Meryn crossed her arms over her chest. "Was there something you wanted?"

"Do I need a reason to come see my family?" Annaliese started toward her, one deliberate step at a time.

Why do you always make me feel like a gazelle in the path of an advancing lion? Meryn forced herself to stand her ground. "When you have betrayed that family, then yes, I think you do."

Her sister stopped a couple of feet from her and drew her flawlessly-shaped eyebrows together. "What are you talking about?"

"I'm talking about you telling the army about the cabin where Jesse and I used to meet."

"I—"

Shane stepped into the doorway of the barn as Brendan came up to stand behind him. "Everything okay here?"

Annaliese glanced over her shoulder before turning back and rolling her eyes. "What a shocker. Your knights in shining armour, swooping in to protect you, as always."

Shane walked around her to stand beside Meryn. He rested a hand against her back. "Sounds like we all need protecting from you, Annaliese, since you were so eager to turn Jesse in and almost get him killed."

"I didn't turn him in."

Meryn gripped the railing. "You didn't?"

"Of course not. There's a severe shortage of good-looking men around here. I wouldn't just toss one away like that." Annaliese zipped up her fitted, black leather jacket. "And now I'm glad I didn't, since rumour has it you *did* just toss him away. Which means the man must be in need of some comfort right about now."

Meryn clenched her teeth together so tightly they ached.

Brendan filled the doorway behind their sister. "Back off, Annaliese."

She let out a cold laugh. "Just like old times, isn't it? The three of you against me. I'm family too, in case you've forgotten."

"Then act like it," Shane said. "Leave Meryn alone, stop fighting against us, and be on our side for once."

For a moment Annaliese didn't answer, then she squared her shoulders. "You three chose the sides a long time ago. I had nothing to do with it. And I'm thankful now that you did, since it means I don't have to be burdened with any sense of *misplaced loyalty*." She spun on her heel and started for the exit.

Brendan moved back from the opening.

When she reached the door, she stopped and looked back, one hand on the frame. "I'll tell Jesse you said hello, Meryn. Although, by the time I'm done with him, I doubt he'll even remember your name." She tossed her hair and pushed past Brendan.

Meryn pressed a hand to her stomach to hold back a wave of nausea.

Shane turned her to face him. "Jesse won't have anything to do with her."

Meryn nodded, her throat tight. "I know. She did kiss him once.

The night he was arrested."

"Really? What did he do?"

"He shoved her away. Then he fired her. Then he tossed her out of the cabin."

Shane grinned. "See?"

"Even if he does decide to have something to do with her, it's not my business anymore."

He squeezed her shoulders. "Why don't you go see him, kid? You obviously still love him, and he's miserable without you. Can't the two of you work it out?"

"No. We can't. Not after what happened with Logan."

"Maybe it's time to let that go." Shane dropped his arms. "I never, ever thought I would say this, but our darling sister did make one good point. Misplaced loyalty can be a terrible burden to bear."

"I think there's a lot to be said for loyalty. And speaking of which, did you go see Abby yet?"

"No, not yet."

"Then maybe you shouldn't be telling me what to do."

"Hey, don't turn on me, okay? If you're upset with Annaliese or Jesse or life in general, just say so. Or take it out on Brendan's punching bag." He inclined his head toward the bag hanging in the corner of the barn.

Brendan lifted a pair of boxing gloves off a nail on the wall and held them up. "Want to give it a go?"

"Really?"

"It's remarkably therapeutic."

Meryn shrugged. "Why not?" Nothing else she'd tried had relieved the deep hurt inside. Maybe this would. She unbuttoned her flannel shirt and handed it to Shane. The tank top she wore underneath would give her more freedom to move. She tugged an elastic from the pocket of her jeans and pulled her hair into a ponytail, then held out her hands.

Brendan carried the gloves over to her and helped her pull them on. When he finished, he stepped back and nodded toward the bag. "Go for it."

Feeling a little silly, Meryn walked over to the bag and jabbed at it.

Brendan snorted. "That's not going to help much. Really have at it."

She shot out her right hand as hard as she could.

"That's better. Now the left. And move your feet a little, like a boxer."

Meryn shuffled her feet. She ploughed her left hand into the bag and then her right. It did feel good. She thought about Annaliese and thrust out harder with her left. When the idea of her sister going to Jesse to offer him comfort flashed through her mind, she pounded the bag three times, hard, with her right hand. That hurt a little, but Brendan was correct; it was remarkably therapeutic.

After a few more jabs with both hands, she was breathing heavily, and she stopped and bent forward, resting the gloves on her upper thighs.

"Okay, that's probably good for your first time."

She straightened up as Brendan came and tugged off the gloves.

His eyes met hers. "Quite a flurry there in the middle. I won't ask what—or who—you were thinking about at that point."

"Thank you." She shook out her hands. "That felt great."

"Well, you know where it is. Use it anytime."

"I just might."

Shane handed her back her shirt, then slid an arm around her shoulders as they walked across the yard toward the house. "Feel better?"

"A little."

"Good. Just so you know, I am planning to go see Abby tomorrow."

She looked up at him. "So if I see you pounding the stuffing out of the punching bag tomorrow night …?"

He grinned wryly. "Then you'll know how it went."

24

Jesse paced the length of his living room. On his better days, he kept himself busy enough that he could push thoughts of Meryn to the back of his mind, the way he shoved the bloody images he'd dragged home from the war zone with him to the outer edges of his consciousness.

Today had not been one of his better days.

An intense pressure was building inside him. He'd give anything to be able to go out for a run, but the sun was setting, and he couldn't take the chance of getting stopped out after curfew.

Every part of him ached. If he didn't do something, he would explode. Jesse dropped to his knees in front of the couch. *God, please. I miss her so much. Help me to let her go.* He drove a fist into the thick cushion along the back of the couch. His knuckles stung, but it helped a little. He pounded it again. And again.

Why did it have to be her husband running across the sand that day? Of the thousands of Canadian soldiers posted in the country, why was it that one particular corporal who went to get help for his platoon?

And why was Jesse the one who had pulled the trigger? He'd been surrounded by trained military personnel. Any one of them was capable of taking out a man at a hundred yards. Couldn't one of them have been in a slightly different position, so another soldier could have been the one to take the shot?

He would never touch Meryn again, never hold her. She would never say his name the way she had the first time, in his quarters. They would never marry. She would never carry his child. Every dream he'd held close to his heart, since the moment he had realized she was the woman he would love forever, was dead.

Jesse propped his elbows on the seat cushions and dropped his head into his hands. *Oh, God.* He couldn't find the words to say, wouldn't have known what to ask for if he did. *Help me*, was the only desperate plea he could form. For several minutes he sat, fingers pressed into his temples, as his heart rate gradually slowed.

A knock on the door brought his head up sharply. *Meryn.* He pushed himself up from the couch and strode across the room. When he yanked open the door, his chest clenched at the sight of Meryn's sister standing on his front step. He started to shut the door.

She stopped him by sliding a leather boot into the opening.

"Get out of here, Annaliese," he snarled. "I'm not in the mood."

She stepped into the doorway, close enough to him that he had to step back to avoid contact. As soon as he did, she slipped through, pushing the door shut behind her and leaning back against it. "I can change that, Captain. It's what I do best." Her voice was low and husky.

Jesse took another step backward. He clenched his teeth at the triumphant smile that crossed her face.

She moved in his direction, lifting her hand to run her fingers along the side of his face.

Jesse grabbed her hand and twisted her around until her arm was pinned behind her back. "I'm not with the army anymore, as I'm sure you know, and my best friend is dead, thanks to you."

"I didn't have anything to do with that. I never would have turned you in, Jesse. I like you too much to want to see you hurt."

He hesitated. The faint, exotic scent of the perfume she always wore clouded his thoughts, and he let her go and moved back. "Then who did?"

She massaged her shoulder as she turned to face him. "I don't know, but I'll find out. They've been encroaching on my territory, so I'm just as anxious as you to find out who they are." As always, her voice wove around him like a web, drawing him in. She had been advancing toward him slowly as she spoke, and when she stopped, she stood so close to him he could feel the warmth of her body along the length of his.

Jesse swallowed hard. "I want you to go." Even to him, the words sounded weak, uncertain.

Annaliese smiled and slid her hands under his black T-shirt and up his torso.

Heat rushed through him.

"Are you sure about that?" When she spoke again, her breath

brushed across his throat. "I know you're lonely, Jesse, and hurting. I can make you feel better. I can make you forget all your troubles."

Somewhere in the fogginess swirling through his head, alarm bells sounded. When she started to unbuckle his belt, he moved to stop her, then let his arms fall back to his sides. He *was* lonely. He hadn't been with anyone since long before he'd met Meryn, and he missed the feel of a woman's soft flesh, of her mouth on his, and her gentle, whispered words. If Meryn wasn't going to forgive him, if there was nothing between them now, why shouldn't he be with someone else?

Annaliese's hands were driving him crazy. No doubt she was more than capable of living up to her claim and helping him let go of everything that weighed him down, all the pain and loss he'd endured the last few months, if just for a while. He needed some comfort tonight, needed to forget just how far down he'd fallen …

Annaliese reached for the button of his jeans.

Jesse's head shot up. He hadn't fallen down. God had lifted him up, further than he'd ever thought possible and way further than he deserved.

She had just reminded him how easily he could drop back down into the mud if he wasn't constantly on his guard.

God, forgive me. He wrapped his fingers around her upper arm, pushed her away, and directed her across the room. Jesse yanked open the door and shoved her out onto the porch. "Get out of my sight. Don't come here again. And if you hurt Meryn, or anyone else I care about, in any way, I won't be responsible for what I do to you."

She rubbed her arm and glared at him. "It's a mistake to cross me. I promise you you'll regret it."

"The only thing I regret is wasting the last five minutes by being in your presence. Go away, Annaliese. Now."

She whirled around and stomped down the stairs, nearly knocking over Ethan, who had just started up. He gripped the railing and watched her until she slid behind the wheel of her red sports car, slammed the door, and squealed out of the driveway.

When he looked back, Jesse held up a hand. "Don't say it." He turned and went inside, leaving the door open for his friend.

Ethan followed him in and closed the door, then locked it with a decisive click.

Jesse shot him a sheepish look as he buckled up his belt. He ran a hand through his hair and blew out a breath. "She's a real piece of work."

"Tell me about it."

Jesse's head jerked. "She went after you too?"

"Once, a few years ago. The night before Kate and I got married, to be exact. Trying to get to Meryn by destroying her best friend, I guess."

"Part of her life-long mission, apparently." Jesse met his friend's gaze. "You didn't fall for her whole"—he waved a hand through the air—"thing, I take it?"

"No, although my situation was different. I knew Kate was waiting for me. I admire your strength of character, under the circumstances, when you don't know when Meryn is going to come around and take you back."

"Or if. And I didn't feel very strong, that's for sure."

"Trust me. That was strong." Ethan clapped a hand on his shoulder. "Listen, Kate sent me over to see if you wanted to join us for dinner."

"That's what you're going with?" Jesse smoothed down the front of his T-shirt. "A dinner invitation?"

"Officially, yes. Unofficially, she'll be glad to hear I didn't have to save you from yourself."

"You almost did."

Ethan's grip tightened on his shoulder. "But I didn't. That's what matters."

"Only through the grace of God."

"Well, we'd all be slogging through the mire without that."

Jesse nodded. "Can we pretend that was a real invite to dinner? I'm starving."

Ethan chuckled and dropped his hand. "Let's go."

25

Shane stared into the window of a store a few doors down from Abby's shop. School had started up a week ago, and the display was still filled with supplies and clothes for the well-dressed student. Not that he had any kids to worry about. He sighed. *Stop stalling.*

Shane made his way to the coffee shop and pulled open the door. *Father, give me the words to say. Help me to know if I can believe what she tells me. I don't want to make a mistake that could cost my family, but I don't trust my own judgement when it comes to Abby. You know her heart. Guide me, please.* He'd stopped by on his way home from work, so it was the end of the day, and Maeve's was almost empty. He scanned the room.

A man sat in a booth in the far corner. Shane couldn't see who the man was talking to, but he laughed and touched the hand of the woman across from him.

Shane stiffened when the woman laughed too. He knew that sound. His eyes narrowed. *I know that man too. Major Gallagher.* Shane had caught glimpses of the commanding officer as he strolled through town as though he was the ruler of the world, but Shane hadn't been this close to him before. Which had suited him just fine.

What was Abby doing with him? And why did the two of them look so intimate? Stomach churning, he started to turn away.

The movement must have caught Gallagher's attention. He shifted his focus toward the door, then said something to Abby.

She leaned forward and looked around the edge of the booth.

Go, Shane. Get out of here. Shane stood frozen as their eyes locked.

The smile died on her lips.

For a few seconds, Shane couldn't move. Then he tore his gaze from hers and yanked open the door. The evening air cooled his burning cheeks as he stalked down the sidewalk. *You're a fool. Should have trusted those instincts and stayed as far away from Abby Wells as you possibly could.*

"O'Reilly." Her voice stopped him, but he didn't turn around.

She reached him and touched his elbow, but he jerked away.

"Shane, listen. Please."

He did turn then, whirled on her, so that she stepped back, surprise flashing across her face. "Oh, I'll listen. If you have any way of explaining why you were meeting with my sister and now Major Gallagher, the two biggest threats to the Christians in town. In fact"—he crossed his arms over his chest—"I'd be extremely interested to hear what you have to say about that."

"He is a customer. I'm friendly to all the customers that come into the shop. It's called good business."

Shane gritted his teeth. "Is that seriously the only explanation you are going to offer me?" He shook his head. "Meryn thought I'd been unfair to you the other day, had possibly even scared you by confronting you the way I did. And if that's true, I apologize. However, what I just saw confirmed that I was right not to trust you. There is nothing good about whatever business you are involved in with those two. Which is why I need to stay away from you, and you need to stay away from everyone I care about."

"Fine. You're the one who came to see me. But like I told you the other day, if you stay out of my life, I'll stay out of yours."

"Don't worry. I won't set foot anywhere near you again."

"Good."

The words were clear, but the hurt in her eyes, the way her lips trembled slightly, confused him.

Almost as much as the fact that, as angry and frustrated as he was, the only thing he wanted to do was pull her into his arms and hold her, tell her that, whatever was going on, they would find a way to work it out.

Shane squared his shoulders. This wasn't something they could work out. Not as long as she was lying to him, withholding information that could potentially put his family in danger. He spun around and stormed toward his truck. *Does she even realize what a precarious position she's in?* In spite of everything, the thought of something happening to her tore at his chest.

Just before he reached the truck, he stopped and came back. Gripping her by both arms, he looked into her eyes. "I don't know what you're getting yourself into, but you are playing with fire. Be careful, or you and a lot of others will get burned." He let go of her abruptly. Without another glance in her direction, he strode around the front of his truck and climbed in, slamming the door behind him as hard as he could. He would have loved to slam it a few more times, but she still stood on the sidewalk, watching him.

He felt her look like a touch on his skin but refused to turn his head. If he did, he wouldn't leave. Jamming the button with his thumb, he started the truck, then pulled onto the street.

His entire body trembled. He couldn't remember ever being so angry, except for the night Meryn came back from the cabin after Jesse had been arrested, and Shane thought Gallagher's men had ... He shook his head to try and clear it of the thought. He'd wondered that day what he would be capable of, if pushed to the absolute limit. If Meryn had been assaulted, would he have hesitated to point his shotgun at the men who had done it, to pull the trigger?

And what would he do if whatever Abby was involved in put his family in danger? Shane forced himself to relax his grip on the steering wheel. Everything was good now. He'd caught this early, tossed Abby out of his life before she had a chance to hurt any of them. Well, much anyway. If he was hurt, it was his own fault for falling for someone he didn't know anything about.

Too many terrible things were going on in their city, in the world, for him to be that careless. *Father, you've given me two jobs—to protect my family and to help Jesse thwart Gallagher's plans for the Christians in town. Help me to put Abby out of my mind, so I can concentrate on both.*

Shane straightened in his seat. That's exactly what he needed to do. What he would do, with the help of God. Put Abby Wells out of his mind. He couldn't allow anything—or anyone—to distract him again.

26

Meryn tugged a book off the shelf and held it out to the woman who'd come into the store to find a good suspense story.

The woman took it from her and turned it over to look at the back.

It was almost closing time, but Meryn never liked to rush a customer out the door. "That one is great, very well written. I've read it three—" Bells jangled, and she glanced over at the front of the store. Her breathing grew shallow. *Gallagher.*

And four other soldiers.

She cleared her throat. "As I was saying, I've read it three times and just loved it."

The woman's face had gone a little pale. She stared at the five uniformed soldiers standing just inside the door, then handed the book back to Meryn. "I'll think about it. Thank you." Before Meryn could respond, the woman hurried to the door. When she drew close, the soldiers moved out of her way.

Gallagher opened the door and held it for her.

After the woman had gone, he shut the door, flipped the sign on the window to Closed, and turned the lock.

Meryn replaced the book as Gallagher walked toward her. She recognized the two privates following him as the usual pathetic puppies traipsing along at his heels. The other two soldiers, a man and a woman, she hadn't seen before. When she spoke, she couldn't keep the contempt out of her voice. "Can I help you, Major?"

He stopped in front of her. "Do you recall that, after your last arrest, you were informed there would be random searches of your store to check for contraband items?"

Last arrest. Like there had been so many. "Yes."

"We're here to conduct one of those searches now. Before we do, is there anything you would like to say? If we were to find illegal items in this building, things would go much easier for you if you were up front with us from the start."

For a fleeting moment, Meryn wondered if she should have listened to Jesse and her brothers. She lifted her chin. "Go ahead and look. I have nothing to hide."

"Suit yourself." The major jerked his head toward the main part of the store. "Search every shelf thoroughly. And pay attention to the floor as you walk. If you find a loose floorboard, feel free to pull it up and check beneath it. That's her favourite hiding spot. If anyone finds anything remotely suspicious, bring it to me."

The other four soldiers scattered around the room.

The major nodded at the barstool-height chair behind her counter. "Take a seat, Ms. O'Reilly."

Stomach twisting, Meryn went around the counter and sat down. *Father, help me. Don't let them find the Bibles. Please.*

"Keep your hands where I can see them."

She folded them on top of the counter. "Do you have a search warrant?"

He laughed.

Meryn waited, but apparently that was the only response she was going to get. From the corner of her eye, she caught a glimpse of Private Smallman peering into the locked cabinet. She had given away nine of the first shipment of ten Bibles in less than two weeks. The only one she kept was the one hidden in *A Tale of Two Cities*, the book she'd taken home to show the others. She'd quickly placed another order, and four of those had gone out in the last few days—was that why the soldiers were here?—but seven books were still on display under the glass. Meryn fixed her attention on Gallagher, refusing to look over in Smallman's direction.

The major leaned a hip against the counter. "I sincerely hope you don't have anything in the store that you shouldn't, Ms. O'Reilly."

"I don't."

"You remember what happened the last time, don't you?"

Her jaw tightened. "Yes, I do."

He pressed both palms to the counter. "I promise you, if we find a single banned book in this place, I'll make what happened to you then feel like a Sunday school picnic. Do you understand me?"

How would you know what a Sunday school picnic feels like? She bit her tongue. Talking back would only make things worse for her. "Yes."

"Good."

Somewhere in the rear of the store, books crashed to the ground. Meryn winced.

Gallagher held up a hand and examined his nails.

Smallman wandered away from the locked cabinet.

Meryn relaxed slightly and studied Gallagher, trying to ignore the crashing sounds that continued to play out in the background. The man could have been handsome once, before bitterness and hatred hardened him and carved out any good that might have been inside him. What had happened to him to make him such a deplorable person?

Only God knew. And only God could heal him from whatever it was.

Pretty sure this one is beyond prayer.

She felt the gentle rebuke deep down inside her. Was any living person beyond prayer? Only God knew that too. It wasn't up to her to decide.

Fighting reluctance, she forced the words to form in her mind. *Father, help him. Soften his heart.*

That would have to do, since it was all she could muster.

For ten more minutes, the soldiers searched her store. When they finished, they gathered back at the front, near the door.

Gallagher pushed himself away from the counter. "No one found anything?"

"No, sir." The female soldier spoke up, and the others shook their heads.

His dark gaze swung back to Meryn. "What's in that cabinet?"

She forced herself to look him in the eyes. "What cabinet?"

He inclined his head toward the Bibles. "The one you were so interested in watching Private Smallman examine. What's in it?"

Meryn drew in a steadying breath. She'd barely glanced in Smallman's direction. Did the major miss nothing? "That's my rare book collection. I'm concerned about them, because they're so valuable."

"Open it."

Don't hesitate. Don't hesitate. "Sure." Meryn pulled open the drawer below the cash register and took out a set of keys and a pair of gloves.

Gallagher followed her over to the cabinet and waited for her to insert the key into the small lock and turn it. When she raised the lid, he reached for a book.

"You should wear gloves." Meryn held out the pair she had grabbed, but he ignored her and lifted out the copy of *A Tale of Two Cities*.

The major opened the book and read from the first page. "It was the winter of despair, we had everything before us, we had nothing before us, we were all going direct to Heaven, we were all going direct the other way ..." He let out a cold laugh and tossed the book back into the cabinet. "That sounds about right." He picked up another book, Charlotte Brontë's *Jane Eyre*, and flipped through it. After a few seconds, he flung it down on top of the other books. He tapped the lid with one finger, and it dropped with a bang that rattled the glass.

Meryn gritted her teeth.

She started to lock the cabinet, but Gallagher waved a hand toward the counter. "Go back and sit down."

Heat rose in her chest. How dare he come into her store without a warrant, when she hadn't done anything wrong—that he knew about—and order her around as if she was one of his subordinates. For a moment she thought about defying him. Better to get him away from the cabinet, though. Or better yet, out of the store.

She spun on her heel and made her way back to the counter.

Gallagher turned to the two soldiers she didn't know. "Coles, Weber, wait for us in the jeep. We'll be right out."

Meryn pressed a hand to her abdomen. Somehow having the two strangers in the store had provided her at least a small measure of comfort. Being alone with the major and the privates was never a good thing.

Her apprehension grew when Whittaker locked the door behind the two soldiers Gallagher had dismissed. Meryn clasped her fingers together in her lap to keep them from trembling. *Father, help me.*

Protect me like you have always done in the past. Give me courage. Please.

Gallagher came around behind the counter and gripped the arms of the barstool. His hooded eyes flicked over her face, like the tongue of a snake.

It took everything she had not to look away.

"All right, Meryn."

She stiffened. On his lips, her name was sullied somehow. Hearing it felt like a brutal violation, as though he was wrenching something away from her that he had no right to take.

"We'll let you off. For now. But know this—we are watching you. I've heard rumours that someone is distributing Bibles in town again, and I strongly suspect it's either you or you know who it is. If you set foot outside the lines, even edge too close to them, we will be on you so fast it will make your head spin. Do you understand me?"

An angry retort sprang to her lips, but she bit it back. Even that might be considered veering too close to the *lines*. "Yes."

He pushed himself up from the stool. "That's good. You've been very cooperative today. Keep that up and you and I will get along very well. In fact"—his hand slid under her hair to cup the back of her neck—"we might even become good friends."

Don't pull away. Resisting him was like waving a red flag before a bull. It only ever spurred him on to greater viciousness.

The rough, calloused fingers touching her skin were the same ones that had pulled the trigger and ended Caleb's life. That thought nearly ripped the last of the self-control from Meryn's grasp, but she clung to what was left of it. The man in front of her could never find out how much his presence unsettled her. How fear and revulsion spun through her like the destructive tornadoes she hated so much. Like a dog, he would feed on that fear, and then there was no telling what he would do to her.

Meryn met his gaze with an icy stare.

His thumb and finger pressed against the artery in her neck. Her pulse pounded.

She got the message. If he chose, he could apply a little more pressure, and she would lose consciousness. Or worse.

After a moment, he withdrew his hand. "We'll be back. And remember, we're watching you." Gallagher marched toward the door, gesturing for the privates to follow him.

The bells jangled behind them, and Meryn slumped against the back of the stool. Forcing herself to take slow, even breaths, she pushed back the sick dread still churning in her stomach. When her heart rate returned to normal, Meryn jumped off the stool and strode to the door. She locked the door and left the Closed sign in the window as she stalked through the store, surveying the soldiers' work.

Books had been tossed to the floor in every aisle, but none of them appeared damaged beyond repair.

Meryn spent twenty minutes cleaning up the mess, then flicked off the lights and made her way on still-shaky legs to the back room. In the past, she had kept the store open later on Friday evenings. Recently, though, she'd started closing at five, the same as the other days, after Shane told her he worried about her being downtown by herself after dark. Tonight, she was glad she had taken his advice and didn't have to remain in the store for four more hours.

She wouldn't tell Shane and Brendan what had happened, or they would renew their efforts to make her remove the Bibles from her store. Still, she needed to be around her brothers, to be with people whose presence could restore the peace that Gallagher and his cronies had just torn from her.

27

Meryn rinsed a plate under the tap and handed it to Brendan as Kate set the orange juice from breakfast into the fridge. "So what's the plan for the meeting this morning?"

Brendan shrugged as he stuck the plate into the dishwasher. "No big plan. When Shane and I bumped into Pastor John in town this week, and he told us he was trying to get a house church organized, I suggested that a few of us meet here this morning and have a small service. Afterward he wants to talk about a more long-term arrangement. He said he'd mention it to a couple of people, and they would come out around ten. I invited Jesse and Hope to join us, and that should be about it."

Meryn glanced at the clock. *9:45*. "All right, then. I'll go make sure the living room is tidied up before he gets here." She shook the excess water from her hands and dried them on the towel hanging on the stove handle.

"I'll help." Kate followed her out of the kitchen and across the hallway to the living room.

Shane sat in the corner reading a magazine, while Ethan tossed a piece of wood into the woodstove.

Jesse and Hope had settled on the couch. Matthew rested his head against Jesse's arm, and Gracie was snuggled on Hope's lap, as the kids watched a show, music blaring loudly, on TV.

Meryn bit her lip and looked away quickly. She picked up a remote-controlled car and several Lego pieces and tossed them into the toy box in the corner.

Brendan flopped down on one of the armchairs.

Jesse looked over at him. "I hope it's okay, but I mentioned that a few of us were getting together to that guy I told you about, Treyvon Adams."

"The lieutenant?"

"That's right. He's not a believer yet, but he's been reading the Bible, and he really wants to learn more. I said I'd try to let him know if we were going to meet."

"Didn't you say you weren't sure if you could trust him?"

"I'm still trying to be careful. My gut says he's a good guy, though. He came by my place a couple of weeks ago to update me on what's happening on the base. He gave me something that could help us too."

Shane closed the magazine he'd been reading. "What's that?"

"Four round metal pieces that attach to the identity bracelets and mess up the GPS coordinates. They're called scramblers."

Ethan leaned a shoulder against the mantel. "Really? What would we use those for?"

"I'm not sure yet. He advised us to only use them when absolutely necessary, to lessen the chances of someone figuring out we have them, but I think they could come in handy if any of us needs to temporarily disappear for any reason."

"Sounds like it."

Shane tossed the magazine on the coffee table. "By the way, Jesse, when Brendan and I were leaving work on Friday, our boss mentioned that he's picked up a few extra projects and could use more help. He asked if we knew of anyone, and we told him about you. Are you interested?"

"Absolutely." Jesse nodded. "That would be great. Should I call him?"

"No, he just said to bring you along Monday, if you want the job. He's a believer too, so when we told him about you and everything you'd been through with the army, he was quite happy to have you come work for him."

"Perfect. Thanks."

Meryn bit her lip. She needed Jesse to have less to do with her family, not more.

No one had asked her, though.

She scooped up the children's books from the coffee table and dropped them with a little more force than necessary into the basket on the floor. "I'll get some chairs from the kitchen in case a few extra people come." She left the room without waiting for a reply. For several seconds, she stood in the kitchen and gripped the back of a chair, eyes closed, praying for calm. When she opened her eyes and turned to take the chair out of the room, she nearly hit Jesse.

"Need any help?"

She cleared her throat. "Sure."

Jesse took the chair from her and set it down. When he leaned toward her, he was close enough for her to catch the faint, citrusy scent of the musk he wore.

Memories of their week in his quarters rushed back to her.

"Sorry, Meryn. I should have asked you before I said yes. Do you mind me working with your brothers?"

She forced a casualness she didn't feel into her voice. "Of course not. You have to make a living."

The corners of his mouth twitched. "All right, then."

"Besides, it's none of my business what you do."

He exhaled. "Do you realize you have been expressing that same sentiment to me, with minor variations, pretty much since the day we met? You need a new line, lady." His voice was low and soft.

Meryn offered him a small smile. "I'll work on that."

"Good. Because I—"

A rapping on the kitchen door cut off whatever he was about to say.

Meryn crossed the room and pulled it open.

Pastor John stood on the porch.

She pulled the door open wider. "Come on in. We're just grabbing a couple of chairs from the kitchen, in case we need them."

His face was a little pale. "I think we're definitely going to need them." He waved her toward the porch. "Come see."

Meryn stepped outside. Her mouth dropped open. A line of cars extended from their barnyard, down the driveway, and about half a kilometre down the road. People were parking anywhere they could find a spot and getting out and walking toward the house.

Meryn pressed her fingers to her mouth. *I'm not the only one who's been missing church.* She'd felt the loss of meeting regularly with other believers to worship God like a gaping hole in her life.

Apparently, others felt the same way. A lot of others.

She spun around.

Jesse had come out onto the porch behind her. He looked as shocked as she felt. Without a word, he went back into the kitchen and called out, "Uh, Brendan, Shane? You better come see this."

Her brothers came outside. Shane's eyes widened.

"I mentioned it to four people," the pastor's voice was hushed. "How many did you guys invite?"

Meryn looked around. Hope and Kate and Ethan had come out to join them. Matthew and Gracie plunked down on the top step of the porch to watch the parade of people. Everyone shook their heads and she turned back to John. "Jesse invited one person, a soldier from the base. Other than those of us already here, and whomever you invited, that's all we were expecting."

Meryn clutched Kate's arm as at least a hundred people streamed toward the farmhouse.

Brendan broke the stunned silence. "I think we're going to need a new plan."

28

Jesse leaned back against the cold stone outer wall of the farmhouse and crossed his arms over his chest. The living room wasn't nearly big enough to accommodate everyone, so Pastor John had suggested they hold church on the front lawn. Thankfully, the mid-September morning was mild, the sun casting a warm glow over the gathering, as if in blessing.

A hum of excitement buzzed through the air as everyone waited for the pastor to call the service to order. A couple of the Sunday school teachers had volunteered to take the kids across the driveway, to the hill leading down to the pond, for their lesson. Several of the children played tag or picked flowers by the water. A series of claps drifted up the small hill, and the kids ran over and dropped onto the grass in front of the teachers. Matthew took Gracie's hand and led her over to the group of children.

Jesse's chest squeezed. *God, prepare their little hearts to hear your Word. They will grow up in a world hostile, even hateful and violent, toward them and everything they believe. It will be impossible for them to hold on to their faith without your help. Let the seeds planted in them today take deep root and grow strong, so that they can face whatever lies ahead.*

The roar of a motorcycle cut through the murmured pre-service conversation. The bike pulled up the driveway and stopped beside the barn. The rider climbed off the bike and kicked the stand down into the dirt. He removed his helmet and hung it on the handlebars before turning toward the house. *Trey.*

Good call on his part not to drive the army jeep. Jesse uncrossed his arms and waved the lieutenant over to stand with him.

Trey lifted a hand in response and picked his way around the people seated on the lawn until he reached the house. His dark eyes were huge when they met Jesse's. "What is going on? I thought you said a few people were getting together."

Jesse laughed. "That's what I thought. Word spread, I guess."

In spite of the mild day, Trey wore a long-sleeved blue shirt. Likely trying to avoid calling attention to the fact that he was one of the few in attendance not wearing an identity bracelet.

Trey sagged back against the wall. "Wow."

Before he could say anything else, Pastor John went around behind the small table Shane and Brendan had set out as a makeshift podium, and cleared his throat. "Good morning." He scanned the crowd in front of him. "It is good for God's people to gather together, isn't it?"

Someone called out a hearty, "Amen," and a ripple of laughter floated through the crowd.

"I think we'll dispense with some of our regular programming for this morning. I don't really have any announcements, except to say that we will be considering various options for the best way for us to continue to get together. We'll contact as many of you as possible when those plans are firmed up. Clearly those of you who get the message are more than capable of passing it along to anyone who might not have received it."

More laughter echoed around the yard.

"Let's begin with a song, shall we?"

A couple of people, a man and a woman Jesse recognized from the worship team at church, had brought guitars, and they led the group in singing, "Surely the Presence of the Lord Is in This Place."

Jesse looked around. It wasn't a typical church service, obviously, but the words of the song rang with truth. The presence of the Lord *was* in this place, filling the open air of the yard as strongly as he had ever felt it inside a church building.

The song finished, and a reverent silence descended over the group as Pastor John took his place behind the table again. "In times like these, it is easy for us to start to think that we are alone in our fear and suffering. The temptation to close ranks, to shut ourselves into our homes, in an attempt to protect ourselves and those we are closest to, is strong. But my friends, look around you. The desire—planted in the heart of every believer by the hand of God himself—to join together in fellowship, is stronger.

"New laws may come—will likely come—prohibiting us from meeting together. But while we hold the law of man in high esteem, while we submit ourselves to it as often as possible, we cannot do so when those laws are contrary to the commands of God. And contrary to that desire that comes from him to be together, to support and encourage one another through these difficult days."

Jesse shot a sideways glance at Trey. Had it been a mistake to invite him here? What the pastor was preaching was sedition. He was openly endorsing breaking the law that the man beside him was duty-bound to uphold. Had Jesse put John and all the people gathered here this morning in danger?

Trey didn't react negatively to what the pastor was saying. His gaze was fixed on the man behind the table, and he appeared to be hanging on every word.

Jesse repressed a sigh as he swung his gaze back to Pastor John. It was too late now. For better or worse, Trey knew the stand that the pastor, and most, if not all, of the rest of them, were prepared to take if they were forbidden to meet together.

The pastor continued, his light Scottish brogue somehow lending an extra measure of history and shared global experience to his words. "In the book of Revelation, the apostle John received a vision of Jesus surrounded by seven lampstands and holding seven stars in his right hand. Jesus himself explained to John that the seven lampstands represented the seven churches. Now, the seven churches did refer to seven actual churches of that day, and Jesus had a message for them, a warning to avoid the unique pitfall each faced. Over the next several weeks, we will be looking at those pitfalls one by one, as Jesus was not only warning the churches of that time, but us as well. Because most scholars believe that, while Jesus was speaking to seven historical churches, he was also making reference to the church around the world in the last days.

"Which means"—Pastor John leaned forward and pressed both palms to the table in front of him—"that Jesus was speaking about us. Every believer here, and every Christian around the world, is a part of the church in the last days, waiting for the return of the Messiah. *We* are the body of Christ. *We* are the seven churches Jesus was talking to. *We* are the seven lampstands, and we cannot, and will not, hide that light from those in desperate need of it."

A powerful feeling rose up in Jesse. On some level, he'd known that none of them was alone, that they had God and each other and that there were others, in town and throughout their country, who believed and would stand up alongside them for the cause of Christ. He hadn't given a lot of thought to the idea of being a part of the church around the world, though. The revelation that all those in other countries who claimed allegiance to Jesus Christ—even though such an allegiance could mean death to themselves or to the ones they loved—were his brothers and sisters. They were his family.

For the first time in his life, Jesse completely understood why people walked for miles to a gathering place or met in secret in underground churches, even knowing that police could burst through the doors any moment and arrest them. An infinite, all-knowing Voice called to that deep, immortal part of them. Told them they were part of something bigger than themselves.

They were part of the church of Christ.

And so was he.

That thought sent courage and strength coursing through him.

The pastor pushed himself up from the table and raised a hand in the air. "The cause of Christ never has been, and never can be, defeated. In the darkest moment in history, when it appeared as though it might have been, he overcame. Death itself could not defeat him. He rose, victorious, our bright Morning Star. And one day soon that Star will shine again, so powerfully that not a single person on the planet will be able to stand in its presence, but all will fall to their knees in acknowledgement that he is Lord. When that day comes, I promise you that no one will give a thought to anything they have gone through here on earth. These 'light and momentary troubles', as the apostle Paul called them, will melt like ice in the sun and will be remembered no more.

"Until that day, we will proclaim the gospel of Jesus Christ, whatever the cost. We will stand with our brothers and sisters around the world. And we will, as our Lord commanded us, continue to meet together and encourage one another, and 'all the more as that day approaches.' As we do, we will find that not only do we have God and each other on our side, but that the angels themselves, the seven stars in the right hand of Jesus, will fight with us and for us."

Jesse's throat was so tight he could barely swallow. He sought out Meryn, sitting beside Kate on a blanket on the lawn. At that moment, she glanced back at Trey, as though checking to see how he was responding to the message, and her eyes met Jesse's. From the look on her face, she was as moved as he was. She smiled faintly and he nodded.

Pastor John gestured for the man and the woman with guitars to join him at the front. "We're going to dust off an old hymn this morning, 'I Surrender All,' a song that is as relevant today as it was when it was first penned over one hundred and fifty years ago. I would caution you, though, not to sing the words lightly. They are a vow, a high-stakes commitment that will require not only God's help, but the love, support, and encouragement of fellow believers to keep. They are a plea, that Jesus will make us wholly and completely his, that we will be filled with his love and power, overcome by his blessing, and empowered and emboldened as the sacred flame is ignited within us. Only then will we be able to persevere. If you are prepared to make that vow this morning, sing with us as we close."

The worship leaders began, singing each word of the verses and chorus with quiet conviction. Distant memories resurrected in Jesse's mind, of Sunday mornings in church, sandwiched between Rory and his dad, his mother's beautiful soprano voice rising above the others. Joy rippled through him. His connection with his family hadn't been severed, even though they were gone from the earth.

They were part of the church of Christ too, and that connection would endure for all of eternity.

He looked over at Trey again. The lieutenant wasn't singing, but a look of intense interest, almost awe, had settled on his face.

God, help him. Open his eyes to see how much you love him and his ears to hear the truth.

Jesse forced his attention back to the words of the song. *Can I make that commitment?* He wouldn't, not unless he could do so with all his heart and soul. When they launched into the chorus for the third time, he joined the rising swell, making the sacred vow without a single reservation. The three words repeated over and over filled every empty space inside him carved out by loneliness and loss, like rain pouring down on parched ground.

I surrender all.

29

"Wow." Meryn sank onto the kitchen chair beside Brendan. "That was unbelievable." She propped her elbows on the table and pressed both hands to her cheeks, head still spinning from everything she had heard and seen that day. People had milled around the farm, reluctant to leave, until well into the afternoon. When the last of them had gone, Brendan and Hope had made dinner for the family and Jesse and Pastor John.

"No kidding." Shane raked his fingers through his dark hair. "I mean, it was great that so many people wanted to meet. We just can't keep having everyone here. We're going to have to figure something else out."

Pastor John stroked his red beard. "You're right. There's no law against us gathering together—not yet anyway—but there is a law against teaching from the Bible and proselytising, and obviously that's what we are doing. It's time to put house churches in place. Meeting in smaller groups will lessen the chances that we'll draw their attention." He pulled an i-com from the back pocket of his jeans. "A few people mentioned to me today that they'd be willing to host one, so I've started a list."

Ethan shifted Gracie to his other knee, and she rested her head against his chest. "Good idea. Put us down to host one as well."

"Me too." Hope looked over at them from the stove, where she was scooping the leftover spaghetti into plastic containers.

Brendan had been drying the cookie sheet he'd used for garlic bread, but now he paused and contemplated her. "Where are you planning to host that?"

A sheepish look crossed her face. "Sorry. I haven't had a chance to tell you yet, but I decided on an apartment and signed a lease."

"Hope, that's great news." Brendan finished drying the sheet and slid it into a cupboard. "Is it the one on Sydenham Street that you liked?"

"Yes. I move in a week and a half, at the beginning of October."

Meryn lowered her hands. If they all hosted churches, they wouldn't be together on Sunday mornings. She sighed. Now that they knew how strong a desire people had to meet—and the pastor had reminded them how imperative it was—they had to start setting up house churches, and they needed places to hold them. Once they got going, they could figure out who was going to be where.

Pastor John moved his finger across the i-com screen. "Okay, with you guys, that makes eight homes so far, which means ten to fifteen people in each group. That's a good beginning, but if we grow any bigger, we'll have to find more homes to meet in." He slid the unit into his pocket.

Jesse leaned back in his chair. "I've started looking into grocery distributors within a couple of hundred kilometres' radius to see if we can find one that will deliver food to us, if it starts to get hard to buy. I'm hoping to find one that's owned by Christians, but so far I haven't come across any. We should start thinking, though, about where it can be dropped off and stored when we do find the right company."

"There's an empty space below the barn floor that we could use." Shane tapped his fingers on the table. "There's a cement foundation and it's underground, so it would be like a cold storage area."

"That could work. It would be far more discreet to deliver it out here than to some place in town too."

Shane nodded. "We can go check it out when we're done here."

More traffic to the farm. *I guess we're all in.* Meryn smiled grimly. *Logan, I hope you don't mind that we're turning your family farm into a stop on the black market.* Somehow she knew he wouldn't.

Ethan nudged Kate. "Gracie's about to fall asleep. We should probably get going."

"Okay." She stood up. "Matthew's playing with the train set. I'll go get him."

Meryn helped her gather up their things and walked them to the door.

Kate hugged her. "Talk to you tomorrow."

Meryn watched them head down the walkway toward their van.

When they had driven out to the road, she went to the fridge and pulled out a pitcher. "I made iced tea. Why don't we take it out to the porch?"

"Sure." Hope opened the cupboard and took down some glasses.

John, Jesse, and her brothers went outside, and Meryn followed them, carrying the pitcher. When she poured a glass of tea and held it out to the pastor, he shook his head. "Thanks, but I should go too."

"All right." Meryn set the iced tea down on the table between the Muskoka chairs and followed him to the top of the stairs.

"Good night, everyone." John went down on step, then turned back. "By the way, Meryn?"

"Yes?"

"Someone mentioned to me, as he was leaving today, that he saw two army jeeps parked in front of your store on Friday afternoon. I take it they didn't find the Bibles."

Meryn gripped the railing. Were there no secrets in this town? "No, they didn't. It was nothing, just a routine check."

"Good." He lifted his hand. "See you soon."

"You too." There was absolute silence on the porch behind her. She waited until he was halfway down the walk before turning around.

Hope sat on the swing. Her toes were pressed into the wooden porch to hold the swing in place.

Shane and Jesse both leaned back against the railing. Neither of them looked happy.

"We didn't have dessert. There are cookies in the kitchen. I'll grab them." Meryn walked toward the door.

Before she could reach it, Brendan, who had propped a shoulder against the wall by the window, pushed away from the house and moved into her path. "Um, something you want to say to us, kid?"

Not really, no. "It was no big deal. One of the conditions the army had when they allowed me to reopen the store was that they would conduct periodic, unannounced searches of the store. That's what they were doing there on Friday."

"And what happened?"

"Not much. They showed up and went around the store, looking through all the shelves. They didn't find anything, so they left."

"Who showed up?" Jesse's voice suggested barely restrained fury.

Toward her or the army? A chill whispered over Meryn's skin. "Five soldiers."

"Did you know any of them?"

She knew what he was asking. The answer wasn't going to help alleviate the thick tension that had descended over the group. "Two of them I had never seen before. The other three were Privates Whittaker and Smallman and …"

Jesse's eyebrows rose.

"Major Gallagher."

Shane crossed his arms. "And were you planning to mention to us at some point that Gallagher and four other soldiers searched the store, where you are keeping outlawed Bibles in plain view? Something that could get you arrested and flogged or even killed?" Her brother sounded calm, but a vein throbbed on his temple.

"Probably …" And then, because Meryn couldn't bring herself to lie to him, she added, quietly, "… not." She lifted both hands, palms up. "Look, we can't keep having this conversation. I'm not risking anything more than anyone else here is going to be. Kate and Ethan and Hope are planning to hold church services in their homes, which could get them into trouble. You guys are talking about smuggling food in and out of here, which is likely to get dangerous at some point. Every time Pastor John stands up to preach, he takes a chance on getting arrested. What I'm doing is no riskier than any of that. And I don't want to have to keep defending myself for doing it."

No one answered.

"I'll get the cookies." Meryn waited until Brendan moved out of her way, then slipped past him and into the house. She flung open a cupboard door. She was an adult and capable of making her own decisions, and if her brothers—or anyone else—didn't like it, they were going to have to find a way to deal with that.

Behind her, someone closed the screen and pushed the kitchen door shut.

Meryn turned around to see Jesse walking over to her. "Look, I'm tired and I don't feel like arguing. I'm not going to take the Bibles out of the store, so please don't ask me to, okay?"

"Meryn, even when we were together, I could never talk you out of doing anything you'd made up your mind to do. I'm guessing I'd have even less luck now."

He stood close enough that she could see the corners of his jade-green eyes crinkle when he smiled. The first time she'd noticed that was the night he walked her to her car after someone had thrown a brick through her store window. The night he'd kissed her for the first time. And told her that forgiveness was the antidote to the suffering in the world. "Then what is it?"

"I just wanted to ask you to please let me know the minute Gallagher comes by the store, or anywhere else near you, again."

"I don't know if I can. On Friday he stayed at the counter with me while the other soldiers went through the store, and he made me keep my hands where he could see them. There was no way I could have sent you a message."

"May I see your i-com?"

She hesitated, then reached into her back pocket and pulled it out. "What are you going to do?"

He took it from her and touched the screen. After a few seconds, he handed it back. "I programmed my number in as an emergency contact. From now on, if anything happens, you just have to hit the number one. A red flag will show up on my screen, and I'll know you need me to come as soon as possible."

Meryn slid the phone back into her pocket. "Thanks."

Any trace of amusement disappeared from Jesse's face. "Did he … harass you or hurt you in any way?"

"No. He made a couple of threats, that's all."

His jaw tightened. "What kind of threats?"

"He said that, if they found any banned books, he'd make what happened to me the last time look like a Sunday school picnic. And he told me they were watching me, and I better not step out of line. That's all."

"Oh well, if that's all, I won't worry, then." He exhaled loudly. "Look, I know it's not my job to protect you anymore, if it ever was, but I do know Gallagher, and I might be able to help. So don't hesitate to use that emergency number, okay? I really do want to be there for you. As a friend."

A friend. The word pricked like the sharp, shocking jab she always gave herself when she tried to sew anything. Should friendship be this much work? This fraught with conflicting feelings? She straightened her shoulders. "I don't know what you would be able to do, but I appreciate you being willing to try."

He shrugged. "That's really all we can do."

Are we still talking about Gallagher? Meryn swallowed. Either way, he was right.

All they could do was try.

30

Meryn tapped a pen on the bookstore counter. She'd had two customers that morning, and it was almost lunchtime. Ever since the water bottle poisoning, business at stores with the fish symbols screwed into the wall above the doors had dropped substantially.

She hopped off the stool. *Time to clean the apartment upstairs.* Her tenant had moved out a week earlier, and she hadn't had a chance to go up and make sure everything was in good shape before she advertised for a new one.

Meryn flipped the sign in the window to Closed and locked the door. Hopefully that would keep the hordes out for an hour or two. She might have smiled at that as she climbed the stairs to the second floor if the situation wasn't getting so dire.

The tenant had left the place fairly clean, but Meryn spent an hour wiping down sinks and counters and vacuuming the apartment. When she finished with the carpets, she switched off the vacuum and swiped the back of her hand across her forehead.

A loud bang echoed downstairs.

Meryn froze. What was that?

Another bang was followed by the sound of running feet and the slamming of the back door.

Heart pounding, Meryn crept toward the top of the stairs.

Flashes of orange flickered against the cream-coloured wall.

Was that … fire? She shook her head. The alarms would have gone off if there was a fire in the store.

Her next breath brought with it a sharp, acrid scent, and Meryn's chest clenched. *Smoke.* She went down one step.

A loud, roaring sound, like a freight train rushing by, filled the air, and a wall of flame swept up the stairs.

Meryn cried out and jumped back, the heat from the flames warming the exposed skin on her arms, face, and neck. *The Bibles.* The thought of the last seven copies burning broke her heart, but there was nothing she could do.

Meryn retreated down the hall of the apartment and dove into the bedroom farthest from the stairs. She slammed the door shut behind her. *Father, help me get out of this alive.* She felt in her pocket for her i-com, but her hands came out empty. She had left the device under the counter in the store. The roaring sound grew louder, and tendrils of smoke crept under the door of the bedroom. *I have to get out of here.* The window was locked, and the adrenaline pumping through her made her fingers tremble so badly it took three tries to pull the tab down and free the window so she could slide it open.

Meryn pressed both palms to the screen and shoved as hard as she could. The smoke curling around her was thicker now, and she coughed into her sleeve. How could the building possibly be consumed so quickly? She gave the screen another hard shove, and it popped out of the window. It bounced off the eight-inch-wide ledge lining the upper floor of the stone building and tumbled to the sidewalk below.

A small crowd had gathered in front of the store, and when the screen landed on the cement, everyone looked up. The looks of horror on their faces sent panic surging through Meryn, but she pushed it back. *I have to get out of here.* She looked wildly around the room. A wooden chair sat in the corner, and she grabbed it and dragged it over to the window.

In the distance, sirens wailed. Thick smoke billowed out the window around her. Meryn climbed up onto the chair and looked out. There was nowhere for her to go but onto the thin ledge. The sirens grew closer. The heat in the room had grown oppressive, and sweat dripped down her back. Meryn forced herself to take shallow, even breaths, but even those drew choking black air into her lungs. She coughed again. Her heart thundered in her chest. *I have to do this.*

She threw one leg over the window frame and slid her shoe down the wall until she felt concrete. Gripping the window frame tightly, she dragged her other leg over the lip and lowered it until she stood on the ledge.

Driving smoke blinded her. She needed to move away from the window, but once she let go of the frame, there was nothing to hold on to but flat stone. *Father, help me. Please.*

Slowly, she lifted her fingers away from the frame and slid a few inches to her right. Below her, people called out but Meryn flattened her hands against the wall in front of her and focused on moving slowly, slowly away from the wall of smoke. The wailing of sirens—the sweetest sound she had ever heard—grew deafening. Red lights flashed off the wall in front of her.

She moved a few more inches and stopped. The air was a little fresher there, and the roar of the fire dulled.

The sirens quieted. A voice pierced the sudden, near-silence. "Stay where you are, ma'am. We're coming."

The reassuring words slowed her heart rate slightly.

A ladder clunked against the ledge three or four feet to her right. It bounced against the concrete.

Someone must be climbing up. I just need to stay here a few more seconds, and the firefighter will help me down.

A tongue of fire shot from the window beside her, as though breathed from the mouth of a dragon.

She stumbled back a step, the heel of one shoe extending past the ledge, as heat and light assaulted her.

A woman on the sidewalk below screamed.

The fire receded again.

Meryn regained her balance and pressed her body to the wall. Blood pounded in her ears.

"Ma'am. Are you all right?" The firefighter had reached the top of the ladder.

Meryn turned her head slightly, so she could see him. "Yes." Her voice was ragged and raw.

"Good." He held out a gloved hand. "Come toward me, slowly. The ledge is wide enough. Just take your time."

Meryn drew in a deep breath, which was a mistake. Another cough gripped her and she leaned against the wall until it passed. *Please help me. I need you now. I can't do this on my own.* Meryn shuffled toward the ladder, an inch at a time.

"That's right. You're doing great. Almost there."

The calm, reassuring voice of the firefighter soothed her, and

Meryn closed the remaining space between them.

"I'm going to take your ankle and guide you to the rung, okay?"

Meryn nodded.

Strong fingers closed around her ankle and showed her where to put her foot. "That's it. Put your other foot on the next rung and come down."

Reluctantly, Meryn let go of the wall. She climbed down another rung, and bent to clutch the sides of the ladder tightly. A loud, cracking sound startled her, but the firefighter gripped both her calves to hold her in place, and she settled back on the ladder.

"It's okay. The front window just broke. Keep going."

A cloud of black smoke billowed up around them from what must be a gaping hole in the front of the store.

"Almost at the bottom. You can do it."

The ladder jerked as the firefighter stepped onto the sidewalk. He guided her with a light touch on her leg and side as she descended. "There you go. Step off now."

Her feet landed on solid cement. Her legs shook violently and might have given out on her, but the man took her by the arm.

"Is there anyone else in the building?"

"No. At least, I don't think so. I was the only one upstairs, and I didn't think there was anyone downstairs. Right before I saw the flames, though, I heard people running through the store and the back door slam."

"People? Could you tell how many?"

"Not for sure. I didn't see anyone, but it sounded like two, or maybe three."

He led her down the sidewalk. "Come over to the ambulance, so they can check you out. And wait here for a bit, okay? The chief will want to speak with you before you leave the scene."

"Okay."

He dipped his head. A paramedic came toward her, pushing a stretcher, and the fireman let her go and turned back to the building.

"Here." The medic draped a blanket around her shoulders and helped her up onto the stretcher.

Even from fifty feet away, she could feel the heat. Meryn sank down on the thin mattress.

"My name is Ben." He nodded at a man coming up beside him, carrying a metal canister. "And that's Owen. We're going to give you some oxygen, okay?"

When Meryn nodded, the paramedic slid a mask over her face. Fresh air flowed through passageways that stung and burned. The tightness in her chest gave a little.

After a couple of minutes, Ben touched her shoulder. "Better?"

She nodded again.

He left the oxygen mask in place as he lifted a stethoscope from around his neck and put it on, then listened to her heart and lungs. "Deep breath."

Meryn inhaled slowly.

"Good." Ben reached for the small, rectangular unit Owen held out to him. "I'm going to check your oxygen saturation levels."

She nodded absently. Over Ben's shoulder, she stared at her store, the shattered front window, the flames leaping out from inside and creeping along the gutters at the top of the building. *The Bibles. And all my books.* Tears pricked her eyes but she blinked them back. Could someone have done this on purpose? There was no other reasonable explanation for the banging and the running she had heard before the fire erupted. It was too much to comprehend, though, that anyone could have intentionally caused so much destruction. Could have taken her life.

Water gushed toward the building. Firefighters fought the blaze desperately, beating back the smoke and flames that poured from her store window. In spite of their valiant efforts, the truth was painfully clear.

It's too late. Meryn pressed her lips together to hold back the sob that rose in her throat.

Everything was lost.

31

Meryn couldn't tear her gaze from the flames still licking broken and blackened glass in the front window.

The paramedic hung his stethoscope back around his neck, a grey identity bracelet clearly visible around his wrist. With a loud ripping sound, he tugged the blood pressure cuff free of her arm. "It's a miracle anyone got out of that inferno alive. God must have been on your side."

Meryn met his eyes and mustered a faint smile. "He always is."

Ben nodded slightly. "How do you feel?"

"Pretty shaky. And it hurts here." She held a hand to her chest.

"Yeah, lungs are funny that way. They really don't appreciate being filled with smoke. Good news is your heart is fine. Any headache or nausea?"

"No."

"Excellent. Those could indicate carbon monoxide poisoning. I'm going to take the oxygen mask off now, see how you feel, all right?"

She nodded.

He slid the mask up over her head and lifted her chin with one finger. "No sign of soot around the nostrils, so you got out before the smoke got too thick in the room. Do you want us to take you to the hospital?" The medic dropped his hand.

Her fist to her mouth, Meryn coughed. "I really don't, unless you think it's necessary."

Ben shook his head. "Obviously you inhaled a fair amount of smoke, but you seem to be breathing well. Fortunately, the flames didn't get close enough to burn you. You'll need to take it easy for a day or two. If you do develop a headache or start vomiting, or if you have trouble breathing or the cough persists beyond a few days, you should go to the hospital right away." He handed the mask and canister to Owen, who carried them back to the ambulance.

"I will."

"Is there someone you can call to come and get you?"

"My i-com was in the store." She glanced over at the flames shooting out the front window, then looked away quickly.

"I have one you can use."

Meryn thought about it. Shane and Brendan were out of town on a construction project, which meant that Jesse was, as well. Not that she would call him. Maybe Kate, although she'd have to drag the kids out …

"Meryn!"

She looked down the sidewalk.

Hope wended her way through the people crowding the street in front of the store, a frantic look on her face.

Relieved, Meryn turned back to the medic. "A friend of mine is coming. She can take me home."

"Great idea. Best not to be by yourself for the next twenty-four hours or so. Like I said, watch for any symptoms that might manifest themselves today. And listen, you went through a harrowing experience. You might have to deal with some nightmares for a while." He touched her hand lightly. "I'll pray for you."

"I guess you have to be careful who you say that to these days."

"Unfortunately, yes. But it doesn't stop me from praying."

Hope reached them and threw her arms around Meryn. "Are you hurt? When I saw the store …" She held Meryn out at arm's length and examined her.

"I'm okay. I breathed in a little smoke, that's all."

"Do you have to go to the hospital?"

"Not unless I start to feel worse. I just have to take it easy for the next twenty-four hours or so."

"My car's at the coffee shop. I'll go get it and take you home."

"I'll walk with you."

"Are you sure?"

"Yes. I—"

A man striding toward them caught her attention.

"I need to talk to the fire chief for a minute. Then I can go, okay?"

"Sure. I'll wait for you." Hope moved out of the way as the chief stopped in front of Meryn.

"I'm Chief Brentwood. Are you the owner of the building?"

"Yes. Meryn O'Reilly."

He unzipped his yellow jacket and pulled an i-com from his pocket. "If you don't mind, I need to ask you a few questions. If it's okay." He shot a look at the paramedic, who nodded. The chief turned back to her. "First of all, I'm very sorry about your store. We did everything we could, but the fire was already out of control by the time we arrived. We won't be able to do much now beyond trying to keep it from spreading to the buildings on either side."

"No one was hurt, were they?"

"None of my people were. And as far as we could tell, there wasn't anyone else in the building. One of my men said you thought you heard people running through the store?"

"Yes. I locked the front door and went upstairs. My back door is usually locked too, although I didn't double-check that before I went up. I heard a couple of banging noises from downstairs, then what sounded like two or three people running across the floor. The back door slammed shut, and right after that, fire shot up the stairs, and I couldn't get down."

The chief entered that information into his i-com. "Anything else you can tell me?"

"I don't think so, except that it all happened incredibly quickly. I had no idea fire could consume a building that fast. And the wall of flames that swept up the stairs sounded like a train roaring through."

"That's helpful. Can you give me a number where we can reach you?"

"My i-com was in the store."

Hope moved closer. "I'll give him my number, Meryn. He can reach you through me until your brothers get back." She recited the number to the fire chief, who entered it into his device.

The chief nodded and dropped the i-com back into his shirt pocket. "When we can get inside and look around, we'll determine if the structure is sound enough to leave it, or if it will need to come down."

"When can I go in?"

"Hard to say. It may not be safe enough for you to go in at all, but whoever calls you with the results of the investigation can confirm that with you. It could be a few weeks before we decide if the building can be left standing. Even if you are allowed back in, there won't be much, if anything, to salvage."

"I'll get in touch with my insurance company right away."

"That would be wise." He lifted his hand to the brim of his helmet and turned away.

Hope touched her shoulder. "Ready?"

Meryn looked over at the paramedic. "Is it okay if I go?"

"Yes. Just remember to give yourself permission to take it easy for a while. You've been through a trauma, and both your mind and body need time to recover."

"I will." Meryn jumped down from the stretcher. She tugged the blanket off and handed it to him. "Thank you again."

Hope slid an arm around Meryn's shoulders and led her across the street, away from the smoke and water and broken glass and gaping onlookers.

When they reached the sidewalk on the other side of the street, Meryn lifted her sleeve to her nose. "I smell like smoke."

"That's not too surprising. How did you get out of the building if you were upstairs when it started?"

"I climbed out a window and onto the ledge, then the fire department arrived with a ladder, thankfully."

"Meryn." Hope's blue eyes, so like Caleb's, widened with concern. "You could have been killed."

"I know. I actually thought I might die for a couple of minutes. But, as the paramedic pointed out to me, God was on my side."

"Your family would have been devastated if anything had happened to you." Hope squeezed her shoulder. "And Jesse."

Meryn shot her a sideways glance. "Hope."

Hope wrinkled her nose. "I'm sorry. I promised Jesse not to say anything to you. I just hate to see him hurting so much."

Now her chest ached from more than just smoke. Why had Jesse extracted that promise from Hope? In fact, why had they been talking about her in the first place? It was all too overwhelming to process, especially with her mind as hazy as the air had been before she'd escaped.

She would have to take Ben's advice, and give herself time to recover before she could begin to deal with any of the thoughts swirling through her head.

32

Jesse poked at the campfire with a stick. It was their last night on their current job, and he was ready to leave their campsite, and the trailer they'd been sleeping in for four days now, and head home to his own bed. Not that he minded the work. In fact, it was a tremendous relief to be back doing manual labour. The more nails he could hammer and two-by-fours he could haul around, the better. Doing was far better than thinking.

Not to mention that it felt good to be making an income again. He'd blown through a lot of savings the last few months, so the opportunity to replenish his resources was welcome.

Brendan carried plates over to the picnic table, next to where Shane stood behind a barbeque, cooking dinner. "Well, the one good thing about everybody being so upset is we get a lot of work done."

Shane frowned. "What are you talking about?"

"You and Jesse. I mean, the two of you work pretty hard anyway, but now that you've both broken up with the women in your lives, you're working like crazy men. This job was supposed to take all day tomorrow, but we're almost done."

Shane flipped a burger and it landed on the grill with an angry hiss. "I didn't break up with Abby. We mutually decided it wasn't going to work out between us. I'm not upset about it."

"And I definitely did not break up with Meryn. She broke up with me. But I'm not upset either." Jesse stabbed viciously at the campfire.

Brendan set a plate down on the table. "I stand corrected. Clearly you're both deliriously happy. The fact remains that we're powering through our work quickly and should be able to be back home by—"

A buzzing sound cut him off.

He pulled his i-com from his shirt pocket. "It's Hope." He lifted the device to his ear. "Hello?"

Jesse grabbed another piece of wood and propped it against the pile in the fire pit.

The smell of cooking meat wafted on a cloud of smoke across their site.

"What?" The last plastic plate Brendan had been holding clattered onto the table. "Is she all right?"

Jesse froze. He speared the stick into the ground and caught Shane's eye.

Shane set down the lifter and came around the barbeque.

Jesse edged toward them. Was it Meryn?

"Are you sure?" Brendan drove his fingers through his dark hair as he listened. "Did she go to the hospital?"

Shane tapped his arm.

Brendan held up a hand. "Do they think it was deliberate?"

Was what deliberate? Had someone hurt Meryn? The thought of anyone doing her harm dragged a murderous rage up from Jesse's belly to his chest.

"Should we come home?" Brendan didn't speak for a moment, then he blew out a breath. "I'm sure she needs rest more than anything. But please have her call one of us as soon as she wakes up. Even if it's the middle of the night." He listened again, massaging his temple with his free hand. "Thanks for staying with her, Hope. I really appreciate it. Good night." He touched the screen and shoved the i-com back into his pocket.

"What is it?" Shane's voice, normally calm, held a hint of panic. "Did something happen to Meryn?"

"Her store burned down."

The warmth drained from Jesse's body. Memories of the night he had been in the bookstore with Meryn when a brick crashed through the window jolted him. "Is she okay?"

"Hope thinks so. Meryn was upstairs cleaning the apartment when the fire broke out." Brendan stalked around the pit. When he reached the stick Jesse had planted in the ground, he grabbed it with both hands and yanked it out.

If someone had set fire deliberately to Meryn's store, it was a good thing he wasn't standing in front of her brother at the moment.

"Apparently, it swept through the building so fast she couldn't get down the stairs. She had to crawl out a second-floor window, where the fire department rescued her from the ledge." In the orange glow of the flames and the setting sun, his knuckles gleamed white around the stick.

Jesse's stomach churned. This was far more serious than a broken window. Meryn could have been killed. "Where is she now?"

"At home. Hope is staying with her. The paramedic said she inhaled some smoke but escaped before it got too bad." Brendan's pacing had taken him to a tree, and he whacked it now, several times, with the stick.

Shane went back to the barbeque and turned the dials to shut it off. His face was grim as he piled the burgers onto a plate and carried it over to the picnic table. "Hope didn't think we should go home?"

Brendan paused his attack on the tree. "No. Meryn just wants to sleep, so there's nothing we can do."

Shane set the plate down and sank onto the wooden bench. He propped an elbow on the table and supported his head with his hand. "Do they think someone did this on purpose?"

Brendan tossed the stick into the fire and went over and sat down across from him. "Meryn heard banging noises downstairs right before she saw the flames. Sounds like it was done on purpose to me." His fist thudded down on the table. "Who would do something like that?"

Jesse wanted to hit something too. Or somebody. Badly. Too worked up to sit, he went back to the fire, found a new stick, and jabbed it into the logs.

One slid from the pile, sending a spray of sparks through the air. A rush of smoke and heat billowed toward him.

He didn't move back.

A cloud of smoke enveloped him, and he coughed. Meryn must have gone through the same thing today, only a hundred times worse. She had to have been terrified.

Shane exhaled loudly. "I guess there's nothing we can do tonight. Might as well eat."

The last thing Jesse felt like doing was eating. Other than commit some sort of violence, he had no idea what he *did* feel like doing. He jammed the stick under the log that had fallen and cranked it back on top of the pile. That was a lie. He knew exactly what he wanted to do. Jump in the truck, head straight for the farm, and see Meryn with his own eyes. Hold her until his heart stopped thudding erratically against his ribs. He wanted … no, he needed to make sure she was okay.

Except that he couldn't.

He tossed the stick into the pit and made his way on not-quite-steady legs over to the table. He slid onto the bench beside Shane, who set a plate in front of him. Jesse picked up the burger from the plate. He stared at it for a moment, until Shane nudged him with his elbow.

"She's fine, Jess."

"Yeah, I know. It's just, as a former law enforcer, this kind of random act of destruction drives me crazy."

"As a former law enforcer."

Jesse shot a look at Shane.

His friend's lips twitched, but his eyes held sympathy.

"That's right."

Brendan swallowed a bite. "Then you think it was random?"

Jesse set down his burger without taking a bite. "I don't know. The store was targeted before, so there's a good chance it wasn't."

"The store was targeted, or Meryn was?" Shane's voice carried an edge.

Jesse hadn't eaten anything, but the smell of the charbroiled burgers, normally one of his favourite aromas, was upsetting his stomach. "Good question."

Shane twisted the cap off a bottle of lemonade. "I told Meryn once before that I didn't like her being downtown anymore, especially by herself. And her smuggling Bibles out of the place made me really nervous. As much as I detest what happened to it, maybe it's for the best that the store is gone."

Brendan ripped a paper towel off a roll and swiped it across his mouth. "I wouldn't put it to her that way."

"I won't. But I can still be silently thankful that she's not so vulnerable now."

"Silence is wise." Brendan crumpled up the paper towel and tossed it onto the table.

Both Shane and Jesse looked at him until he lifted both hands.

"What?"

Shane managed a tight grin. "It just doesn't quite match up, somehow, you advocating silence. Or wisdom, for that matter."

In spite of the rage still pulsing through him, Jesse snorted a laugh.

Brendan threw them both a scornful look. "Obviously, there are greater depths to me than either of you realize. Anyway, Hope thinks so, and that's all I care about." He gathered up his plate and stood. "I'm going to bed."

"Okay." Shane stood too and picked up his plate. Like Brendan's, it still contained most of an uneaten burger. "Let me know if you hear anything from Meryn, okay?"

"Of course."

Shane pointed a thumb in Jesse's direction. "Tell Jesse too. As a *former law enforcer*, he'll want to hear all the details of the case, see if he can contribute to solving it in any way."

Brendan lifted a hand before disappearing into the trailer and letting the door slam behind him.

Jesse's jaw tightened. It wasn't quite as funny when he was on the receiving end of the harassment. Not that he didn't deserve it for lying to one of his closest friends—poorly—about why he was upset. But still.

Shane nudged him again. "Eat something. You'll be hungry in the night."

Jesse looked pointedly at Shane's plate.

Shane set it back down on the table with a sigh and sat. "Hope will let us know if there are any problems. If we go home we won't be able to do anything except hover, and Meryn would hate that."

Yeah. Especially if the person hovering is me. He sighed. "I know." He picked up his burger and took a half-hearted bite. The food tasted like Styrofoam in his mouth, but he choked it down. "So, not buying the former law enforcement bit?"

Shane laughed. "You are a terrible liar."

"Your mother once told me she considered that a point in my favour."

"She would. And she's right. Although maybe I'm not the one you're lying to."

Jesse set down the burger, the one bite he'd taken not sitting very well. Was Shane right? Had he been lying to himself all along, thinking he could keep seeing Meryn, hearing her voice, being in the same room with her while knowing that she would never be his? Had he really believed they could be friends? His shoulders slumped. "You could be right. Maybe I've just been kidding myself all along, fooling myself into believing that I could ever move on. Meryn is a part of me, and not being with her feels like something deep inside of me has literally been ripped out. I have no idea how to let her go." He shifted in his seat until he faced his friend. "But I have to, Shane. Us not being together isn't my choice. It's Meryn's. And I have to respect that."

"Well, you've admitted it. That's a positive step. Now you can stop the self-deception and cling to the truth." He reached for a bottle of water from the centre of the table and tipped it in Jesse's direction, a serious look on his face. "May it set you free."

Jesse grabbed his own bottle of juice and tipped back his head to drink. It did feel good, admitting the truth out loud that he'd tried so hard to hide, even from himself. The load he'd been carrying felt different somehow, as if it had shifted and now rode a little more comfortably on his back.

God, please let Shane's words come true. The prayer was a desperate plea. Jesse may have taken a big step tonight, but the last thing he felt was free.

33

Meryn shut the door of the car and followed Hope across the parking lot of Maeve's Coffee Shop. The morning air was fresh and cool, and she breathed deep, grateful that the burning sensation in her lungs had eased. She stopped outside the door. "Hope, thank you for taking me home and staying with me last night. I can't tell you how much I appreciate it."

"I was happy to do it, Meryn. I was so worried about you yesterday, I doubt I would have slept much if I hadn't been there."

"I hope Brendan knows how lucky he is."

"Feel free to remind him any time." Humour sparkled in Hope's eyes.

"Don't worry, I will. Although, given the way he looks at you, I don't think he needs a reminder." For the first time since she had walked away from the fire the day before, Meryn allowed herself a glance up the street at her burned-out store.

Streaks of black climbed the walls above the boarded-up windows on both storeys.

Hope grasped the door handle. "Do you want coffee before you go?"

"No, thanks. I had a cup at home. I'm going to check out the store on the way to my car, see if the fire department is still conducting their investigation. If so, I might be able to get someone to give me an idea of the extent of the damage and when I can get inside."

"Okay." Hope pulled open the door. "I better get to work. I'll see you later."

She nodded. When the door closed behind Hope, Meryn forced herself to walk toward the store. *Father, thank you that I was not alone in that building, that you were there with me. Thank you for helping me get out alive. Show me now which path to take. If you want me to rebuild the store and open it back up, make it clear that's your plan for me. And if you don't, then help me to let it go.*

Tears stung the corners of her eyes. Why had her life become all about letting go? Had she been clinging to things—or people—she shouldn't have? Had she lost perspective on what was truly important, and now God was reminding her of what she needed to value most highly?

Meryn swiped the moisture from her eyes. *Maybe.*

No one appeared to be at the store when she reached it. She held the side of her hand to her forehead to block the glare, and peered through the small window in the door that had somehow survived the intense heat.

Nothing moved inside.

I need to see if I can salvage the Bibles. Meryn shot a look up and down the street. A few people strode along the sidewalk or wandered in and out of stores, but no one seemed to be paying attention to her. She'd just go in for a minute. If she sensed it wasn't safe, she'd come right back out, and if an investigator showed up and questioned her, she would simply apologize. It *was* her property, after all.

Meryn examined the entryway. The frame was splintered and a crack zigzagged across the door from top to bottom, where one of the firefighters had kicked it in. Meryn had to shove her shoulder against it a couple of times before it popped open. When it did, she stepped inside and pushed the door shut, just until it touched the frame.

The charred remains of books crunched beneath her hiking boots as she moved deeper into the store. The smell of smoke still permeated the air, and her eyes watered. She coughed and pulled her jacket higher, zipping it to the top to cover her mouth and nose.

Most of the shelves had toppled over and burned. Water still dripped from the ceiling and from any shelf left standing.

This place had been a second home to her, the fulfillment of a lifelong dream. Here she had shared her love of books with every person that had come through the doors. She had read stories to children and served tea to patrons who had curled up with a novel on one of the many armchairs tucked into corners and arranged around the fireplace.

She and Jesse had discovered a strong connection here, and she'd experienced his wrath in this room when he'd stormed in and arrested her for smuggling Bibles. So many memories crashed through her mind she couldn't begin to sort them out.

The Bibles. Meryn picked her way carefully over to the locked cabinet along the wall. Even before she reached it, she knew it was hopeless. The glass was scorched and broken, and black soot coated every inch of wood. Choking back a sob, she reached through the gaping hole in the lid and lifted out one of the books. It was so badly damaged that when she tried to flip the pages, they crumbled into dust in her hands. Another loss beyond measuring.

Footsteps thudded toward her from the back room, behind one of the shelves.

Probably one of the inspectors coming to survey the damage. Meryn pulled her jacket from her face and swiped at a tear that had started down her cheek. "I'm sorry. I know I'm not supposed to be here. I was just—"

Jesse came around the end of the shelf and stopped.

Meryn clutched the burnt Bible to her chest.

He lifted his hands, palms up. "Meryn. I'm so sorry."

She swallowed hard at the tenderness in his voice. "It's just stuff."

He tilted his head, emerald eyes dark with sadness. "This place was a lot more than that to you, I know." He walked toward her, stopping a couple of feet away. He glanced at the book in her hands and winced. "This is a terrible loss. Terrible and senseless."

She nodded, throat too tight to speak.

"Your brothers headed straight to the farm from work to see you. They may not be too happy to find that you aren't in bed, resting. I only knew because I stopped in at the coffee shop on my way home, and Hope told me you'd come here."

"I needed to see what was happening with the store. And, as you can see, I'm fine. It was a close call, nothing more." Her forehead wrinkled. "If Shane and Brendan went straight to the farm, how did you get here?"

"I bought myself a truck. My first vehicle, if you can believe it. I've never needed to own one of my own before. I always just drove an army jeep." He looked around the store. "Do they know what happened?"

"I haven't heard from the fire department yet, so I have no idea when they'll be done with their investigation." Her gaze lifted above his shoulder, and she gasped.

Someone had scrawled two-foot-high words in neon-orange spray paint across the wall behind Jesse. The letters were partially obscured by streaks of black smoke, but the water that had streamed down had washed away some of the soot, and she could make out the first three letters—*Jes*—and the last two words—*You Now*.

"What is it?" Jesse swung around to look. For a moment he didn't move, then he strode over to the wall, pulling off the denim shirt he wore over a navy T-shirt. He crumpled up the shirt in one hand and scrubbed it hard over the rest of the letters.

Meryn went over to stand beside him.

As soon as they could make out all the words, he stopped scrubbing and they both stared at the wall.

Jesus Can't Save You Now.

When he turned to her, anger flared in his eyes. "If there was any doubt that this was deliberate, it's gone now." He pointed at the wall behind her. "And that explains the banging noises you heard."

She turned to look. The smoke detector hung loosely against the blackened wall, held by one wire. The rest of the wires had been torn from their places, the frayed ends poking in all directions. Meryn turned back to Jesse. "Someone tampered with it."

"Yeah. They hit it with something. A baseball bat, maybe."

"They meant to hurt me."

"They meant for the store to be completely destroyed anyway." His face softened. "You'll miss this."

"Miss it?"

"The store. What will you do?"

"If they decide the structure is sound enough, I'll rebuild it."

He blinked. "That's an unbelievable amount of work, Meryn. And time and expense, even with insurance."

"I don't care. I won't let them win, Jesse. I won't let them defeat me, drive me away. Not if there's any way for me to stay."

He studied her for several seconds before reaching out and

rubbing her cheek with his thumb. "You have some soot, here." His fingers stilled on her face. "Stubborn Irishwoman."

Neither of them moved. Her heart thudded so loudly she was sure he could hear it.

The front door creaked open.

Jesse dropped his hand quickly and stepped back.

Meryn felt the gaze that lingered on her face like she'd felt the heat of the encroaching flames on her skin. She inhaled a quivering breath and turned toward the door.

Drew stood in the opening.

She held up a hand. "Wait. Don't come in, it's a mess. I was just coming out."

Jesse nodded. "I'm leaving too. I have a meeting to get to. I'll go out the back way."

"Okay." Her voice shook slightly.

His eyes met hers briefly before he nodded toward the entrance. "Drew."

Drew lifted a hand but didn't speak as Jesse headed for the back of the store. Drew looked over at Meryn. "Should you be here?"

Because of the fire or with Jesse? Meryn shook her head. Same answer either way. "Probably not. I just came in for a minute to assess the damage." She made her way carefully through piles of ashes and debris, both still warm through the soles of her boots.

Drew stepped back so she could come out.

Meryn went onto the top step and turned to pull the door shut behind her. She bit her lip as her gaze fell once more on the words Jesse's scrubbing had revealed.

Meryn pushed back her shoulders. That lie had no power over her. The words of Isaiah—*when you walk through the fire, you will not be burned*—swept through her mind as she closed the door.

That was a promise from God. And, unlike the words scrawled across her wall, those words were truth.

34

Drew stopped in front of a store a few doors down and pointed to her cheek. "You have soot on your face."

"Yes, I know." Her finger trembled slightly as she reached up to touch the spot. How could she still react so strongly to Jesse's touch, to his eyes searching hers? Wasn't she getting over him at all? Would she ever? Fear clutched at her chest. "I mean, I'm not surprised." She held up one hand, black from the Bible she still clutched in her fingers.

"Can I take you home?"

She shook her head. "My car is just around the corner, and I don't want to get yours all dirty. Walk me there?"

"Sure." Drew fell into step beside her as she headed for the street where she'd left her car. Was that only yesterday?

"I'm sorry about your store, Meryn. I heard there'd been a fire downtown, but I didn't realize it was your building until I happened to overhear two clients talking about it in the bank a few minutes ago. You could have called me." His look was mildly accusing.

"I didn't call anyone. My i-com was destroyed in the fire."

"Then how did *he* know to come?"

Her eyes narrowed. "*He* works with my brothers. They must have told him what happened."

Drew blew out a breath. "I apologize, Meryn. You don't need me jumping all over you." He stopped and pulled her to him. "And I don't have any right to tell you who you can and cannot see."

His hand cupped the back of her head, and Meryn relaxed against him, letting the feel of his strong arms around her push back the confusion and uncertainty that seeing Jesse had stirred up in her. She lifted her head and contemplated him. Drew was a good man and a good friend. And he cared about her. If she spent time with him, if they could get back to the way things used to be, her feelings for him might deepen. Maybe that was the only way for her to move on, to put the past behind her once and for all. Everything she and Jesse had once had was destroyed now, as completely as the flames had decimated her store. But her life didn't have to be over. She could rebuild it, create new memories. With someone else.

The ache that thought caused was for the store. Not for him. It couldn't be.

Drew grasped her upper arms lightly. "What is it, Meryn?"

"I told you, when you came out to the farm after the water poisoning, that when I was ready to move on, you would be the first to know."

"Yes, you did."

"If you still feel the same way you did then"—the words threatened to stick in her throat, but Meryn forced them out—"I am ready."

His hazel eyes lit up. "Of course I feel the same way. But ..." He threw a glance back in the direction of the store. "Are you sure?"

She didn't look back. "I'm sure."

"I never thought I would hear you say those words. You've made me very happy, Meryn."

"I hope we can make each other happy."

"I'll do everything in my power to make that happen, I promise." Leaning in, Drew pressed his lips to hers gently. When he pulled back, he searched her face. Looking for doubts? Second thoughts?

It was too late for those.

A light breeze blew past her, carrying with it a hint of smoke. And a reminder.

Fire destroyed, but it also cleansed and purged. It took away, but it also gave.

And today, it had provided what Meryn needed the most. A brand new start.

35

"Where's Meryn?" The screen door banged shut behind Shane as he came into the kitchen.

Brendan closed the silverware drawer. "She went to bed early. She's had a long couple of days."

Shane turned on the tap and squirted soap onto his hands. "Yeah, I guess she has. When I was talking to her before going out to do the chores, she seemed pretty exhausted." He rinsed off his hands and dried them on the towel hanging on the oven door handle.

Brendan handed him a plate filled with meatloaf, mashed potatoes, and carrots. "Did you see the store?"

Shane's grip on the plate tightened as he carried it over to the table and sat down. How anyone could wilfully cause that kind of damage was beyond him. "Yeah, I drove by this afternoon. What a disaster."

"It really is. Hope and I went over and looked through the window in the door after she finished her shift at the coffee shop." Brendan reached for his fork. "Are you praying?"

"You go ahead."

Brendan's eyebrows rose but he bowed his head and gave thanks for their meal before digging in.

Shane moved the food around on his plate. It had smelled good when he walked in, but a strange restlessness plagued him, and his appetite had disappeared. "Did she tell you about her and Drew?"

Brendan reached for his water glass. "Yeah."

"What do you think?"

He shrugged. "Does it matter? Meryn's going to do what she's going to do. And Drew's a good guy. Personally, though, it feels a little messed up. I thought she and Jesse would find a way to work things out."

"So did I." Shane tossed his fork onto the plate. "We're all pretty messed up, I guess."

"Not me. Things with Hope are going great."

"That's good. I'm happy for you." The words sounded far more sarcastic than he'd intended.

Brendan set his fork down too. "What is the matter with you tonight?"

"Sorry. I didn't mean that. I really am happy for you. Hope's great. It's just that everything else feels wrong lately, upside down or backward or something."

"Why don't you call her?"

"Who?"

"Are we back to that again? You know who."

"I can't." Shane pushed his chair back. "Thanks for making dinner. I really appreciate it. Do you mind if I eat it later, though?"

"Why? What are you going to do?"

"I need to go out for bit."

Brendan glanced toward the window. "You know it'll be dark in an hour."

Shane got up and carried his plate to the fridge. "I won't be long."

"Be careful. After we got that warning last week coming home from work, they won't hesitate to take you in if you get stopped again."

He shut the fridge door harder than necessary. "Brendan, I'm thirty-seven years old. I can take care of myself. Really don't need you telling me what to do."

His brother lifted both hands. "Just trying to avoid having to bail you out."

"I believe you owe me a couple of bail-outs."

Brendan grinned. "Still, be careful."

"I will." Shane studied the sky over the barn as he headed for his truck. Much as he hated to admit it, Brendan was right. The sun was already drifting pretty low. He shouldn't stay out long. A night in jail would not improve his mood. Especially since it was impossible to predict what could happen to a Christian who was arrested and taken to the base. That could get ugly fast, as Meryn had found out. And Jesse.

Shane drove the streets of Kingston for a few minutes, no definite plan in mind other than getting out of the house. The church was a dark and silent silhouette against the orange-streaked horizon, and an aching sense of loss assailed him as he drove by.

He slouched in his seat as he approached Maeve's. On some level, he'd known this was where he would end up when he left the house. Or maybe ever since he'd accused Jesse of not being honest with himself the night before. *Hypocrite.* Shane gripped the steering wheel as he slowed the truck. The Closed sign hung in the door, but the café was still well-lit. He caught a glimpse of Abby wiping down a table by the window.

Shane chewed his lower lip. Like Jesse, he'd tried to pretend he could let go of what he and Abby had. Of course, he wasn't as deeply into anything with Abby as Jesse had been with Meryn. Still, something connected the two of them powerfully. He'd felt it the moment his gaze had been drawn to her that first day in church.

He pulled into the lot and parked in a shadowy corner where he could see the back door of the café. Abby would have to come out soon herself, if she wanted to be home by curfew. Shane drummed his fingers on the dashboard.

It was getting dark fast. He should probably go home now and forget this whole thing. He bent and straightened his fingers, trying to get rid of the excess adrenaline pumping through him.

He and Brendan seemed to have switched personalities the last few weeks. Brendan was pretty calm these days, likely from the influence of Hope, while Shane's emotions had been far more volatile than usual.

His brother had asked a fair question. What *was* the matter with him?

The back door of the coffee shop opened, and Abby came out clutching a full black garbage bag in one hand. She set it down and locked the door, then picked up the bag and tossed it into the Dumpster behind the shop. Without a glance in his direction, she headed for the Kev and climbed in.

Shane leaned forward to look up at the sky. Almost pitch black. He sighed. Since there was no way to get home before curfew now, might as well follow her to see if she went straight home.

Making sure to stay well behind her, Shane tailed the Kev for five or six blocks. When Abby made her third left turn, he pulled over to the side of the road and stopped. *This is ridiculous. She's heading back to Maeve's. She knows I'm following her.* Halfway down the block, Abby turned into the coffee shop parking lot. With a heavy sigh, Shane signalled and pulled back onto the street. Time to go home before he got nabbed for being out after curfew.

Red and blue lights flashed in his rearview mirror.

Too late. Gritting his teeth, Shane swerved to the side of the street again and turned off his engine.

A soldier approached his window and rapped on the glass. Shane rolled it down.

The man glanced at Shane's wrist and moved back. "Step out of the vehicle." A second soldier came up behind him, hand on the butt of his weapon.

Shane pushed open his door and got out of the truck.

"License."

He pulled his wallet out of his back pocket and retrieved the laminated card. He handed it to the soldier, who passed it to the man behind him.

The first man pulled an i-com from his shirt pocket. "Hold up your identity bracelet."

Shane complied.

"What are you doing out after curfew?"

"I went for a drive and lost track of time. I was heading home when you pulled me over."

The soldier looked up from his i-com, eyes hard. "You received a warning about being out late a week ago."

"Yes, sir."

"Is there a reason you feel the law doesn't apply to you like it does everyone else?"

Shane's muscles tensed at the man's tone. Somehow, he didn't think he was going to be let off with a warning this time. *So much for being careful.* "No, sir. I don't think that."

"Then, can you explain your wilful disregard for the rules?"

"I've been careless, I guess. It won't happen again."

"No, it won't. We'll make sure of that." The soldier pulled a set of handcuffs from his belt. "I'm placing you under arrest for curfew violation. Turn around and put your hands behind your back."

Seriously? A movement across the street caught his eye, and Shane glanced over.

Abby stood on the sidewalk, watching them.

What did she think she was doing?

"Turn around now." The soldier barked out the command this time.

The other man stepped closer, as though expecting trouble.

Shane sighed and turned around.

Cold steel snapped around his wrists.

Unlike Brendan, who'd been a little wild as a teenager, Shane had never been arrested. He didn't like the feeling one bit.

The soldier took him by the arm and nodded at the jeep parked behind Shane's truck. "Let's go."

Before they could start forward, Abby stepped just off the curb and lifted her arm, so her bracelet could be clearly seen. "Excuse me, gentlemen."

"Stay with him." The soldier who had scanned Shane's bracelet let go of him.

The other soldier moved to his side and grasped his elbow.

The man walked across the street to Abby. Shane couldn't hear what they were saying, but Abby held something up to show the man, and he nodded. The two of them spoke for a couple of minutes, then Abby pulled her i-com from her jacket pocket and detached a stylus from the side of it. She held both out to the soldier, who wrote something on the screen.

Shane's brow furrowed. Would she be arrested too?

If so, it was all his fault.

36

The soldier with Abby turned and gestured for the man holding Shane to bring him across the street.

"Come on." The man tugged on his arm.

Shane narrowed his eyes as they reached the other side. The soldier hadn't slapped handcuffs on Abby. He must not have arrested her. Then, what was happening?

"Thank you, gentlemen." Abby shoved her i-com back into her jacket pocket. "I'll take care of this myself."

"Yes, ma'am." The soldier she'd been speaking with nodded respectfully and handed her a small key before he and his partner headed back to their vehicle.

Shane stared at Abby. "What is going on?"

Shaking her head, she grasped his arm. "Let's go inside."

"Abby. What—?"

She glanced back at the soldiers. "Inside."

Exhaling loudly, Shane followed her to the front door of the coffee shop.

Still holding his arm, Abby yanked a set of keys out of her pocket and unlocked the door. When they had gone in, she let go of him, shut and locked the door, and pulled the blinds down over the glass. All the other blinds in the shop had already been lowered. She whirled back around to face him. "Just couldn't stay out of my life like I told you to, could you?"

"You were threatening my family."

Abby held up a finger and took a step toward him. "No. You *believed* I was threatening your family. That's not quite the same thing, is it?"

Shane didn't answer, but he took an involuntary step back.

She moved forward and stopped in front of him, standing so close he could see the tiny flecks of green in her grey eyes.

Focus, Shane.

"Why were you following me?"

"I wanted to see if you were going straight home, or if you had any other clandestine meetings set up in town."

"I thought we agreed that what I did or didn't do was none of your affair."

"I decided to make it my affair." The double entendre was not lost on him. "And why did the soldier agree to leave me here with you? What was that you showed him?"

"In good time."

Was that *amusement* in her voice? Before Shane could toss out the irritated retort that sprang to his lips, she stopped him with a hand on his chest.

"Sit down, O'Reilly."

"I don't want to sit down."

"Then you don't hear my story. Your choice." She pulled back her hand and crossed her arms, waiting.

Shane berated himself for missing the warmth of her palm against his T-shirt. He held out for five seconds before moving back a few feet and sinking onto a red stool at the counter with an exasperated sigh. The cuffs dug into his wrists. "Was that the handcuff key he gave you? Any chance you could take these things off of me?"

She shook her head again, and this time he definitely detected humour in her eyes. The sight of it sent an odd mixture of annoyance and desire coursing through him.

"I don't think so. You and I are going to have a chat. And by chat, I mean that I'm going to talk and you're going to listen. I have some things to say, and I kind of like the idea of having a captive audience."

"Could you at least sit down? I'm getting a sore neck trying to look up at you."

"Welcome to my world," she said dryly, but she did walk over and sit down on the stool beside him.

"What did the soldier write on your i-com?"

"He was signing a non-disclosure agreement. I'd have you sign one too, but ..." She inclined her head toward the hands pulled behind his back. "In lieu of that, I need you to give me your word that nothing

I tell you will leave this room."

Curiosity overrode his irritation. Barely. "Fine."

"All right." She crossed one ankle over the other. It took everything in him not to glance down. "Here it is. I was sent to Kingston on assignment."

"By?"

"The organization I work for. The Canadian Security Intelligence Service."

Shane almost choked on the breath he'd just taken. "CSIS?"

"That's right. Even with all the craziness in the country, it's becoming clear that things are happening at a lot of the bases, including the one at Kingston, that are not strictly by the book."

"You mean Gallagher."

"I can't go into details, but suffice it to say, I was sent here to carry out an undercover operation to find out what has been going on and whether or not the law is being broken by those in command."

"Which it is."

"As my investigation is on-going, I can't comment on that. In fact, I've already told you far more than I should have."

"Why?"

"Because your pulling crazy stunts like following me around in the dark is putting my investigation in jeopardy. Now that you know what I'm doing here and why I've been looking into what certain people, including your sister, have been up to, I'm hoping you will back off and let me do my job. Incidentally, I wasn't meeting with Annaliese the day you saw me at her warehouse. We'd received a tip that she was out of town, so I just went in to take a look around."

Shane's head was spinning. Abby was one of the good guys? That opened up a number of interesting possibilities. "You're a spy."

"That's right."

"A spy. With CSIS. *The* CSIS. You."

She shifted on the stool. "Getting a little insulting, O'Reilly."

"I'm sorry. It's just that you don't look like a spy."

"Believe it or not that's actually considered an asset in my line of work."

"Yeah, I guess it would be. But a spy ..."

"It's agent, actually. And why were you really following me tonight?"

He measured his words carefully. "It never did sit right with me, the idea that you could be involved in something questionable with my sister. I guess I wanted to make one more attempt to figure out what you were really up to."

"Why?"

"Because I wasn't ready to give up on us." In the silence that followed the words he hadn't meant to say, at least not the way he'd said them, something crystallized in the empty space between them. Something he could almost reach out and touch if she hadn't insisted on keeping him a *captive audience*. Shane twisted his wrists, trying to relieve the pressure, then stilled as a new thought occurred to him. "Your name isn't Abby, is it?"

Her hesitation answered the question.

"What is it?"

She didn't reply.

He wasn't surprised. He'd unwittingly put her in danger. Revealing her name on an undercover operation would only increase that danger a hundred—

"Leah."

"Leah." He almost whispered the word as it rolled off his tongue for the first time.

She bit her lip, the first chink he'd seen in her tightly fastened armour since she had brought him into the coffee shop. "Yes, well. You understand, of course, that is highly confidential. If anyone else finds out, my job—and my safety—will be on the line."

"So basically your life is in my hands now."

The armour clinked back into place as she lifted her chin. "Should you decide to break that confidence, I'm perfectly capable of dealing with whatever consequences may follow. Right after I toss you in jail."

"I have no doubt." He was the one amused now, and from the hard glint in her eyes, she didn't appreciate it any more than he had. "Does that mean you're not going to toss me in jail now?"

"Not this time." Leah stood up.

"I'm glad to hear it." He rose too and moved toward her.

It was her turn to take an involuntary step backward.

"Could you take these things off me, then? Not exactly designed for comfort, are they?"

"No." The steel was back in her voice. "They're designed for subordination and compliance. So frankly, I'm not in any hurry to take them off. It will do you good to remember who's in charge around here."

"Oh, don't worry. With or without the cuffs, I won't forget that." Shane took another step toward her. "Please, Leah."

"Don't do that."

He wasn't sure if the tremor in her voice was anger or something a lot more vulnerable. "Don't do what?"

"Don't use my name like a weapon. That's not why I gave it to you. In fact, don't use it at all. It's dangerous."

That's true. His lips twitched. "In what way?"

"As I said, my life could be at risk."

He smiled and took another step.

When she moved back this time, she met solid wall behind her.

Shane pressed his advantage and closed the gap between them, stopping just short of touching her. "Just your life?"

"What else?"

"I don't know, your heart, maybe?"

"That's ridiculous. I am a pro—"

He stopped her with his lips on hers.

For a moment, Leah held herself rigid, then she lifted her hands to his face and responded to his kiss with an eagerness that stole his breath.

Once he stepped back, she shook her head. "I can't do that."

Shane grinned. "Don't underestimate yourself. I thought you did it pretty great."

"You know what I mean."

He lifted his shoulders. "I understand the words you're saying. Your lips, however, are saying something else entirely."

"Well, listen to the words. They're always more sensible."

"But your lips are considerably more honest."

Leah sighed and twirled her finger in the air. "Turn around."

187

"Gladly." Shane turned his back to her, wincing as the cuffs tightened slightly before loosening with a loud click. He faced her again, rubbing one wrist, and she slipped the handcuffs into her jacket pocket. "When can I see you?"

"It's really not a good idea for me to get involved with you, O'Reilly. I'm here to do a job, then I'll be gone."

The lack of conviction in her voice encouraged him. "You haven't been thinking about me?"

"That's not the point."

"I think it's exactly the point. You've been thinking about me, and I've been thinking about you. Now that I know what I know, there's nothing standing in our way."

"There are all kinds of things standing in our way."

Shane ran a finger along her jawline. "Name one."

She didn't respond.

He laughed softly. "Let's have dinner soon. But early. I can't be out after curfew again."

"No, you really can't. I played the get out of jail free card for you tonight, but I won't be able to do it again." She exhaled. "All right. Dinner. But I can't do it before Monday."

"Monday works. I'll pick you up here at five." Shane followed her to the door. "Leah."

She turned back. "Call me Abby. You're the only one I've told about my name."

"Why did you?"

She met his eyes. "I suddenly couldn't stand for you not to know."

Good answer. Shane touched a curl. "You'll be careful?"

"I'm afraid it's a little late for that."

His stomach was doing strange things again.

"But if you mean at work, then always." Leah tugged her i-com from her pocket and inputted something. "There. I put it on your record that you have permission to be out for fifteen more minutes. That should give you enough time to get home." She slid the device back into her pocket and pulled open the door. "I'll see you Monday."

Shane nodded and went out into the cool September evening. For a long moment after he'd climbed into his truck, he stared out the front window, trying to process everything that had just happened. Then he smiled and shook his head.

A spy. Of all the theories he'd come up with to explain her mysterious behaviour, that one hadn't even crossed his mind.

37

Jesse closed the door behind the last of the fourteen people, besides him, Brendan, and Hope, who had come to the house church at Hope's apartment.

Pastor John had spoken to them earlier, but for the next few weeks they'd be on their own as he made the rounds to the other groups.

Jesse grabbed two empty mugs and carried them into the kitchen.

Hope leaned back against the counter. Brendan stood in front of her, and the two of them were kissing.

Jesse rolled his eyes. "Discussing this morning's sermon, are we?"

Brendan stepped back. "Sorry."

"I doubt that." Jesse nudged him in the arm, and Brendan grinned. Jesse set the mugs in the sink. "You two heading out to the farm for lunch?"

Hope, cheeks pink, exchanged a look with Brendan.

Jesse cocked his head. "What?"

She walked to the fridge and pulled open the door. "Nothing. We just thought we'd eat here, with you."

"Hope."

She shut the door and turned to him with a sigh. "All right. Brendan and I want to talk to you about something."

Jesse braced himself. From the look on her face, he wasn't going to like what they had to say. "What?"

"Why don't we talk over lunch?"

Eating was the last thing he felt like doing. "I'd rather you tell me now."

Hope looked at Brendan again. He'd been pouring himself another cup of coffee, but he replaced the carafe and turned to Jesse. "Good news first. Shane and Abby have talked. I don't know how she explained her visit to our sister, but somehow she did to his satisfaction. He's assured us that she's not up to anything. In fact, they've gotten back together."

Jesse nodded. "That's good to hear." He swung his gaze back to Hope. "And the bad news?"

She hesitated.

Just say it. Jesse gripped the counter behind him.

"Meryn and Drew have started dating."

Jesse blinked. From a distance, he heard the words, but they wouldn't register in his brain, as though they'd been spoken in another language. "Dating?"

Brendan cleared his throat. "Yeah. They got talking after he came to the store on Friday afternoon, and decided they're going to start seeing each other."

Friday afternoon. *Right after I was there, and the two of us ...* The two of them what, shared a moment? He'd thought they had anyway. Obviously, she hadn't felt the same. Jesse's grip on the counter tightened until his knuckles ached.

Hope was watching him closely. What did she think he was going to do, put his fist through her wall? Meryn wasn't his, not anymore. She was free to see whomever she wanted to. Just because he felt like he'd been kicked in the gut didn't mean he was going to lose it. Probably.

Jesse forced himself to let go of the counter. "All right, then. Thanks for telling me. What are we having for lunch?"

"Jess."

He lifted a hand. "It's all good, Hope. I have no say in anything Meryn does. I do want her to be happy, though, and if Drew can make her happy, that's great."

There wasn't a chance Hope would believe him.

Jesse forced himself to meet her gaze. *Please, let it go.*

Hope looked as if she was about to say something, but Brendan walked over to her. "Hope and I will throw something together for lunch. Why don't you go relax? We'll call you when it's ready."

Jesse nodded and headed for the living room. *Drew.* From the moment Jesse had met Meryn, Drew had hovered on the periphery of their relationship. In spite of Meryn's protests that they were just friends and that Drew couldn't compete with him, Jesse had never been able to shake the feeling that Drew was always there, waiting for his opportunity to jump in and try to take Meryn from him.

And now he had. Even if she and Jesse weren't together anymore, the thought sickened him.

Jesse stopped in front of the window and shoved both hands in the pockets of his jeans. *God, help me. Let the words I said to Hope—that I want Meryn to be happy, even if it's because of someone else—come true. I'm tired of wanting what I can't have. I'm tired of feeling like my heart is being ripped out over and over again. I'm just ... tired.* He rested his forehead against the cool glass.

A movement outside caught his eye, and Jesse straightened quickly and pulled his hands from his pockets.

Soldiers.

Two men and two women in khaki combat fatigues, weapons strapped at their waists, milled around on the sidewalk across the street from Hope's building. Three of them watched the entrance. The fourth, a corporal Jesse recognized but whose name he couldn't remember, glanced up at Hope's apartment window. His eyes met Jesse's and his features hardened. He said something to his companions, and they all looked up.

Come and get me. For a wild moment, Jesse wished they would. He was in a fighting mood, and there was no one he would rather take on than Gallagher. His fists clenched.

None of the soldiers moved.

Jesse uncurled his fingers. He didn't really want them to come up. If they did, it was more likely they would arrest Hope, since this was her place. Not that they could prove that she, or any of them, had broken any laws. Unless they had bugged the place.

His brow furrowed. That was unlikely, although it wouldn't hurt to look around. He'd do that before he left. As Jesse watched, the soldiers conversed for a moment before they turned and made their way toward two jeeps parked a little ways down the street. The corporal threw one last glance over his shoulder—a warning?—before sliding behind the wheel of one of the army vehicles.

Jesse exhaled.

Why were soldiers in front of Hope's building? Had they heard that there was going to be a church service there that morning? Did they know about the other services going on? Had they questioned anyone who had left the building after meeting up here?

He grabbed the i-com from his pocket and inputted a message to Pastor John. *Did you see soldiers on the way out of Hope's place? Did they stop you?*

When the device vibrated seconds later, he snatched it up and scanned the screen. *I was just about to message you to warn you they were there. I saw them. They kept an eye on everyone as they left the building, but they didn't detain us.*

He touched the screen. *Will need to discuss what to do about that this week.* Jesse slid the i-com back into his pocket.

At least they hadn't stopped anyone. The soldiers were just watching them.

So far.

38

Meryn opened the carved lid of the wooden jewellery box on her dresser. Her fingers trembled slightly as she reached inside, but she pushed back her shoulders and lifted the necklace out of the box. The light from the lamp on her dresser glinted off the gold heart hanging from the delicate chain. Meryn swallowed hard and dropped the necklace into a small plastic bag, then zipped it shut and added it to the pile on her bed.

She reached for the white cloth sack that she had stuck on the shelf in her closet the day she'd come home after being held on the base as a prisoner months before. Holding the sack open with one hand, she shoved the items on her bed into it: Jesse's copy of *Moby Dick*, the necklace, and the royal-blue T-shirt and plaid, flannel pyjama bottoms that she'd laundered and folded neatly after the last time she'd worn them. Everything she still had in her possession that needed to go back to him now that they were no longer together.

Meryn picked up the bag and strode down the stairs.

Gracie and Matthew played with the train set in the corner of the living room.

The ache in her chest eased slightly at the sight of them. She had Drew now, and her family. Plenty of people who loved and cared about her. They were all she needed.

Kate reclined on the couch, several colourful pillows tucked behind her back. She looked up when Meryn came in, and closed the book she'd been reading, keeping her finger between the pages to hold her spot. "Hey, you."

"Hey, yourself." Meryn forced a lightness she didn't feel into her voice.

"What's wrong?"

"Nothing." Meryn dropped the bag on the floor.

Kate reached for a bookmark on the coffee table and slid it into the book before setting it down. She contemplated the bag. "What's that?"

Meryn picked up a pillow from the other end of the couch.

Kate pulled her knees up, giving Meryn room.

She sat down and settled the pillow on her lap. "Just a couple of things I thought Jesse might like back. Would you mind dropping them off to him when you go home?" It took everything in her to make the request sound casual, off-hand.

Kate twisted her head to look around the room. When her gaze came back to Meryn, the corners of her mouth twitched. "Who *do* you think you are talking to?"

Meryn picked at the crocheted flower pattern on the pillow, not quite meeting her friend's eyes. "I hope I'm talking to the one person in my life who promised to always support me, no matter what."

"No matter what? I don't think I ever promised you that."

"I think you did."

"No, I'm pretty sure I would have remembered." Kate held out her hand. "Let me see."

Meryn picked up the bag. Clutching it to her chest, she looked at Kate. "Are there any circumstances under which you would just take this bag, not look in it, hand it over to Jesse, and say no more about it?"

Kate's face softened. "Meryn. I love you like a sister. You're my closest friend in the world, and you very likely saved my life when you brought me into your family. I owe you a debt I can never hope to repay."

Meryn pursed her lips. "That's a no, isn't it?"

Kate smiled. "Yes, that's a definite no." She held out her arm again and waggled her fingers. "Come on. Hand it over."

With a sigh, Meryn held out the bag.

Kate snatched it from her and pulled it onto her lap.

Meryn's throat tightened as Kate rifled through the contents.

"Well." Kate lowered the bag back to the floor. "I'm sure he'll be glad to get his book back."

Meryn clutched the pillow tightly. "It's not right for me to keep the other things when I'm seeing someone else. And speaking of which, I'm in a new relationship, which is very exciting. Are you ever going to ask me about that?"

Kate wrapped her arms around her knees. "Of course, Mer. I want to hear all about it. But how about we finish our other conversation first? Are you sure you need to hurt Jesse more by throwing his stuff back at him?"

"I'm not throwing it back at him. I'm not giving it back to him at all. You are."

"Yeah, about that. Maybe this is something you should do yourself."

"It is, I know. But I can't."

"Why not? Don't you think you owe him that much?"

"I'm sure I do. It's just that …"

"What?"

"I'm so certain I made the right decision, Kate. That ending things with him was the only thing I could have done. Then I see him or hear his voice or …"

"Or?"

"Or he touches me or looks at me, and suddenly I'm not sure about anything anymore."

Kate's eyebrows lifted. "He touches you?"

Heat flared in her cheeks. "Not in any intimate way or anything, just, you know, sometimes he walks by me or hands me something and his fingers brush mine, that sort of thing. Accidental touches. They don't mean anything, but they … confuse me." She drew in a shaky breath. "All I'm trying to say is that I think it's better if I avoid situations where I'm alone with him, or even in the same room with him, as much as possible."

Kate regarded her somberly. "Because you know it's not over, don't you?"

Tears welled in Meryn's eyes. "You know what? Forget it. You're right." She tossed the pillow onto the coffee table and reached for the bag. "I'll take it to him myself."

Kate grabbed Meryn's hand. "No, I'll give it to him. You know I will. If I can catch him at home. He seems to be out a lot lately."

That sent an unexpected pain darting through Meryn. "Where does he go?" *And who does he see when he's there?* She flung up her hand.

"Never mind, don't tell me. It's none of my business."

"You're probably right, although I couldn't tell you even if it was. I don't know where he keeps taking off to. I haven't asked him, because it really isn't any of my business either."

Meryn pressed both palms to her eyes and groaned. "Why does everything always have to be so complicated? I just want simple for a change."

"If you want simple, then Drew's your man."

Meryn dropped her hands.

Kate grinned. "I'm sorry. I meant your relationship with Drew must be simple. Relatively anyway. He's always liked you, and now you're together. You're good friends, which is always a great foundation to build on."

"Exactly." Meryn swiped at a tear that had started down one cheek.

"Aunt Meryn?" Gracie came around the end of the couch and rested little fingers on Meryn's arm. "Are you sad?"

"I am a little sad, sweetie. But I'll be okay."

"I give you hug." Gracie clambered up onto the couch and flopped onto Meryn, wrapping her arms around Meryn's neck.

"Oof." Meryn pulled her close and pressed a cheek to the soft, red curls. "Thanks, Gracie. You always know what I need, don't you?"

The toddler lifted her head, earnest brown eyes inches from Meryn's. "You need Jesus."

Meryn laughed. "You're absolutely right. I do need Jesus." She pulled Gracie close again and met Kate's gaze over the head of the little girl.

A smile played around Kate's mouth. "There you go, Mer. Maybe things are simpler than you think."

39

Shane took Leah's hand to help her into the cab of his truck. She dropped onto the seat with an exasperated sigh. "You *would* drive a truck that sits eight feet off the ground. There is no way to gracefully enter or exit a vehicle like this."

"Not for you, maybe." Shane closed the door. He rounded the front of the vehicle and slid easily onto the seat behind the wheel.

"Show-off." She threw him a look of mock disgust. "Is it absolutely necessary to flaunt those good genes of yours?"

He started the truck and pulled out onto the street. "There's nothing wrong with your genes, trust me. Definitely superior stock. And I can say that with all sincerity, now that I know Cameron doesn't actually share them." His brow furrowed. "He doesn't, does he?"

"No, he definitely doesn't. We aren't related in any way, just partners."

"Do you have any real siblings?"

The question hung in the air. Probably shouldn't be asking her personal questions. Like she said, she'd already told him far more than she should have. Of course, she'd only given him her first name, so it's not like he could track down her family, even if he wanted to. "You don't have to tell me anything."

"No, it's okay. I have two sisters."

"Are you close to them?"

"Yes, actually. We're very close." Her voice carried the same wistful tone it had when she'd talked about her grandparents' farm, and mentioned to Ethan how nice it was to be around a family. Just how much had she sacrificed in service to her country?

"But you don't see them much."

"Not nearly as much as I'd like."

"Let me guess: marine sniper and search-and-rescue pilot?"

She laughed. "Accountant and librarian. I got all the daredevil tendencies in the family, much to my mother's horror. Both sisters are happily married, with five kids between them—three boys and two girls—who are growing up way too fast." Leah rested her head against the seat. A small sigh escaped her.

"Long day?"

"A long couple of months, pulling double duty with the coffee shop and my work outside of that. It's been a good cover. It's amazing how willing people are to open up and tell you things when you're serving them coffee and food."

"It is exceptionally good food."

A sheepish look crossed Leah's face. "I have a confession to make. We don't actually do most of the baking at the shop. It gets delivered to us every morning, and we just stick it in the oven to finish it off and to make the place smell authentic. By the time Hope arrives, everything is ready to set out. I'm sure she thinks we're there at the crack of dawn preparing all those goodies." A shadow darkened her features. "That's the part of my job I hate the most, having to deceive everyone."

"I'm sure." Shane stopped the truck at a four way stop and looked in every direction before pulling forward. "And I'm sorry to hear about the baked goods. I was looking forward to having those cinnamon buns served to me every weekend for the rest of my life."

Leah lifted her head. "Okay, first of all, getting a little ahead of yourself, O'Reilly. And secondly, not to get your hopes up, but the cinnamon buns are the one thing I actually do make. My grandmother's recipe."

He grinned. "That is excellent news." He pulled into the restaurant parking lot and eased into a spot. "Shall we?"

"Yes, please. I'm starving."

Shane took her hand as they walked toward the building. He pointed to her bracelet with his thumb. "I'm kind of surprised they let you keep your job after you put this on."

"So far, I think they've found it valuable. I can get into places other people can't and gain confidences I wouldn't if I wasn't wearing it."

"What about Gallagher?"

Her brow furrowed. "What about him?"

"The two of you seemed to be deep in conversation the other day. Why do you think he was willing to talk to someone he knew was a believer, since he hates us so much?"

"He had an agenda of his own. I mean, he pretended he was interested in me, but I could tell he was trying to get information out of me, like I was trying to get information out of him. We were just using each other. Thankfully, I had the upper hand, because I knew who he was and what he was after, but he had no idea who I really was." Her face grew serious as she glanced around the parking lot and lowered her voice. "And I'd like to keep it that way. Please remember to call me Abby, or that could cause problems. Other than that, I'm not an agent while we're here, just a normal girl out with a relatively normal guy."

"Sounds good to me." They reached the door and Shane opened it and held it for her.

The hostess seated them at a table for two by the fireplace and handed them each a menu. Classical music played softly in the background.

Leah's grey eyes met his over the flickering candle in the centre of the table. "This is a nice place, O'Reilly. I'm impressed."

"That was the idea." He set down the menu. "Actually, this isn't all about impressing you. It's also an attempt at an apology."

"Apology? For what?"

"For not listening to my gut about you. Besides knowing you wouldn't be involved with my sister, I also knew, deep down, that you wouldn't be colluding with the major. Unfortunately, I let my emotions overrule my head in both those situations. I said some awful things to you and treated you badly. I'm still not entirely sure why, since that isn't like me, honestly. And I'm truly sorry."

"I know."

"That I'm sorry?"

"That it isn't like you."

The flickering flames in the fireplace beside them reflected off her curls, turning them a gleaming gold. "How do you know that?"

Leah closed her menu. "I know how much your family means to

you and how responsible you feel for them. I understood that you were just protecting them when you lashed out at me. And I guess, in a way, it's a good sign that I evoke such deep emotions in you."

"Oh, you do that, believe me."

Her cheeks flushed but she smiled.

"So, you forgive me?"

"Yes." Leah took a deep breath. "But—"

"What can I get you tonight?"

Shane searched Leah's face as she ordered. What had she been about to say? For such a small word, *but* could do a tremendous amount of damage. After everything that had happened between them, was she going to tell him she didn't want to pursue a relationship?

The server turned to him, and Shane ordered the prime rib, but his mind was almost completely preoccupied.

When the woman left, Leah finally looked over at him. "I'm sorry. That was a bad place to leave off."

"It really was." He managed a weak grin.

"I was about to say that I forgive you, but only if you'll forgive me."

"For?"

She clasped her hands together on the table. "That first Sunday, when I came home from having lunch at your place, I did a background check on you."

Shane mulled that over. It made sense, given that she was a spy. *Still feels a little like someone's been watching me through a peephole.* "Just on me?"

The three-second hesitation gave him his answer.

Shane frowned. "Who else?"

"Meryn. Brendan. Your parents."

"Not Annaliese?"

"No. I already knew everything there was to know on her. Except that she was your sister. I didn't put that together until you gave me her name in the barn."

So, she'd checked him out. *I guess that makes us about even.* And maybe her looking into his past to make sure there was nothing that could cause her any trouble just showed that she'd sensed, even that first day, that the two of them could possibly have a future together, like he had. "I don't suppose you can tell me if you found anything on the rest of my family."

"No, I can't." She offered him an apologetic smile. "Except to say that I'm still here."

Which meant they were clean. Or that she wasn't worried about Meryn's record. He shifted on his chair. "Find anything interesting on me?"

Her lips quirked. "Not a thing. Definitely not the bad-boy type, are you?"

"Hey, I got arrested yesterday."

"Then whined for half an hour about the cuffs and ended up getting your charge dropped by a girl. Doesn't count, sorry."

Shane grinned. "All right, I admit it. I never really had a rebellious streak, and I don't have a hidden past. What you see is what you get with me."

"Which is the real reason I'm still here." Leah unclasped her fingers and pressed her hands to the black tablecloth. "Look, I want to be as honest with you as I can possibly be from now on."

"Great. I want that too."

"All right, here goes. It's a bit early to toss this word around, but trust me, you don't want me as a girlfriend."

Shane would have laughed, if she didn't look so serious. "I'm pretty sure I do."

"No, really, I mean it." Her gaze darted around the room before she leaned in and lowered her voice. "My job is dangerous. Anything could happen. And I'm gone a lot, often at a moment's notice. Besides that, I ... I haven't dated anyone in a long time. I'm not even sure I remember how to be in that kind of relationship anymore."

"You don't have to be anything except yourself."

"That's the thing. I feel like my life is some kind of maze. When I'm on assignment, I'm right in the middle of it. When the assignment is over, I have to try and find my way out again. In the beginning, it was easy. I always knew which path to take. The longer I do this, though, the harder it seems to be to take the right turns. Sometimes, I worry that one time I won't be able to find my way back out again, that

I'll hit dead end after dead end and eventually forget who the real me is."

Shane reached across the table for one of her hands. He turned it over and slowly and deliberately traced the letters *L-E-A-H* in her palm, then closed her fingers over them and held her hand in both of his. "I know who the real you is. I'll remember for you."

For a moment, she didn't speak. Then, she lifted her shoulders. "Maybe you're right, O'Reilly. Maybe you can bring me back."

"I can. And I will. Every time."

"Do you really want to have to work that hard?"

"Believe me, I knew from the moment I met you that you were going to be work. I'm still here, aren't I?"

"But …"

Shane shook his head firmly. "No more buts. And I don't think it's too early to toss around the word *girlfriend*. I think that's exactly where we're headed, now that there are no more big secrets between us."

Leah studied him.

"What is it?"

"This is a strange feeling. Like the walls I've carefully constructed between myself and every other person in my life don't exist between us."

"That sounds like a good thing."

"It is. And I know, in my head, that transparency is a beautiful thing. It's just going to take a bit of getting used to."

He squeezed her hand, then let her go as the server arrived at the table, a steaming plate in each hand. Yes, he was going to have to work hard. They both were, if this was going to happen between them. But he had no doubt it would be well worth the effort.

40

Jesse opened the front door of the in-law suite.

Hope stood on the top step, clutching a paper bag. "I brought dinner."

Jesse took the groceries from her and stepped back, waving a hand in front of himself to direct her inside. "That's an automatic in at my place."

She went into his apartment. "It always got me into Rory's place too."

"Pretty sure that had very little to do with the food."

Hope laughed as she followed him to the kitchen. "You didn't have plans, did you?"

"Who, me? What plans could I possibly have?" Jesse set the bag down on the kitchen counter.

"I don't know. Kate says you've been disappearing a lot lately. There's speculation you're either moonlighting with a second job or you have a new woman in your life."

He shot her a look. "Who's speculating?"

"Kate and I."

"Well, sorry to disappoint you both, but I don't have time for another job."

"What about the new woman?"

He winced. "Not there yet."

"Will you ever be?"

"I can't imagine it. But you never know." He tipped the bag toward him and peered inside. "What are we having?"

"I brought steaks, since we didn't get to have them last time, and potatoes and salad."

"I'll start the barbeque." Jesse let go of the bag and headed for the door. As soon as he opened it, a loud crack of thunder shattered the early-evening calm. With a sigh, he closed the door and went back to the kitchen. "You and I are destined not to barbeque steaks, apparently."

Hope took the package of meat out of the bag and set it on a shelf in the fridge. "It's okay. We can have them another day. I brought a few things, because I didn't know if you'd found another store to shop at yet."

"Yes and no. I was refused service at two other grocery stores, but then I found one on the other side of town that hadn't heard about my terrorist leanings yet. And actually, this has turned out to be a good thing. I've been meaning to look into companies with warehouses in the area that might deliver food to us if we stop being able to buy stuff, and being banned from some of the stores here motivated me to start seriously looking. I found one just this side of Toronto that's owned by a Christian family. I've been talking to them, and they're open to delivering food to us, if and when we need it."

"That's fabulous. Good to know we have a back-up." Hope pulled a package of chicken from the paper bag. "How do fajitas sound?"

"That works for me. What can I chop?"

She grabbed a yellow pepper and handed it to him. "Have at it."

Jesse took the chopping board down from the cupboard and slid a knife out of the holder on the counter.

They worked in silence for a couple of minutes.

Not holding my breath that the reprieve will last. Hope never had been one to be put off when she was on the trail of something.

"Are you going to tell me?"

He repressed a smile. "Tell you what?"

"Why you've been disappearing so much. Where you go and what you do when you're there."

"I don't have to share every little detail of my life with you, you know."

Still holding on to the handle of the frying pan she'd placed on a burner, she turned to face him, planting her free hand on her hip.

Uh-oh.

"You'd like me to respect your privacy."

Jesse hesitated. *She's setting me up.* Even knowing it was bait, he took it. "Yes."

205

"Like you respected my privacy the day you stole my diary from the tree house and read it to every single boy in your class at recess."

"Hope, that was twenty-five years ago."

"It still hurts."

He set down the knife. "I have to admit it's a bit of a relief."

"What is?"

"Not to have that hanging over my head anymore. I knew it would come back to bite me at some point; I just didn't know when."

"I have a very long memory."

"I'm well aware." He picked up the knife and started chopping again. "Still not telling you, though."

"Fine. I'll find out on my own."

"How?"

"I have my ways."

"I wouldn't devote too much time or energy to it, if I were you. It's not a big deal, just a project I'm working on."

"When are you going to let me in on it?"

"When I'm done."

"And when will that be?"

"When all the speculating females in my life leave me alone and let me get to it."

It was a bit harsh, but it bought him three more minutes of quiet. Then, Hope went to sit down on one of the barstools at the counter and found the white bag he'd set there after Kate had dropped it off that afternoon. The sight of it sent fresh pain prickling through him. Jesse's heart sank.

"What's this?"

He rinsed his hands under the tap, swiped them on a towel, and held out a hand. "It's nothing. I'll put it in the bedroom, so it's not in your way."

She pulled the bag out of his reach. "Interesting."

"What?"

"You actually went a little pale there. What aren't you telling me?"

"Nothing."

Hope pursed her lips. "Did I mention it still hurts that you shared my most personal thoughts with half the school?"

Jesse rolled his eyes. "Do you realize that every time you've told that story tonight, my audience has gotten bigger?" He exhaled loudly. "All right. But this clears my tab. I owe you nothing after I tell you, got it?"

"Got it." She handed him the bag. "What is all this stuff?"

"Just a few things from Meryn that Kate gave back to me today." Kate had been sweet and apologetic when she'd brought the bag to the door, softening the blow as much as possible. Would it have been easier or more difficult if Meryn had returned the things herself? He still wasn't sure.

"Ah. What things?"

"A copy of *Moby Dick* I loaned her, a pair of my pyjamas, and a necklace."

"Your pyjamas?"

"Yes. And it's not what you think." He set the bag on the counter and sat down on the other barstool. "They're part of the story I said I'd tell you one day."

Hope rubbed her hands together. "Let's hear it."

Memories rolled over him in waves, and he steeled himself against the poker-hot pain of them. "As soon as I met her, I knew Meryn was going to get herself into trouble. When we found out she was smuggling Bibles, I had to arrest her and bring her in, and she was held in my quarters, because we weren't equipped for female prisoners then."

Hope's eyes widened. "Caleb allowed that?"

"He wasn't happy about it at first. I finally managed to talk him into it, but he was still concerned that I was either going to fall for her completely or that she would brainwash me into becoming a Christian while she was there."

"And which of those happened?"

He offered her a wry grin. "Both, actually."

"Caleb must not have been too thrilled."

"He was remarkably good about it. He was just worried that I had made my life a lot more complicated and dangerous, on both counts, and of course he was right. To his credit, he was supportive, and risked his own life and career on numerous occasions after that to cover for me."

"Where do the pyjamas fit in?"

The biggest wave crashed over him—the memory of that terrible, beautiful night that changed everything. "Three men broke into my quarters one evening and threatened Meryn. She was pretty shaken up when I found her. Until then, she'd been sleeping in her clothes, so in an effort to help her feel better, I offered her a pair of my pyjamas, so she'd be more comfortable."

"Poor thing."

He almost smiled, remembering. "Yeah, I'm sure it was terrifying, although I think she was more mad than anything. Anyway, when she went home, I sent the pyjamas with her. She told me she put them on whenever she was thinking of me or missing me, and they made her feel better."

"And now she's returned them."

"Yeah. I guess she's not thinking about me or missing me anymore."

"I seriously doubt that's true." Her gaze dropped to the bag. "And the necklace?"

Really hoped she wouldn't ask. He did owe her. It had been a lousy thing to do, showing her diary to other kids, even if it was really only four or five and not half the school. Even at the time, he'd felt bad. Besides, it helped a little, talking to Hope about all this. They'd given each other a hard time all their lives, like real siblings, but she'd always been there for him when he needed her. Had somehow managed to make him feel better, no matter what he was going through.

With a sigh, he reached into the bag and pulled out the necklace. Looping the chain over two fingers, he held it up. The gold heart dangled in front of his wrist.

Hope touched it. "You gave her your heart."

"Twice."

"Twice?"

"Yeah. Right after I gave it to her the first time, we had a disagreement. She ripped the necklace off and threw it back at me."

Hope chuckled. "I'm liking her more and more." She climbed off the stool and went over to check on the chicken frying in the pan on the stove.

"She's something, all right."

"I take it you made up and gave Meryn the necklace again."

"Yes. And she wore it until she broke up with me. Then, it disappeared, but she didn't give it back to me. Until today." He nudged the bag with his fingers. "It's actually a good thing Kate dropped this stuff off."

Hope scooped up the peppers he'd chopped and tossed them into the frying pan, along with some broccoli and onions. "How do you figure that?"

He swivelled the chair around to face her. "I think, even though Meryn is seeing Drew, as long as she kept my stuff, especially the necklace, I still clung to the illusion that she might come back to me." He dropped the necklace into the little plastic bag and stuck it into the cloth one, with the book and pyjamas. "But if she was keeping the door open, just a little bit, it's shut firmly now. She's moving on with her life, Hope. And that frees me up to do the same."

Hope set down the lifter and came over to him. She wrapped her arms around him. "I'm sorry, Jess."

He rested his cheek on top of her head. "Me too."

"How does this project of yours figure into your new plans?"

He took her by the arms and gently pushed her away from him. "Shameless attempt to take advantage of a moment. Forget it. I've paid my debt. I'm not telling you anything more."

She laughed and went back to the stove.

A flash of light lit up the apartment, followed by a crack of thunder so loud it rattled the windows.

Jesse stood and crossed the living room to look outside.

The sky had darkened while they were talking. Almost-black clouds scuttled across a backdrop tinged a sickly yellow. The last time he'd seen the sky that shade was the night he'd gone to Meryn's to warn her that Annaliese was watching her.

Where is Meryn now?

Wherever she was, she'd be a little freaked out.

God, watch over her, please, since I can't. When he returned to the kitchen, Hope was scooping chicken and vegetables onto a wrap. She held a plate out to him.

"Thanks." Jesse set it on the counter. "Looks a little ominous out there."

Hope carried her own plate over to the counter and settled back on the barstool. "Do storms bother you?"

"Not me, no."

"Who, then?"

He sighed. "I shouldn't worry about this anymore, but Meryn hates them." Not that it was any of his *business*.

"Another story?"

"Yes, for another day. Or maybe I need to get some new stories. Or better yet, listen to yours. What's going on with you?" He took a bite of the fajita wrap and listened as she told him about her day at Maeve's.

Tried to listen anyway. In spite of his attempts to rein them in, his thoughts drifted occasionally to Meryn and the night he'd spent at her farm talking her through that terrible storm. *Is she alone now? Is she okay?*

When he'd finished the last bite, Jesse grabbed a paper towel off the roll on the counter and wiped his mouth. He tossed the towel onto his plate and leaned back. "That was really good, Hope. Thanks."

"I'm glad you enjoyed it. I wondered if you were even tasting it, when your mind was on other things."

"I was paying attention to you."

"I know. But you were also thinking about Meryn."

"No, I …" The protest died at the look of compassion on her face. She knew him too well.

"Why don't you message her, see if she's all right? It might set your mind at ease."

"I don't think I should."

"Why not? You're still friends, right?"

"In theory." He tapped a finger against his chin. "Do you believe that ever really works?"

"I think it's hard, but it is possible. You showing her that you still care about her, that you're not angry with her for returning those things, could go a long way toward that."

"I'm not angry. I'm just … sad."

"I know." She nodded at the i-com he'd left on the counter. "Ask her if she's okay. She'll appreciate it, and you'll feel better."

Jesse thought about it for a few seconds, then picked up the device. He sent a brief message and set it back down. "If this blows up, it's all on you."

"Fair enough." She grinned and reached for his plate.

The i-com buzzed just as she returned from putting their plates into the dishwasher. Jesse looked at Hope. She made a grab for the unit, but he snatched it out from under her fingers and read the words.

"Well?"

"She's good. Her brothers are with her." He slid the device into his shirt pocket.

"Do you feel better?"

"Actually, yes. Thanks for pushing me on that. I did figure she'd be okay. Shane and Brendan know how she feels about storms. There's no way they'd let her go through this one alone."

"Pretty protective of each other, those O'Reillys, aren't they?"

"Yeah, they are."

Her smile held a hint of melancholy. "It's quite lovely, isn't it?"

"Yes, it is." He studied her. "And you may as well get used to it, because they're equally protective of the ones they bring into the family. You'll be taken good care of, don't worry."

"And who's going to take care of you?"

Jesse slid off the stool and gathered up their silverware. He dropped them into the holder in the dishwasher, closed the door, and leaned back against the counter. "You know what? Someone else has always felt the need to take care of me—my parents, then Rory, then Caleb. I'm thirty-six years old. Maybe it's time I took care of myself."

Hope lifted slender shoulders. "Taking care of yourself isn't what it's cracked up to be. We all need someone watching out for us."

"I'm afraid that's going to have to be you, then, because I'm fresh out of other options."

"Don't make it sound like you're scraping the bottom of the barrel."

"Sorry."

"We're going to be all right, both of us."

"I know." Except that he didn't. "I'm really glad you came tonight. I didn't realize how much I needed you to be here until you showed up at the door."

"It was the least I could do after getting you banned from—"

The buzzing of his i-com cut her off.

"Sorry." Jesse fished it out of his pocket and scanned the screen. "Ethan says we should come over and hang out in the basement with them until this storm blows over."

"All right." Hope rinsed her hands under the tap and dried them on the towel hanging on the stove handle. Thunder rumbled again and the lights flickered. "We better go soon."

Jesse followed her to the door.

Hope went out and stopped on the top step. "Is there anything you need to grab before we head over?"

A gust of wind nearly ripped the door knob from his hand. Jesse surveyed the room. His gaze fell on the white bag on the counter. Ignoring the pang that shot across his chest, he stepped outside and wrestled the door shut. "No, let's go."

41

Meryn stared out the window at the darkening sky, fighting the trepidation tightening every muscle in her body. They hadn't had a storm this bad since the night Jesse had stayed with her at the farm. She shook her head, trying to clear it of the memory. The last thing she wanted to be thinking about today, after she'd finally mustered the strength to send him back his things, was how sweet he'd been that night.

Brendan nudged her in the shoulder, and she jumped. "Sorry. Didn't realize you were so far away."

Meryn swallowed and turned from the window. "It's okay. I was just ... daydreaming. What do you want for supper?"

"Don't worry about that. I'll throw something together in a bit. I was thinking that it's been awhile since I beat you at pool. Feel like a game?"

"You don't have to take care of me, Bren. I'm fine." Lightning flashed, followed by a sharp crack of thunder, and Meryn sucked in a quick breath.

"Clearly. Still, it would be fun to have a game. Why don't we go downstairs for a while?" He waved a hand at the basement door.

She headed toward it. "Where's Shane?"

"Feeding the cows. He said he'd just be a few minutes."

Meryn stopped at the top of the stairs and shot a worried glance at the front door. Just as she did, it opened and Shane came inside, dripping wet.

"It's getting nasty out there." He looked over at her. "I think it's going to blow over soon, though."

"Look, I appreciate what you're both doing, but it's not necessary. Like I told Brendan, you don't need to take care of me. I can handle a little storm."

A gust of wind whipped around Shane. A vase of flowers on the windowsill crashed onto the counter.

He turned and shoved the door closed.

Icy tremors moved through Meryn in waves, but she worked to keep her features even. She started toward the vase.

Brendan grabbed her arm. "Leave it, kid. We'll get it later. Let's go down." He looked back at his brother. "We're playing pool, Shane. Want to take on the winner?"

"Sure. I'm just going to change. Be right there."

Meryn forced herself to take slow, even breaths as she descended to the basement. They were perfectly safe down here. This old farmhouse had stood for eighty years and through who knew how many storms. It wasn't going to come down today. Probably. She shook off the thought. Was Jesse somewhere safe? Was he thinking about her? Remembering that night like she was?

Stop it, Meryn. He wasn't the one she should be thinking about. She reached into the back pocket of her jeans and pulled out the i-com Shane had picked up for her to replace the one that had been destroyed in the fire. He'd had to go to three stores before he found one that would admit to having i-coms in stock. Meryn rubbed a thumb over the slim gold device.

What would happen when this one stopped working? Would they be able to buy another one to replace it, or would it be even harder then for anyone with a bracelet to purchase items? She sighed. *We'll deal with that when the time comes.*

Meryn touched a finger to the screen. *Are you home from work? Be careful of this storm, okay?* She tapped the Send button and dropped the device back into her pocket.

Brendan stood at the pool table, leaning on a cue. His eyebrows rose when she looked at him.

"Just messaging Drew to see if he got home from work okay."

"Ah." Brendan reached for a cube of chalk and rubbed it over the end of his cue. "Are you breaking?"

"Go ahead." Meryn selected her favourite cue from the rack on the wall and applied chalk to it. Her i-com vibrated and she tossed the chalk back onto the shelf and reached for the device.

Got home, no problem. Not worried about the storm. Dinner

tomorrow?

She responded with a quick *sure* and stuck the i-com in her back pocket.

"What is it?" Brendan tapped the white ball into the other ones sharply, and they spread out across the table. Two of the solid-coloured ones dropped into pockets.

"Nothing." Meryn propped the cue on the side of the table and sent the blue ball into a corner pocket.

"Thanks, but you might want to go for a striped one next time. And wait your turn." Brendan leaned over the table and tapped a yellow ball down a hole.

"Sorry. I'm a little more distracted by the weather than I thought." Meryn rested the end of the cue on the floor and glanced over at the small window set high up in the wall. Raindrops pelted the glass and she looked away.

"Of course, the weather. That must be it." He missed on the next shot and straightened up.

"What else?" She set up her shot and this time dropped the striped orange ball into the pocket she was aiming for. She walked around the table, eyeing the balls and debating her next move.

"Was that a response from Drew?"

"Yeah, why?"

"You had a funny look on your face after you read it."

"No, I didn't." She hit another ball, harder than she'd intended.

It bounced over the side of the table and clattered onto the floor.

"Meryn." Brendan bent down and picked up the ball. He set it down on the green velvet but didn't let go of it.

"It's nothing. I thought it was a little strange that he didn't ask how I was, that's all. I guess he's forgotten that I don't like storms much. No big deal." Except it kind of was a big deal. Somewhere, down deep, it hurt that, after all their years of friendship, he didn't remember that about her.

He took his hand away from the ball. "Good thing you don't need to be taken care of, then." He offered her a wry grin before sinking two more solid balls.

"Yes, it is, since you're clearly not going to do it." She frowned and scrutinized the table, largely populated now by striped balls.

"Well, I'm sure not going to let you win. Last time I did that, you pummelled me." He rubbed his upper arm. "Still aches there when it rains, you know."

Meryn laughed. "You deserved it."

"Very likely. And I did learn my lesson." He proceeded to send the rest of the solid balls into the pockets, followed by the eight ball. "See?"

Meryn made a face at him. Her i-com vibrated again. She yanked it from her pocket.

Drew. *You all right?*

An afterthought. She tossed the device onto the table at the end of the couch.

Shane came down the stairs and set a box on the coffee table. "A few provisions to keep us going while we wait this thing out."

Meryn looked into the box. Meat and cheese and buns for their dinner. And graham wafers, chocolate, and marshmallows for dessert.

"I thought I'd make a fire, and we could have s'mores later."

"Excellent idea."

"We have candles down here, right? There's a pretty good chance the power could go out."

She waved a hand toward the kitchen area. "In the cupboard." Her i-com vibrated again, and she snatched it up, impatient now. "Sorry, Brendan, I'll tell Drew …"

It wasn't Drew. Prickles skittered across her arms. Why would Jesse message her? He hadn't done that since things ended between them.

Just checking to see if you're okay. You're not alone, are you?

Meryn pressed her fingers to her mouth. How could he do something like that, right after Kate had dropped his things off to him?

Throat tight, she touched the screen. *I'm good. Brendan dragged me to the basement on the pretext of urgently needing to play pool, and Shane brought down stuff to make s'mores in the fireplace, so I'm not alone. Thank you for thinking of me.*

Before she could second-guess the wording, she pressed Send and set the device back down. Adrenaline coursed through her system, and she rolled up her sleeves. "All right, Brendan. That round was just practice. Rack 'em."

"Uh-oh. You're in trouble now." Shane brought two candles and a lighter over to the coffee table. "She's got her serious game face on."

Meryn won the next game, then beat Shane before Brendan finally took her down again. The storm raged around the house, but she barely noticed.

After another hour of play, Shane stuck his cue back into the rack on the wall. "Why don't we eat?"

Meryn washed her hands in the small washroom off the recreation room, then sat down on the couch, suddenly realizing she was famished.

Brendan dropped down beside her. "Are you going to tell me?"

"Tell you what?" Meryn reached for a bun and a paper plate.

"Who that last message was from."

"Oh." Her cheeks warmed as she set down the plate. "It was just Jesse checking to see if I was okay."

Shane handed her a can of soda. "Really."

"Don't make a thing out of it. He happened to be here the last time there was a storm this bad, and I told him about the chicken coop, so he knows how I feel about weather like this."

Brendan moved the meat and cheese closer to her. None of them spoke for a moment as they passed around the food and put their sandwiches together. Then Brendan elbowed her lightly in the arm. "It's not so bad, is it?"

"What?"

"Being taken care of a little."

Meryn glanced over at the window. A soft-pink sunset glowed through the glass. The storm had passed. She blew out a breath and smiled at Brendan. "All right, I admit it. Once in a while, it's really not that bad."

42

Jesse pressed a hand to the small of his back and groaned as he leaned backward. He and Shane and Brendan had spent the entire day helping Hope put all her new furniture together and get it set up in her apartment.

Raindrops pattered against the living room window of the in-law suite. He straightened and his gaze fell on the white bag, still lying on the counter where he'd tossed it after showing its contents to Hope four days ago. *Really need to take care of that soon.* The problem was he couldn't figure out what to do with the things Meryn had returned. He couldn't see himself keeping them or giving them away. Or ever wearing the pyjamas again. It didn't seem right to toss them out, though.

A light rapping noise pulled him from his musings. Jesse walked over to the door. When he pulled it open, his eyes widened. "Michael!"

Michael Stevens, the commissioner who'd helped him get Matthew and Gracie back after Kate and Ethan had been charged with child abuse just because they'd read the kids Bible stories before bed, stood on the front step. His dark hair and goatee glistened, and his expensive suit was rumpled and damp.

Jesse held out his hand and clasped Michael's. "It's good to see you. I can't believe you're here."

Michael gripped Jesse's elbow. "It's good to see you too, my friend. When I heard you'd been arrested a few months ago, I thought I'd never have the chance again." He let go of Jesse's arm.

"I didn't think you would either." Jesse moved back. "Come on in."

Michael stepped inside. "I left my vehicle several blocks away, because I didn't think parking a government car in the driveway of the main house was the best idea. I thought I could beat the rain here, but apparently I was wrong."

"Make yourself at home. I'll grab you a towel." Jesse went into the washroom off his bedroom, head spinning. It really was great to see Michael, but what was he doing here? A social call would be welcome, but it was unlikely that was the reason he'd driven here from Ottawa. Was he bringing bad news? A warning? Jesse grabbed a thick beige towel from the shelf and brought it out to the living room.

Michael had been studying the shelf of books, but he turned when Jesse approached him, and reached for the towel. "Thanks." He'd loosened his tie, removed his jacket, and slung it over the back of a kitchen chair. The light-blue, long-sleeved dress shirt underneath was relatively dry. He rubbed the towel over his face and hair before tossing the towel over his jacket. "That's better."

"Can I get you a drink?"

"No, thanks. I can't stay long."

"How did you find me?"

"A buddy of mine works in one of the tracking stations. I called him when I got out of my last meeting, and he pinpointed your location."

"Ah. No hiding anymore, is there?"

"Not when you're wearing one of those." Michael inclined his head toward Jesse's bracelet.

Jesse held a hand out toward the couch. "Please, sit." When Michael complied, Jesse took the chocolate-brown armchair across from him. "Is everything okay?"

Michael tapped his fingers on the arm of the couch. "Tricky question to answer. I was in Kingston today, as part of an investigation I'm involved in, so I thought I'd take the opportunity to come by, see how you are, and fill you in on some things that are happening."

"I'm glad you did. I'm doing all right. It's challenging here for believers, with Gallagher in charge, but we're coping as well as we can."

"Gallagher's actually the reason I'm here. I can't say much about it, but after what happened to Major Donevan, I recommended an inquiry into his death. That has led to a much bigger investigation of questionable activities going on at a lot of the bases across the country. I was asked to come to town today to talk to a few people. There's not much more I can tell you before it's all wrapped up, but I wanted you to know that something is being done."

"That's good to hear. Let me know if there's anything I can do to help."

"I will. I'm sure you'll be called to testify. Until then, I would advise you to be very careful. Stay out of Gallagher's cross hairs, if at all possible."

"I'm trying."

"Good. We're at a dangerous point. Although this is a highly classified operation, it's difficult to keep an investigation as involved and complicated as this one completely secret. Certain people are going to start to realize that they are under scrutiny, and things could get ugly. If Gallagher finds out he's the object of an investigation, he could become even more aggressive, like an animal backed into a corner."

"I understand."

Michael shifted in his seat. "There's something else."

Pretty sure I don't want to hear it. It had been an emotionally draining week. More bad news was the last thing he felt like getting at the moment. "What is it?"

"The terrorist threat in the country has been raised to its highest level since 10/10."

"Why? Has something else happened?"

"In the last two weeks, there have been ten confirmed-credible terrorist threats, eight against oil pipelines or refineries and two against nuclear power plants. All issued by The Horsemen."

A knot formed in Jesse's stomach. This was bad. "I haven't heard anything about that."

"The government and military are keeping a tight lid on it, hoping to avoid public panic. After the infiltration of the water bottle facility, Ottawa hired some high-powered international company, LADON Security, to protect the resource sector. That company is now responsible for securing all water, oil, and nuclear plants and refineries in the country. It's next to impossible to guard the thousands of kilometres of pipelines, but they're doing the best they can."

"LADON?"

"Yeah. It's an acronym. Stands for 'leased agents defending our nations,' or something like that."

"Must be quite the company."

"Apparently, it is. Tens of thousands of employees, mostly ex-military. A bunch of countries employ them for security. Their rates are staggering, but for the sake of public safety, the Canadian government is hoping they're as good as advertised."

"Personally, I hope so too. We're not that far from either the Pickering or the Darlington nuclear plants."

"I know." Michael ran his fingers through his damp hair. "I'm sorry to dump all this on you. I just want to make sure you and the other Christians in town are as prepared as you can be for what may come. Since The Horsemen are connected to these threats, you can expect the army to come down hard on anyone they perceive to be affiliated with that group, however loosely."

"What do you think they're going to do?"

"According to the buzz going around the capital, the military is planning to clean house, so to speak. They will start making more and more arrests for lighter and lighter infractions. Hearings could become shorter and even less thorough, and sentences harsher. A whole lot of believers could be rounded up and *dealt with* in an attempt to frighten the rest into absolute compliance."

Jesse slumped against the back of his chair. "That doesn't sound promising."

"You will have to encourage everyone you know to be especially vigilant and cautious, to not take any unnecessary chances."

"Are you suggesting we hide away and do nothing?"

"Absolutely not. Only that, before you do anything that could be considered remotely subversive, you count the cost and make sure you're willing to pay it if you get caught." Michael leaned forward, eyes gleaming. "We're in a war, my friend. You of all people understand what that means. Yes, the risks are high. But the cost of doing nothing, of falling back and allowing the enemy to advance, is far higher."

Jesse's heart pounded the way it always had the night before he shipped out, headed for battle. Michael's assessment was accurate. They were in the midst of a war, and there was no way Jesse would camp out miles from the action. He wanted to be on the front lines, engaged in hand-to-hand combat with the foe, however outnumbered and outgunned his side appeared to be. God fought for them. And that was good enough for him.

He glanced at his friend's wrist. It was still bare. "They don't know about you yet."

"Actually, I'm not sure about that. I've been getting the feeling lately that several of my colleagues are distancing themselves or looking at me suspiciously when I speak up at a hearing. I think the truth is about to come out. Which, at this point, would almost be more of a relief than anything."

"Maybe it's time to get out of Ottawa for a while."

"Possibly. I can't go anywhere until this investigation is concluded, though. Once that happens, I should be able to carry on with my life, figure out what Julia and I are going to do now."

"Julia?"

"My fiancée." Michael pushed to his feet. "Sorry to cut this short. I'm not sure why, but I feel as though I need to head home now, not hang around Kingston any longer. I had the same sensation before I came here, and I probably shouldn't have taken the time, but I really wanted to see you." He lifted the towel and pulled his jacket off the chair, then replaced the towel.

Jesse followed him to the door. "Thanks for coming by. I hope it doesn't end up causing trouble for you."

Michael slipped on his jacket. "It was a risk I was willing to take. It really was good to see you. I'll be praying for you. There's no easy place to be a believer these days, but Kingston is one of the most difficult. For now. I'm hoping that will change soon."

"I hope so too." Jesse pulled him in for a hug and clapped him on the back a couple of times. "I'll be praying for you. And I expect to get a wedding invitation before long."

Michael grinned. "Count on it." He turned and went down the stairs.

Jesse leaned a shoulder against the doorframe, uneasiness suddenly swirling through his chest. Had Michael made a mistake, stopping by? *God, help him to get out of town without running into any problems.*

For several seconds, as he strode across the lawn, Michael was bathed in the light flowing out of Jesse's apartment and falling onto the grass. Then, both he and the light disappeared, swallowed up by the thick darkness.

Would the light they carried—that seemed so dim and wavering at times—be enough to withstand the approaching night? Could it beat back the blackness that threatened to overwhelm them?

Jesse tipped back his head. The rain had stopped, and a half-moon hung in the sky, a halo of soft yellow encircling it. The tension left his shoulders. Like the moon, none of them produced their own light. They only reflected a much greater one, one that could never be overcome by the darkness.

43

Jesse pounded another nail into the floorboard of the deck their boss had assigned Shane, Brendan, and him to build. It was early October, but the sun beat down on his neck and back with mid-summer intensity. The heat and the exertion helped drive thoughts he didn't want to be thinking from his head, and he pounded harder.

A strong hand clapped down on his shoulder. "Pretty sure that one's in, Jess." Brendan pulled back his hand. "How about we give these poor boards a break and have some lunch?"

Jesse rocked back on his haunches. He had driven the nail in pretty hard. In fact—his gaze swept over the deck—he'd driven all of them in pretty hard. None of these boards were going anywhere soon.

He set down the hammer and rose, arching his back to stretch out tight muscles. Then he followed Brendan and Shane across the lawn to a picnic table in the shade of a big maple tree at the side of the house.

Brendan held out a bottle of juice.

Jesse took it and sank onto the bench. He twisted off the cap and tipped his head to swallow half the cool liquid, then swiped at a bead of sweat sliding down the side of his face. "We're almost finished with the deck. Should be able to start on the roof this—"

The sound of wheels crunching on gravel cut him off.

Jesse glanced in the direction of the front of the house. His blood ran cold at the sight of an army jeep pulling into the driveway. "That can't be good."

A man in full camouflage gear climbed out of the vehicle and slammed the door shut.

Jesse's shoulders relaxed. "It's okay. It's Trey."

The lieutenant strode across the lawn toward them.

Jesse lifted a hand. "Hey, Trey. Good to see you." He'd ask how the lieutenant knew where to find him, but it seemed like pretty much anybody could access his GPS coordinates these days.

Trey exchanged greetings with Brendan and Shane before turning back to Jesse. "I need to talk to you. Do you want to go somewhere private?"

Jesse shook his head. "I'll just tell them what we talked about afterward anyway. Might as well discuss whatever you came to tell me with all of us."

"All right." Trey slid onto the bench beside him. He pulled off his beret and ran a hand over his tight curls. "It's not good news."

"Of course it isn't." Jesse set down his drink. "What is it?"

"It's Michael Stevens. He's in custody."

A heavy weight dropped into the pit of Jesse's stomach. "Where?"

"Here in Kingston. He was brought in Friday night."

The night he came to see me. Jesse felt sick. "He came to my place that evening, but he didn't stay long, because he said he felt like he needed to get out of town before it was too late."

"Well, unfortunately, he didn't."

"Why did they arrest him?"

"I followed the messages back and forth between Gallagher and General Burns at Headquarters. Apparently, they found out the commissioner was involved in some sort of investigation here, and they both took exception to that. The general fast-tracked an arrest warrant, and Gallagher caught up to Michael as he was leaving town."

Because he stopped to talk to me. A weight, like a rock, settled in Jesse's stomach. "What did they charge him with?"

"Their old standby—treason. They're claiming he was here to meet with representatives of some anti-government group in order to smuggle them classified documents."

The rock in his gut bounced around a little. "When is his hearing?"

"If they had one at all—and I'm not convinced they did—it's already over. A sentence has been handed down."

"They're going to execute him, aren't they?"

"Yes. Tomorrow morning. The general sent the warrant over a few hours ago. After Gallagher gave Michael the news, I offered to take him his lunch. I wanted to see if there was anything I could do for him. He asked me if I could get in touch with you and let you know what was happening. Until then, I didn't realize there was a connection between the two of you, or I would have told you what was going on sooner."

Jesse studied him. Time to decide, once and for all, if he was going to trust Trey fully. "Is there any way to break him out?"

"I figured you'd ask, so I've been giving it some thought. It would be incredibly risky, but it might be possible."

"How?"

"The alarm system is wired up separately in each wing. If I can override the system in the death row area and rig up a loop to play on the security camera footage, I might be able to get in there and get Stevens out of his cell and the building. Two guards will be doing rounds. It takes approximately ten minutes to circle that part of the building, so that's all we'd have for me to take him outside, pass him off to you, and get back in."

Shane replaced the cap on his bottle of lemonade. "Where would we meet you?"

"In the woods on the other side of the east wall, down by the lake. Jesse knows where they are."

Jesse nodded. *And if we can't trust you, you'll have half the company with you instead of Michael, won't you?* He straightened on the bench. Somehow he knew that wasn't going to happen.

Trey's eyes met his, and a small smile crossed the lieutenant's face, as though he understood he'd just passed some sort of test. "If you wait for me there, I might be able to get him to you and get back inside before the guards go by again and realize he's missing."

Jesse pushed away the lunch he'd brought in a paper bag, appetite gone. "That's risky, all right. Everything would have to go perfectly for you to get in and out in ten minutes."

"I know, but I'm pretty sure I can do it."

Brendan set down the sandwich he'd been eating. "How do we get him away from the base?"

"He'd have to cross the lake. As soon as he reached the American side, he would be home free. As long as they don't pick him up over there, of course. He must stay hidden, or the Americans will send him right back. They don't have any more sympathy for Christians across the border than they do here."

So, not a foolproof plan. Probably the best they could come up with, though, given the time frame. At least it would buy them some time to try and figure out a more long-term solution. Jesse sighed. He didn't have a choice. It was his fault Michael was behind bars. He was all in, whatever the risks. "Too hazardous to try to take a military boat. It would be better to get one of our own."

Shane and Brendan looked at each other.

Jesse raised a hand, palm up. "What? Do you know someone with a boat?"

Shane nodded. "Our boss has been trying to sell his fishing boat for a while. It's a beauty, with a one-fifty-horsepower motor. We could buy it and use that. I'll call him as soon as we're done talking and arrange to pick it up after work today."

Jesse's mind raced. "It could work, especially if we use the scramblers, but we're all taking a big chance. With no time to plan anything out properly, we'll be flying by the seat of our pants, without a contingency plan if things go bad. Really think about whether you're willing to put yourself in that kind of peril."

"Jess, he helped our family. Kate and Ethan might have lost their kids for good if he hadn't put his career on the line and met with you." Shane's voice was firm. "We have to do everything we can to help him."

Brendan wiped his hands on a napkin. "I agree."

Jesse contemplated them both. Meryn wouldn't like it, but the one good thing about not being with her anymore was that he didn't have to run everything by her before he went ahead with it. "Okay." He turned back to Trey. "You tell us when you'll be bringing him out, and the three of us will be there."

44

The moon was a sliver in the sky, barely breaking through the dense clouds to cast a pale, watery light onto the farmyard. Perfect for what they were about to attempt. Jesse really hoped that was a good sign. He flipped open the box and withdrew one of the tiny, round scramblers. He handed the box to Brendan before sliding the metal disc under the grey identity bracelet on his wrist. "Let's go over the plan again."

Brendan took out a scrambler and held the box out to Shane. "We'll put the boat in the water on the other side of the woods from the base. I'll row it closer from there and wait with it. In the meantime, you and Shane cut through the trees to the spot where you're supposed to meet Trey. Forty-five minutes from now, at one fifteen a.m., Trey will shut off the alarm and get Michael out. At one twenty, they should meet up with you. Trey will leave Michael and return to the base. If Michael has a bracelet on, you give him the last scrambler and bring him down to the boat. He'll row as far out as he can, then start the motor and power his way across. The three of us can sneak back to the truck, drive home, and go to bed."

Shane gave the box with the last scrambler in it back to Jesse. "It's a perfect plan." His tone was dry. "What could possibly go wrong?"

Jesse snapped the box shut and shoved it into the pocket of his jeans. "Better not to ask ourselves that. If we start coming up with a list, we'll call the whole thing off."

"We can't do that. A man's life is at stake."

"That's true." Jesse glanced at his watch. "We should head out in a couple of minutes. How about we say a prayer first?"

"Good idea." Shane glanced upward. "We're going to need all the divine help we can get."

The screen door creaked and Meryn padded out onto the porch in a pink T-shirt, jean shorts, and bare feet. "Are you ready?"

Shane draped an arm around her. "As ready as we can possibly be."

"I don't like this."

"It's something we have to do."

Meryn drew in a shuddering breath. "I know."

Shane squeezed her shoulder. "Pray with us?"

She nodded.

The four of them stood in a circle as Jesse prayed. "God, we know that what we are about to attempt is dangerous. But we all feel it is what you want us to do. So, we ask for your presence with us. We pray that everything would go smoothly, and Michael would get away safely. Let Trey get back to the base okay, and help us to get home without being discovered. Give us courage, so we can honour you in this and in all we do. Amen."

"Amen." Brendan clapped his hands together. "Let's do this."

Shane pressed a kiss to the top of Meryn's head and let her go.

Brendan pulled her into a hug. "We'll be back before you know it."

"You'd better be."

Jesse started after her brothers.

Meryn grabbed his arm. "You'll be careful?" In the dim porch light, her blue eyes were pleading.

His chest clenched. "We will be, I promise."

She managed a shaky smile and dropped her hand.

Jesse felt her gaze on him as he made his way down the cement walkway. *Is she wondering, like I am, whether this is the last time we'll see each other?* He pushed back the thought. If they were going to make it out of this escapade alive, he had to be completely focused.

None of them spoke as Shane drove toward the lake. He took the long way around, so they could come in from the other direction and avoid driving past the base. Still, Jesse held his breath as they drew closer to the old psychiatric hospital, praying no one would drive out through the gates and catch them on the road after curfew. He exhaled when they reached the dark, shadowy woods and Shane pulled off the road onto the lane that wended its way down to the water.

He circled the truck around and reversed down the ramp until the trailer was nearly submerged and the boat floated on the surface of the lake.

Jesse and Brendan jumped out and freed the motorboat from the trailer. Brendan carefully climbed on board, bracing himself with a hand on one side as he dropped onto the white leather seat in front of the motor. When he was settled, Jesse pushed the small craft farther out in the lake.

Brendan picked up an oar, lifted it in the air in salute, then dipped it below the surface of the water. The boat glided along near the shore, heading for the stretch of land that fronted the army base.

Shane pulled the truck forward until the dripping trailer was clear of the water. He parked close to the trees and climbed out.

Jesse opened up the back door and grabbed the two pairs of night vision goggles he and Meryn had worn when they used to meet in secret. He held one out to Shane, who took it and pulled it over his head.

Jesse slid his on and inclined his head toward the trees, not wanting to speak, even this far from the base, in case his voice carried over the water.

Shane headed into the woods, stepping over stones and twigs and holding branches until Jesse was close enough to grab them. When they had crept through the brush for several minutes, Shane stopped and pointed.

Ten yards ahead, the woods ended, and grass stretched beyond that all the way to the stone wall that surrounded the base.

Jesse checked his watch again. Five after one. If all went well, Trey and Michael would meet them in fifteen minutes. He and Shane picked their way carefully to the meeting point, a group of three trees just inside the edge of the woods, and settled in to wait.

Jesse strained to hear any noises. A rush of wings overhead startled him, and he breathed deeply to slow his heart rate. A mosquito landed on his bare arm, and he swiped it away. A barely audible splash broke the stillness of the night. Brendan, making his way to the shore in front of the base. The trees Shane and Jesse stood under were twenty yards from the water. Through the breaks between branches in front of him, moonlight glimmered faintly on the surface of the lake.

The door in the wall creaked open.

Jesse scanned the area between the wall and the trees. Two figures, draped in green through the lens of the goggles, came into focus.

Michael and Trey. Their mission was nearly over.

Jesse nudged Shane, and they moved closer to the edge of the woods. Trey made his way directly toward them, Michael striding behind. When they were ten feet from the edge of the woods, Jesse reached into his pocket. From this distance, he could see the identity bracelet Gallagher must have forced Michael to put on, even though he was planning to kill him. The sooner Michael could slip the scrambler under the bracelet, the better, because the army would start to trace him as soon as they realized he was gone. Jesse pulled the box out and opened the lid.

Trey stopped in front of him.

Jesse touched his arm and spoke in a low voice. "Everything go all—?"

A piercing siren wailed through the night, shattering the calm.

Trey whirled around, knocking the box onto the forest floor. "They know we're gone."

Footsteps thudded along the grass, coming from the direction of the lake. Brendan reached them, breathing heavily. "What should we do?"

Jesse crouched down and felt around the leaves and twigs lining the ground. He found the box and tipped it toward him. His heart sank. The scrambler was gone.

Shane sank down beside him. "What are you doing?"

"I dropped the box when the alarm went off. The first thing they'll do is start a trace on Michael's bracelet. We have to find that scrambler."

Shane straightened. "There's no time. He has to leave now." He dug under his own bracelet. "He can use this one."

"Shane, no." Brendan stepped closer.

Jesse pushed to his feet and shoved the empty box into his shirt pocket. "He can have mine."

"We don't have time to argue. If you're caught, Gallagher will kill you for sure. Better he take mine." Shane pulled the small metal disc out and handed it to Michael.

He took it and slid it under his bracelet. "Thank you."

Trey shot a look back at the base. "I'll go with him. I can't get back into the base now—they'll have it on complete lockdown."

"You know the shortest route across the lake?"

"Yeah. I've done a lot of patrolling out there. I can get us across quickly."

"Do you have a knife?"

"Yes."

"Cut off his bracelet when you reach the halfway mark and toss it into the lake. Michael, if you stay out of sight, you should be safe after that—they have no jurisdiction past that point."

Michael clasped his hand. "Be careful, my friend."

Jesse nodded. "You too." The sounds of shouting and boots tromping across packed earth echoed from behind the walls of the base.

Jesse jerked his head toward the water. "Go."

Trey and Michael sprinted toward the lake. Jesse, Shane, and Brendan shrank back into the shadows of the trees.

The siren continued to shriek, the eeriness of it sending chills up and down Jesse's spine. He waved his arm in the direction of the truck.

Shane started toward it, and Brendan followed.

Jesse brought up the rear, all three of them moving cautiously, trying to avoid twigs and branches. He cast a glance behind him every few seconds. They'd only gone fifteen feet into the forest when the gate in the wall crashed open.

Jesse whispered an urgent, "Wait!"

Shane and Brendan stopped and looked at him.

Jesse gestured toward the trees and all three of them pressed against the trunks. He lifted a finger to his lips. They faced the water, but by turning his head a little to the right, Jesse could make out eight soldiers coming through the opening in the wall. Although it was dark in the woods, the property between the wall and the lake was fairly well lit by lampposts, and the soldiers hadn't taken time to grab night vision goggles.

The men drew even with them and passed by, spread out in a line, three feet apart.

"Check down by the lake."

Every muscle in Jesse's body froze at the harsh command. *Gallagher.*

The major stopped at the edge of the trees, in a direct line out from where Jesse stood with Brendan and Shane. Gallagher clasped his arms behind his back. He stared out at the lake as four soldiers broke away from the others and headed for the water.

For several long minutes, the soldiers searched along the shoreline. Then, they thudded onto the dock. The sound of the motor on the military boat starting up cut through the night. One soldier walked along the dock, loosening the lines.

Before he could toss the ropes into the boat, the answering roar of another motor echoed across the surface of the water.

All four soldiers turned toward the sound. The soldier on the dock threw the ropes into the boat and jumped in after them. The boat reversed past the end of the dock and circled around until it was facing the centre of the lake. The driver must have shoved it into high gear, as the boat surged ahead.

Gallagher stood as if cast in bronze.

Could he sense them nearby somehow? For what seemed like an eternity, but was likely only fifteen or twenty minutes, Jesse concentrated on drawing in one slow, agonizing breath after another. His back was shoved up against the rough bark of a tree, and sweat trickled between his shoulder blades. The high-pitched squeal of mosquitoes buzzing around his head nearly drove him out of his mind, but he didn't dare swat them away. Whenever he risked a sideways glance at Shane and Brendan, the brothers looked as uncomfortable as he was, but neither of them moved or spoke.

Finally, the roaring of a motor grew louder.

Jesse's fingers curled into fists, the nails digging into his palms. Was that one motor or two? It was almost impossible to distinguish over the sirens. Had the soldiers caught Michael and Trey?

The roar grew louder and then dropped off suddenly, idling at low speed as the boat with the soldiers in it glided to the dock.

Jesse let out a breath. Trey and Michael's boat was not with them.

One of the soldiers leaped onto the dock as soon as they were close enough, rocking the boat so the others had to grip a side to keep their balance. He retied the ropes and the other three men disembarked. They trudged toward Gallagher, who, as far as Jesse could tell, hadn't twitched the entire time they had been gone.

"Well?" he demanded, as soon as the soldiers were in range.

"They got away." The voice of the soldier held a slight tremor.

"Get inside and wait by my office. I want a full report."

"Yes, sir." The soldiers continued past him and disappeared through the door in the wall.

For a few interminable moments, Gallagher continued to stare out at the water. Then, he turned and slowly scanned the woods.

Jesse held his breath. Could he see them? *God, hide us. Cloak us in darkness and shadows. Don't let Gallagher find us.*

A thick cloud drifted across the face of the moon, and even the weak light it had been valiantly trying to emit faded.

Gallagher spun around and stalked toward the wall. In seconds, the heavy wooden door crashed shut behind him.

Shane gestured to Jesse and Brendan. "Let's go. The siren will cover any noise we make."

They moved cautiously yet quickly through the woods. Brendan, who wasn't wearing goggles, stumbled over a root in his path and nearly fell. He managed to catch himself on the trunk of a tree, then stayed close behind Shane the rest of the way.

When they finally broke through into the field on the other side, Jesse's heart was pounding as though he'd just run a marathon. The three of them headed for the truck and jumped in. Shane started the engine and drove down the lane. At the road, he again turned in the opposite direction of the base and drove the long way back to the farm. None of them spoke until they drove up Meryn's driveway and parked the truck behind the barn.

Jesse pulled the box that had held the scramblers out of his pocket and flipped it open. "Here, Brendan."

Brendan slid the metal disc out from under his bracelet and pressed it into one of the slots.

Jesse stuck his in the slot beside it and returned the box to his pocket.

"That was way too close." Shane propped his elbows on the

steering wheel and pressed his fingers to his temples.

Jesse rested his head against the window. "They got away, that's the main thing."

"How weird was that, Gallagher just standing there, only a few feet away from us, the whole time?" Brendan sounded as spooked as Jesse felt. "Do you think he suspected we were there?"

"He would have sent those soldiers in after us if he thought anyone was near."

Shane pushed open the door of the truck. "Jess, you better sleep on our couch. You don't want to take a chance and drive home now."

"No, I guess not. Let's hide the trailer first, though."

The three of them disconnected the trailer, pushed it through the double barn doors to the mow, and covered it with hay.

Jesse ran over the events of the evening in his mind as he and Shane and Brendan walked toward the house. *Thank you, God, that you answered our prayers and brought us home safely. And that Michael got away. Help him and Trey find a place to stay.* Jesse had no idea how long they would have to be gone. Poor Trey hadn't counted on leaving the country that night. Neither of them had passports on them. Hopefully Trey had his wallet with enough cash to see them through for a while. They were smart men; they'd figure something out.

There wasn't anything Jesse could do for them now, except maybe try to contact someone with enough authority to overturn the death sentence. *But who?* Definitely not anyone at Headquarters, since the general himself appeared to be helping Gallagher every step of the way.

The problem was, with Jesse's contact in the army and his contact in Ottawa both gone, he had no idea whom he could trust.

45

Meryn carried her coffee over to the table and sat down. "So, they got away?"

She'd stayed up until they got home early that morning, but they had all been too exhausted to discuss the details. As soon as they'd assured her they weren't hurt, the mission was a success, and they'd tell her all about it in the morning, she had let them get some sleep.

"Looks like it." Brendan poured cereal into a blue ceramic bowl. "They chased them across the lake but came back without Michael and Trey. They must have reached the halfway point before the soldiers could catch up with them."

"Won't the authorities be waiting for them on the other side?"

Jesse spread jam on a piece of toast. "There are hundreds of kilometres of coastline. It would be next to impossible for the Americans to predict their landing site. I'm sure the authorities will be looking for them, though, so they will have to lay low for a while. I'm going to try and figure out who I can talk to about having the execution order overturned, see if there is anyone who can help get them back to Canada without either of them facing the death penalty here."

"No one saw you on the property?" When none of them responded, chills shivered across Meryn's skin. She stopped stirring her coffee. "Shane?"

He sighed. "The whole time the soldiers were out on the water, fifteen or twenty minutes, Gallagher stood at the edge of the woods, not far from where the three of us were. It was dark and he wasn't wearing night vision goggles, so I'm sure he didn't see us. Besides, if he had, he would have come in after us or sent his lackeys in to drag us—"

The sound of vehicles roaring up the driveway cut him off.

Brendan jumped to his feet and strode to the window. When he looked at them, his face had gone pale. "Army jeeps."

Shane reached out a hand and covered Meryn's clasped fingers on the table. "I'm sure it'll be all right, kid. Even if they suspect us of helping Michael escape, there's no way they can prove ..." His eyes met Brendan's.

The chills intensified to icy pinpricks. Meryn struggled to draw in a breath as she unclasped her fingers and gripped his hand. "What? Did something happen?"

"We lost one of the scramblers, so I gave mine to Michael. I figured the chances of them checking my location at that exact time were slim, but Gallagher is just evil enough to have thought of checking the data recordings."

Boots tromped up the porch stairs.

"Whatever happens, Meryn, I know we did the right thing." Shane spoke with quiet urgency. "We couldn't have just sat here and let Gallagher kill the man who helped bring Matthew and Gracie home. You know that."

Meryn nodded, throat tight.

Shane let go of her and stood up.

Meryn and Jesse rose too.

A fist pounded on the screen door, banging the wood against the frame. "Army! Open up."

Brendan spun away from the window, marched to the door, and flung it open. "Yes?"

Through the small space to one side of Brendan, Meryn could see Private Whittaker standing on the other side of the screen. Gallagher and Smallman hovered behind him. Meryn moved to Brendan's side.

Two other soldiers waited at the bottom of the stairs.

Gallagher tossed a small object up over and over, snatching it repeatedly out of midair.

Meryn was mesmerized by the movement. She hadn't seen the scramblers. Was that one of them? A hard ball formed in her stomach. Gallagher knew Jesse and her brothers had been at the base. *He'll kill them all.*

Whittaker held up his i-com. "We have a warrant for the arrest of Shane O'Reilly."

Meryn pressed a fist to her lips to suppress a moan.

Brendan's hands closed into fists. "On what grounds?"

"We can only convey that information to Shane O'Reilly."

Shane brushed by Brendan. "I'm Shane O'Reilly. What are you charging me with?"

"Aiding and abetting a fugitive." Whittaker pulled open the screen door. "Step outside."

Shane went out.

Gallagher dropped the object he'd been playing with into his pocket and stepped in front of Shane to read him his rights. "Turn around and put your hands behind your back."

Shane did as he was told. His eyes, surprisingly calm, locked on Meryn's.

Jesse shoved through the screen door as Gallagher snapped handcuffs around Shane's wrists.

Brendan followed Jesse out onto the porch, and the screen door slapped shut.

Smallman, Whittaker, and the soldiers at the bottom of the stairs all withdrew their weapons.

Meryn moved closer to the screen and grasped the metal handle. *Father, help us. Don't let them do this.*

Gallagher jerked his head toward the jeep. "Take him."

The soldiers at the bottom of the stairs holstered their weapons as they came up to grasp Shane by the arms. They dragged him off the porch and down the walkway.

"Gallagher, leave him alone." Jesse's voice was thick with rage. "I'm the one you want. Why don't you just take me in and have done with it?"

The major let out a cold laugh. "You're right. You are the one I want. And I'll come for you, rest assured. But first, I'm going to take in a couple of others you care about." He sent a look in Meryn's direction that burned like a just-spent match against her skin. "Guess who's next?"

Jesse shrugged. "I don't care about her. We're not together anymore. She's nothing to me."

Even though she knew the words were for Gallagher's benefit, they struck Meryn with the force of a clenched fist.

Gallagher snorted. "We'll see about that." He spun on his heel and headed for the stairs.

Brendan lunged forward.

Meryn gasped as Whittaker and Smallman both shifted their weapons to aim them at his chest.

Jesse caught Brendan's arm and yanked him back. "Don't. You'll just get yourself shot."

The privates kept their weapons trained on Brendan as they backed down the front walk. The jeep Shane was in wheeled around and drove down the driveway.

Gallagher slid behind the wheel of the second jeep. Whittaker and Smallman jumped into the backseat. The major circled around the farmyard and sped away.

Jesse let go of Brendan.

White-hot anger poured through Meryn as she slumped against the doorframe. *This isn't happening. Not Shane.*

Brendan let out a roar of frustration and slammed the side of his fist against the wall of the house, hard enough to rattle the glass in the kitchen window.

Meryn flinched. When the second jeep had gone, she pushed open the screen door.

Brendan turned when she came out. His locked jaw and wild eyes reflected the fury coursing through her.

"I'm going to do the chores." She pushed past him.

"I'll come with you."

"No, thanks. I can handle it."

"But ..."

She gripped the post at the top of the steps and looked back at him. "Bren, I need to be alone for a bit." Without waiting for a response, she went down the stairs, praying neither of the guys would follow. They wouldn't like her going off on her own, but she didn't care. If she didn't have a chance to work off some of the emotions building inside of her she would explode. Or scream. Or break something.

Meryn reached the barn entrance and lifted the wooden bar. Flinging it to one side, she whipped open the doors and stormed in. One of the cows lowed softly when she entered. They did need to be fed and have fresh straw tossed into their pens, but there was something she needed to do first.

She wrestled the boxing gloves on and laid into the punching bag, landing blow after blow on the hapless piece of equipment. She'd come out here a few times since the night Brendan had shown her how to do it, but she had never attacked the bag with such vehemence.

She pictured Gallagher's face on the dingy white bag and landed a flurry of punches with both fists. What would Gallagher do to Shane? Have him flogged? He wouldn't kill him, would he, just for helping someone Gallagher knew to be innocent?

Meryn groaned, holding the bag in place with both gloves, so she could rest her forehead against it. Sobs rose but she swallowed them back.

That man was not going to reduce her to tears. Even if he wasn't here to see them, he'd know, somehow. He always seemed to know everything, and she refused to give him the satisfaction.

Meryn pushed away from the bag and landed another round of punches before throwing off the gloves. She walked over to the pitchfork propped against the wall. Holding a palm to the rough barn board, she took in several slow breaths. Finally, the erratic thudding of her heart eased. The punching bag had helped, but until Shane was free, nothing would take away the deep ache that slashed across her chest. *Father, bring him home. Please.*

Meryn picked up the pitchfork and stabbed it into a pile of straw.

46

Jesse stood at the living room window, staring out at the barn. Meryn had been out there for forty minutes. He gritted his teeth, wishing he could pick up the lamp on the table beside him and send it crashing through the glass. *What is she doing?* He spun around. "How long should we leave her alone?"

Brendan stopped his pacing and braced himself against the fireplace mantel. "I'd have gone out there half an hour ago if I didn't think she'd take my head off."

"We need to talk to her. I don't believe Gallagher is bluffing about coming for her next. She has to go somewhere safe."

"Right. And where would that be?"

"I don't know. But if she'll discuss the possibilities with us, maybe we'll come up with something."

"I'm game to try if you are."

"Would you give me five minutes to talk to her before you join us?"

"Sure. You can take the first round of bullets, no problem."

"Thanks a lot." Jesse studied Brendan carefully. The heat he'd radiated when Gallagher took Shane away seemed to have fizzled quickly. Fire still smouldered in his eyes, but it was contained, not the out-of-control blaze Jesse had expected. "You're not giving up, are you?"

Brendan's head jerked. "Of course not. The next time Gallagher shows up here, I'll be ready for him. I'm just trying to stay calm and focused and come up with a way for all of us to get out of this mess. Doing what I'd really like to do—put my fist through a wall or smash a piece of furniture into bits or go after Gallagher—isn't going to help Shane much. Or Meryn."

"I guess not." Jesse started for the kitchen. "I'll see you out there. Wish me luck."

"I do. You'll need it."

He stopped with a hand on the doorframe and looked back at Brendan. Under other circumstances, he might have been amused. "How did a big strong guy like you get to be so afraid of his little sister?"

Brendan looked sheepish. "I'm not afraid of her. I just … don't like it when she's not happy with me."

Jesse's stomach tightened. "Yeah, I get that."

"I guess you do. It's not getting any better for you, is it?"

"Not yet. But I'm trying to stay calm and focused too." He smacked the doorframe a couple of times before heading outside. The barn doors hung open and he stepped inside, taking a moment to inhale the scent of warm, sweet hay in an attempt to settle his nerves.

Meryn stood in front of one of the stalls, stroking the forehead of a cow. She looked a million miles away and jumped when his shoes crunched on straw. She glanced over at him and frowned. "You don't need to check up on me. I'm …"

"Fine. I know."

She shoved herself away from the metal railing. The inferno he'd expected in Brendan's eyes flared in hers. "You know what? No, I'm not fine. Why Shane? He's the kindest, gentlest …" She bent forward, both hands low on her hips, like a runner at the end of a gruelling race. "He would never hurt anyone. And now they're going to …"

His muscles tightened. He couldn't finish that thought either. "I'm so sorry, Meryn. And I'm sorry for what I said to Gallagher about you. It wasn't true."

She straightened up and waved her hand through the air, as though his words were a swarm of gnats she could swat away. "I know that. Don't worry."

"I am worried. Gallagher could come back for you anytime. You have to leave here, go somewhere safe."

The fire in her blue eyes died when they met his. "There is nowhere safe."

The words sucker-punched Jesse in the gut. *No safe place. Just like the note on the brick that came through her store window that night had said …*

Brendan came through the doorway. "What about Mom and Dad's?"

"There's no way I'm dragging them into this. Gallagher will use my bracelet to track me down there, then he could easily turn on them. Even if he didn't, it would kill Mom to see me arrested and taken away."

Jesse felt sick. "What if we removed your bracelet and then you took off?"

"What good would that do? I'm sure Gallagher is already having me tracked, expecting me to bolt. If I tried, an alarm would go off immediately. The army would be here in minutes and they would hunt me down like an animal, just like you said they would do with Ethan and Kate if they ran with the kids. And when they caught up to me, I'd be arrested for sure. At least this way there's a slight chance Gallagher's bluffing, trying to drive all of us, especially you, crazy by leaving this threat hanging over our heads. Other than distributing the Bibles, which I don't think he figured out I was doing before the evidence burned up, I haven't broken any laws. If he does arrest me, it will have to be on completely made-up charges. It's possible even he won't sink that low."

Jesse worked to keep the scepticism from his face. Personally, he didn't think there were any depths to which Gallagher wouldn't sink.

She cocked her head, dark hair falling down over one shoulder. "You think he'll do that, don't you? Manufacture phony charges and somehow get a commission to rule against me."

"That's exactly what he did with Michael Stevens. I wouldn't put anything past him. And I can't stand the thought of us just sitting around here waiting to find out what he's capable of."

"Me neither. Which is why I think you should go." Meryn nodded toward the door.

"What?" Jesse shook his head. "No way. I'm not going anywhere."

"Then you're playing right into his hands. He *wants* you to witness him taking us in. That's the part that's giving him such sick pleasure. If we can't stop him from doing whatever he is planning to do—and we can't, whether you're here or not—then maybe we can take some of the fun of it away from him."

Brendan smacked both palms on the railing of the stalls. "This is insane. There has to be something we can do."

"There is. We can pray. For Shane and for us." Meryn waved a hand through the air. "That's not nothing, you know. And whatever happens after that, we won't be alone. God will be with us."

Jesse searched for some kind of argument but came up empty. There was no safe place for her, for any of them. And it might actually be better if he did leave. Maybe, if Gallagher checked the GPS data and realized Jesse had gone home, he'd leave Meryn alone and come straight for him. It wasn't likely, but it was possible.

Even if Gallagher did come for her, Jesse wouldn't be able to stop him, and if Jesse attempted to, he'd be doing just what Gallagher wanted him to do.

Meryn was right. There was absolutely nothing any of them could do.

Except pray.

47

I'm never going to fall asleep. Meryn tossed back the covers and sat up in bed. After Jesse left, Brendan had insisted on spending the night in the rocking chair in her room, his shotgun propped up against the table beside him. She eased herself off the bed, freezing in place for a few seconds when the mattress springs creaked.

Brendan's breathing stayed deep and even.

Meryn tiptoed across the room, slipped into the washroom, tugged on a pair of jeans, and pulled on the pink T-shirt she'd left there the night before. She crept back out of the washroom and went into the hallway, pulling the bedroom door shut behind her. Her chest tightened when she reached Shane's door, and she stopped and pressed a palm to the wood for a few seconds, blinking back tears. *Father, watch over him. Keep him safe. Please.*

Darkness cloaked the house. Heart heavy for her brother, Meryn made her way down the stairs carefully, avoiding all the spots that would creak beneath her bare feet. When she reached the bottom, she stood for a moment, listening, but didn't hear a sound from upstairs.

Good. Brendan would never let her go outside, not alone anyway. Not tonight. And she desperately needed fresh air and solitude to clear her head. She glanced at the clock as she entered the kitchen.

Midnight. Meryn went to the window and peered out. A yellow quarter-moon hung in the sky above the barn, draping soft light over the yard. Everything was still and quiet. *It's safe. I'll just go out for five minutes.*

She slid her feet into her sandals. Hopefully Brendan wouldn't wake up and come looking for her. He would not be happy if he found her on the porch. *Neither would Jesse.* Pushing back the thought, she opened the door and stepped outside.

The smells of damp earth and fallen leaves filled her senses. The coolness in the air flowed over her, clearing out the cobwebs that had draped themselves over her thoughts.

Meryn walked over to the railing and closed her eyes. *Father, I don't know what is going to happen tomorrow or the next day or the day after. But you know. Help me to trust you. Take away my fear. Watch over Shane and protect Brendan and Jesse and me and anyone else that Gallagher might go after. Thank you that you are here, and that, whatever happens, you will be with us. I—*

A thudding on the porch step turned the blood flowing through her veins to ice. Meryn opened her eyes.

Gallagher stood on the cement walkway, one booted foot resting on the bottom step. Two other soldiers had stopped just behind him. Whittaker and Smallman.

Of course. Meryn looked back at the house.

A cruel smile crossed his face as Gallagher waved a hand toward the door. "By all means, scream, cry out, alert your brother. Nothing would make me happier than arresting him and taking him in too. You could have your own family reunion, right there on death row."

Meryn's pulse raced. She couldn't call out for Brendan. He'd come flying out of the house with his gun and end up dead, more likely, than arrested. No one could help her now. *Father, give me courage.*

Gallagher came up the stairs slowly, his gaze raking over her.

Meryn crossed her arms and forced herself to hold her ground when he stopped in front of her.

He trailed a finger down her cheek. "I've been looking forward to this moment, gorgeous. You must have been too, since you couldn't even wait for me to come in and get you."

She shuddered, but didn't answer.

He moved closer. "No need to play coy. I know you and Christensen ended things a while ago. If you're lonely, we can easily fix that."

"I'm not—"

His hand shot out and he gripped her chin and shoved his mouth against hers.

Shock and revulsion coursed through her. Meryn uncrossed her arms and planted both palms against his chest and shoved against him in an attempt to free herself.

Finally, he let her go and stepped back.

Meryn wiped her mouth hard with the back of her hand.

His hooded eyes gleamed. "We can continue this later. Unfortunately, I have another appointment I really need to keep, so let's get on with it." He yanked a set of handcuffs from his belt. "Turn around."

When she hesitated, Gallagher grabbed her arm and spun her around. He snapped a handcuff around one wrist and then reached for her other one and yanked it behind her back, so he could close the cuff around it.

Meryn suppressed a groan at the darting pain in her shoulder. She whirled to face him. "What are you charging me with?"

"How about harbouring a fugitive, for starters? Resisting arrest. And, in all likelihood, smuggling Bibles."

"I didn't resist arrest—I resisted your disgusting advances. Last time I checked, good taste wasn't a crime."

"Well, that *good taste* might have cost you your life. A little more willingness to accommodate me could have earned you a lighter sentence."

"I'll take my chances with the justice system."

His laughter was mocking. "Suit yourself. I can come up with more than enough on you to ensure you receive the punishment you deserve."

"I don't see a warrant."

He raised his hand, the back of it toward her. "This is all the warrant I need."

She lifted her chin, daring him to hit her.

After several seconds, he lowered his hand. "I think I'll save that for later too. I always prefer to perform before a wider audience." He grasped her elbow, his fingers digging into her flesh. "Let's go, sweetheart. It's showtime." He dragged her down the porch stairs.

Meryn struggled to stay on her feet.

The two privates moved back as Gallagher pulled her down the walkway, then their footsteps echoed on the cement behind her and the major.

She craned her neck to look back. "Does it ever get cold there in

Gallagher's shadow?"

Gallagher jerked her forward, and she stumbled and nearly fell. Where had they parked? He directed her down the driveway. A jeep sat on the shoulder of the road. No wonder she hadn't seen or heard anything in time to alert her brother.

It's just as well. Brendan would be furious when he woke up in the morning to find her gone, but at least he hadn't been arrested along with her. Maybe one of them would live through this. *Mom and Dad.* Meryn pushed back a surge of panic. What would happen to them when they found out about her and Shane? If Gallagher killed them, would her mother survive the news?

They reached the jeep. Still clutching her elbow, Gallagher opened the back door and shoved her down onto the seat. Whittaker slid in after her, while Smallman climbed into the back from the other side. Gallagher rounded the front of the vehicle and slid behind the wheel.

The tires spun as he pulled onto the road.

Her mouth and elbow throbbed. The handcuffs dug into her wrists. Meryn shifted, trying to get comfortable. Would Gallagher lock her up close to Shane? At least then she would know what was happening to him.

They reached the base and the major flashed his identification at the guard in the booth.

He nodded and waved them through.

Gallagher wheeled into a parking space and cut the engine. "Bring her."

Whittaker got out and leaned in to grasp her arm and pull her from the backseat. Smallman took her other arm.

Gallagher stalked toward the nearest building, and the two privates led Meryn along the pathway after him. At the door, the major entered a code and pressed his thumb to the pad.

The lock clicked open.

Once inside the building, the privates, hauling Meryn between them, followed Gallagher through the maze-like hallways. It seemed to take forever, but they finally reached a metal door with a large Restricted Access sign on it.

Was this the death row Gallagher had referred to earlier? Meryn's chest clenched. Would she come back out that door alive? *Father, I know you are with me, even here in this evil place. Give Shane and me strength. Help us get out of here alive. Please.*

Gallagher unlocked the door and held it open. Whittaker and Smallman pulled her through the doorway. Six cells lined the right side of a long walkway. Nothing but bars separated them. The first three cells were empty.

Shane stood at the front of the fourth cell, watching them approach. He gripped the bars with both hands as they walked by. "Gallagher, let her go. She wasn't involved in anything I did. She's completely innocent."

Gallagher stopped outside the fifth cell and touched his thumb to the pad before cupping Meryn's chin in his hand again. "Maybe your precious sister isn't as *innocent* as you'd like to think, O'Reilly." He slid open the door.

Meryn jerked away from him, and he laughed and took her elbow to pull her into the cell.

She swallowed. *What is he going to do?*

"Turn around."

Gallagher was like a wild animal, ruthless and unpredictable. Meryn would far rather be facing him, where she could gauge his actions and try to guess what he might do next. However, her desire to have the handcuffs removed overrode her apprehension, and she did as he'd told her.

He removed the cuffs from her wrists.

Meryn spun back around.

Gallagher tucked the cuffs into his belt. "Time to keep that other appointment I told you about. I'll be back before you have time to miss me."

Relief weakened her knees as he went out into the walkway. He closed the door behind him with a clang.

After all three soldiers had gone out the door at the end of the walkway, Meryn looked at Shane and lifted both hands helplessly in the air.

His eyes flashed with anger, but he held his arms through the bars, and she went to him. He cupped her shoulders and searched her face.

"Did he hurt you?"

"Not really, no."

His eyes darkened. "Not really?"

Meryn exhaled. "I'm fine, Shane."

"How did he get past Brendan?"

She bit her lip. Shane wouldn't be any happier about the risk she'd taken than Brendan or Jesse.

"Meryn?"

"I couldn't sleep because I was worried about you. I thought some fresh air might help."

"No. Tell me you didn't go outside and walk right into Gallagher's clutches."

"He was about to come into the house. If I hadn't gone out, Brendan would have gotten himself arrested or killed trying to keep Gallagher from taking me into custody. There was nothing he could have done."

He ran a hand over his eyes. "You're right, I know."

"So what do you think this appointment is that Gallagher keeps talking about?"

He dropped his hand and met her gaze.

Her shoulders slumped. "He's gone to get Jesse, hasn't he?"

"That would be my guess. They've left me alone since they put me here, so I'm thinking he wants all three of us locked up before he carries out whatever plans he has."

Another shudder moved through her at the thought of what those might be. "Do you think he'll go after anyone else? Brendan or Kate and Ethan?" She drew in a sharp breath. "What if he does something to Matthew or Gracie?"

Shane grasped both her arms. "I doubt he'll bring in too many of us or he'll start to arouse suspicion, especially if he drags children in here. But whatever happens, God is in control. We have to remember that, kid."

Meryn nodded. *Help me to remember. Help us all through this, please.* She rested her head against the bars.

There was no sense even speculating what Gallagher's plans for them were. Once he brought Jesse in, they would all find out.

48

Jesse bolted upright in bed. What was that? He snatched the i-com from his bedside table. He'd refused to leave the farm yesterday until Meryn had promised to send him a red flag if anything happened. He squinted at the screen. No message. *Then, what woke me up?* He glanced at the alarm clock. Almost one in the morning.

He sat up and swung his legs over the side of the bed. Was it the wind? He listened a moment, straining to hear a rustling or creaking, whatever had caught his attention in the first place. Silence.

Jesse pulled on the jeans he'd tossed over the chair in his room and strode to the bedroom door. The living room was shrouded in darkness. He started for the front door but froze after a few steps, apprehension prickling across the back of his neck. *He's here.*

A click sounded and soft light flooded the room, illuminating Gallagher's face in an eerie glow. "Hello, Christensen." He sat on the couch, his pistol resting on one knee.

Jesse glanced over at the door. Whittaker and Smallman stood on either side of the only exit from the building. He looked back at Gallagher. "What do you want?"

A mirthless smile crossed the major's face. "Same thing I always want. To see you suffer."

Jesse drove his fingers through his hair. "Are you ever going to tell me why you detest me so much? Because it's getting a little old, to be honest."

Gallagher pushed to his feet. He shoved his pistol into the holster that crossed his chest and paced the living room floor. "Does the date June twenty-fourth, 2050 mean anything to you?"

The question ripped the air from Jesse's lungs. "Should it?"

"Yes. It should. It should mean something to you like it means something to me."

Jesse fought for calm. Gallagher couldn't know about that, could he? No one did. Almost no one anyway. Just the ones who'd been there that day, in the scorching desert. And Meryn.

Gallagher advanced toward him slowly. "Shall I refresh your memory?"

I'd much rather forget. Not that he ever could.

"June twenty-fourth, 2050. The day you single-handedly killed fifteen people. Quite the feat. Under normal circumstances, you might have been given a medal for an act like that. But the circumstances weren't normal that day, were they?"

"What are you talking about? I didn't kill fifteen people."

"Not directly, no. But you killed Logan Phillips, the one who was trying to get help for the rest of his platoon that was under fire. And because you did, help never arrived, and thirteen more soldiers died."

Jesse's eyes dropped shut for a few seconds. How could Gallagher know all this? Even he had never heard the numbers, had never found out what happened to Logan's platoon.

"Did you ever see the names of the soldiers whose blood still drips from your hands?"

He shook his head slightly, tremors of horror reverberating through him. "No."

"Well"—Gallagher yanked an i-com out of his shirt pocket—"I think it's about time you did, don't you?" He slid a finger over the screen. Light flashed from the unit as he activated the projector app. A list of names appeared on the wall.

He scanned them quickly. None of them looked familiar, until ... Jesse sucked in a quick breath. *Christopher Gallagher.* Could that be …?

"That's right." Gallagher's voice was cold enough to send shards of ice skittering across Jesse's skin. "My son."

Jesse's heart pounded. Hope was right. The nightmare of that fateful day continued to send one part of his life after another crashing into rubble, like the aftershocks of a devastating earthquake. "Your son?"

Gallagher touched the screen again, and a picture of a young man in army fatigues flashed onto the wall. His eyes were Gallagher's, without the scornful hatred. "I dated Sierra all through high school. In our junior year, she told me she was pregnant. A few months later, our son, Christopher, was born. The birth was difficult, and for a while it looked like I might lose them both. Thankfully, they survived, but the doctors told Sierra she could never have another child." He turned off the projector and slid the device back into his pocket.

Jesse leaned against the wall behind him, legs weak. The thought of Gallagher as a father, as someone capable of loving another human being, of being loved himself, had never crossed Jesse's mind. He studied the man who had made his life miserable for so long, pieces of that puzzle finally starting to click into place.

Gallagher's eyes had gone distant, unfocused. He wasn't standing in front of Jesse now; he'd gone back to another time and place. Even his voice, when he spoke, sounded far away. "After we graduated, we got married, and I went to RMC Saint-Jean and then enlisted in the army. Sierra lived for Christopher. He was her whole life. When he turned eighteen and decided to enlist as well, she wasn't happy about it. I took leave and came home to spend time with her, help her adjust to the idea of having another person she cared about in the line of fire. Two months after he'd been sent to the Middle East, we got the phone call."

The pain in Jesse's chest was so intense he couldn't draw in a breath. He lowered his head. Every one of those soldiers who died that day had a story, people who loved them and had been devastated by their loss. He'd only heard two of those stories, and already the load pressing down on him threatened to break him. Summoning every ounce of willpower he had left, he raised his gaze to meet Gallagher's. "You said I killed fifteen people that day. Logan and the thirteen soldiers in his platoon only make fourteen. Who was the other person?"

Gallagher didn't answer.

The truth struck Jesse with the burning, shocking force of a lightning strike. "Your wife."

"She was gone from the moment we got the news. It only took her three more weeks to take the pistol I'd brought into our home and make it official."

Jesse closed his eyes. *God, help me. I can't take any more.*

"We'd been together twenty-five years. We had our ups and

downs, like everyone else, but I cared about her. We were looking forward to watching Christopher settle into his career, meet someone, marry, give us grandchildren. We wanted to grow old together. It was a beautiful plan."

Jesse's throat had gone so dry he couldn't swallow. Like it had been that day ... "And I got in your way."

Gallagher's eyes sharpened back into intense focus. "Yes, you did. In every possible, conceivable way."

"How did you know it was me?"

"Christopher's platoon was ambushed that day. They were outnumbered three to one and under heavy fire. Logan Phillips was the only one who got away. One other soldier, Christopher's best friend, Max, was badly wounded but managed to survive by crawling under a tank and pretending to be dead. When the army finally medevacked him out, the soldiers transporting him thought he was unconscious and talked freely about what had happened. I tracked him down in a hospital a month later. For the sake of his friendship with my son, he took a huge risk and told me everything. I found out that you'd been sent back to Canada, and I requested a transfer. I've been tailing you ever since, waiting for the opportunity to destroy your life like you destroyed mine."

Gallagher's dark eyes burned with hatred. Jesse hadn't only destroyed lives; clearly he'd also destroyed a soul. He did have blood on his hands. And the tally of the dead could grow by three in the coming hours.

"Thomas." Jesse lifted both hands in a helpless gesture. "I'm sorry." The words were as weak and meaningless as they'd been when he'd said them to Meryn.

Gallagher's features went hard as flint. "Not nearly as sorry as you're going to be." He pulled a set of handcuffs from his belt.

The fight had been knocked out of Jesse. Feeling as though he were slogging through mud, he pushed away from the wall, turned around, and bent his arms behind his back. *I deserve this.* He lifted his head.

Was that true?

For the first time since that terrible day in the desert, he wondered.

Yes, I have blood on my hands, but your blood was shed so I could find forgiveness and healing. Help me to remember that. To remember that your blood is enough. Not just for me but for Gallagher too. Soften his heart. Help him to understand your mercy, so he can show mercy to us.

It would take a miracle, but Jesse believed in a God of miracles, a God of the impossible.

Gallagher clicked the cuffs closed. "I'm arresting you for a slew of things I'll write up and submit to make all this nice and legal-sounding." He didn't bother patting Jesse down, like he hadn't bothered with Shane the day before.

Jesse frowned. Why was he being so lax with the regulations? Was he trying to show them that the rules didn't apply to him in order to increase their fear and trepidation?

If so, it was working. A man with unlimited power and no accountability was capable of anything.

Jesse sighed. He no longer cared what Gallagher did to him. No one else should have to pay for his actions, though. Especially not ... His jaw tightened. "Did you arrest Meryn?"

"I promised you I would, didn't I? I always keep my promises. And the most important one is the promise I made while standing in the rain at my wife's graveside four years ago. I vowed that I would do everything in my power to make sure you experienced every last drop of the pain and loss she endured at your hands." Placing his palm between Jesse's shoulder blades, he steered him to the door. "Not that such a thing is possible, but"—he swept an arm in front of him, motioning Jesse outside—"let's go see what we can do, shall we?"

49

Meryn shifted on the hard bed. In the cells on either side of her, Shane and Jesse were quiet. Other than checking to make sure Gallagher hadn't hurt either of them, Jesse had hardly spoken since he'd been brought in a couple of hours earlier. Whatever had happened between him and Gallagher, when the major arrested him, seemed to have really shaken him.

The door at the end of the walkway crashed open.

Meryn sat up. *What is going on?*

In the dim fluorescent lighting, Gallagher strode down the walkway toward them.

Her breath caught in her throat. She got up off the bed.

Jesse and Shane both stood up too.

When Gallagher stopped outside her cell and pressed his thumb to the security pad, they moved to the bars on either side of her.

"Gallagher, what are you doing?" Jesse's voice held a warning.

Gallagher grinned as he slid open the door to her cell. "I'm going to give her a taste of a real man."

"Meryn, come here." Shane held out his arm, voice urgent.

She took a step toward him, but Gallagher snatched the gun from the holster across his chest and levelled it at her. "Don't do it."

Meryn froze.

Still holding the weapon on her, he advanced slowly.

She backed up.

Jesse moved along the bars, staying even with the major. "Gallagher, do not touch her."

"Or what?"

Jesse didn't respond.

Meryn's eyes locked on Gallagher. Her heart pounded as she clenched and unclenched her fists.

When he shoved the weapon back into the holster, she broke

toward Shane, but Gallagher lunged for her. Grabbing her around the waist, he dragged her toward the bed at the back of the cell.

Both Shane and Jesse yelled, but Meryn couldn't make out what they were saying through the words screaming in her head. *Father, help me!* She repeated the desperate plea over and over in her mind as she struggled to break free of Gallagher's hold.

He threw her down on the bed. Her head bounced against the metal, and for a few seconds, a shower of stars shimmered behind her eyes.

Gallagher clambered on top of her.

Meryn pushed against his chest with both hands. Her fingers bumped a hard object, and she closed them around the butt of his pistol. Yanking it from the holster, she pointed it at his face, gripping it tightly in shaking hands.

Gallagher let out a derisive laugh. "Do you think I'm stupid enough to bring a loaded gun into a cell with a prisoner when I don't have backup?"

Heat surged through her chest. *There's more than one way to use a weapon.* She brought the gun back, and swung it with all her might against his temple.

Gallagher tumbled off of her and onto the cell floor.

Meryn scrambled off the bed and ran toward the open door.

Gallagher grabbed her ankle from behind, and she fell to her hands and knees.

The gun clattered across the cement.

He got to his feet and tackled her, driving her over onto her back on the cold floor, and climbed onto her again. "Fine. We'll do it here. Gives everyone a better view anyway." He unbuckled his holster and tossed the gun belt to one side, then undid the buttons on his jacket. He yanked it off and dumped it on top of his belt.

"Jesse!" Shane called out.

Something grated across the cell floor.

Over Gallagher's shoulder, Meryn saw Jesse crouch down to pick it up. They'd landed closer to his cell than Shane's, and Jesse reached through the bars, straining to get to the major, but falling a few inches short.

Gallagher's smile was vicious as he undid the button on his camouflage pants.

Rage roared through her, so thick and strong she could taste it on her tongue. This man had tormented her long enough. Someone needed to show him he couldn't just take what he wanted whenever he wanted it. With a furious cry, Meryn flung herself upright and drove her fist into Gallagher's jaw.

Pain exploded across her knuckles.

He arched back, just enough for Jesse to grasp his shirt at the back of the neck and haul him off of her.

Jesse slammed him up against the bars and shoved the blade of a knife against his throat.

Was that what Shane had slid across the floor to him?

"Meryn!" Shane held out his arm again.

She staggered across the cell to him. When she reached him, she turned and pressed her back to the bars, and he wrapped his arm around her. Meryn shot a glance at the open doorway. Should she make a break for it and lock Gallagher in her cell? Her heart sank. If she did, he'd just reach through the bars and use the thumb and key code pads to unlock the door, and then she would be trapped in the walkway with him, too far away from Shane and Jesse for either of them to be able to help her.

Blood trickled down Gallagher's neck as Jesse pressed the blade in farther. "Are you going to leave her alone?"

"Yes." The major gasped out the word.

Jesse didn't pull the knife away.

Meryn stood frozen in place. Would he kill Gallagher?

None of them moved for several seconds, until Jesse dropped his hand.

Gallagher spun around to face him. His laugh was mocking. "You can't even kill me right, can you?"

Jesse snapped the blade shut. "God will be your judge, Gallagher, not me."

The major smoothed down the front of his shirt. "All right. I'll give you this round. I'll let you pretend you're some big hero, saving her. You know why?"

Jesse didn't answer.

"Because, the irony is, before you *saved* her, I was prepared to let her live." Gallagher stepped away from Jesse's cell.

Shane tightened his hold around her, but the major ignored them as he gathered up his gun, jacket, and belt. "Drop the knife and kick it to me."

"Not until you are out of her cell."

He stalked to the door and went out, slamming it shut behind him.

Jesse tossed the knife onto the floor and kicked it into the walkway.

Gallagher bent down and grabbed it, then dropped it into his pocket. Blood dripped from his temple and throat. "You can have this battle, Christensen, but tomorrow I win the war. Once and for all." He stormed toward the exit.

Jesse leaned an arm against the bars and dropped his forehead onto it.

The adrenaline that had carried Meryn through the attack dissipated. She shook.

Shane turned her to face him and rubbed his hands up and down her arms. "Are you okay?"

She nodded, teeth chattering.

"Meryn." He brushed the hair back from her cheeks. "We're in God's hands. Not Gallagher's. You know that, right?"

She drew in a long, shuddering breath. "Yes."

He pulled her to him.

Meryn rested her cheek against a bar. The metal was cool against her heated skin. She stood there as her brother held her with one arm and stroked her hair with his other hand. Gradually, the trembling stopped.

Shane took her by the shoulders. "You sure you're all right?"

"I'm sure."

"Good." He inclined his head toward Jesse.

Meryn looked over her shoulder.

Jesse sat on the floor, leaning against the bars. His elbows were propped on his bent knees, and he'd lowered his head into his hands.

"Talk to him," Shane whispered as he let her go. He walked over to his bed and dropped onto it.

Meryn crossed to the other side of her cell and sank onto the floor beside Jesse.

When he didn't move, she slipped her arm through the bars and rested her hand on his chest.

His heart pounded beneath her fingers. He lifted his head. "I just sentenced you to death."

Her throat tightened at the agony in his voice. "No." Meryn shook her head. "If I die tomorrow, Gallagher will have killed me, not you."

"But I led you into this." He waved a hand around the cell. "All of you."

"Jesse." She cupped his chin to turn his face until their eyes met. "You weren't the one we were following when we got involved in all this."

The tension in his muscles gave a little. He reached up and took her hand, enclosing it in both of his. "You're right. Thank you for the reminder." He turned her hand over and ran his fingers over her tender knuckles. "Quite the right hook you've got."

Meryn mustered a weak smile. "Brendan recently introduced me to the cathartic wonders of the punching bag."

"Really? What motivated that?"

"I was upset and frustrated one day when …"

"When what?"

"I'd rather not say."

His lips twitched. "I take it I was somehow involved."

She exhaled. At this stage of things, was it worth keeping anything from him? "It was the day Annaliese stopped by to let me know she was going to find you and offer you 'comfort,' because things had ended between us."

"Ah. So, was it your sister being your sister that got you upset, or the idea of her being with me?"

Meryn tried tugging her hand from his, but Jesse held on and she gave up. "You're going for full disclosure tonight, aren't you?"

"Why not?"

She sighed. "All right, then, it was both."

He studied her for a moment. "Nothing happened."

"I know. Kate told me. Although …"

"It wasn't any of your business."

"Exactly."

His face grew serious. "Are you really okay?"

"I really am, thanks to you and Shane."

He let out a short laugh. "I don't know. You were holding your own pretty well." He dropped his gaze to their clasped hands. "If Gallagher had … finished what he started, I don't know if I would have dropped that knife."

"I don't know if I would have wanted you to." She squeezed his fingers. "What you said was correct, though. It is God's place to judge him, not ours."

His jade-green eyes probed hers. "I've never stopped loving you."

Everything had been stripped from them. She only had one thing left to give him. The truth. "I've never stopped loving you either. There was just so much …" Her voice broke.

"I know." Jesse lifted her hand to his mouth and kissed it. "But just so you know, lady, whatever happened between us in the past, and whatever happens after tonight, you will always be my business, and I will always be yours."

50

Meryn raised her head. She still sat on the floor next to Jesse, her hand in his. A dull light sifted through the barred windows set high up in the wall.

Boots thudded down the walkway toward them.

Jesse let go of her and stood.

Meryn scrambled to her feet too and backed up to the bars. The feel of him behind her, his breath warm on her head, infused her with strength.

Gallagher walked toward them, Whittaker and Smallman shadowing him.

Meryn's stomach tightened. Was this it? Were they here to kill all three of them? She glanced at Shane. He had moved to the bars closest to her cell, gripping one of them as he watched the men approach.

They stopped outside Shane's cell.

Gallagher entered a code and pressed his thumb to the pad. The lock clicked and he slid open the door.

Jesse's fingers found hers through the bars, and she clutched them tightly.

The two privates followed Gallagher into the cell.

Shane didn't move.

The major stopped in front of him and shot a sideways glance at Jesse. "Well, this is it, Christensen. You and your little friends have been the bane of my existence for far too long. I've indulged your game-playing until now, but it's time to end this." He held up a pistol.

Stifling a sob, Meryn started forward, but Jesse slid his free arm around her waist and pulled her back gently. "Wait."

The major nodded curtly at her brother, and Whittaker pulled the cuffs from his belt and moved around behind Shane.

Meryn pressed a hand to her abdomen as Whittaker cuffed Shane's wrists.

Gallagher grasped Shane's arm. He directed him to the middle of the cell. "On your knees."

Behind her, Jesse jerked. He had to be reliving what had happened here just a few months earlier, when Gallagher had executed Caleb in front of him. The memory he had shared with her ripped through Meryn too. Obviously Gallagher was capable of putting a bullet into all of their heads. And nothing was likely to stop him at this point.

Shane knelt down. His eyes found Meryn's and he offered her a small smile before mouthing, *It's okay.*

The major pressed the pistol to the back of Shane's neck.

"Gallagher." Jesse spoke up behind her.

"What?"

"Let them go. Neither of them has done anything wrong. If you want me dead, then kill me. The more innocent blood you shed, the greater the chances you will be found out and stopped."

"Maybe so."

Meryn's eyes narrowed. The words made it sound like the major was capable of rational thought, but the smirk on his face told her he was enjoying the game too much to give it up now.

Gallagher looked down at Shane. "Perhaps I *should* give him a second chance. Tell you what, O'Reilly. Renounce your faith in Jesus Christ—right here, right now—and I might let you live. Can you do that?"

Shane's gaze rested on Meryn. When he spoke, there was no trace of uncertainty in his voice. "No."

For a few more seconds, Gallagher stood there, the pistol still pressed to Shane's head. Then, he pulled it back.

Meryn's knees weakened. Would he let them go like Jesse had asked?

"All right, then, let's try something else, shall we?" Gallagher waved a hand in Shane's direction. "Watch him, Whittaker."

The private stepped closer and pulled his own weapon out of its holster, pointing it in Shane's direction.

Meryn swallowed as the major went out into the walkway and strode over to Jesse's cell. After entering the code and shoving open the door, he nodded for Smallman to go inside.

The private walked into the cell, and Gallagher shut and locked the door behind him. Smallman drew out his weapon as he approached Jesse.

Jesse's arm tightened around her waist as Gallagher pressed his thumb to the pad outside her door and opened it.

The major ambled over to her, as though out for a leisurely stroll through the park. When he reached her, he grasped her arm and tugged her toward him. "Let go of her."

Jesse didn't loosen his grip.

Meryn twisted her head to see what was happening.

Gallagher nodded at Smallman. "Kill him."

The private's face blanched, but he lifted his gun to Jesse's temple.

Meryn's heart stopped beating. "No." She wrenched herself away from Jesse.

"Meryn!"

Jesse's cry was anguished, but she didn't look back as Gallagher dragged her to the middle of the cell.

He stopped and yanked her in front of him, wrapping one arm around her throat and shoving the barrel of the pistol against the side of her head. He turned her a little, until they both faced Shane. "All right, O'Reilly. I'll give you one last chance. Think very carefully. If you refuse this time, your sister will die." He spoke slowly and deliberately. "Do you renounce your faith in Jesus Christ?"

The colour drained from Shane's face. Horror flashed through the dark eyes that met hers.

Father, help him. Give him strength like you gave it to me when I needed it most. Meryn shook her head slightly.

Gallagher increased the pressure on her throat.

She clutched his arm with both hands, her vision dimming.

"Well?"

Help him.

"No." Her brother choked out the word.

"Well, then, I guess she gets to go first."

God, give me strength. Peace flooded through her, and she let go of the major's arm and straightened.

Gallagher lowered his head until his mouth was close to her ear.

"Jesus can't save you now, sweetheart."

He set fire to the store. Or ordered someone else to. Fury swept through her. *Father, help me. Fill my last moments with forgiveness, not hatred. Mercy, not vengeance.* Meryn kept her eyes on her brother's face. *I'm ready.*

The door at the end of the walkway flew open.

Gallagher jerked but kept the pistol pressed to her head.

Who is that? She blinked, trying to make out the people marching down the walkway.

Six soldiers came toward them, led by …

Her forehead wrinkled. Was that … Abby? And Cameron? What was going on?

Abby reached Meryn's cell and took one step inside.

"Don't." Gallagher's short command stopped her.

"Lower your weapon, Major."

He glared at her. "So, not a coffee shop owner."

"That's right."

"Then who are you?" He snarled the question at her.

Abby reached slowly into her pocket and withdrew something that she held up in Gallagher's direction. "Agent Leah Winters, Canadian Security Intelligence Service."

Meryn stared at her. *Agent? Leah?*

Gallagher didn't relax his hold. "Agent Winters, these prisoners have all been tried and convicted under the Terrorist Act. Had you done your homework, you would know that my men and I are carrying out lawful executions and have no choice but to follow the orders we have been given."

"Those highly questionable *orders* have been countermanded by CSIS. As soon as you stand down, I will be more than happy to show you the official paperwork signed by the Prime Minister herself."

Gallagher's grip on Meryn's throat eased, then his muscles tensed again.

"Major." Abby's—or Leah's?—voice grew hard. "You will let the prisoner go immediately or face another murder charge to go with all the other charges that are pending as a result of the investigation we have been carrying out here the last several weeks."

Gallagher pressed the gun harder to her head.

Meryn flinched.

"If that's true, you're going to execute me anyway. And if I'm going down"—his gaze shifted to Jesse—"I'm taking her with me, Christensen. You can live the rest of your life with the knowledge that you killed all three of them as surely as if you had pulled the trigger yourself."

All three of them?

Abby—or whatever her name was—took another step forward.

Gallagher spun to face her as he spoke into Meryn's ear. "Say goodbye, gorgeous."

Meryn's eyes met Leah's. *She doesn't have a clear shot.*

The loud crack of the pistol firing was deafening in the confined space. Meryn gasped. Had she been hit?

Gallagher's arm dropped from around her neck, and he staggered backward. The pistol he'd held to her head crashed onto the cell floor.

Leah moved in and picked it up. Two of the soldiers rushed to the major and hauled him to his feet.

Gallagher clutched his upper arm with one hand, blood seeping through his fingers. His eyes, flashing with contempt, looked past Meryn.

Jesse. Meryn whirled toward him. He stood stock-still, a pistol gripped in both hands and still pointed at Gallagher. He shifted his gaze to Meryn and slowly lowered the weapon.

The men holding Gallagher led him over to stand in front of Leah.

"This arrest won't stand, Agent Winters. I promise you that. When the charges against me are dropped, I will come after you. And I won't rest until I have your badge."

She stepped closer to him. "If you are holding out hope that the person who has been protecting you and colluding with you to this point will be able to do anything for you, you should know that he is also under investigation and will have been brought in by now. It's over, Gallagher. Your reign of terror has come to an end. All that remains now is for you to face the consequences of what you have done and pay the price for the lives you have destroyed. And the price will be astronomically high, *I* promise *you.*"

Gallagher's cheeks paled but he didn't reply.

The other two soldiers brought Whittaker and Smallman over to stand on either side of him.

A numbing shock spread through Meryn as Leah informed all three of them that they were under arrest, and read them their rights.

She finished and jerked her head toward the walkway. "Call for an ambulance and take him to the front doors to wait for it to arrive. I want four of you with him at all times, two in the room and two outside his door. I'll take care of releasing the prisoners in this wing and meet you at the hospital shortly."

One of the men nodded, and the soldiers led Gallagher into the walkway, where they were joined by two more soldiers.

Cameron turned to the men standing with Whittaker and Smallman. "Bring them."

Private Smallman glanced back over his shoulder as he was taken from the cell.

Jesse nodded at him.

Meryn frowned. *What is that about?*

Cameron conducted the group down the walkway and out the big door at the end.

Meryn's legs refused to hold her up any longer, and she sank onto the bench and pulled her knees up to her chest. Her gaze drifted over to Shane.

He got to his feet awkwardly and slumped against the bars. He didn't meet her eyes.

The numbness moving through her deadened her limbs until she could barely move. She dug her elbows into her knees and dropped her face into her hands. Shudder after shudder swept over her, terror and relief combining to sap every ounce of energy in her body.

Could it finally be over?

51

"Shane?" Meryn stepped through the barn doors.

Shane shovelled a forkful of straw over the rails. "Hey." His gaze slid to her briefly, then back to the pile of straw on the floor in front of the stalls. "You escaped."

"Yeah." She let out a short laugh. "It wasn't easy. I had to wait until Brendan went to the washroom before I could flee the house."

From the moment Brendan had pulled her from the army jeep that had driven them home after dropping Jesse off at his apartment a few hours earlier, her brother hadn't let her out of his sight. She understood. It was great to spend time with him when she hadn't been sure she'd ever see him again, but a little room to breathe felt good too. "What's going on?"

Shane jabbed the pitchfork into the straw. "Nothing, why?"

"You've been pretty quiet since we got back."

"It's been a nightmarish couple of days. I can't remember the last time I slept. I'm worn out, I guess." Sweat glistened on his arms and soaked through his light-blue T-shirt.

How much straw had he hefted in the last hour? Meryn cocked her head. "Is that all?"

"That's enough, isn't it?" He carried his load down to the last stall and tossed it over the bars.

When he went back for another one, Meryn grabbed the sleeve of his shirt. "Can you stop for a minute?"

He stuck the fork into the straw and swiped his arm across his forehead. "I haven't been out here since Wednesday. I need to make sure they have everything they need."

"They're good. They have food and water and"—she glanced over at the cows—"at least a month's worth of straw to sleep on."

"But—"

"Shane. Why don't you tell me what's really bothering you?"

"Fine." He grasped the pitchfork by the handle and whipped it toward the back wall of the barn. It thudded against the wood and dropped onto the cement floor. "He attacked you, Meryn. Almost raped you, right in front of me. And I couldn't do anything to stop it. I couldn't protect you." His chest rose and fell rapidly.

The memory of the night before slammed into her. Meryn shoved it back before the trembling could take hold of her again, like it had done off and on all day. She seized both his arms. "You did protect me. You smuggled in the knife and got it to Jesse."

"Which only made Gallagher decide to kill you after he'd planned to let you live."

"He just said that to mess with your head, and Jesse's. He was toying with all of us. There's no way he would have let any of us live if Abby … Leah hadn't come in and stopped him."

He didn't speak for a moment. Then, the muscles under her fingers relaxed slightly. "Still, having to say the word I knew would kill you ripped me apart."

"I understand. But you couldn't have done anything else. And now you know."

"Know what?"

"That under the most horrific circumstances imaginable, you still wouldn't deny your faith."

"I almost did. I … I wanted to. For a few terrible seconds, I wanted to."

"But you didn't. Every believer wonders if, faced with torture or death or threats to the people they love, he'll stay strong until the end. You've been given a gift, Shane, we both have. We found out the answer to that question."

He contemplated her briefly before he nodded. "That's true. When Gallagher asked me that second time if I renounced my faith, I couldn't do it. I couldn't say the word. All I could do was cry out to God to help me. And I felt it."

"What?"

"A peace flowing through my whole body. A strength that I knew didn't come from me. That's why I was able to refuse, even knowing how high the cost would be."

Meryn's chest tingled with warmth. "I felt that too, when Gallagher had his gun pressed to my head. And when I was being flogged. God was there, giving me the strength to endure, to do what I had to do. I couldn't have done it on my own, but I didn't have to. Neither did you."

"Good thing." Shane touched her elbow. "So, you forgive me?"

"Absolutely not."

His eyebrows rose.

"There's nothing to forgive. You did everything right."

He managed a weak grin. "Okay. Thanks, kid."

"If you really want to thank me, you can stop calling me—"

"Forget it. Not gonna happen." Shane walked over, grabbed the pitchfork, and propped it against the wall. "I better hit the shower before Leah gets here."

"Not a bad idea." Meryn followed him out of the barn and waited for him to drop the bar into the slots on the door. "How long have you known?"

"Known what?"

"That Abby was really Leah. And a CSIS agent."

"Oh. She told me a couple of weeks ago."

"I'm glad she told you the truth."

"I was too. It's the reason we got back together." His eyes searched hers. "The truth isn't always enough, though, is it? You and Jesse told each other the truth last night. Do you think that resolved anything?"

She lifted a hand. "I don't know, Shane. It's complicated. And there's Drew ..."

"Maybe Drew has a right to know the truth too."

Tears pricked Meryn's eyes. What a mess it had all become.

Shane sighed. "I'm sorry. I know you've been through a lot. Probably not the right time to get into this. Just promise me you'll think about it, okay?"

Meryn nodded and followed him into the kitchen. Jesse's voice carried across the hall from the living room, and she stopped and bit down on her thumbnail. Leah had told them before they left the base that she would come by later that afternoon to discuss everything that had happened with them, and answer some of their questions. Jesse must have driven here so he could hear what she had to say.

After everything that had passed between them in the night, she had no idea how to be around him. Shane was correct; the circumstances might have been extreme, but she and Jesse *had* told each other the truth. Unfortunately, her brother had also been correct about the other thing he'd said.

Sometimes the truth just wasn't enough.

52

Jesse felt Hope watching him as he flopped onto the chair in the corner of the farmhouse living room. He was as physically and emotionally drained as the night he'd stumbled into this room after witnessing Caleb's murder. The memory didn't help improve his frame of mind.

He met her gaze and tried to smile, but the effort required more than he had in him. The smile she tried to return to him was just as forced, and loaded with questions. He appreciated the fact that she wasn't bombarding him with them at the moment. He'd have to tell her everything that had happened soon, though, as the uncharacteristic patience was unlikely to last long.

A movement on the other side of the room caught his eye. Brendan walked over and grabbed some clothes out of a laundry basket sitting at the bottom of the stairs. He carried them over to Jesse. "You look done."

Jesse didn't even try to straighten up. "I feel done."

"Well, if you need a pick-me-up, go ahead and use the punching bag in the barn. That'll get the blood pumping again." He lifted the clothes. "You can borrow some workout stuff if you want."

Jesse didn't have the energy to shake his head. "Thanks, but I'm good. I just need to hear what Abby or Leah, or whatever her name is, has to say, then I'll head home and sleep for a couple of days."

"Suit yourself." Brendan went over to the couch and dropped down beside Hope, setting the clothes on the arm of the couch beside him. He glanced over his shoulder in the direction of the kitchen.

Hope touched his arm. "Meryn's with Shane. She's safe."

Brendan grimaced. "I know." He straightened on the couch. "When's Leah supposed to come by, Jess?"

"She was going from the base to the hospital to check on Gallagher first, but I would think she'd be here anytime now."

Brendan nudged Hope. "Did you have any idea she was a spy?"

"No, not at all. The more time I spent with her, the more convinced I was that she wasn't doing anything shady, but it didn't occur to me that she worked for CSIS."

"Me neither." Jesse looked over at her. "I was as happy as anyone to find out what she was doing at the base, though."

"I'm sure you were. I know you probably don't feel up to talking about it yet, but whatever happened there the last couple of days must have been pretty horrific."

"It was." Jesse scrubbed his face with both hands. "On top of everything that was going on, which was bad enough, a lot of terrible memories came rushing back."

Sadness flooded Hope's face. "Of course they did. I'm sorry you had to go through all that again."

Brendan slid his arm around her. "Me too. I'm just thankful the three of you came out of it alive. When I found out you'd all been taken in …" His free hand tightened into a fist on his knee. "Well, it wasn't easy being on this end of things either, I'll say that. I've never felt so frustrated and helpless in my life."

Hope covered his clenched fist with her hand until he uncurled it and twined his fingers with hers.

The screen door slammed in the kitchen. A moment later, Shane came into the room. "I'm going to take a quick shower."

Brendan glanced behind him. "Where's Meryn?"

"Relax. She's in the house. She's making tea."

Gravel crunched and Jesse looked out the window. "It's Leah."

"I'll be back in five minutes." Shane headed up the stairs.

Jesse rested his head against the back of the chair.

A minute later, a knock sounded at the kitchen door before it creaked open. Leah's voice mingled with Meryn's.

He couldn't make out the words, but the sound of Meryn's voice filled him with equal parts comfort and pain. He sat up as Meryn and Leah came into the room.

If Leah wondered where Shane was, she didn't show it. "Hi, everyone. I'm sorry to have kept you waiting."

"No problem." Brendan waved a hand at the brown leather armchair by the fireplace. "Please, sit. Shane will be right down."

"I'll get the tea while we're waiting." Meryn turned and left the room.

Too tired to fight the urge, Jesse followed her with his eyes until she disappeared from view.

Shane came down the stairs as Meryn entered the room again. He took the tray from her and carried it over to the coffee table in front of the couch. The aroma of spices rose from the teapot in a cloud of steam. He set it down and went to stand by the stone wall of the fireplace.

Meryn didn't look over at Jesse as she poured the tea into mugs and handed one to everyone. When she carried a green mug over to him, her gaze barely brushed his face, just lingering long enough for him to take the mug from her.

Jesse repressed a sigh. What had happened between them the night before may have gotten them back on more stable footing, but it appeared as though nothing substantial had changed, as far as the two of them getting back together. Had he really thought it would? He lifted the mug to his lips. Hoped, maybe.

Leah opened the brown leather briefcase she'd brought with her and pulled out a file folder. "Please understand that everything I am about to tell you is highly confidential. I shouldn't be revealing it to you when it's not yet public knowledge, but I believe there is some information that all of you need to know in order to understand what happened to you and what is going to happen next." She set the file folder in her lap, then lowered the briefcase to the floor and pulled her i-com from her jacket pocket. "Before we start, I need everyone to sign this non-disclosure agreement. If anyone is not comfortable signing, and that's your prerogative, we will move this briefing to a secure location, and those of you who do sign the agreement can meet with me there. Does anyone wish to abstain from signing?" Abby slid the stylus from the side of her i-com as she scanned the room.

No one spoke up.

"All right, then. As soon as everyone signs the form, we can begin." She held out the device to Shane, who pushed away from the stone wall to cross over and take it from her.

He signed the screen and handed the unit and the stylus to Hope.

Leah leaned back in her chair and sipped her tea as everyone passed the i-com around.

Jesse was the last to sign. He read the form quickly and added his name to the bottom of the screen, below the others, before handing the unit back to Leah.

This should be interesting. Were they finally going to get some answers about Gallagher and everything that had been going on in Kingston since he had taken over the base?

Leah set down her tea and pocketed the unit. "I'm sure you were all—or almost all—surprised to find out that I'm not who I led you to believe I was."

She picked up the file folder from her lap and flipped it open. "I'm sorry I had to deceive all of you like that. I had no choice about keeping my identity secret while on this undercover assignment, at least until I was forced to reveal it at the base today. I've been involved in an investigation that has focused on several military bases across the country, including the one at Kingston. We've had several breaks recently, and we're getting close to wrapping up the investigation. Here in town, Major Thomas Gallagher is facing numerous charges, and his case will go before a commission sometime in the next few days."

Brendan leaned forward. "Was this all about him?"

"No. It appears as though Gallagher was part of an international terrorist group called Thrakon."

"The Dragon." Jesse murmured the name of the group Caleb had told him about when Meryn was so sick with the Red Virus. Thrakon was suspected of unleashing the virus on North America and eventually the rest of the world. As far as he knew, the connection had never been proven.

Leah tilted her head. "You're familiar with this group?"

"I first heard about it a few months ago, during the Red Virus epidemic. At the time, almost nothing was known about them."

"We've begun to get a clearer picture. Thrakon has been linked to the bottled water poisoning, as well as numerous threats against oil refineries and nuclear plants in this country, and several others. A number of members were active in this area. Gallagher has only been involved with the group for about four years, but he is a fairly high-ranking member."

Four years ago. After what happened with his wife and son. Jesse's skin grew clammy.

"He ran a cell out of Kingston?"

"Actually, no. The cell leader was someone else in town."

Shane scrutinized her. "Who?"

Leah looked apologetic. "Your sister, Annaliese."

Jesse's gaze swung to Meryn.

She looked stricken.

Personally, he was glad they'd finally figured out what Scorcher—the code name assigned to Annaliese when she became an informant for the army—was really up to. And that, if she was arrested before she could skip town, she'd pay for all the pain she'd inflicted. Meryn wouldn't fully share his sentiments. She'd always held out hope that her older sister would repent of her evil ways and want to be part of their family. Jesse would have given anything to be able to go to her, but he stayed where he was.

Shane came over, settled on the arm of the couch beside her, and wrapped an arm around Meryn's shoulders. "So, Gallagher and Annaliese were working together?"

"Theoretically. Although, it appears they were not exactly united in purpose. Gallagher's interests seem to have been more local and"—Leah's eyes flicked over to Jesse—"personal. Once he became the base commander, that seemed to be enough for him. That might have changed, of course, if he'd been able to get rid of you as he had intended, but up until now he appears to have had a singular focus and used Thrakon to achieve his own goals. It sounds like he was far more likely to take directions from the cell leader in Ottawa, who not only gave him orders but also provided the means, through false arrest and sentence warrants, to do whatever he liked here to whomever he liked."

General Burns. Jesse didn't ask for confirmation, since Leah was already giving them more information than she should. If and when the general was arrested, they would hear about it.

Leah looked at Hope. "That unholy alliance resulted in one wrongful death being carried out, and very nearly four more."

Hope's head jerked. "You can prove that Caleb's execution order was not legitimate?"

"Yes. The army will be issuing a formal apology to you shortly, Hope. And they have already ruled that they will be removing the terrorist status given to Caleb and wiping his record clean. In addition, with your permission, they would like to move Caleb's body to the Beechwood Cemetery in Ottawa, where he will be buried again, this time with full military honours."

Tears glittered in Hope's eyes, and Brendon tightened his hold on her. Her gaze met Jesse's and he offered her a sad smile that she tried valiantly to return.

"Has Annaliese been arrested too?" Shane's voice was tight.

"Yes. Unlike Gallagher, Annaliese had set her sights on rising higher in the organization, and was doing so fairly rapidly. There was no love lost between her and Gallagher. In fact, he hasn't stopped talking since he was brought in and has given us quite a bit of information on her activities and those of others in the area involved with Thrakon." She lifted the file folder in Jesse's direction. "One of the many things he mentioned was something we already suspected, that the cell leader in Ottawa arranged to have Caleb assigned to security duty at the G7 summit in Germany, to get him out of the way so Gallagher could arrest you. If Caleb hadn't come back early, there's no doubt he would have followed through with his plan to execute you."

Michael was right. "Yes, Commissioner Michael Stevens mentioned that he thought that order was highly irregular, and he was going to launch an investigation into what happened."

"Which he did. And, incidentally, we are aware that Commissioner Stevens and Lieutenant Adams were forced to flee to the States. Now that we know the circumstances surrounding the commissioner's arrest, both of them will be brought back, and any outstanding charges against them will be dropped. CSIS is very grateful to Commissioner Stevens. It was his investigation into Caleb's assignment to Germany that led to this one, and has ultimately allowed us to infiltrate Thrakon here in Canada. That has enabled us to figure out who a number of the key players are, as well as what the group was trying to achieve internationally."

"Which was?" Jesse sat up straighter, wide awake now.

"Domination of the world economy by gaining control of the two most valuable and precious commodities on the planet: water and oil. They've carried out operations in almost every country that has a plentiful supply of both. Their MO was to move in and draw attention away from themselves and onto marginalized groups, usually faith-based ones. In North America, the scapegoat for them was Christians. In fact, Christians were targeted in about seventy-five percent of the countries they infiltrated. After making sure the military was occupied with maintaining control over that group, they then carried out further attacks. They targeted water and oil resources, then turned their attention to the nuclear plants, knowing that having control of the nuclear power gave them a chokehold on a country."

Jesse tugged the i-com from his shirt pocket. "Let me guess, when the governments of those countries were looking to hire a private security firm to guard those resources, Thrakon was happy to provide LADON Security."

"Exactly. It was a brilliant strategy, really, and we're only just beginning to realize how deep it went and how many people and countries were involved."

Jesse played a hunch that LADON was more than an acronym and did a quick search on his device. What he found didn't shock him. *In mythology, the name of a hundred-headed dragon who guarded the garden of the Hesperides.*

And, in reality, the name of the organization hired to guard priceless treasure against itself.

Jesse shook his head as he dropped his i-com back into his pocket.

Leah checked something in the folder before continuing. "We're working with the CIA and MI5, and other intelligence organizations around the world, to piece all of this together, which is another reason everything I've told you must be kept confidential. Of course, the high profile arrests of Gallagher and your sister will make the news shortly, so you would know that they were involved then anyway."

Shane set his mug on the coffee table. "So these terrorists aren't 'radical Christians,' and The Horsemen isn't an actual group?"

"That's right. It was a fictional organization created by Thrakon to perpetuate the story that Christians had become a terrorist threat in

North America."

"What does that mean?" Meryn's voice rasped and she cleared her throat. "Will the restrictions against Christians be dropped, so we can go back to the way things were before 10/10?"

Leah grimaced. "Things should get better, in Kingston anyway, now that Major Gallagher is gone. And it's possible the army will decide to lift the curfew. But I doubt that a whole lot will change otherwise, to be honest. Even before 10/10, there was an extremely high degree of hostility toward Christians. No conclusive proof was ever found linking Christianity to the bombings, but rumours alone were enough to push that hostility into absolute intolerance.

"The general public has responded favourably to the bracelets and other restrictions levelled against Christians. While Kingston was the first city to close its churches, that move spread quickly across the country and was greeted in most towns and cities with what could only be called a celebration. In fact, the government's approval rating has never been higher. I can't say for sure, since all of this has just broken open, but it's unlikely Ottawa will move quickly to ease sanctions that have received such support among the majority of voters, especially with an election looming. However, time will tell."

"What about Whittaker and Smallman?" Jesse had a promise to keep, and he might as well get it over with.

"At the very least, they'll be charged as accessories to whatever crimes Gallagher committed." Leah tapped the file folder against the coffee table. "How did you manage to wrestle the gun away from Private Smallman? I was so focused on Gallagher, I didn't see what happened."

"I didn't wrestle it away from him. When you told Gallagher he was being charged with murder, Smallman panicked. He sidled up to me and whispered that he didn't want to go down with Gallagher. He asked if I'd try to help him if he gave me his gun. Obviously, I told him I would, and he handed it over."

"Do you think he should be let off?"

"Not let off, no, but he has always been the weak link in Gallagher's chain. The first time I was arrested, I almost had him talked into helping me. I would have, if Whittaker hadn't intervened. He's a follower, nothing more, and he probably only ever went along with what Gallagher and Whittaker were doing, because he was too scared to cross them."

"Are you willing to testify to that and to the fact that he voluntarily helped you take down Gallagher?"

"Yes."

"All right. I need to talk to you and Meryn and Shane individually at some point in the next day or two, take down all of your statements. We'll write up that testimony then." Leah flipped through the papers inside the folder and pulled one out. "Apart from what Thrakon has been doing, there have been a number of reports of other base commanders carrying out questionable activities since 10/10. CSIS plans to continue assigning undercover operatives to various bases around the country to look into this."

She set down the paper. "I have been authorized to offer you a job, Jesse. With your qualifications and your knowledge of military procedures, only minimal training would be required to qualify you as an agent. It would mean travelling all over the country, but it would enable you to uncover and put a stop to practices going on at other bases that would be similar to the kinds of things Gallagher was doing here."

Jesse glanced over at Meryn. "I'll think about it, Leah, thanks."

"Good. In addition, the army has ruled that your dishonourable discharge and your level-three classification were also unwarranted and will be expunged from your record, effective immediately."

Relief poured through him. He was done with the military. If he hadn't been discharged, he would have retired. Still, having his record cleared meant personal vindication, and access to veterans' services and a pension, both of which would make his future easier. "That's great news."

"It's justice, or at least as much as the army can do for you, and for Caleb, to try to make up for everything you have been through."

Hope crossed her legs and clasped her hands over her knee. "Can you do anything about the fact that Gallagher had Jesse banned from several stores in Kingston?"

"I don't know anything about that. Which stores?"

"It started with The Hundred-Mile Market, but Gallagher encouraged the manager to spread the word to other stores. Not sure how far that got."

"Ah. The Hundred-Mile Market." Leah shook her head. "I'll talk to him, but I'm not sure I'll be able to do much. I didn't realize it started with Jesse, but the manager there has been stirring up quite a bit of support for a proposal to ban all Christians from the stores downtown. And a law has been proposed in Parliament to that effect."

Time to set up those food deliveries. Jesse sighed. Other than Gallagher and Scorcher being gone, it didn't sound like a whole lot would be different.

Leah picked up her mug and wrapped her fingers around it. "I think that's everything I had to tell you today. Hopefully, you can all rest a little easier, knowing that whoever takes over for Gallagher will be watched much more closely and held to much stricter guidelines and regulations than he was."

Meryn tucked her hair behind one ear. "How did you know we'd been arrested?"

"I didn't. Not until this morning. Only Gallagher and his lackeys, and of course his contact in Ottawa, knew what was going on. When Brendan woke up to find you gone, he came straight to the coffee shop to talk to Hope. She took him into the back, but he was so worked up, I could still hear everything. As soon as I realized what he was saying—basically that he was about to go to the base and tear the entire place apart, brick by brick—I called it in and headed over there."

Shane punched Brendan in the shoulder. "Hey, your bellowing accomplished something productive, for a change."

Brendan whacked him back. "You're welcome."

"Hello?" Someone rapped on the doorframe leading into the living room.

Jesse looked over and his stomach muscles tightened. *Drew.* He'd been so absorbed in what Leah was saying, he hadn't heard a vehicle drive up or the kitchen door open. Clearly, no one else had either.

"Sorry to interrupt. I knocked but no one came to the door."

"It's okay, Drew." Meryn stood up and walked across the room to him.

He pulled her into his arms. "I'm happy to see you're home. I texted Brendan earlier when I couldn't reach you, and he told me you'd been arrested. I was so worried."

A stabbing pain shot through Jesse. He'd known that they were seeing each other, but he hadn't actually witnessed them together until this moment, hadn't seen him touch her ... Blood rushed through his veins now, pounding so loudly in his ears he could barely hear Meryn when she spoke.

"It's all right. Everything worked out." She stepped away from Drew, cheeks flushed.

Drew reached for her hand. "Can we go somewhere and talk?"

Meryn nodded and looked back over her shoulder. "I'll see everyone later."

He led her from the room.

No one moved until the screen door slammed shut.

In the awkward silence that followed, Shane started loading empty mugs on to the tray.

Jesse pushed back a surge of nausea and got to his feet as Drew's car drove past the window, heading for the road. "You know what?" Jesse walked behind the couch and rounded the end where Brendan sat. "I think I might ..."

Without a word, Brendan reached for the workout clothes and held them up.

"Yeah. Thanks." Jesse grabbed them and headed for the barn.

53

Shane carried the tray of mugs out to the kitchen and set it down on the counter. His mind spun with the effort of processing everything he had just heard as he opened the dishwasher door and set the mugs inside.

Brendan and Hope came into the kitchen. Brendan leaned his hip against the counter as Shane straightened and closed the dishwasher door. "We're going for a walk."

Shane nodded. "All right."

"When we get back, I'll call Mom and Dad, let them know that you and Meryn were arrested but everything is all right now. I know I can't tell them more than that, but I'm sure they'll want to come for a visit, and it would be good for them to be here when the news about Annaliese comes down."

"Good idea." Shane waited until the screen door had shut behind Brendan and Hope, then went back into the living room.

Leah still sat on the leather chair. She'd propped an elbow on the arm and rested her head on her hand. She looked up as he approached. "That was a marathon."

"No kidding."

She shoved the file folder into the briefcase and snapped the case shut.

When she started to rise, Shane took her hand and helped her up. He reached out and brushed back a wayward curl. "You were magnificent today."

"I didn't feel magnificent."

"Why not?"

"I've never been in a situation like that before. I mean, I've negotiated my way through more stand-offs than I care to remember, but never when the hostages were people I cared about. Totally different feeling."

"And yet, you stayed completely focused and in control. I was proud of you."

She touched his elbow. "There is something I've been wondering about."

"What's that?"

"When Gallagher arrested you, why didn't you tell Meryn or Brendan to let me know? I could have gotten there a lot sooner."

"I thought about it, believe me. But I didn't want to tip Gallagher off to who you really were, not when you were so close to uncovering everything he's been doing here."

"You were willing to risk your life to protect me?"

He lifted one shoulder. "You and all the other people Gallagher would have harmed in the future if he'd stayed in power."

She studied him. "You might not be the bad-boy type, but there's nothing weak about you, is there?"

"That's not true. I have one big weakness, at least."

Leah's lips twitched. "So do I." Her i-com buzzed. She held up a finger as she fished the unit out of her jacket pocket. She looked at the screen and wrinkled her nose. "Cameron. I better take it."

"Do you want me to go?"

She grabbed his arm. "No, stay. I'll just be a minute." She pressed the unit to her ear. "Yes?"

He studied the fingers splayed over his skin. Her hands were small, like the rest of her, but, when she had stood in the doorway of his cell, calmly pointing a weapon at Gallagher and speaking with such authority, she hadn't seemed small at all. She had been an agent very much in charge of a tense, hostile situation. Maybe he wouldn't worry about her when she was off doing whatever she was doing, most of which he would likely never know anything about. *Not much anyway.* He managed a grim smile.

Leah's thumb rubbed his arm lightly.

He swallowed and looked up.

Frustration contorted her features. "Yes, I hear you. I'm sure half the city can hear you."

Shane frowned. Cameron's voice, loud and angry, was carrying into the room, although Shane couldn't make out the words. *What is he saying to her?*

"I'm on my way." Leah disconnected the call and shoved the device back into the pocket of her jacket. "Sorry about that." She let go of his arm, and his skin, where her fingers had been, went suddenly cold.

"What is it?"

She shrugged. "Just Cameron being Cameron. He's not happy that I'm out here."

"Because the investigation isn't wrapped up yet?"

"No, because of you."

"Me?"

"Yes. He's been pressuring me to date him for months. That time at Maeve's when he jumped down your throat, it wasn't because he was trying to protect me, it was because he was jealous."

"You're kidding."

"I wish I was." She shook her head. "I've been considering asking for a new partner for a while now. I'm going to do that as soon as possible."

"So, all those fights you two had, that wasn't about you spending time with Christians?"

"Mainly, it was about the time I was spending with you, but he also wasn't happy about the other. He really doesn't like us; he just keeps holding out hope that I'll turn my back on my faith to be with him. He views every minute I spend in church or with you or your family as a step away from that." Leah picked up the briefcase and started for the kitchen.

Shane followed her. "I take it Maeve isn't your grandmother?"

She stopped and turned around, a sheepish look on her face as she set the briefcase down on the kitchen counter. "No, she's me, actually."

"You?"

"Yeah. It was my father's nickname for me when I was a child. Apparently, I liked to call the shots then too. He'd always laugh when I'd plant my fists on both hips and stand up to kids twice my size. That's when he started calling me Maeve, his warrior princess."

Shane grinned. "I love it. Very Irish."

"Yeah, I know. My dad had some Irish blood in him, so I guess I do too, a little."

He snapped his fingers. "I knew there was a reason I liked you so much."

Leah went very still.

Shane bent his head and kissed her gently, his fingers tangling in her copper curls.

When the kiss ended, she stepped back and held both hands to her flushed cheeks. "Wow. That was a lot of honesty."

Shane grinned, remembering the first time he'd kissed her and told her that her lips were more honest than her words. "That's right. No more lies."

"I'm glad to hear that. Because, like you said one time, I'm also a big fan of transparency. Except, of course, for having to keep my current alias, where I am, and what exactly I'm doing a secret." Her face grew serious. "Do you really think you can live with that, and the fact that I'll be gone a lot of the time?"

"That is a pretty *tall* order, Agent Winters."

"Well, life's too *short* to play it safe, O'Reilly."

"That's true, it is. So, if you can live with me worrying a little, then yes, I can live with what you do. Because I tried living without you, and, you can ask Brendan, it wasn't pretty."

"Then, I guess I can handle a little worrying." Leah reached into her pocket and pulled something out. "I would appreciate you treating my gifts with a little more respect, though." She held out the knife she'd given him. "Don't worry, they sanitized it in the lab."

Shane took it from her and slipped it into the back pocket of his jeans. "I have nothing but respect for this knife. It saved Meryn. I'm very happy to get it back. I thought I'd lost it for good when Gallagher took it."

"Unfortunately, Gallagher took a lot of things that can't be given back as easily as this knife."

He nodded. "It's going to take Jesse and Hope and Meryn, and probably a lot of other people, a while to heal from all the damage he did, but they can start the process now, thanks to you."

"All kinds of people were involved in this investigation. It wasn't just me."

Shane shrugged. "In my mind, it was."

Leah flashed him a smile that weakened his knees before she grabbed the briefcase off the counter. "I should go before Cam—" Her grey eyes sought out his. "Before my partner blows a gasket."

Good. More honesty.

"I have reams of paperwork to file on this case, and I need to talk to Gallagher again."

A chill moved through Shane. "I wish you didn't."

"Me too, but there are plenty of soldiers guarding him. It will be safe. I want to catch him while he's still in the mood to chat. And I need to talk to my boss about getting a new partner."

That I do want her to do. The sooner, the better. Shane walked her to the door.

Leah started to push open the screen and stopped. "It is too bad Maeve's is going to close. Something about it really seemed to appeal to people. It was starting to get busy."

"And Hope will be out of a job."

She pursed her lips. "Good point. I should talk to her. Maybe she'd be interested in taking over the lease and continuing to run the shop. Of course, she'll have to actually do the baking, or hire someone to."

"She might be interested. The way things are going with her and Brendan, I doubt she'll be leaving town any time soon."

Leah clutched the handle of the briefcase with both hands and looked up at him. "She might not be, but I have to."

A tiny pang shot across his chest. *Better get used to it, Shane. This is what you signed up for.* Besides, it might be advisable to put a little time and distance between them. It would allow them to slow things down, really get to know each other. "Are you going home?"

"I don't have a home, not really. But I do need to head back to Ottawa in a couple of days."

He drew in a deep breath. "All right. You go. Do what you have to do. But you do have a home now. And whenever you are able to come back to it, I'll be here, waiting."

54

Jesse strode up the walkway toward the farmhouse. He froze halfway to the house when he saw Shane and Leah standing together in the doorway. Without a word, he spun around and headed back toward the driveway. He'd changed back into his own clothes in the barn, and he could return Brendan's clothes to him later.

Jesse pulled open the door of his truck. Everything at the farm seemed to be settling down. Scorcher and Gallagher were out of the picture. Brendan and Hope were going strong, Shane and Leah were good, and—Jesse climbed into the truck and slammed the door behind him, somewhat harder than necessary—Meryn and Drew seemed happy too. Time for him to go home.

A sad smile crossed his face as he manoeuvred the truck down the driveway and onto the road. *I'm happy for Shane*. He and Leah were meant to be together. And now they were.

He gripped the steering wheel tighter. Life didn't always work out that neatly. He believed, with all his heart, that he and Meryn were meant to be together, but she was off with some other guy, and Jesse was driving home. By himself. To his empty apartment.

How had everything spiralled so far out of control?

Jesse had known since high school exactly what his life would look like. He and Rory and Caleb would have long and distinguished military careers, meet and marry wonderful women, have all kinds of kids, and the three of them would retire together and spend their days playing darts and reminiscing about their various exploits, which would grow bigger and more heroic as the years went on.

Jesse scrubbed his forehead with the side of his hand. Like Hope had said that day at Caleb's grave, nothing had happened like it was supposed to. Caleb and Rory were gone. There were no wives, no kids. Their military careers might have been distinguished enough, but they certainly hadn't been long. And, of the three of them, only he had a hope of living a long life. Somehow, heartbroken and alone, that seemed more of a Sisyphus-like curse—having to endlessly roll the same rock up a mountain—than any kind of achievement.

Without realizing it, he'd driven to a piece of land where he'd spent a lot of time the last few months, while everyone was *speculating* about where he might be. Jesse parked and climbed out of the cab. For a long time, he stood, both hands shoved into the front pockets of his jeans, surveying the property. The hope that had ignited the night he'd talked to Meryn in her kitchen, and realized she wasn't completely happy that things had ended between them, flickered and threatened to go out.

Maybe it *was* time for him to go. Not just back to Ethan and Kate's place, but to really go. Seeing Meryn all the time, watching her with someone else, being so close to her and yet a chasm apart, was like going through their breakup over and over again. He couldn't take that much longer.

Should he accept the offer CSIS had made him? It was a good job. Nothing would make him happier than going undercover and rooting out all the other Gallaghers out there and helping to bring them to justice.

Almost nothing anyway. His fingers closed around the silver heart Meryn had given him and that he still dropped into his pocket every morning. Jesse pulled it out and stared at it. He'd held on to that heart so desperately, thinking that, if he didn't let go of it, the possibility that Meryn would give him her actual heart again—for good this time—still existed.

He still couldn't quite let go of that hope, but maybe, if he stopped carrying a constant reminder of her and everything they had once shared around with him, someday he might reach that point. With a heavy sigh, Jesse reached out and slid the heart into a small hole in a nearby birch tree. There was a chance someone else would happen along and find it sometime. He prayed it would bring that person all the joy and none of the sorrow it had brought him.

Hope might have been right that day. But he'd been right too. He felt that down in his very soul.

God was still on his throne. And he had not abandoned any of them.

That thought gave Jesse the strength to lift his fingers to his lips and then press his hand to the small hole in the tree. After one last glance around, Jesse turned and made his way to the truck.

55

Trees and houses streaked past the car window. Meryn touched her fingertips to the glass. "Where are we going?"

"I thought I'd take you to my place. It's quiet there and we can talk. I want to hear about everything that happened to you the last couple of days." Drew reached over and grasped her hand. "I was so worried, Meryn. When I heard you'd been arrested, I thought I might never see you again."

She sighed. "You almost didn't. Gallagher had every intention of executing all three of us, but thankfully he was stopped just in time."

"By whom?"

She turned her head to offer him an apologetic smile. "I can't get into details, not yet. There's an ongoing investigation, so I'm not really supposed to talk about any of it."

"I understand." Drew pulled into the driveway of the home he'd grown up in. He'd inherited the grey-brick bungalow when his parents died.

A wave of nostalgia washed over Meryn as she glimpsed the garage where she and Drew had spent so much time when they were both in university and he was working on his dad's car. They were so young and innocent then, just kids. Never suspecting for a moment that life could turn so uncertain, so ugly.

Those days seemed far away now, almost another lifetime.

"You okay?" Drew rounded the front of the car and stopped in front of her.

"I'm fine." The response was automatic, but she wondered as soon as she heard it if it was the truth. Was she okay? So much had happened in the last forty-eight hours, and in the year since 10/10. Everything had changed. She had changed. What would happen next? Where would she go from here? Would she rebuild the store? Marry Drew? Have children? With all the craziness in their country—in the world—

could they even seriously consider taking a leap of faith like that?

"Meryn?"

The concern in Drew's voice called her back. "Sorry. I haven't slept for a couple of days. My mind's a little muddled at the moment."

He rested his hand on her back and guided her to the back door. "No problem. We can relax. I just need to be with you for a little while."

Relaxing sounded good at the moment. Sleeping sounded even better, but that could wait a while longer. When he unlocked the door and held it open for her, Meryn wandered into the house. The house looked the same as it had when she used to hang out here. Memories flooded through her, of Drew's mother inviting her to stay for dinner, and his father going on and on at the table about the latest baseball scores and trades until finally his wife shushed him and changed the subject. Even now, Meryn could picture them both there, in the kitchen, arguing in that good-natured, obviously-still-in-love-with-each-other way that they'd had. She stole a glance at Drew. Could she find that kind of love with him?

A chill gripped her and she rubbed her hands over both arms.

"Are you cold?" Drew walked over to the thermostat and peered at it. "My mother used to complain about it being cool in the house all the time. I'll turn it up a degree or two." He punched at a button.

A distant whirring sound testified to the furnace's willingness to accommodate his request.

He turned around. "Can I get you anything? Tea? Coffee?"

"Tea would be great, thanks." Meryn felt a sudden need to wrap her fingers around something warm, something that would banish the lingering cold that had settled deep inside her. She sank down on the couch as she waited for him.

A few minutes later he returned, handed her a steaming mug, then settled down beside her.

Meryn pulled the mug to her chest, letting the heat soak through her red blouse and spread across her skin.

Drew slid an arm around her shoulders and tugged her closer. "You must have been terrified. I know you can't say too much, but do you want to talk about how you're feeling? Maybe it will help to get it out."

"It *was* pretty scary." She wanted to tell him how God had answered their prayers and given them the strength to get through what was happening, to face certain death with calm acceptance, but something held her back.

"What is it?"

Meryn forced a smile as she set the mug on the table beside her. "Nothing. I just don't feel like talking about any of it yet, if you don't mind."

"Of course." He leaned in and pressed his lips to hers. He'd kissed her before, but had never pushed himself on her. His kiss was demanding now and stirred up a deep unease in Meryn. His hand moved to the back of her head, and he pulled her closer.

Images assaulted her like physical blows. Gallagher shoving his mouth against hers on the porch, dragging her toward the metal bench, stripping off his gun belt and jacket, the feel of his hands on her, his breath hot against her skin. Panic tightened Meryn's throat so that she couldn't breathe. She planted her hands on Drew's chest and shoved him away.

His eyes flashed. "What's wrong?"

Her heart pounded. "I'm not sure. I just don't want …"

"What? You don't want what, Meryn. Me?" Quiet fury laced his words.

Meryn stood up.

"This is about *him*, isn't it?" Drew scrambled to his feet.

"Who?"

"You know who. The captain. Jesse. The one you've never quite been able to get over."

"This has nothing to do with him. He's not even in my life anymore."

Drew gaped at her. "Not in your life anymore? What are you talking about? Every time you turn around, he's there. You see him more now than you ever did when you were dating him. Frankly, it might be the worst breakup in the history of breakups."

The revelation jolted through her. He was right. With Jesse still so much a part of her life, it didn't feel like they were broken up. Just … broken.

And, like she'd told Jesse when she'd ordered him out of her kitchen that terrible day, some things were too broken to be fixed. Weren't they?

Drew ran a hand over his head. When he dropped his arm, his hair was mussed and disheveled. "That's why you agreed to go out with me, isn't it? So you could try and convince yourself that you were over him."

"No, of course not. I *was* over him. It was time to move on."

He grasped her upper arms. "Stop lying to me, Meryn." His voice rose. "After all we've been to each other, don't I at least deserve the truth?"

Shock reverberated through her as Shane's words came back to haunt her. What *was* the truth? She didn't even know anymore.

Drew let go of her abruptly. "We were always meant to be together. When Logan died, I thought it was just a matter of time before we would be. Then *he* came into the picture. He had no right to come storming in and take you away from me. I'd lost you once, and I swore there was no way I was going to lose you again. That's why I …"

A tight fist gripped her insides. "You what?"

Drew looked away.

Meryn stared at him, trying to work out what he was saying. If he felt that strongly that Jesse had taken her away from him, how far would Drew have gone to get revenge? She sucked in a sharp breath. "You're the one who turned him in, aren't you? You told Gallagher we were at the cabin the night they came and arrested him."

"We were supposed to be together," Drew repeated, his voice dull. "I had to get him out of the way."

Meryn stepped back. *Drew* had betrayed them? She'd been so sure it was Annaliese … "Drew, he almost died. His best friend was executed. Because of you."

His jaw tensed. "That was on him. If he hadn't interfered in our relationship, none of that would have happened."

Meryn pressed a hand to her abdomen. "We weren't in a relationship, Drew. We were friends. And now we can't even be that. Not ever."

His eyes filled with agony. "Don't say that, Meryn. I still love you.

I always have and I always will." He reached for her.

Meryn stumbled backward before he could touch her. "That's not love. That's some twisted form of control and manipulation." A new, horrifying thought struck her. "All those times, out at the farm, when I felt like someone was spying on me ... that was you, wasn't it?"

His face darkened. "I wasn't *spying* on you, Meryn. I was watching out for you, trying to protect you. I knew he was no good. And I was right, wasn't I? He must have done something terrible, broken your heart somehow, or you'd still be together."

"That's none of your business. *I'm* none of your business." Meryn didn't look at him as she headed for the door on trembling legs. After the dim interior of the bungalow, the bright daylight nearly blinded her, and she shaded her eyes with one hand as she rounded the corner of the house. *Where can I go?*

Meryn blinked away the hazy fog that draped itself over her mind as she strode down the driveway and onto the sidewalk. She had no idea where she was going until she saw it—the spire of the church gleaming white in the sunshine. Meryn fixed her gaze on it as she made her way toward the building that had been her sanctuary for so many years.

A large padlock secured the massive wooden doors that had always been open to anyone looking for hope and peace, a cup of coffee, a listening ear, redemption. Now those doors were locked, and no light glimmered through the stained-glass artwork etched in every large, arched window. The building was completely silent.

Meryn climbed the stairs at the front of the church. When she reached the top, she turned and sank down on the cold cement porch. She bent her knees to her chest and wrapped her arms around them.

One of the things she had loved the most about this church was that it had always offered love and acceptance to the lost.

But if some things were too broken to be fixed, wasn't it possible for them to be too lost to be found?

She and Jesse couldn't make their way back to each other. Finding happiness with the man who had killed her husband would be a complete betrayal to Logan.

Wouldn't it?

Meryn let go of her knees and covered her mouth with one hand. Had she been lying to herself about that? Logan had loved her. He would have wanted her to be happy. And he would have understood what had happened in the desert, how much Jesse regretted pulling that trigger. Logan would have forgiven Jesse.

Could she?

She dropped her hand. She did forgive him. She had the minute he'd confessed to her that he'd killed Logan, when she'd seen how sorry he was, how that moment in time had haunted him for years.

So, who was it she hadn't forgiven? The weight of unforgiveness still tugged at her, threatened to pull her into some abyss she might never be able to climb out of. That unforgiveness had caused her to shut the door on her relationship with Jesse.

The answer struck her. She hadn't forgiven herself. She'd fallen in love with Jesse, while somewhere, in the hidden recesses of her mind, she'd harboured doubts about her husband's death. Until Jesse had confirmed it that day in the kitchen, she still wondered if the army had been lying to her. If they weren't really sure what had happened to Logan but had told her he'd been killed, so they could close the book on his life, on his service to them. Even though she'd known it was unlikely, the remote possibility that he wasn't dead, that he was just missing and might someday come home looking for her, had lingered. And in spite of that, she'd allowed herself to love another man.

A sob rose in her throat. Maybe refusing her second chance at happiness, when it was what her late husband would have wanted for her, had been the true betrayal of the love she and Logan had shared.

What have I done? She had hurt Jesse so badly, put him through so much. Meryn moaned as she dug her elbows into her knees and dropped her face into her hands. *Father, forgive me. Give me the strength to forgive myself. Help me to let go of everything that has happened in the past, to cast this burden I've been carrying around on you. It's too heavy for me. I can't bear it any longer.*

For several long minutes, she sat, heart crying out to God, her thoughts too painful to put into words. Gradually, like the first rays of dawn slowly piercing the black of night to break over the horizon, pinpricks of peace broke through the heaviness weighing her down.

What should she do now? She needed to find a place to work through what she had survived and figure out where she would go from here. This building was closed to her. The church, the bookstore, Drew's family home … she had run out of places to seek refuge.

She lifted her head. No, she hadn't. There was one other place. Her parents' home. The fate of the store was still unknown. Her relationship with Drew was over. And with Jesse moving on with his life—likely planning to take the job with CSIS and shake the dust of Kingston and everything that had gone on here from his feet, which she couldn't blame him for—there was nothing keeping her in town. She could go, leave the events of the last year behind her, and begin a new chapter in her life.

But, before she left, there was one more door that she needed to close.

56

Meryn sat beside her father on the hard bench in the hallway outside the restricted area on the base. Leah had let them know that Annaliese had been brought here, to death row, twenty-four hours earlier, two days after she had told them what Annaliese had been up to. Just being this close to the place where she and Jesse and Shane and Caleb had experienced so much horror and pain sent tremors rippling through her. Her father drew her closer, and she rested her head on his shoulder.

She looked up when the door beside them opened. Her chest squeezed as her mother came out, clinging to Shane's arm. She looked thin and frail as she leaned against her elder son.

Meryn jumped to her feet and went to her. "Mom?" She reached for her mother's hands. The fingers that gripped hers were cold and trembling. "Are you okay?"

Her mother's smile was weak, but the steel that had seen her through every challenge in her life appeared in her eyes. "I will be."

Meryn's father held out his arm. "I'll take her back to the farm to rest."

"All right." Meryn squeezed her mother's hands, then let her go.

A soldier led her parents down the hallway toward the exit.

Shane touched her arm. "Are you sure you want to see Annaliese, Meryn? You don't have to. You don't owe her anything. She's responsible for most of the hardship you've experienced in your life."

"I know. But she can't hurt me anymore. If I don't see her and say goodbye, I'll always regret it."

"Do you want me to come with you?"

She shook her head. "This time I need to face her on my own, without you or Brendan there to defend me."

Shane hugged her. "I'll be praying."

Another soldier opened the door and waited for Meryn.

She hesitated, staring down the long walkway. Shane was right.

She didn't have to do this. *Maybe I don't have to, but I need to.* Meryn pushed back her shoulders and started forward.

Annaliese was alone in this section of the base. She was in the last cell, and she got up from the metal bench and walked toward the bars at the front as Meryn approached. Even now, dressed in an orange jumpsuit—regulations clearly being followed again, with Gallagher no longer in charge—she looked stunningly beautiful, like that doll Meryn had thought her sister was when they were children.

Annaliese gripped the bars. "Ah, Meryn, my greatest adversary. Have you come to gloat?"

"I'm not your adversary, Annaliese. I never have been."

"Then, why are you here?"

"To say goodbye. And to tell you it's not too late for you."

Annaliese stared at her. "Not too late?" She let go of the bars and held up both hands. "Look, Meryn. Do you have any idea how much blood is on these? Hundreds, maybe thousands of people."

"The apostle Paul also had blood on his hands. It wasn't stronger than the blood of Christ."

Her sister's blue eyes grew hard. "There it is, my biggest and most spectacular defeat."

"What are you talking about?"

"I've dedicated my life to taking everything from you, and the thing I most longed to strip from you—your faith—you still hold on to."

"That's because I don't hold on to it. I'm not strong enough to. It holds on to me. And no one, not even you, can take me or any other believer from God's hands. If you had read even a little of the book you had me arrested for passing out, you would know that."

Scorn flickered across Annaliese's perfect, porcelain features. "Lies and fairy tales. No one can love that much."

"No person can. They will always let you down. Only God won't."

Her sister tossed her long blonde curls over one shoulder. "I found him, you know."

"Who?"

"My father. Do you know what he is?"

Meryn shook her head.

"A bricklayer." Annaliese laughed coldly. "I am the daughter of a bricklayer. All those dreams of royalty, of vindication, ground into the dust that covers him from head to toe, that will never be dug out from underneath his cracked and broken nails."

"It doesn't matter, Annaliese. That never mattered. You had a father here. And a family. None of us cared where you came from. We only wanted you to be one of us. But that was never good enough for you."

"No, it wasn't. I was made for something much greater. I always knew that. I could never have what I have—my looks, my intelligence, my ability to bend others, especially men, to my will—if I wasn't supposed to use them for some great purpose." She studied Meryn through the bars. "You have those things too, although you never did know how to use them. You couldn't even hold on to the one man I've ever met who might actually be worth holding on to." Annaliese let out a long breath. "I tried to take him, you know, and failed. I guess he was holding on to a fairy tale too."

The ache carved into Meryn's chest months ago, the night she had ordered Jesse out of her life, deepened.

Annaliese rested her forehead against two bars. "That's the irony of all this. I spent my entire life trying to defeat you, and in the end, without even trying, you have beaten me in every possible way."

"It was never my intention to beat you. I would have loved you if you had let me."

"Love comes at too high a cost."

"The cost of a life without love must be far greater."

Annaliese pushed herself away from the bars. "You might be right about that. You were always right about everything."

"I've been wrong about a lot of things. But I'm right about you and God. It's not too late. Turn to him, while you still have time."

Her sister lifted a pale, slender hand. "Goodbye, Meryn."

An unexpected grief twisted through her. She didn't move until the guard behind her shifted, impatient. Then, she nodded, once. "Goodbye, Annaliese." She turned and headed for the door, her sandals echoing on the concrete floor.

Shane waited for her on the other side of the door. He searched her face. "Are you all right?"

"No." Her attempt at a laugh came out more like a sob.

"What do you need?"

Her eyes met his dark ones. "I need to see my sister."

Shane's face softened. "All right, let's go. I'll take you to Kate."

57

Jesse rapped on the sliding glass door, then slid it open and stepped into the kitchen. He'd had a lot of time to think in the last four days, since Leah had met with them at the farm and told him CSIS was offering him a job. It had taken most of that time to make a decision, but sometime in the early morning, he finally had. *God, let it be the right one.* The same words he'd been saying over and over in the hours since drifted through his mind again. Somehow, he still didn't feel complete peace about the decision, but hopefully that would come.

Kate and Ethan stood at the sink doing the lunch dishes. They both turned toward him when he came inside.

"Sorry to barge in, but I wanted to talk to you guys."

Ethan glanced at Kate as he tossed the dishtowel onto the counter. "Come on in."

Jesse walked over to them.

"Jesse, there's something you should—"

He lifted his hand. "Wait. I have to get this out. I came to tell you I'm going away."

"Going away? For how long?"

"For good."

His friend reached out and gripped his arm. "You can't go. We need you here."

"I don't think you do. Gallagher and Annaliese are both gone. The house churches are all set up. I've made the arrangements for food delivery, when that is needed. Things should be okay around here, for a while anyway."

"But …"

"I can't do it, Ethan. I can't stay here. I thought, if Meryn was happy, if he was good to her, I could handle it, but I was wrong."

"Jesse …" His friend let go of his arm and glanced over Jesse's shoulder.

"No, don't try to talk me out of it. I have to go. It's just too painful to see her with someone else."

"I'm not."

Jesse froze at the sound of Meryn's voice behind him, then his gaze met Ethan's.

His friend winced and mouthed the word *Sorry*.

Kate grabbed Ethan's elbow. "We're just going to ... check on the kids." She pointed outside and Ethan followed her out onto the deck, sliding the door shut behind them.

Jesse turned around slowly.

Meryn stood in the doorway leading into the hall.

"Meryn. I didn't realize you were here."

She wore the long-sleeved blue shirt she had worn the morning after he'd held her in his arms all night as that terrible storm raged around the farmhouse. The shirt that brought out the incredible ocean-blue of her eyes.

Even now, knowing she wasn't his and would never be, the sight of her sent a rush of longing through him that weakened his knees.

A faint smile crossed her face. "I gathered that."

"What did you mean, *you're not?*"

She swallowed hard and crossed the room, stopping a few feet in front of him. "I mean, I'm not with anyone else. It's over with Drew." She rested a hand on the back of a kitchen chair. "I want you to know I didn't end things with him because I had any expectation that you would take me back. I don't. I know I hurt you terribly and ..." Her voice broke.

It took everything he had not to reach for her.

"I've put you through so much. I wouldn't ask you to consider it. But, Jesse ..." She took a step closer to him. "You don't have to go."

"I don't?"

"No. That's what I came here to tell Kate and Ethan. *I'm* leaving."

The words ripped through his body like an electric current. "You're leaving? Where are you going?"

"Back to Ottawa. I still have friends there, and my parents. I can start over. But the Christians here need you. I know it's quiet right now, but it probably won't be for long. I can't be responsible for driving you away. Please stay."

He shook his head. "There are too many memories here, Meryn. Everything I see, everyone I talk to, reminds me of all the things that have happened since I arrived in town. So I can't stay."

Meryn's shoulders slumped.

"Not unless you stay with me."

Her head jerked up. "Jesse … Can you really forgive me after everything I've done?"

He closed the space between them and grasped her arms lightly. "There's nothing to forgive, Meryn. I understood why you couldn't be with me after what I did. I never blamed you for that."

"And I know that what happened with Logan wasn't your fault, that you were just trying to protect the soldiers with you. Staying away from you wasn't about what you had done. It was about what I had done."

"What you had done?"

"Yes, falling in love with you when I still had doubts about my husband's death. Somewhere, deep inside, I believed that not being with you was the price I had to pay for my unfaithfulness."

"It had been three years, Meryn. I think God and Logan would have understood that you needed to move on. And Logan would have wanted you to be happy."

"I finally figured that out. And I realized that I could never be happy with Drew. Especially after I discovered …"

"What?"

"That my sister was telling the truth, for once. She wasn't the one who turned you in."

He let out his breath in a rush. "Drew."

She nodded. "He said he had to get rid of you, because you had taken me away from him, but that isn't what happened. I was never in a relationship with him before I met you, only after, and that was a mistake for so many reasons."

He grimaced and let go of her arms. "That did hurt."

She closed her eyes. "I'm sorry. I was trying to forget you."

"How did that work out for you?"

Meryn opened her eyes and let out a short laugh. "Not so great."

"Good." Almost-extinguished hope flared to life. Meryn met his gaze steadily, and in the depths of her eyes, he discovered what he was looking for. Jesse took her face in his hands and found her mouth. All those weeks and months of missing her, of longing to feel her soft skin under his fingers, her lips on his again, poured into his kiss.

Finally, he ended it and rested his forehead against hers.

They stood like that for several moments, until he pulled back and looked at her. "Marry me."

"What?"

"Marry me, Meryn. I love you, with all my heart. I don't want to spend another day away from you."

She bit her lip and then nodded. "Yes."

"Yes?" He was almost scared to believe that everything he had dreamed of since the day he had met her might suddenly be within reach.

A smile broke across her face. "I love you too. And I don't want to be apart from you either. So yes, I will marry you."

"Tonight."

She inhaled sharply. "Tonight?"

"I told you I don't want to be away from you another day, and that includes not wanting to spend another night without you in my arms. Besides, do you know what today is?"

Her brow furrowed. "No."

"It's 10/10. One year ago, our country changed forever. And our lives. Let's ask God to redeem this day for us, to bring beauty from ashes and turn it from a day of terror into a day of joy."

Meryn clasped her hands in front of her. "But can we pull everything together that quickly?"

"Since the rules changed and the government no longer considers a marriage covenant legally binding, it's not necessary to get a licence. If Pastor John is willing, all we have to do is find a place and let our family and friends know when and where to show up."

"All right, if the pastor agrees, let's do it. Let's get married tonight."

"I'll see if he can come on such short notice." Jesse pulled his i-com from the back pocket of his jeans and touched the screen to send a short message, praying fervently for a positive response as he did.

Now that she had agreed, it would be devastating to have to wait.

He pulled Meryn to him again, just as his i-com buzzed. He lifted it up and read the message over her shoulder. Relief flooded through him. "He says he's been waiting for this text for ages and to just name the time and place."

She laughed, the sound like cool water flowing over him after a day in the hot desert.

Jesse sent the time, waited for confirmation, then looked down at her. "It's all set. Five o'clock tonight. I told him I'd message him the location." He kissed her again, then reached for her hand. "I'll drive out to your place and tell your brothers what's happening. And I'll ask them if they'll stand up with me." A shadow passed over his face.

Meryn squeezed his hand. "I'm sorry Rory and Caleb won't be there."

"I have a feeling they will be." Jesse touched a finger to her pink-tinged cheek. "Are you sure, Meryn?"

"I've never been surer of anything in my life."

"Neither have I."

"Then, let's find Kate and Ethan—I doubt they've gone very far—and tell them the news." Jesse led her to the door and slid it open. Just before they stepped outside, he kissed her once more, gently this time. "To tide us over until the ceremony," he whispered in her ear. "And after ..."

The flush on her cheeks deepened.

"Well, that looks promising." Ethan leaned against the wooden railing, one foot propped on the bottom porch step, a huge grin on his face.

Kate's elbows rested on the post on the other side of the stairs, and both hands covered her mouth as she looked up at them.

Jesse gripped Meryn's hand tighter as they went down the stairs.

Ethan clapped a hand on Jesse's shoulder. "Can we assume that neither of you are leaving?"

Jesse grinned. "No, we're staying. Although we might be ... unavailable for a few days."

Kate looked at Meryn. "Why, where will you be?"

"Um." She wrinkled her nose. "On our honeymoon?"

Kate clapped her hands together. "You're getting married? When?"

Jesse glanced down at his watch. "In about four hours."

"Meryn ..." Kate's eyes widened. "Is he serious? You're getting married *today*?" She clutched Meryn's arm. "We have to get busy. There's so much to do."

Jesse laughed. "I'm going to pack and head out to the farm. Ethan, if I message you when I figure out where the wedding is going to be, will you and Kate bring my beautiful bride to me?"

"It would be my pleasure."

Jesse let go of Meryn's hand, reluctantly. "I'll see you later."

When she nodded, her eyes glowing, it took every bit of willpower he had to leave her and go to his apartment.

He threw a few things into a backpack and slung it over his shoulder. After grabbing the white cloth bag from the counter in his kitchen, he went out onto the small wooden porch.

With one last look around the small building he'd called home for some of the most difficult weeks of his life, he pulled the door shut behind him.

58

"Kate, I can't see anything." Meryn grabbed her friend's elbow when she stepped on a patch of uneven ground and nearly stumbled.

"I believe that was the idea." Kate patted her hand. "Keep your eyes closed. We're almost there."

"Almost where?"

"Nice try. Your brothers want to surprise you, and I'm not about to ruin that."

Meryn held up the long skirt of Kate's wedding dress and took several cautious steps forward. "All right. I'm not going to argue with you. Not tonight."

"Well, that's a nice change. Okay, here we are." Kate stopped and took hold of Meryn's upper arms. "This has all happened pretty fast, Mer. No second thoughts?"

Eyes still closed, Meryn shook her head. "None. I never dreamed I could be so happy. Especially after everything that's happened. And I believe Logan would be happy for me too."

Kate squeezed her arms. "So do I. All right, then, let's go inside and get you married." She let go of Meryn and took her arm to guide her the last few steps. "Ethan, can you get the door?"

"Sure." He'd been walking behind them, but now Meryn felt him brush past her and heard the creaking sound of rusted hinges being forced open. *Where are we?* "Can I open my eyes now?"

"Not yet. Almost there. But be careful, don't fall. I want Gracie to wear my dress someday too." Kate tugged her forward and into a building of some kind.

A damp, musty smell permeated the air.

Meryn reached out and her fingers brushed a cold cement wall. Was this really a good place for a wedding? She trusted her brothers, though. Shane and Brendan knew how much this day meant to her.

"Okay. You can look now." Kate's voice was hushed.

Meryn opened her eyes and drew in a quick breath. They stood in the doorway of the little storage room in the basement of the church, where she had encountered Jesse for the first time. *Was that only a year ago?* So much had transpired, it felt like a lifetime.

The boxes that had been stacked to the ceiling that day were gone. The people they'd invited to join them sat on chairs that had been set up in rows, with a space between to form an aisle. Everywhere she looked, there were lights: dozens of candles and countless strings of twinkling mini-lights draped everywhere. The room had been transformed into a fairyland.

"I can't believe it. I've never seen anything so beautiful."

Jesse stood at the front of the room, Pastor John on one side of him and Shane and Brendan on the other. Her future husband wore a dark suit and tie, and he looked so handsome that, for a moment, she couldn't breathe. His gaze locked on hers, and as incredible as the setting was, she suddenly didn't see any of it.

He was all there was. *And he is all there will ever be.*

"Ready, Meryn?" Her father stood in front of her, one arm held out.

Meryn smiled up at him. "I'm ready." She slid her hand through the crook of his elbow.

Soft music played from a sound system somewhere, and everyone in the room stood up as she and her dad started up the aisle. *I should look around, see who's here.* She couldn't take her eyes from Jesse, though, as she walked toward him. She leaned closer to her dad and whispered, "Am I dreaming?"

He chuckled and covered her hand with his. "No, darlin'. You're more awake today than you've been for a long time."

When they reached the end of the aisle, her father gently extricated her hand from his arm and held it out to Jesse, who took it in his. Her father kissed her cheek and went to sit in the front row with her mother.

Jesse cupped the back of her head and pulled her to him. He pressed his lips to hers.

"Hey, hey, hey." The pastor's voice held amusement that was echoed by a wave of laughter in the room. "It's not time for that yet."

Jesse lifted his head. "Sorry. I've been patient for weeks and weeks."

"Then you can be patient a while longer."

The pastor spoke for several minutes about the sanctity of marriage, but Meryn hardly heard a word.

Jesse's eyes, glowing jade in the softly-lit room, never left hers. When John asked him if he had any vows to say to her, he reached into the pocket of his suit coat and pulled something out. "You told me once that some things are too broken to be fixed. And you were right. Some things *are* too broken to be fixed. By human hands. But not by God's. Only he can take what is broken and restore it completely." The corners of his eyes crinkled as he smiled. "Meryn, you have had my heart since the moment we first met, right there in the back of this room." He nodded toward the door he had yanked open to find Gracie clutched in her arms, the two of them attempting to hide from him in the darkness. "Whatever might have happened in the months since, you have still had it, every moment. And you always will." He held up his hand. The heart necklace he'd given her twice before dangled from his fingers. "May I?"

Meryn turned and lifted her hair out of the way. His fingers brushed her neck as he did up the clasp. When she dropped her hair and turned back to face him, he winked at her. Warmth flowed through her as she closed her hand around the heart at her throat.

She didn't let go of it until John asked them to exchange the rings. A twinge of panic shot through her. Did they have rings? Could they get married without them? Someone tugged on the skirt of her dress, and Meryn looked down. Gracie clutched a gold ring between her thumb and forefinger and held it up to her. Meryn pressed a kiss to the top of Gracie's head as she took the ring from her.

Matthew, solemn in a shirt and tie, hair slicked down, handed another ring to Jesse. Meryn's heart squeezed. When had Jesse gotten the rings? All this time, no matter how hard she'd pushed him away, how much she'd hurt him, he hadn't gotten rid of them. Hadn't let go of hope.

I'll spend the rest of my life making up for all the pain I caused you and showing you how grateful I am that you never gave up on us. She made the silent vow with all her heart.

He smiled at her, as though he could read the words in her eyes, as he lifted her left hand and slid the simple ring onto her finger.

She slipped the matching band on his finger, repeating after the pastor, "With this ring, I thee wed."

And then she was lost again, until John's voice, the faint Scottish brogue undermining his serious tone, called her back. "By the power vested in me by the Province of Ontario, I now pronounce you husband and wife." He nudged Jesse and inclined his head toward Meryn. "*Now* you may kiss the bride."

Soft laughter rippled through the room again as Jesse leaned in and kissed her.

Music filled the room and everyone applauded.

As some of their family and friends filed toward the back of the room, where a table had been set up with food and drinks, Jesse inclined his head toward Meryn's parents. Her mom and dad stood up as the newlyweds approached.

Her mother placed soft palms on Meryn's face, blue eyes glistening. "I have never seen you so beautiful or so happy."

"I've never been so happy." Meryn studied her mother, as lovely as ever in spite of the health issues that plagued her. What had happened with Annaliese couldn't have helped. "How are you doing?"

Her mother patted Meryn's cheeks before dropping her hands. "I'll be all right. I lost your sister years ago. I just wasn't forced to admit that to myself until yesterday. But we won't talk about that today." She pushed back her slender shoulders. "Today is a day for celebrating and joy." She rested a hand on Jesse's arm. "I was right about my younger daughter, wasn't I? I told you it might take some time for her to get over everything but that she would. And she did. Now you have a whole new family. The two of you must come to Ottawa to visit us."

Jesse covered her hand with his. "Thank you, Isabelle. You gave me hope the day I came to see you, and I've held on to it ever since."

"And here we are."

"Here we are. We'll come and see you both, very soon."

Meryn's father slapped him on the back. "Welcome to the family, son."

"Thank you, sir."

Her father hugged Meryn. "I need to take your mother home now. But we'll see you again before too long."

She watched them until they had left the room.

A soldier walked toward them.

"Trey!" Jesse grasped the man's hand. "How did you get back?"

Trey nodded toward Leah, who stood in the back corner between Michael Stevens and Shane, a glass of punch in her hand. "Michael has been supplying information to Agent Winters for a long time. When we first got to the States, we found a motel and laid low for twenty-four hours. As soon as he could get to a payphone, Michael called her. She told him everything that had gone on since we'd left—that Gallagher had been arrested and it was safe to come home. They sent two agents over to pick us up yesterday. We debriefed with her this afternoon. She mentioned you were getting married this evening, and we decided to crash the wedding. I hope that was okay."

"More than okay. I'm thrilled to see both of you. Meryn, you remember Trey?"

"Of course. From our first impromptu house-church service."

He grinned. "That's right. Congratulations to you both." He turned back to Jesse. "Michael and I had a lot of time to talk while we were in hiding. He answered a ton of questions for me." Trey held up his arm. A grey identity bracelet circled his wrist. "Looks like I'll be a regular at your house church."

Jesse pulled him close and slapped him on the back a couple of times. "That's great news, Trey."

Michael came up behind Trey.

Jesse hugged him too. "I can't believe you're here."

Michael waved a hand around the room. "There was no way we were going to miss a shindig like this." He drew a tall, blonde woman to his side. "Jesse, Meryn, I'd like you to meet Julia, my fiancée."

The woman's smile was sweet and genuine "Congratulations. Michael has told me a little about you and Jesse and what you both have been through. I'm very glad for you that everything has worked out."

Jesse wrapped an arm around Meryn's waist. "Have the two of

you set a date?"

"Not yet."

"Well, don't wait too long. I highly recommend married life."

Michael laughed. "The voice of experience talking. What do you think, Meryn?"

She smiled up at her husband. "So far, so good."

Michael's face sobered as he looked back at Jesse. "I hear you and Meryn and her brother were nearly executed for helping me escape."

Jesse shook his head. "That final confrontation with Gallagher had been in the works for a long time before you came into the picture. If you hadn't given him the excuse to take us in, he would have found another one, or manufactured something. You can rest easy on that."

"I hate to break up the party"—Trey pointed to his watch—"but it's going to be dark soon."

Michael nodded. "You're right. We should get back to the hotel." He held out his hand, and Jesse clasped it. "Julia and I wish you all the best, my friend."

"You too."

The three of them left the room. Jesse squeezed Meryn's shoulder. "We should probably go soon. Do you want something to eat or drink before we leave?"

"A glass of punch would be wonderful."

They crossed the room to where her brothers, Hope, and Leah stood talking to Kate and Ethan. Jesse poured Meryn a drink and handed it to her.

Kate rested a hand on Meryn's back. "That was so beautiful, Mer. Can you believe how Shane and Brendan transformed this room?"

"No, actually, I can't." She turned to her brothers. "How did you get into the church?"

Brendan looked proud of himself. "They never changed the lock on the back door. Pastor John still had the key, so he let us in."

"Well, I don't know how to thank you. I never would have thought of holding the ceremony in this room, but it was perfect."

"Consider it your wedding present, since you didn't give us enough warning to buy you anything." Shane kissed her on the cheek. "I'm thrilled for you and Jesse, kid."

"Thank you."

"Here's another gift, Meryn. I just received this message a couple of hours ago." Hope held up her i-com to show Meryn the screen.

She scanned the words quickly, ecstatic when she realized what they meant.

Jesse touched her arm. "What is it?"

"They've wrapped up the investigation of the fire at my store and ruled that the building is still structurally sound. I can rebuild."

He squeezed her elbow. "That's great news."

Hope slid the i-com into her purse and looked at Jesse. In a dramatic stage whisper, she said, "Well, you got your act of God. I knew you would."

Meryn tilted her head. "Act of God?"

Jesse glared at Hope. "I've been married twenty minutes, and you're already getting me in trouble with my wife."

His wife. Joy rippled through Meryn.

"You can't help yourself, can you?" Jesse nudged Hope's arm.

"Nope." Hope's eyes twinkled. "Someone has to fill in for Caleb and Rory. If they were here, you know they'd be giving you a hard time right now."

He grinned. "That's true."

Brendan pulled Meryn close. "Well done, Meryn. You deserve all the happiness in the world after everything you've been through." He stepped back and pointed a finger at Jesse. "You take care of her, you hear? Or Shane and I will—"

"Take me out and teach me a lesson, I know." Jesse draped an arm around her. "Don't worry. I'll take good care of her." He glanced toward the window. "We all better head out soon. It's getting late."

Shane cleared his throat. "I know you probably haven't had time to think about this, but if you want Brendan and me to move out of the farmhouse, we can. It's really Meryn's place."

"Actually, I have something else in mind for us."

Meryn looked at him. "What do you have in mind?"

He tapped a finger on her nose. "A surprise. Do you have a suitcase?"

Ethan nodded. "I put her things in your truck."

"Great." Jesse leaned closer to Meryn. "I brought that outfit I told you I wanted you to wear tonight."

Heat flared in Meryn's face as she bit her lip. The memory of that night by the pond—when she'd been wearing his T-shirt and flannel pyjama bottoms, and he'd told her that she wouldn't have to worry about any fancy lingerie on their wedding night, because he loved her in his pyjamas—flashed through her mind.

Brendan frowned. "Dude, that's our sister."

Jesse shrugged. "Well, she's not my sister, so I don't see what the problem is."

Ethan snorted a laugh that turned into a cough when Brendan scowled at him.

"Shall we?" Jesse pointed at the door.

"All right." Meryn hugged Kate and waved at the group. "Goodbye, everyone."

Jesse captured her fingers in his, and she followed him out of the room and down the damp corridor to the back of the church. He opened the screeching door and held it until she went through, then he came out and pulled it shut behind them.

A patch of light spilled from the basement window, pushing back the encroaching dusk to fall, soft and warm, on the grass outside the old limestone church as they made their way across the lawn to Jesse's truck.

59

Jesse helped Meryn up into the vehicle and tucked the long, ivory dress around her. "Ha. Look at me. I'm getting all *hands*y, and there's nothing Brendan can do about it. Not anymore."

Meryn laughed, and his chest tightened.

Was it really possible that he could be this happy? The way he felt right now made every moment of pain and heartache disappear, as though they had never happened.

Meryn—his wife—leaned in to kiss him.

The faint scent of lavender drifted from her, and he breathed it in.

She trailed a finger down the side of his face. "Where are we going?"

He caught her hand and pressed her palm to his mouth. "You'll see." He forced himself to let her go, shut the door, climbed in beside her, and started the truck.

She shifted in her seat to face him. "I have three questions for you."

"Yes."

She blinked. "You haven't heard the questions yet."

"It doesn't matter. Whatever you ask me right now, I'll say yes."

She pursed her lips and studied him. "Hmm. Intriguing. Unfortunately, these aren't those types of questions. I do claim the right to hold that offer in reserve to be used in the very near future, however."

"Anytime." He grinned as he pulled away from the curb and onto the street. "So, what do you want to know?"

"First of all, what did Hope mean when she said you got your act of God?"

Jesse gripped the steering wheel. "We were talking about you one night, and she said she thought you were lovely and sweet. I agreed but added that you were also stubborn, and it would take an act of God to get you to change your mind about us." He shot her an apologetic look.

"Sorry."

"Don't be. You're right. I am stubborn. I know that. If I hadn't been so stubborn, we could have gotten here a long time ago."

He let go of the wheel with one hand and rested his hand on her knee. "We got here exactly when we were supposed to, don't worry about that."

"What about the job with CSIS? Will you take it?"

He contemplated the question. Earlier that day, he'd made up his mind to accept the offer. But he finally understood why he hadn't felt a peace about that decision. "No. I need to be here, Meryn, with you, doing the work you told me that last night in my quarters that God had for us to do, whatever that might be." *This is the right decision. Thank you for showing me the way. Please continue to lead and guide Meryn and me in the days and years to come.*

Meryn touched his hand. "I need you to know that part of that work will involve using the store, once it's rebuilt, to keep moving out Bibles. It's the best way for us to do that, and with more and more people asking questions about Christianity, there is a desperate need. I know you don't like it, but this is something I—"

Jesse squeezed her knee. *I could lose Meryn. For good this time.* If Leah was right, executions could still be carried out for offences like the one Meryn was talking about. "All right."

She stared at him. "All right?"

I surrender all. Even her. "Yes. If that's what God is calling you to do, who am I to stand in your way? I'll help you any way I can."

Meryn leaned over and kissed him. "Thank you."

He smiled at her. "What's your other question?"

"When Gallagher had the gun to my head, he told you that he was going to take me down with him and that you would have to live with the knowledge that you'd killed all three of us. Who was he talking about? Who were the other two people?"

The question pricked a hole in the bliss he'd been floating in and deflated it a little.

She must have seen that on his face, because she frowned. "I'm sorry. We don't have to talk about it tonight if you don't want to."

"No, you should hear this." He wove his fingers through hers.

"When he came to arrest me, Gallagher told me a story that finally helped me to understand why he hates me so intensely. It turns out that his son, Christopher, was part of Logan's platoon. When I shot Logan that day, his platoon ended up being massacred, and Christopher was killed."

Meryn's face paled. "Oh no."

"That's not all. Christopher was their only child, and shortly after his death, Gallagher's wife took her own life. Those were the two other people he was referring to when he made that comment."

"Jesse." She undid her seatbelt and slid over to him. "Neither of those deaths were your fault. You know that, right? You did the only thing you could with the information you had when you shot Logan. You had no way of knowing who he was or what he was doing when he was running toward you. By the time he reached you, his platoon was probably already gone. Even if he had been able to tell you what was going on, you likely would never have gotten to them in time. And if you'd tried, the soldiers in your platoon might have been killed as well. And Gallagher's wife made the choice to end her life. Their blood isn't on your hands. Don't believe that lie."

Shock jolted through him. Somehow, through all those years of carrying this load around, of tormenting himself with thoughts of all the lives he'd destroyed, that idea—that, even if Logan had been able to reach them, it was unlikely there was anything Jesse and his platoon could have done to help—had never occurred to him. The fact that it had come from Meryn, the one whose husband he had stolen, was almost too incredible to comprehend.

The load that had pressed down on him for years eased. "Thank you for that." His throat tightened, and he couldn't say any more. *Thank you, God, for the gift of this woman beside me. For the rest of my life, I'll do everything in my power to be worthy of it, of her.*

She rested her head against his arm. "My mind is spinning."

"In a good way, I hope."

"In an amazing way. I'm trying to catch up with how much my life—our lives—have changed in the last few hours."

Jesse flicked on the turn signal. They were almost there. "Believe me, no one knows better than I do how much your life can change in a day, or in an instant. This time, thankfully, it's in the best possible way."

"Yes, it is."

Jesse pulled onto the property he'd been heading for and stopped the truck. She straightened, and he slid a finger under her chin to tip up her face. "We're here."

"Where?"

"Come and see." Jesse pushed open the door and jumped out. He rounded the front of the vehicle and helped her climb down. "Leave your things. I'll come back for them." He took her hand. A strand of birches blocked their view of the back of the property. They walked past several trees before Jesse stopped. "Wait. I need to grab something here." He reached into a hole in the tree and pulled out the object he'd left there the last time he'd come to this place.

Jesse held out his hand toward his wife. The silver heart she had given him lay on his palm. "I almost gave up, Meryn. The other day, when I was here, I convinced myself that I didn't have your heart anymore, that it was finally time to let go of the dreams I'd held on to for so long."

She took his hand in both of hers and closed it over the heart. "Never let go of it. You have always had it. And you always will." Her gaze drifted past him. She let go of him and gathered up the skirt of the wedding dress as she walked toward the edge of the bush.

Jesse followed her.

When she reached the grass beyond the trees, she stopped and looked up at him. In the silvery moonlight, her eyes glistened with wonder. "You built it."

"Yes."

"It's just the way you described it in your story."

"As close as I could make it. Well, me and the contractor and crew I hired several months ago."

She grasped his arm and pulled him toward the little log house, built on the edge of the stream that ran through the property. They went up the steps of the wide, wooden porch that surrounded the house on three sides. The smell of newly hewn wood hung in the air.

Jesse pulled the keys from his pocket. His fingers trembled as he inserted one into the lock and pushed open the door. Would she like it? Was it the way she had pictured it when he told her the story of the old man and woman that night in his quarters? The rustic house she had always imagined having one day?

He'd stopped by here before going to the church and turned on a lamp. The living room with the large, stone-walled fireplace, couches and chairs arranged around a soft, earth-toned area rug, glowed softly. After he'd built a fire, the flames flickering off the pine walls would make it even cosier. Other than that, all that was missing was the dog curled up on the rug. Something they would remedy as soon as Meryn was ready to help him choose one. For tonight, though, they would be the only living things in the house. Which suited him just fine.

"Jesse." Meryn's voice was filled with awe. "I can't believe you did this. It's perfect. Far more beautiful than I dreamed it would be." She started to step inside.

"Wait." Jesse bent down to scoop her up into his arms. The satin dress was cool and smooth against his skin.

Meryn clasped her hands behind his neck.

He tightened his hold, deeply aware that, at that moment, he held everything in his arms that he had ever wanted. "You know how you keep telling me that there is no safe place anymore?"

She nodded.

"Well, that's not true. There is one." He carried her over the threshold of their new home. "For tonight, there is one safe place."

Bio

Sara Davison, author of the romantic suspense novel, *The Watcher*, and the romantic suspense Seven trilogy, has been a finalist for three national writing awards, including Best New Canadian Christian Author. *The End Begins*, the first book in the Seven trilogy, was long-listed for the 2016 INSPY Award and was a Daphne du Maurier Award finalist. Sara has a degree in English Literature from Queen's University and is a member of The Word Guild. She currently resides in central Ontario, Canada, with her husband, Michael, and their three children, all of whom she (literally) looks up to. Her favourite way to spend her time is drinking coffee and making stuff up. Get to know Sara better at www.saradavison.org and @sarajdavison.

Acknowledgments

To my great blessings in life. Michael, Luke, Julia, and Seth, you are always on my side, cheering me on and sharing every joy and trial that comes our way. I could not do what I do without you.

To my extended family. Your love, support, and encouragement make the hard days easier and the good days that much more joyful. I thank God daily for the gift of each one of you.

To the Reverend Paul Carter, First Baptist Orillia, whose series on Revelation inspired the idea for this trilogy in the first place. I pray God will bless and keep you and your family as you continue to preach boldly from his Word and inspire others to do the same.

To my early readers, especially Simon Presland and Mary-Jo Wilson. I am deeply grateful for your time and for the invaluable feedback you always offer. You help me believe in my work and in myself.

To my agent, Sarah Joy Freese, and to Greg Johnson and all the wonderful people at WordServe Literary. I can't tell you how much it means to me to have all of you standing behind me.

As always, deepest thanks to Christina, Sherrie, and the amazing team at Ashberry Lane. Thank you for seeing the diamonds in the rough, early versions of my books, and for having the courage and patience to chip and polish until the manuscripts shine. These books are a team effort and would not be what they are without your wisdom, guidance, and expertise. I look forward to continuing to walk this road with you!

Discussion Questions

1. Pastor John preaches a sermon on how imperative it is for Christians to gather together. How important do you believe it is for Christians to meet together in a church setting? If it ever became illegal for believers to gather together, how willing would you be to take the risk and meet in a house church or other location? Why do you believe that Christians do this even when threatened with imprisonment or death?

2. After visiting Caleb's grave, Hope asks Jesse if he thinks it's wrong to question what God does. Do you think it is okay to question God? Can you think of a biblical precedent for your answer? If so, is there a right and wrong way to do so?

3. In spite of the horrific things they have gone through, Jesse tells Hope that he knows two things to be absolutely true: that God is still on his throne, and he has not abandoned them. Do you believe God is in control of everything that happens? What do you say to someone who believes that, if God were really in control, terrible things would not happen to the people who follow him?

4. Meryn wonders what horrible thing she did to make God take away both of the men she loved. Then she reminded herself that God doesn't work like that. Do you believe that is true? What other possible reasons could there be for believers to suffer unimaginable loss and pain?

5. After Trey tells Jesse that people have been showing up at the base, asking for bracelets, Jesse says that, when he was still on the base, it bothered him not to wear one like other believers. Do you think you would feel the same under similar circumstances, or can you see the value in keeping your faith a secret as long as possible?

6. When Michael Stevens comes to see Jesse, he leaves quickly because he senses he should get out of town. Have you ever felt the Holy Spirit warning you to do or not do something in this way? Did you listen? What happened?

7. When Meryn talks to Shane after they are released from prison, she tells him that every believer wonders if they will have the courage to withstand severe persecution without denying their faith. Have you ever considered what you would do in a situation like they found themselves in? How much would you be willing to sacrifice for your faith?

8. Do you believe you would receive strength from the Holy Spirit if you ever faced a situation where you, or someone you loved, could die for your faith? Have you ever received this strength in times of severe trial or testing? How did you know that's what it was? Share your story.

**Did you miss the first book in the Seven trilogy?
Read *The End Begins* now!**

THE SEVEN TRILOGY BOOK 1

THE END BEGINS

SARA DAVISON

Bookstore owner Meryn O'Reilly and Army Captain Jesse Christensen are on opposite sides of a battle. After a series of terrorist attacks in 2053, martial law has been declared in Canada and the military has taken over. When a radical Christian group claims responsibility, Jesse and his platoon are sent to Meryn's city to keep an eye on the Christians and ensure they are not stepping outside the confines of the law.

Fiery and quick-tempered, Meryn chafes under the curfew and other restrictions to her freedom. Jesse is equally amused, intrigued, and terrified by her spirit. She could find herself in prison if she shows defiance to the wrong soldier, namely Lieutenant Gallagher.

Jesse watches out for Meryn when possible, although she wants nothing to do with him. His worst fears are realized when she commits a crime he cannot protect her from. Now they both face an uncertain future and the very real threat of losing everything, including their lives. With time running out, Jesse works feverishly to convince the authorities to show leniency to Meryn. And to convince her that love can overcome any barrier that lies between them.

ASHBERRYLANE.COM

ASHBERRY LANE

**Follow that with the second book in the Seven trilogy.
Read *The Dragon Roars* now!**

THE SEVEN TRILOGY BOOK 2

THE DRAGON ROARS

Sara Davison

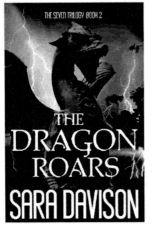

No one in the army can find out that Captain Jesse Christensen has become a believer. He and bookstore owner Meryn O'Reilly are forced to meet in secret, facing imprisonment or worse if they are found together.

Meryn wants to give her heart to Jesse fully, but her past holds her back. Although circumstances conspire to keep her silent, she needs to tell him her secret.

The year is 2054. As the world descends into chaos around them and Christians in Canada and around the world face tighter and tighter restrictions, Jesse and Meryn wage a battle against forces of darkness – both physical and spiritual. They face the threat of being ripped apart forever as Gallagher closes in on his favourite target. Jesse's life hangs in the balance.

Jesse, Meryn, and all believers must decide if their faith is strong enough to carry them through these dark days, or if the cost of declaring allegiance to Jesus Christ is just too high.

ASHBERRYLANE.COM

ASHBERRY LANE

Enjoy another Ashberry Lane book!

The Journey of Eleven Moons
Bonnie Leon

A successful walrus hunt means Anna and her beloved Kinauquak will soon be joined in marriage. But before they can seal their promise to one another, a tsunami wipes their village from the rugged shore … everyone except Anna and her little sister, Iya, who are left alone to face the Alaskan wilderness.

A stranger, a Civil War veteran with golden hair and blue eyes, wanders the untamed Aleutian Islands. He offers help, but can Anna trust him or his God? And if she doesn't, how will she and Iya survive?

Ashberry Lane
ASHBERRYLANE.COM

The Memoir of JOHNNY DEVINE

CAMILLE EIDE

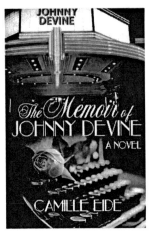

In 1953, desperation forces young war widow Eliza Saunderson to take a job writing the memoir of ex-Hollywood heartthrob Johnny Devine. Rumor has it Johnny can seduce anything in a skirt quicker than he can hail a cab. But now the notorious womanizer claims he's been born again. Eliza soon finds herself falling for the humble, grace-filled man John has become — a man who shows no sign of returning her feelings. No sign, that is, until she discovers something John never meant for her to see.

When Eliza's articles on minority oppression land her on McCarthy's Communist hit list, John and Eliza become entangled in an investigation that threatens both his book and her future. To clear her name, Eliza must solve a family mystery. Plus, she needs to convince John that real love — not the Hollywood illusion — can forgive a sordid past. Just when the hope of love becomes reality, a troubling discovery confirms Eliza's worst fears. Like the happy façade many Americans cling to, had it all been empty lies? Is there a love she can truly believe in?

ASHBERRYLANE.COM

ASHBERRY LANE

Daughter of the Cimarron

Samuel Hall

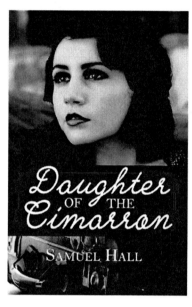

Divorcing a cheating husband means disgracing her family, but Claire Devoe can't take it anymore. Forced to provide for herself, she travels the Midwest with a sales crew. Can she trust the God who didn't save her first marriage to lead her through the maze of new love and overwhelming expectations? The long twilight of the Great Depression—with its debt, disgrace, drought, and despair—becomes the crucible that remakes her life.

Ashberrylane.com

BROKEN Wings

THE Thistle SERIES
BOOK ONE

DIANNE PRICE

He lives to fly—until a piece of flak changes his life forever.

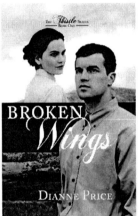

A tragic childhood has turned American Air Forces Colonel Rob Savage into an outwardly indifferent loner who is afraid to give his heart to anyone. RAF nurse Maggie McGrath has always dreamed of falling in love and settling down in a thatched cottage to raise a croftful of bairns, but the war has taken her far from Innisbraw, her tiny Scots island home.

Hitler's bloody quest to conquer Europe seems far away when Rob and Maggie are sent to an infirmary on Innisbraw to begin his rehabilitation from disabling injuries. Yet they find themselves caught in a battle between Rob's past, God's plan, and the evil some islanders harbor in their souls.

Which will triumph?

ASHBERRY LANE
ASHBERRYLANE.COM

CPSIA information can be obtained
at www.ICGtesting.com
Printed in the USA
LVOW12s1520301016
510907LV00002B/235/P